F.G. Hibbard

Biography of Rev. Leonidas L. Hamline

Late one of the bishops of the Methodist Episcopal Church

F.G. Hibbard

Biography of Rev. Leonidas L. Hamline
Late one of the bishops of the Methodist Episcopal Church

ISBN/EAN: 9783337097981

Printed in Europe, USA, Canada, Australia, Japan

Cover: Foto ©Raphael Reischuk / pixelio.de

More available books at **www.hansebooks.com**

BIOGRAPHY

OF

REV. LEONIDAS L. HAMLINE, D. D.,

LATE ONE OF THE BISHOPS OF THE METHODIST
EPISCOPAL CHURCH.

BY

REV. F. G. HIBBARD, D. D.

———————⋆———————

CINCINNATI:
HITCHCOCK AND WALDEN.
NEW YORK:
PHILLIPS AND HUNT.
1880.

PREFACE.

THE present work was undertaken in compliance with a general call for a biography that should bring out more fully Bishop Hamline's personal and ministerial character, and the just proportion of his historic merit. Bishop Hamline lived in the most important epoch of the history of the Methodist Episcopal Church, and no man, since Asbury, has done more than he to shape its character and guide its fortunes over the roughest of navigable waters.

Nothing was left by him which was prepared with reference to a biography. Even his diary was written for his family and private friends. When solicited to prepare material for a biography, he declined. But while his modesty was a marvel even to those who knew him best, his sincerity was never doubted. Yet the material for a biography lay scattered among his papers, or registered in the archives of the Church, requiring only an extra measure of care and labor to call them forth and put them in order. Many things, indeed, might have been better supplied and arranged by his own hand had health and leisure permitted. Still the reader of the following pages, we trust, will be able to grasp the proportions and apprehend the genius and godly spirit of the man. Since the days of Fletcher the Church has not been blessed with a brighter light, whether viewed in relation to spiritual life and experience or ministerial talent and labor, while for wisdom in Church law and

PREFACE.

government he was thoroughly a son of Wesley. "The biography and writings of the late Bishop Hamline," says the late Bishop Thomson, "should by all means be given to the Church. It will make a work of great value and permanent usefulness. It would give me pleasure," he adds, "to edit the publication if I could find the time. I could do it *con amore*, but my engagements are such as to leave me no time for such labors, especially in my feeble health."

The object of the following pages is to put this "burning and shining light" in its proper relations before the world for the present and future generations. Such lights never grow dim with age. The volume edited by Dr. Palmer, with pious care and affection, is a thesaurus of spiritual knowledge and maxims of life. While we would not impair the spiritual element of the biography, we would give the hilstoric more fulness; yea, the historic becomes a medium of the clearer effulgence of the spiritual. Besides, other material had come to light which it was due to posterity to publish. But in attempting this it has been a subject of unceasing care that his wonderful spiritual experience should suffer no eclipse or dimness by neglect or omission.

Our task of love is done. It was begun and continued in prayer, and with prayer that it may be a blessing to the Church, it is now committed to the guidance of that Providence without whose favor and blessing all work and device must fail.

F. G. HIBBARD.

CLIFTON SPRINGS, N. Y., *March* 8, 1880.

NOTE.—The reader will find the full headings of the chapters in the Table of Contents.

CONTENTS.

CHAPTER I.

CHAPTER II.

CHAPTER III.

CHAPTER IV.

CHAPTER V.

CHAPTER VI.

CHAPTER VII.

CHAPTER VIII.

CHAPTER IX.

CHAPTER X.

CHAPTER XI.

CHAPTER XII.

CHAPTER XIII.

CHAPTER XIV.

CHAPTER XV.

CHAPTER XVI.

CHAPTER XVII.

CHAPTER XVIII.

CHAPTER XIX.

CHAPTER XX.

CHAPTER XXI.

CHAPTER XXII.

CHAPTER XXIII.

CHAPTER XXIV.

CHAPTER XXV.

CHAPTER XXVI.

CHAPTER XXVII.

BIOGRAPHY

OF

REV. LEONIDAS L. HAMLINE.

CHAPTER I.

EARLY HISTORY.

HISTORY and biography stand related as *genus* and *species*, having a common origin, and subject to the same laws of development and decay. The latter deals with individual character as its theme; the former with the growth and destiny of masses or nations of men. History, in its broadest sense, is little else than the record of the doings of individuals; that is, it is their biography so far as their acts affected the public welfare: while biography, on the other hand, is the record of a man's life and doings so far as it bears on his individual character and destiny. Thus the moral object of all human history and biography is the same, namely, to instruct, caution, and encourage men in that which is right, by showing how certain principles of ethics, in religion or polity, in individuals or nations, affect character and human happiness. All ethical principles are tested only by experience. When incorporated into either individual or national policy they develop after their kind in

13

good or evil effects. The laws of material nature are not more certain and uniform in their effects than are those of the moral government of God. Indeed, they are not so certain. It is more certain that the principles of ethics, founded in the nature of God, and developed in moral government and redemption, shall abide immutably, than that the material "heaven and earth" shall continue. The interest we have, therefore, in Christian biography and history is unspeakably great, inasmuch as they are crucial tests, an infallible demonstration of the verity, power, purity, and blessedness of divine moral truth. We see how certain causes lead to certain results by the most satisfactory and only certain test of all ethical philosophy, that of experience.

In the subject of the following memoir we see the working of divine truth and grace with uncommon clearness and fullness. His marked qualities and aptitudes of mind, his high positions of official responsibility, his great sufferings, his culture and tastes, the natural, and we may say of his early life, skeptical, cautiousness of his mental processes, the perfect humanity, and reasonableness of his acts, conspire to invest his life and experience with a wonderful force of evidence of the verity and power of that all-conquering grace which bore him so triumphantly to the end.

Mr. Hamline was of French ancestry, of the Huguenot Protestant type. His grandfather, Ebenezer Hamline, was born in Burlington, Hartford County, Connecticut, about 1740. He was a lieutenant in the Revolutionary war, noted for his bravery; was at Fort Edwards, Ticonderoga, and other places, and died a Christian in 1810. He had six children, three sons and three daughters—Mark, Daniel, and Lent, and Rosa, Hannah, and Lois. His wife was a woman of character, possessing great energy and courage. The children were reputable and pious. Mark Hamline, the eldest, and father of the subject of this memoir, was born in 1764. He, too, served in the Revolution while yet but a boy. His wife was daughter of Captain Othniel Moses. They were pious, and settled in Burlington, Connecticut. He was a school-teacher, managing also a small farm; was of marked ability and a prominent man in the Congregational Church, and among his neighbors. His great decision of character, sound judgment, and unconquerable resolution caused his opinion to be much sought after in matters of special importance. A strict observance of the holy Sabbath marked his Puritanic integrity. If he lent a horse on Saturday he strictly required that it should be returned the same night. While living some three miles from the church he was absent but one half day in ten years. He always took his children to church. Gentlemanly and dignified he blended kindness in all his social intercourse. The young loved him no less than the aged, and his appearance among the former in their moods of gayety and mirth would always command silence and respect. As a teacher of youth he was successful, and when in later life his daughter moved to a college in Ohio, men of distinction, in many instances, called on her, learning she was a daughter of Mark Hamline. He was the early instructor and friend of Rev. Heman Humphrey, afterward president of Amherst College. Character and courage ran in the blood. A granddaughter of Mark

Hamline, who had a son in the recent war sick at Washington, hastened there to attend him. She was withstood by the surgeon, and denied a permit to take him to a private residence to nurse him. Her remonstrances were in vain. "I have charge of the hospital," he said, "and shall exercise my power." Looking him full in the face, she replied, "Sir, you will find that I have more power in Washington than you have." She obtained that day an interview with President Lincoln, who gave permission for the removal of her son. That day, also, the surgeon was removed.

Leonidas L. Hamline, son of Mark Hamline, was born in Burlington, Connecticut, May 10, 1797. His parents being of the Congregational order, and his father an admirer of the Hopkinsian phase of Calvinism, he was brought up after the genuine manner of the New England Congregationalism of the day. Little is preserved of his early life beyond the simple facts of his great reverence for religious doctrine and worship, his obedience and devotion to parents, his amiable deportment, his precocity, and his strong love of study. Impressed that his natural genius and religious bent suited him better for the pulpit than to secular callings, his father, in conformity to the custom of the times, early proposed to educate him for the sacred office. It was probably this that encouraged the ardent and ingenuous mind of Hamline, before his conversion, to turn the early current of his thoughts and study in this direction. When ten or twelve years old he wrote a sermon on the text, "Why seek ye the living among the dead?" The ability and tact which it displayed surprised his parents and friends, and encouraged their hopes. At that age, when plowing in the field, his father "often found him resting his team while he sat on the plow so absorbed in his book as to have forgotten his work." His great reverence for the Sabbath, and his scrupulous observance of its sanctity, were marked features of his life in childhood, and not less in his last years. Before his conversion a Presbyterian ministerial friend used to say, "Some good will yet come to Hamline for his observance of the Sabbath."

Of his supposed early conversion he thus speaks in later life: "My parents designed me for the ministry, and I was partly educated for that purpose. When sixteen years old I was convicted of sin, and was thought to be converted; but, probably from the want of evangelical instruction, I came short of it. But encouraged by friends, I joined the Congregational Church, and became a warm youthful advocate of religion. I found I was not born again, but judged I was much like others around me, and 'hoped.' In a few years I was satisfied that I had no religious fitness for the ministry, and ambitiously turned to the law."

When about seventeen he engaged in teaching portions of the year to enable him to pursue his education. At this time he introduced religious service in his school. The awakening was so strong that at times the school exercises were suspended. Many were hopefully converted. A Christian lady living in East Barrington, Massachusetts, informed Mrs. Hamline that there were elders in the Church in that village, who were then living, who had been converted through Mr. Hamline's labors, when he was a

2

young man of seventeen or eighteen, teaching classical school, with anticipations of the ministry. The pastor of the Congregational Church where Hamline, with his parents, worshiped was once asked what he thought of Leonidas. He replied, "How do you think I would feel to see my son standing on the spire of the church?" thus intimating the danger of young Hamline from the precocity of his genius. He early became popularly noted for his ability and tact in public speaking and debate. While at the Academy at Andover (not the Theological Seminary), he was so marked for classical taste in language and style that he was appointed censor of compositions. In New York, at one time, while staying a few weeks, he was urged to accept the challenge of a Universalist preacher which the latter was offering in his lectures from evening to evening. He at length consented, and after a few evenings, the interest of the debate rising and the audience increasing, the champion feeling the day was lost began to be rude and abusive. The chairman expressed his regret that the youth who had behaved with such decorum and propriety should receive such treatment. When the meeting broke up a lady said to Hamline, "You have saved my soul, sir. I am a member of the Presbyterian Church, and led on by the sophistry of that Universalist preacher was about to leave my own and join his Church."

At another time, a debating club had proposed as a question, "Is there a God?" Hamline was not on the programme, but was alarmed when he saw on the negative a member of the bar of known intellectual strength and power in debate. He knew, also, those on the other side. When the debate closed the chairman announced, "If we take the vote now, we must vote there is no God." Hamline trembled for the effect on his friend, and said to a mutual friend sitting near, a Presbyterian gentleman, "If you will move to continue the debate and place me on the affirmative I will consent." The motion was immediately made and passed, and the debate continued through most of the night. When the vote on the question was finally taken, it was in the affirmative. Mr. Hamline remarked afterward that he did not take up the argument or meet objections on the ground commonly taken, knowing that his friend on the negative had thoroughly gone over that already, and had accordingly fortified himself. But he drew upon resources and modes of thought which were his own, and much of it extempore. He had feared that his noble opponent had been troubled with doubts, and hoped that his arguments had relieved them.

"Once when he was passing up the Ohio River the company in the gentlemen's saloon on the steamboat were engrossed for an hour or two by a noisy infidel, who had gathered a crowd around him, and was entertaining them with jeers at the Christian religion. Mr. Hamline was walking back and forth through the saloon, not seeming to notice what was passing, though he observed that the speaker was eying him, and evidently wished to attract his attention. As he turned from time to time he drew nearer the scene of discourse. At length the boaster said, 'When I die there will be no more of me than of my old white horse. Can you prove

otherwise, stranger?' appealing to Mr. Hamline, who
turned quickly, and said, 'If, when your old white
horse is reposing under the shade in a hot Summer
day, I should approach and whisper in his ear arguments to prove that he is immortal, would you not
deem me a fool?' The company broke up in a roar
of laughter, leaving the chagrined boaster to hide
himself as best he could."

When about eighteen years of age, from hard
study and continued strain upon the nerves, his
health failed, which sympathetically affected his
brain. The first symptom of mental aberration
which was discovered was in the jovial relaxation of
his characteristic and scrupulous observance of the
holy Sabbath. It soon became plain enough that
his habit of life must be suspended. A voyage
South was determined on, hoping that sea air and
change of climate would prove effectual. His nervous temperament had not been understood by his
parents, and his amazing precocity had been imprudently stimulated by his admiring, but most imprudent, friends. He remained in South Carolina till
his father's limited means forced his recall. While
abroad, as at home, his mind was habitually calm
and chiefly ran upon religious themes. Serious conversation and discourses which were called preaching mainly occupied his time. On his return home
he came by land, in the care of a military gentleman, who was coming North for his health. On the
way Hamline attracted attention and won good opinions by his conversation, and being ever ready to
speak in public or any other place on religious
themes, his traveling companion very imprudently

and improperly represented him privately as a candidate for the ministry in the Presbyterian Church. For doing this he had no other authority than the facts that his parents were Congregationalists, and had designed him for the sacred office. Hamline himself had often spoken in public, and it was popularly considered he would be a preacher. But he was not a licentiate, and there is no evidence that he knew that his companion had thus informed concerning him.

On this ground, while in Pittsburg, he was invited by the Rev. Dr. Herron, of the First Presbyterian Church, to occupy his desk. Hamline did so. His services were so well accepted that other Presbyterian pulpits were opened for him. Without guile or thought of evil Hamline consented. His success was satisfactory and his popularity at Pittsburg unquestioned. What he had done was on his part sincere, and in ignorance of any impropriety. He himself, at that time, believed he had experienced a change of heart, and had the ministry in view. It is authentically stated that his senior traveling companion privately brought Hamline thus into notice at this time. The excitement of the effort, however, was unfavorable to his health. Some trifling symptoms in conversation indicated that his brain had been overdrawn. There is something inimitably touching in all this. But as a proof of the good impression left upon the minds of the clergy of Pittsburg whom he had served, in later years, when Mr. Hamline entered the ministry and opened his itinerant life, Dr. Herron once and again sent him an invitation to visit him. But Hamline found no time

to turn aside from his work. When, however, in
1848 his duty as Bishop called him again to Pittsburg to General Conference, Dr. Herron, as will be
noticed in its place, met him with great cordiality,
and at once engaged him to preach in his pulpit.
Other Presbyterian Churches did the same.

Mr. Hamline's convalescence was slow. He continued his studies as he was able. But in the lapse
of time he became dissatisfied with the evidences of
his conversion and changed his plan of life. He
says of himself, "I gradually became convinced that
I was not converted, and finally gave it all up and
went to studying law." On his return from the
South, or soon after, he went West, and, in 1824,
we find him at Zanesville, Ohio. Here he became
accquainted with Miss Eliza Price, an amiable, well-
reported, and carefully educated young lady, an only
child and an heiress. Her father, now a widower,
came to this country from Ireland, when a young
man, with high recommendations and experience in
the mercantile profession. He was a member of
the Protestant Episcopal Church. His promptness,
probity, and ability soon gained him friends, and
at Zanesville he rose to high repute and respectable wealth. To Miss Eliza Mr. Hamline was married. They lived together in much affection and
harmony in the elegant paternal mansion, with an
easy competence, but now without God. In 1827
he took licence as a lawyer, at Lancaster, Ohio, and
returned to his profession. Four children were
given them, two sons and two daughters, of whom
three died in infancy, one only still surviving, Dr.
L. P. Hamline, of Evanston, Illinois. With an in-

come of respectable competency, an honorable profession which he entered with ambition and high
qualifications, a social standing of the first quality,
an æsthetical taste which drew from all sources the
purest earthly enjoyment, a faultless human morality,
a wife worthy of his affections, and a home like an
earthly paradise, Mr. Hamline, to all worldly eyes,
seemed the pet of fortune and the successful candidate for happiness.

> "But mortal pleasure, what art thou in truth?
> The torrent's smoothness ere it dash below."

CHAPTER II.

[1828–29.]

CONVERSION.

NOTWITHSTANDING his uncommon resources for content and earthly happiness, Mr. Hamline was not happy. His own language afterward, in a letter to a friend, best describes his state: "I was," he says, "unhappy. My days and nights were restive. I could not complain of my earthly lot. Neither poverty, sickness, nor solitude made me wretched, for I was removed from all these common occasions of sorrow. I knew no one around me whose means were more competent, whose home was more alluring, or whose intellectual tastes had larger means of gratification. My fireside was attractive, my friends were faithful, my library liberally supplied me the choicest entertainments, and my allotment was a life of easy leisure for the unalloyed fruitions of all these means of comfort. But with all these appliances which seemed to promise me a paradise, I was the prey of unaccountable heart dissatisfactions which I was sure grew upon me with the progress of time; for though at first they were the mere *ennui* which almost passed unnoticed in my memory, they slowly grew into serious annoyances, which I found my outward advantages could neither heal nor assuage."

Mr. Hamline's education had been rigidly Calvinistic, yet, through the Edwardean and Hopkinsian channel of reasoning, he supposed he had found a harmony of predestination and free will which reconciled him to the system, while the doctrines of total depravity and effectual calling, as Calvinistically taught in those days, lulled him to sleep with the belief that he could do nothing till God had renewed his heart. He was at this time living a life of religious indifference, and at the same time of irreligious unrest. His love of metaphysics made him an easy disciple and admirer of Edwards, while his educational prejudice against, not to say his contempt for, the Methodists left him no doctrinal antidote to his pernicious speculations. But he was a child of Providence, and wonderful were the steps by which he was brought to Christ, in the personal assurance of his complete salvation.

In the fall, or early winter, of 1827, Mr. and Mrs. Hamline came to Perrysburg, Cattaraugus County, New York. It appears that Mr. Hamline was called there on legal business which detained him for a length of time. He had also started to see his parents in New England. His usual way of traveling was in a gig, with baggage wagon, driven by a boy, following. He first took board with a Mr. Edwards, whose wife, an intelligent Methodist lady, with Mrs. Maphet, also a Methodist lady of culture, residing in the same place, became important instruments in leading him to Christ. Subsequently Mr. Hamline took board with the family of Mr. John Kent, in Villanova, an adjacent village in Chautauqua County. The Kent family were relatives of Chancellor Kent, of New York, and were also Methodists. Without being aware of it, Mr. Hamline found himself in a neighborhood where he saw Methodism in its original simplicity and power. He soon became known in the social circles, and with the leading men, and his influence was felt. It was felt also that his influence must be for good or evil upon a large scale, according to his choice or rejection of spiritual religion. As he had providentially fallen within Methodistic circles, to that Church he became a subject of special solicitude and prayer. The first steps toward his conversion were taken by the pious women above named. We give the account from Mr. Hamline's own pen:

"What can be done," said Mrs. Maphet, "for a gentleman who listens to all you say, admits his obligations, confesses his sins, yet goes on, careless to eternity, plunging his soul into perdition?"

"Indeed, Mrs. Maphet, you mistake. He is far enough from these pliant admissions. True, he will not dispute with ladies, because he is too polite; but he is a subtle Calvinist, as I learn from his conversation with my husband."

"Don't you think, Mrs. Edwards, that he talks this way merely for argument?"

"O no; there's no mistake. He's a Calvinist, and one of the rankest sort. He told my husband yesterday that if he were to stab a neighbor at midnight, God would inspire him with the malice, and create the volition of the deed."

"That is Calvinism with a vengeance."

"Yes; but my husband says it is true, honest Calvinism, just as Calvin himself taught it, and as the standards of Calvinistic Churches maintain it, though its features are veiled or softened in the pulpit, so as not grossly to offend the public taste."

"I suspect, Mrs. Edwards, that there is little hope of Mr. Hamline's conversion; but he is here a stranger, and from his cast of mind will do much good or evil in the world. Let us make an effort to save him. I think he is a man of dreadful principles, and were his heart as bad as his head, I should be afraid he would turn out a murderer. This Calvinism is a dreadful thing."

"I think badly enough of Calvinism, Mrs. Edwards; that you may be sure; but let it pass at present. I wish you would take this book to Mr. Hamline, and tell him that a lady requests him to read it; and while he reads, will you join with me in secret supplication that God will bless its perusal to his conviction?"

"'Fletcher's Appeal!' Mrs. Maphet, he won't read it."

"Try him, and if he declines I have no hope. If he reads it he will not escape without some serious reflection. Its philosophical cast will suit his taste, and must arrest his attention. You know, too, that, like Moses's ark, it was woven with many prayers. Carry it to him, and if possible get him to read it."

Mrs. Edwards returns home and finds Mr. Hamline and her husband engaged in earnest conversation on free will, predestination, and human accountability, in which Mr. Hamline took high Calvinistic ground. When the conversation closed, and Mr. Hamline rose to retire, Mrs. Edwards entered the room, and handing him the book, repeated Mrs. Maphet's request that he would "do her the favor to give it a reading." He accepted it politely and retired.

A few days after Mrs. Maphet called at Mrs. Edwards's to know the result of reading the book. Mr. Hamline said:

"I received a little volume from you, Mrs. Maphet, for which I return you my sincere thanks."

"Excuse the liberty I took, Mr. Hamline. I thought the philosophy of the treatise would entertain you; and permit me to add, that I hoped a *higher* good would grow out of its perusal."

"Mr. Fletcher is a lively writer, madam. There is French in his style. Not quite so profound as the Calvinistic school. Edwards is my favorite. His work on the Will is the glory of the human mind. Do not by this understand that I underrate Mr. Fletcher. He is a fine, flowing writer, and I thank you, madam, for sending me the book."

"Did you read the 'Address,' sir, which follows the argumentative part of the volume!"

"No, madam. I supposed the argument was what you designed for me?"

"I would be pleased, sir, if you could read the 'Address.'"

"I saw that it was designed for 'seekers of religion,' and as I am not a seeker, I did not think it applicable to my moral state."

"Perhaps, Mr. Hamline, it would induce you to be a seeker That is my hope, and in it I solicit you to finish the volume."

"Do you think, Mrs. Maphet, that we can become seekers when we wish?"

"Yes, sir, I am of that opinion."

"I thought, madam, this serious state of mind was induced always by a supernatural influence—by the Holy Spirit."

"Yes, sir; of that I do not doubt; but the Holy Spirit is waiting, unless I greatly err, to impart his gracious influences to every willing heart. He already moves you to seek a Savior; and if you yield to his gentle drawings, he will greatly increase the influence until it becomes a soul-converting energy."

"There are so many differing opinions, Mrs. Maphet, that one not skilled and experienced is at a loss what to conjecture. Some, you know, hold that the divine efficiency operates all moral changes, and that conversion is an unsought blessing, which none can gain by pursuing, or evade by resisting."

"But surely, Mr. Hamline, as you do not act on this principle in the affairs of life, you would not make a practical application of it in the weightier matters of religion. I can not undertake to argue the disputed points of Christian theology. As to the nature of God's supervision of all things, and its harmony with our freedom, you can discourse much better than I; but do not think it presuming when I say that I sought the different states of mind through which a stupid sinner journeys into the fellowship of God, and I sought not in vain. This makes me solicitous to see others seek, and causes me to believe that they will meet with like success."

"Perhaps, Mrs. Maphet, your seeking and receiving were connected only in point of time, and not in the order of cause and effect."

"That might be the case if I were the only successful seeker. But many of my acquaintances have sought with similar results."

"But have you not known some converted who did not seek?"

"Never one."

"You will recollect better than I; but I was considering the case of Saul of Tarsus."

"True, sir, he was *convicted* before he sought, and that may sometimes happen. But after his conviction he waited three days before the scales fell from his eyes. In the mean-time he was put upon seeking, and going into the city he prayed, and God showed him what he would have him to do."

" But Mrs. Maphet, this overwhelming conviction has never fallen on me."

" Nor is it probable that it will. Saul's was an extraordi-nary case. You know that some become rich without trade, and some honorable without effort; but this is not the common course of things. Wealth generally comes from business and economy, and fame from enterprise and prudence. So a few are convicted of sin without studied diversion of mind from the world, or a diligent application to the means of grace. But, generally, efforts at devotion go before serious and deep con-viction. Let me ask you one question : Did you ever know a man become rich without effort ?"

" Indeed, madam, perhaps—I scarcely know—I think—I believe I am not a competent judge. If you please, madam, I will excuse myself, and attend to a little writing in my room."

Mr. Hamline retired. Mrs. Maphet felt some suspicion that his conscience was disturbed, and was encouraged to hope that prayer in his behalf was not wholly in vain.

This first sally, if it failed to conquer, at least greatly dis-turbed and disconcerted him, which was some gain. Some months after, when Mr. Hamline was practicing a game of chess with Dr. C., in the midst of the game two gentlemen were introduced as Methodist ministers. After a brief salutation they resumed the game. At this time Mr. Hamline was wholly under the influence of his New England education, and scarcely conceded that Methodist ministers held any legitimate title to the profession. At the close of the game one of the ministers opened the following colloquy :

Minister. That must be an intricate game, judging from the *deep attention* you bestow on it.

Hamline. (Slightly embarrassed.) It is intricate, and per-haps, gentlemen, we owe you an apology.

Min. Is it a *useful* game ?

H. So it is accounted by many judicious persons.

Min. To what good account may it be turned ?

H. It is an *intellectual* game. Chance can do nothing for the parties. The skill of the player is tested by its result.

Min. It is, then, like "billiards" or "nine pins."

H. O no, sir, not at all; mind has nothing to do with these. They tend to weaken rather than strengthen the intellect. Chess is a means of mental discipline; its influence is like that derived from the study of mathematics.

Min. I see, sir; chess is a game of intellectual, billiards of mere *manual*, skill.

H. Exactly sir.

Min. Do you not think, sir, that Euclid would be a safe substitute to train the opening mind?

H. O yes; but Euclid is too severe for unremitting study. We must have relaxation; no man can endure to plod at science always.

Min. But, Mr. Hamline, if chess is so much like mathematics, how can it subserve the ends of relaxation? I should think, from your account, that it would only be exchanging one heavy burden for another. As a means of mental discipline, I can not approve the game. You know that study has two objects; one is to train the mind to the vigorous use of all its powers; if chess, as you aver, accomplishes that end, another of great importance it never can subserve, namely, the acquisition of knowledge.

H. It has not all the uses of science, but it has one peculiar advantage; by provoking to emulation it rouses mind to its best efforts; and it also blends relaxation with mental discipline.

Min. What relaxation can it give? If you were preparing to address a jury, would you not prefer a walk in the garden to a game of chess just before you commenced the argument?

H. You drive me to close quarters. The relaxation it affords is somewhat general, and I can not just now specify particulars.

Here the conversation took a new turn, whether by design or accident, is immaterial. But another blow upon the pride and prejudice of Mr. Hamline had been given, and a new idea of the tact and type of Methodist preachers.

The next topic was camp-meetings. Mr. Hamline was invited to attend one just about to commence in the neighborhood. He declined. He did not "approve of such meetings." He had heard much of "the unseemly confusion which prevails at these forest gatherings," and could not think it right to encourage them.

"Have you ever attended a camp-meeting?" said the Minister.

H. No, sir; I was not willing to invade others' rights, and was aware that if I went I should be provoked to levity. I therefore resolved not to go near them.

Min. But ought you to condemn them on the testimony of others, when you might have made your own observations?

H. My witnesses were unimpeachable, and, I presume, stated facts.

Min. But I submit it to you, as a lawyer, whether inspection is not better than report.

H. I suppose it is.

Min. Then you have unwarrantably condemned us. I think, Mr. Hamline, you should come to our meeting. We may surely claim that our trial, as the instigators and supporters of camp-meetings, be according to the "rules of evidence" which require the best evidence that the nature of the case admits.

H. That is not unreasonable; and now I will either come to your meeting, or say no more on the subject of disorder.

After dinner the clergyman departed. Mr. Hamline was surprised, not to say mortified to find an "ignorant Methodist preacher" so well informed, and withal so shrewd in conversation, that even on topics concerning which he supposed clerical men knew very little, the argument was rather against himself.

"You caught a Tartar," said the doctor, as the gentlemen withdrew and left Mr. Hamline and his companion to trifle away another hour at chess.

The third day after this, as Mr. Hamline was walking in the yard, the doctor rode up and asked him if he would visit the camp-ground.

H. You are not serious?

Dr. Get into my carriage, and I will show you.

H. Then I answer no; I can not ride in that direction. Anywhere else, if you please.

Dr. But they have got into difficulty with the rowdies, and want your advice.

"Go, husband," said Mrs. Hamline, who, overhearing the conversation, had come to the door, and was listening to the proposal with deep interest.

Mr. Hamline looked first at the doctor and then at his wife, as uncertain what to do, or whether either was in earnest.

H. Doctor, you say they are in trouble?

Dr. Yes, and they ought to be protected in their rights. I wish you would go over and help them.

H. Well, this is the legitimate result of camp-meetings; yet, as you say, they have the right—that is, the *legal* right—to worship God or Satan, if they will, undisturbed. I will go with you in ten minutes.

The camp-meeting was held on what was called Lake Circuit (then Pittsburg Conference) near Wright's Corners, Chautauqua County, New York. Job Wilson was preacher-in-charge, and William Swayze presiding elder. The doctor, with whom Mr. Hamline rode, was an infidel. In an hour they were on the camp-ground. The voice of singing as they approached, the order and solemnity of the proceedings, made an unexpected impression upon Mr. Hamline's mind. The congregation were assembled for preaching. After the singing, the preacher, who had so lately challenged the utility of chess, arose to address them. The discourse was earnest and evangelical. It was not perfect, yet it was manly and convincing, and so superior to Mr. Hamline's views of Methodist preaching that he was taken by surprise, and was compelled to admit that not one in fifty of the sermons from the trained theologians of the day possessed half the merit. Prayer-meeting within the railed space, which was as usual constructed before the stand, followed the sermon. The description which Mr. Hamline himself gives of the proceedings of the prayer-meeting indicates that it far exceeded in external demonstrations and spiritual results the average of such meetings. It was, indeed, a season of extraordinary power.

Hamline watched the progress of the scene with emotions which he could scarcely endure, yet could by no effort suppress. He had heard just such scenes described. He supposed that a view of them would provoke in his bosom no other feeling than disgust. But it was otherwise. He felt a solemnity, an awe so great that a faintness came over him; and unwittingly he leaned, pale and trembling, against a tree, and every now and then his hand was upon his heart, as though it were uneasy and pained within him. Nor did he observe that his friend, with a *sang froid* peculiar to himself, eyed him closely, and read in his manner the perturbations of his mind. At length the doctor said:

"Mr. Hamline, suppose we step forward and see what is going on?"

"Doctor, I am sick of it. This is a singular scene, and I am at a loss what to think. I believe we had better return."

"Tut! we must stay long enough to speak with these ministers, and hear one or two more of them preach."

So saying, he seized Mr. Hamline by the arm, and, casting at him a significant glance, as much as to say, "Are you frightened?" drew him along to a position where more than a hundred sin-sick souls were crying for mercy.

The sight was wholly new to Mr. Hamline. He had never until then seen a sinner convicted to the point of crying aloud in the presence of others for the pardon of sin. He fixed his eyes first on one, then on another, tracing them along to see if any tokens of affectation or hypocrisy could be detected. He grew dizzy as he gazed, while his convictions of the sincerity of the awakened ones at the altar increased. He became sick and faint. His friend, the doctor, saw it, and, though an infidel, was, for a moment moved. They retired a little, where they could hear but not see what took place. Two hours had scarcely passed, and he had experienced a solemn conviction of the error of his former opinion that Methodist camp-meeting scenes were only adapted to excite vulgar mirth or curiosity. He had no longer any fixed opinions in regard to what he now first saw in respect to the reported disorders of Methodism. The confusion of his mind had set afloat all his preconceived views of religion. This confusion arose from the stirrings of his heart. He was smitten, and the blow had reached and wounded the "inward parts." The doctor, too, was disturbed. Mr. Hamline was interested for him, and observed, with lively satisfaction, a shade of slight concern spread along the lines of his changing countenance. Little was said by either. But the doctor never came to Christ.

The scene at the altar had spread religious concern among the witnessing multitude, and checked the purpose of the rioters. Still it was considered best that the statute protecting religious meetings should be read from the stand. A few loud blasts of the horn gave signal for closing the prayer-meeting and for the assembling of the people for preaching. Mr.

Hamline and his companion ascended the stand with the preachers. As the gathering throngs dropped into their seats, their eyes were directed to the stand. Mr. Hamline seemed the special object of interest. Some took him for a minister; others knew him, and knew his dislike of camp-meetings. He grew uneasy at his position, but in the crisis of his embarrassment he was told to "proceed." As he arose and stood before them, hundreds of prayers ascended to God on his behalf. For the incidents of that hour he afterward praised God. It is not to be supposed that he himself premeditated any grave defense of camp-meetings. He proposed to expound the statute and retire from observation. But as he proceeded he grew confident, and went on to say that this was his *début* upon a camp-ground; that he had looked for repulsive exhibitions, but that the very things which, in description, had disgusted him, appeared inoffensive to the eye. He then spoke to the disorderly, assuring them that "he who had the cowardice to interrupt these solemnities was too mean to be cursed by any decent man."

The sermon followed, and after it, again, the prayer-meeting. The presiding elder, "Father Swayze," invited Mr. Hamline to go to the vacant place at the altar and kneel with him before God. The following conversation ensued:

H. Excuse me, Mr. Swayze; I am a hardened sinner, and dare not approach a place so sacred while my heart is unmoved.

S. That, sir, is Satan's device. He would rob you of God's pardoning mercy. If your heart is hard, you should go to the altar to get it softened. The more obdurate it is, the more you need the prayers of God's people, and the more prompt you should be to assume the attitude in which you may enjoy them.

H. Surely Mr. Swayze, you would not have me assume the *posture* without the *spirit* of mourning.

S. Surely I would, if you can not otherwise assume it. Do you not *wish* to mourn?

H. I suppose not, or I *should* mourn.

S. And do you always, then, feel as you wish to feel?

H. In religion I suppose I do. That is the view I have taken of religion when skepticism has not prevailed over belief. I have heard it said that "*every man has just as much religion as he desires.*" Is it not true?

S. No, sir. The habitual state of a devout heart is that of desire; and one of the most conclusive, indirect evidences of a gracious state is a thirsting after God and his salvation.

H. But if God does not satisfy holy desires is he not tyrannical, and a violator of his promise?

S. What promise?

H. "He that hungers and thirsts after righteousness shall be filled."

S. Mr. Hamline, excuse me to-day from all doctrinal and metaphysical discussions. I urge upon you a simple effort to seek religion, assuring you, from God, "they that seek shall find." My duty toward you now lies in a narrow compass. Will you go with me and kneel down at the altar?

H. I repeat, sir, that to do it would be hypocrisy. Sinful as I am, I should fear to desecrate that altar by approaching it without tempers befitting such a posture. I have no just conceptions of my depravity, no proper desires for renovation, and to do what would indicate such desires would be adding deceit to insensibility.

S. What do you mean by *proper* desires for renovation?

H. I mean a desire for renovation for its own sake, not for its resulting benefits.

S. Will you never seek religion until you can do it without regard to its benefits?

H. Indeed, sir, to tell the truth, I know not what I shall do. But I confess that I am all wrong, or these people are not right. I can not, however, go with you to the altar; I am selfish, and my nature seems worse than common natures. If I wish for religion, it is merely as a step to heaven—mark that— as a mere step to heaven. I have no love for religion's self. I want not its purity, but its peace; not its sore travail of duties and self-denials, but its escape from the maelstrom of perdition to the beatific rest.

Mr. Hamline's Calvinism was educational and honest. A mind like his could not rest in simple dogma, he must have a metaphysical ground work for his theology, which, indeed, if well laid, is right and immovable, but in this case it had proved seductive, and with an unconscious pride of intellect, had nearly proved his ruin. He did not approach the altar, but remained at the meeting until its close, his mind growing more and more perplexed. He seemed careworn and sad.

When he returned, his wife met him at the door; but her eye no sooner fell upon his features, as she was advancing with great cordiality to welcome him, than she uttered an exclamation of concern and said, "Husband, what ails you? Surely you have been sick." On his assuring her that he was well, she exchanged her look of alarm for an expression of humor, and said, "Then you must have got the power." The reply was embarrassed, and in a manner so serious that they soon fell into a grave and quiet conversation.

Mr. Hamline had now passed repeated warnings, entreaties, and opportunities, while his heart remained proud and resistant. He was awakened, condemned, restless, and unhappy. All his old foundations of half-skeptical, metaphysical reasonings had been shaken, and his strong prejudices rebuked and confounded. One more test remained to be applied. Pharaoh yielded upon the death of the first-born. Two months had passed, when Mr. and Mrs. Hamline, at two o'clock in the morning, September 10, 1828, might have been seen in earnest conversation over the sick cradle of their only child. "Suppose, husband, we send for Dr. D.," said Mrs. Hamline; "he is highly spoken of, and is as near as any physician."

H. I have no objection; but I assure you there is no hope. I believe that the child will die, and I have felt so from the beginning. It is a deeply wrought impression in my bosom that she will be taken from us on *my account.*

Mrs. H. How on your account, my dear?

H. I can not explain. If I live you shall hereafter know.

While the physicians were in consultation over the case, Mr. Hamline walked rapidly back and forth, with his eye constantly turned to the cradle. Suddenly the child exclaimed: "I fall! I fall!" The frantic mother pressed the child's forehead, and said, soothingly, "No, my baby shall not fall." For a moment it quieted, and the spasm returned. Mr. Hamline rushed to the door to call the physicians, and the mother sprang wildly up, and exclaimed, "My baby will die!" The little one caught the words and repeated, "Baby die! baby die!" and, as if comprehending the whole, she handed her little doll to her mother, and falteringly repeated, "Baby die!" till she became insensible. The doctors hurried in and exclaimed, "She is gone!"

The mortal agony of the parents was great, but greater was the agony of the father for having resisted the Holy Ghost. While the little frame was being prepared for the grave, he took the mother by the hand, led her into an adjoining room, knelt with her, and tried to pray. Retiring to a grove for meditation, he said, "And now, what have I left? Should God come down again in his wrath, what could he lay his hand upon? Ah! heaven can strike *one heavier* blow, and it will come unless I turn. There is no way of escape but by repentance. God has now only plucked the fruit, or, rather, has broken off a twig. If he comes again in judgment he will cut down the tree." Two full hours passed in these reflections, and then he seriously set himself to form the *purpose* of seeking God.

A conflict with skeptical suggestions as to experimental religion, and with election decrees having been first endured, he turned to what he considered the regular business of seeking religion. For three weeks he attended upon duty in a formal, regular, and business-like way, with no other result than a deeper consciousness of sin and helplessness. One day Mrs. Maphet called, and, seating herself near Mr. and Mrs. Hamline, sat for a time in silence.

"What is the matter, Mrs. Maphet?" said Mr. Hamline.

Mrs. M. I am concerned, sir, at your condition.

H. Why so, Mrs. Maphet? I am trying to seek the kingdom of God.

Mrs. M. Yes, Mr. Hamline, so I understand; but, from all I can learn, you seek in such a manner that you will never obtain.

H. Please explain.

Mrs. M. You spend half an hour or so, two or three times a day, in your closet. The rest of your time, if I understand, you give up to miscellaneous reading and conversation. Now, sir, can a man accomplish any great worldly thing by devoting to it an hour or so each day? Suppose you had studied the languages an hour a day in your boyhood, or had read law at that rate when a student, what would have been the result?

H. Why, Mrs. Maphet, you know we are not to be saved by works. Would you have me drudge all day at my devotions? for, unwilling as I am to confess, or even to *know* it, I find that all my efforts to pray are mere drudgery, affording me neither peace nor hope.

Mrs. M. I fear, Mr. Hamline, that you labor under a great mistake. You say we are not saved by works. Now this is both true and false. It is false in the sense just now suggested by you, and it is false in any sense which lends the least countenance to inaction or supineness in the pursuit of religion.

H. Please, then, Mrs. Maphet, to tell me how it is true.

Mrs. M. It is *true* only in the sense of denying *merit* to our works. We *are* saved by works not at all meritorious in the sight of God. This is the true relation of works to human salvation, if I can understand the Bible.

H. This is a new idea. I suppose, then, I am to work just as though I could purchase salvation.

Mrs. M. Yes, and feel just as though your works were of themselves mere sin and death; for this is true.

H. Then you would have me read and pray more.

Mrs. M. Yes; I would say, do nothing else. Throw away every thing: law books, newspapers, history, poetry, conversation, and, if possible, the very memory of your afflictions— forget your child and her grave in the all-absorbing efforts of your soul to find Jesus. In a word, no longer *seek*, but *strive* to enter in at the strait gate. O, sir, it is rather insulting than honoring God to profess an intention to serve him, and then show so little regard for his favor as to pursue it with less zeal and diligence than you would the veriest trifle on earth.

H. Mrs. Maphet, I am convinced of my error; I have insulted God, and by my conduct shown small regard for his favor. But I will do differently; I will from this moment do nothing but implore his mercy.

Mrs. Maphet wept during this conversation, and Mrs. Hamline avouched a cordial concurrence in all she had said. From that hour Mr. Hamline threw aside every thing else, and gave himself wholly to the pursuit of religion. For two days he was much of the time alone upon his knees; but, alas! it grew darker and darker. Time passed heavily, while in various forms of humiliation and earnest seeking he seemed only to sink into deeper darkness. Returning from church one rainy Sabbath, wet and cold, after peculiar self-denials and labor, he entered through a back door alone and passed unobserved into the garret, where he yielded to the most agonizing reflections.

"And this," said he to himself, "is seeking religion. And this agony, which no demon could endure, I am to receive as an illustration of God's mercy. He says, 'Seek, and ye shall find.' Indeed I *have* found—what? A heart incapable of loving God, fierce in its enmity toward my Maker, uncontrollable by any power of mine, and equally so by any aid vouchsafed me from above." Then it occurred to him, "If any man love not the Lord Jesus Christ let him be *anathema maranatha*." "Well," he exclaimed, "I love not Christ. My heart is as empty of all such love as a deserted, falling mansion is of elegant furniture. I can not love him. And I shall be cursed, nay, am cursed; cursed by the Father, cursed by the Son, cursed by the Holy Ghost! And is there a worse hell?"

As he uttered the closing sentences in an agitated frame he raised his voice, and was overheard by Mrs. Hamline, who hurried up stairs and interrupted his painful soliloquy. Wet and cold as he was, he followed her, with some hesitation, to the chamber, and seated himself by the fire. In a few minutes Mrs. Maphet announced that the preacher was below, and was about to have prayers, inviting Mr. and Mrs. Hamline to join in the devotions. "Excuse me," said Mr. Hamline; "to me prayer is useless, and I must give it up." Mrs. Maphet burst into a flood of tears and retired. "Husband," said Mrs. Hamline, "let us go down." Partly relenting, and moved by his wife's entreaties, he yielded and joined the praying circle. In the progress of the prayer, under some common devotional expressions, a softening influence suddenly touched his heart. It was not overwhelming, but gentle—a small rivulet in the desert of his heart—a distilling dew on the parched waste of its affections. Yet it was refreshing. Hope in an instant recovered its lost dominion, and Mr. Hamline said within himself, "Perhaps I am not lost. I will go to meeting once more, and make another effort to find a reconciled God." He accordingly went that very evening to a prayer-meeting. It was a small assembly of twelve praying souls, met to plead in Christ's name. The minister was there, and having given out a hymn, he said, "If our afflicted friends," meaning Mr. and Mrs. Hamline, "will come forward and kneel down we will all pray for them." It was the first proposition that had been made of

the kind, and probably Mr. Hamline had never until then been
in a state of mind to act upon it; but the words were no sooner
uttered than he hastened forward and fell upon his knees.

Earnest pleading in his behalf now arose from as many
believing hearts as were in that little assembly. The voluntary
outward humiliation of Mr. Hamline as a "mourner" greatly
moved them. Their strong desires in his behalf were unre-
strainable, and in a few minutes every tongue seemed to be
employed in loud invocations for God's mercy upon him. After
a time the special struggle of his soul abated, and he lapsed
into the calmness of indifference. A young man came and
knelt by his side and whispered, "Mr. Hamline, I fear you are
not anxious enough for salvation." "No, sir," said Mr. Hamline. "I am not anxious at all." "I feel," said the other, "that
if you do not embrace religion to-night you never will." "So I
think," said Mr. Hamline. The young man paused a little, and
then exclaimed, "I can not give you up!" and commenced
praying aloud. Suddenly a divine influence was shed on the
assembly. Again all fell upon their knees, and in a few minutes every voice was once more pleading in prayer. Hamline
felt the descending power. For a minute or two he retained
his kneeling posture, but his desires for salvation grew more
and more vehement, till at last, forgetful of every thing but the
wants of a soul making its last effort for eternal life, with one
unrestrained outcry for mercy, he threw himself on the floor.
Mrs. Hamline flew to him in great consternation, and others
gathered round, ready, if there were need or opportunity, to do
what might be done to soften the features of a scene so bold and
rugged. But God was also there, and Mr. Hamline had naught
to do with any other. He did not know, until afterward informed, that his wife had hung over him so long in silent agony.

The witnesses say that for one hour and a half Mr. Hamline continued in this prone posture. The time was almost
wholly spent in exclaiming in full voice, "Come, Jesus?" or
"Help me, Jesus!"

In the midst of his struggles it came suddenly to his mind,
as though whispered by the lips of the Savior, "Will you now
give up your child?" and instantly his whole heart, with a new,
strange outflow of consenting emotions, said "Yes, yes; I do,
I do!" After a little time it was again suggested, "Can you
now forgive your enemies?" and in the same full, hearty man-

ner he exclaimed, "Yes!" feeling at the moment that he would fain have all his worst enemies in his arms at once that he might press them to his bosom. After a little it was again suggested, "Can you now give up *yourself* and all you have forever to Christ, to do with you and with it as shall please him?" and again, with an unspeakable fullness and freeness, his heart replied. "Yes, all—all—I give up all forever!"

At this point, had his faith taken strong hold of Christ, he might have gained the witness of renewing grace. But the peace and quiet of mind which supervened he took for stupidity. "'T is done!" he says. "This was my last effort, and Christ, who came so near, has left me forever!" "How do you feel now?" inquired a venerable saint. "Stupid! stupid!" said Mr. Hamline. "Ah!" said she; "you'll feel better to-mórrow." She had penetrated his real state better than he had. He returned home. Before retiring he says to his wife, "Let us once more try to pray." A gentle melting came upon him in prayer. "Perhaps," thought he, "all is not lost." In the morning, alone in his room, he opened his Bible to these words, "Let not your heart be troubled: ye believe in God, believe also in me." John XIV, I. His whole soul seemed in a moment absorbed in meditating the force of this language. "Why am I troubled?" thought he. "Does not *Jesus* utter these words? Why did I not think and feel that it was his own language addressed to a wretch like me? Yes, I believe in God, the Creator, the Judge, the Avenger, and my heart is 'troubled.' Why have I not believed also in Jesus, the Savior, the bearer of my sin and punishment, and thus eased my troubled conscience?" He fell upon his knees in prayer, crying "Jesus, I can not let thee go." "Jesus, thou can'st not cast me off." As he repeated this, Christ came down to him and within him in fullness and sweetness, and he exclaimed "O Jesus, thou art *within* me," and that Scripture was borne to his mind, "Christ in you the hope of glory." Doubts were gone. He rose exulting in the fullness of this life. This great event and era of his life was on October 5, 1828. He now first begins to live. Thirty-six years later, on the anniversary of his being "born from above," he says, "I am thirty-six years old to-day."

At the first meeting he attended after his conversion, at the close of the sermon the minister requested him to exhort. He

4

arose, and related the history of the "Prodigal Son," bringing the whole scene in vision before the audience, until they
seemed to behold the poor, tattered, forlorn wretch tremblingly
approaching the paternal mansion, and the venerable father
first espying him in the distance, and watching with intense
interest his approach, till at length, recognizing his returning
son, he ran to meet and embrace him. He then said, "That
prodigal son is before you in the person of the speaker. *I* am
that prodigal; I have returned to my Father's house. For me
the fatted calf has been killed, and on me the best robe has
been put," etc. The affecting manner in which he presented
his conversion told on the hearts of the hearers, and a number
were converted that night.

At the first love-feast he attended, the presiding elder sat
down, after opening the meeting, saying, "Let the man most
deeply indebted to grace be first to rise and speak for Christ."
Mr. Hamline was instantly on his feet, exclaiming, "I am
that man." As he went on speaking, a sister, whose husband
had been defeated in a suit in which Mr. Hamline was the lawyer for the prosecution, and who had on that account been
very bitterly prejudiced against him, asked Mrs. Maphet, who
sat next her,

"Who is that?"

"Why, it is the lawyer of whom you have said, 'he can
not be converted unless he makes restitution to my husband.'"

"Well, I believe he is converted." And a little time after
she exclaimed, "Bless the Lord! he is converted."

Mr. Hamline thus again narrates his experience:
"On the 10th of September, 1828, my little daughter,
Eliza Jane Price, yielded her spirit into the hands of
Christ. She had been our idol. When she was gone
from us, with an aching heart and solemn mind I walked
out, with my senses nearly bewildered by distracting
grief and want of rest, and in the midst of both said
within myself, I shall see no more earthly good. God
has closed upon me the gates of terrestrial happiness.
Let me now seek 'the kingdom of God,' and prepare to follow my sainted dear one to the heaven of

saints. From that time I received her death as a
providence which must work a revolution in my feelings, hopes, joys, prospects, wishes, and destiny.
Still I went lazily to work to improve the dispensation. I knelt morning and evening with my body
to pray, and cold and heartless utterances broke the
silence of the hour of prayer. I continued thus until
Friday, the 3d of October. At that time my dear
wife, Eliza, became more anxious about her soul,
and deep conviction fastened upon my mind. This
continued until Sunday evening, the 5th, when at a
prayer-meeting at father Whipple's my struggles became extreme. I now believe God then changed my
heart, and on Monday, the 6th, gave me evidence of
his love. With few interruptions I enjoyed God's
presence, until Thursday morning, the 9th, when I
became sorrowful, and continued by times despairing
and calm until Friday evening, the 24th of October,
when fresh light burst into my soul. Saturday, 25th,
was a day of peace. Sunday, October 26, 1828, was
a day of days. I joined the Methodist society on
trial. God blessed me in it. 'One thing have I
desired of the Lord, that will I seek after; that I
may dwell in the house of the Lord forever to behold the beauty of the Lord.'

"Monday, October 27th, was a day of sweet enjoyment. My soul was like a well-watered garden.
God's grace is sufficient for me.

"Monday, November 3d. Have just returned
from Perrysburg Quarterly Meeting. I saw the fields
and streets and lanes where I had walked to meditate
upon myself, upon my own worldly prospects, and
lay my schemes of worldly ambition. But O! how

changed! Three months had wrought miracles in my
behalf, during my absence from this place. I have
lost my moral identity, and resumed it in a new,
and I trust lasting, character since I left this place.

"O for this love let rocks and hills
    Their lasting silence break.

"Sunday, attended the holy Eucharist, and ate
the flesh and drank the blood of Jesus. O my Savior! I feel that I have a part and lot with thy followers. This thy son was dead and is alive again,
was lost and is found. Holy Redeemer, help the vile
dust which thou hast redeemed to praise thee with
his latest breath, and shout thy praise on hills of
light in worlds beyond the grave!"

CHAPTER III.

[1829-31.]

EARLIEST PREACHING—OLD OHIO CIRCUIT—MOUNT VERNON.

A MIND like that of Mr. Hamline's could not be inactive. Activity was the law of his being. Hitherto he had moved in the direction of his ambitious schemes, but now, with a change so wonderful, an experience so clear, like the converted Saul, "immediately he was not disobedient to the heavenly vision." He began to speak and address the people upon the all-momentous concerns of religion. As he says: "I began to talk to the people, and they were convicted and converted." "He began speaking in public," says Rev. J. W. Nevins, "immediately after his conversion, and continued to do so till he returned to Ohio. His wonderful conversion might lead us to expect wonderful results. He seemed to spring into the new life fully armed for the great conflict. A few junior months sufficed for preparatory discipline, and he burst upon the world like a new star in the firmament. Immediately all things were counted loss for Christ. Home, wealth, worldly honor, ambition, the pride of social position, all were laid upon the altar. From his palace home he was called to sleep often in cabins, where, in the bleak winter night, he had only to draw aside the hanging blanket in order to thrust his hand between the logs into the storm without. His meager income, after meeting his necessary traveling expenses, he gave to his poorer brethren. His easy pleasure-rides he exchanged for long, tedious, and often perilous traveling, fording streams, crossing prairies, threading forests which sometimes were not even blazed.

Several weeks were spent, after his conversion, among the loving friends to whom, under God, Mr. Hamline owed so much, after which it became necessary to return with the dear remains of their beloved little one to Zanesville, to place them in the family vault. The fame of his conversion and public exercises had preceded him. There was at this time a great revival in progress at Zanesville, and the excitement increased by the coming of two students of the Ohio University, Joseph M. Trimble (afterwards Dr. Trimble) and Wm. Herr. The former was the son of Governor Trimble. They were both students of high standing, and afterwards men of mark and high repute. They were fresh from college, and had just entered the itinerancy. Their coming awakened public interest, and the multitudes came out. "But," says Finley (in his "Sketches of Methodism"), "the wonders did not stop here. It was rumored that the most eloquent divine that ever addressed a Zanesville audience had become a Methodist preacher, and was coming back from the East, whither he had gone on a visit, to identify himself with Methodism, in a place where before he had wondered at the audacity of a Methodist preacher in daring to ride along the main street. He came, and listening, wondering thousands hung upon his lips, if possible with greater interest than they had

done before. Under these circumstances Methodism
gained an influence and standing which it has not
lost to this day." Wm. Herr, above named, in his
semi-Centennial sermon, 1878, speaking of 1828, and
the noble army of ministers that arose at that time
in the Ohio Conference, says: "A few years later
two stars of the first magnitude appeared in the ministerial horizon—L. L. Hamline and Edward Thomson, the one from the legal and the other from the
medical profession, both of refined tastes, classic
culture, and rare pulpit eloquence. After years of
successful ministerial and literary labor in the editorial and educational departments, they were both
elected to the episcopal office, which they adorned
with peculiar meekness and dignity."

At this time, the beginning of 1829, Mr. Hamline felt no call to devote his life to the ministry.
He was a member on probation, and could not hold
an office within six months from the date of joining
the Church. Meanwhile, he turned his attention to
the practice of law. Hitherto he had been successful—had never lost a case. We are not informed that he subsequently lost a case, but he felt
a growing incongeniality with the profession. The
Church, too, believed him truly called to the sacred
office. If he felt it difficult to pursue his profession
under the present state of mind, still he could not
retire without adequate reason. He had not been
inactive since his conversion, but had become distinguished for his labors at camp-meetings, protracted meetings, and other occasions, besides the
ordinary means of grace. But the time had come
to decide the sphere of his life-work. One day,

while conducting a suit before a single justice, an
overwhelming conviction fell upon him that he must
quit the law and preach the Gospel. This he endeavored to overcome or dismiss for the time, but it
returned again and again, and so embarrassed him
that he was forced to shorten his argument and close
his speech. He never attempted another. Here
ended his legal pleading, thenceforward to turn to
the sublimer calling of "beseeching men to be reconciled to God." He received license to exhort
about six months after his conversion, and license to
preach at the expiration of his first year of membership, November, 1829. The balance of that year,
till September, 1830, he spent in varied labor as a
licentiate, wherever a Providential door was opened.

At the session of the Pittsburg Conference, August, 20, 1830, Robert Hopkins (who still lives at this
writing) was appointed Presiding Elder of the Mo-
nongahela District. The District lay mostly in West
Virginia, "including, also, Washington and Greene
Counties in Pennsylvania. The narrow strip of land
lying between Pennsylvania and the Ohio River,
called the 'Pan Handle,' was of course included in
the District. Here were situated the West Liberty
and Ohio Circuits, the Rev. Jacob Young being appointed to the former, and Robert C. Hatton to the
latter." Hatton refused to go to his appointment on
principles relating to antislavery preaching, and, after
consultation, the two circuits were united, with Jacob
Young preacher-in-charge, and an assistant to be
supplied. Young recommended Mr. Hamline, and,
after the Presiding Elder had taken further advice
with David Young, also a Presiding Elder, who lived

in Zanesville and knew Hamline well, the call was issued. Though unexpected, it was promptly obeyed. Mr. Hopkins, from whom we derive this information, says: "His first appearance made no unfavorable impression on our mind, though it was clear that he had not been long associated with Methodists. His humble teachableness spoke volumes in his favor. It was the time of our Quarterly-meeting. After preaching and business of Saturday, Brother Hamline was announced to preach in the evening. The congregation assembled. Anxiety was on tiptoe to hear the new preacher. All things conspired to make the occasion one of profound interest. He rose in the pulpit at the proper time, and, with gravity and dignity, went through the opening services. He announced his text in Luke xviii, 29, 30, A few sentences were sufficient to convince us that we had before us a man of no ordinary ability, possessing a mind highly cultivated and great power of language. To say we were all pleased with the performance, is language too tame for the occasion. We were in ecstasy, carried beyond ourselves, half crazy with delight.

"We met next day for the services of the Sabbath, and, as we wished the people to have the best preaching available, I asked Brother Hamline. But his modesty was equal to his greatness. He shrunk from the very idea of taking the place of the Presiding Elder, and could not entertain it for a moment. So we yielded to his wish, but appointed him to preach again at night, which he did. His text was Gal. iii, 26. He described the relation between parent and child, he dwelt on the patrimony which the

5

former provides for the latter, when suddenly he
paused, his arms dropped to his sides, and, looking
on the congregation, he asked the unconverted man
what kind of patrimony he expected. The solemnity was almost oppressive. He then portrayed the
future condition of the sinner. The scene was awful.
One man who sat near the aisle in front was so
frightened that he fled for the door and disappeared."

After this Mr. Hamline attended at a Quarterly-
meeting at Washington, on the District, and preached
from Hos. xi, 8, "How shall I give thee up?"
Waterman, the Pastor, himself a preacher of note,
said, "it was the best sermon he ever heard." At
the camp-meeting on the District he preached from
Psa. viii, 3. "He carried the attention and feelings
of the congregation with him," says Hopkins. "It
was a heavenly time. Rev. W. Lambdin followed
in exhortation, and invited mourners to the altar."
"They did come," says our informant. "We can
not describe the scene. The altar would hold no
more. They knelt outside, all over the ground.
The whole was a prayer-meeting. As the result of
the meeting we took in one hundred and thirty-eight
probationers. Some three or four turned out ministers of the Gospel. Thank God for even the remembrance of it." "In fine," concludes Brother
Hopkins, "we spent much of our time when on that
part of the District with Brother Hamline, were with
him in the pulpit and on the platform, in private
families and secret devotions, in the prayer-meeting
and the social circles, and in all found him invaria-
bly what we ought all to be—pious and devoted
and humble. And we are tempted to close this

sketch with the language of Mr. Wesley, in the close of his sermon on the death of the sainted Fletcher, 'I shall never see his like again.'" Hamline was, indeed, as yet unfamiliar with Methodistic government and usage, but his wonderful experience in coming to Christ, his powerful conviction and conversion, his naturally incisive mind now baptized with the Holy Spirit, made all his former studies and knowledge of men available to the pulpit, while in social life he was every-where at ease.

At one of the appointments on this circuit, while preaching with great power, his audience suddenly burst into tears, rising simultaneously to their feet. A scene of power and mercy ensued. Among the converts of the day was one who became a preacher of the Gospel. His field of labor was now seventy miles from his family, to whom his visits were necessarily rare and short. After a few weeks spent on the circuit, he thus writes to his wife, under her burden of solitude and care:

"My Dear Eliza,—I trust you will not permit the affairs of home to make you unhappy. For my part I think if we can obtain and keep our Savior we will do well. Oh, that we might serve God and enjoy him. Your letter came to hand Sunday evening, November 14th, just as I was entering the pulpit. I have been enabled to preach to acceptance, and, I hope, to some little profit. At Wellsburg the prospect is flattering. I am now on my way round the circuit. Hope to see you a couple of days early in December.

"Keep courage, and may God bless you and the little boy. If we serve God he will make all plain. Oh, may we have Christ in the soul! I leave it all and commit my cause to God, and trust we shall yet reach heaven. I say again, my dear Eliza, do not grieve and mourn about our affairs. Oh, how much worse off we might be! I fear more for you than the property. I fear for your nerves and headache. Rest in the confidence of divine mercy and protection. I am resolved to commit all my griefs and fears into the hands of Jesus. Good-bye, dear. May you be happy in your God."

While here the Rev. Z. H. Coston, who had taken a deep and friendly interest in Mr. Hamline, came seventy miles to see him, and to know for himself whether in truth he had been converted. He came in an opportune moment. The preacher-in-charge was sick, it was quarterly-meeting with them, and Hamline knew not how to preside in a quarterly conference. Coston instructed him. His visit was convincing. His friend was truly converted. Coston was a life-long friend of Hamline, and himself and wife accompanied him to Mt. Pleasant, Iowa, in the latter part of his life, living till the death of the Bishop in the same village square, and helped, at Bishop Hamline's request, to dress him for the grave.

The savor of Mr. Hamline's influence on this first circuit remained. Later, in 1836, Bishop Morris passed over this region, and wrote to Mr. Hamline his observations. The Bishop says: "I intended to write you long since, and have frequently been reminded of this duty by hearing your name kindly spoken of by inquiring friends as I crossed your old paths at different points. Yet, like other sinners, I have been slow to carry my good desires into practice. On my way to Wheeling, Virginia, I stopped at Athens and Zanesville, and from Wheeling to this place (Pittsburg). I came through your old circuit about Wellsburg and called on father Worthington. In all these places brethren inquired after your welfare. While in Beaver I met with sister Lee [afterward Mrs. Jacob Young], who informed me it was in her house, in the State of New York, you were converted. She showed me her little son, named for you, and was not a little pleased when I informed her that you wore a Methodist coat and a 'broad-brimmed hat.'"

In 1845, when Mr. Hamline (then Bishop) was passing over the same ground, he thus writes to his son:

"We are now on 'Old Ohio Circuit,' in the place where I first traveled. Wellsburg, Virginia, is a beautiful place on the south bank of the Ohio, a few miles above Wheeling. Here we have received a truly warm greeting, and have been often overwhelmed by the pressure of friends. I would be delighted to have you travel with us through this part of Virginia. Your dear mother left you fourteen years ago in the hands of Mrs. Kent four weeks when you were about eighteen months old, and went around this circuit with me. It is a sad gratification to think of this as we visit along among friends. Let us be sure that we prepare to rejoin our dear friends who now look down and watch us in the kingdom of God."

To Rev. Jacob Young, his senior colleague on the circuit, he writes, at the same time.

"I have enjoyed the privilege of meeting many of our old friends. I preached at Wellsburg three times, at Worthington's once, and once at Liberty. I intended to go to Short Creek, but feared I was laboring too much. The Virginia friends were most hearty and kind in their welcome, and made me feel that it was good to see them."

Mr. Hamline's appointment to Mt. Vernon Circuit the following year (1831), we need only say, was equally auspicious. His senior colleague was Rev. J. M'Mahon. With his Presiding Elder, Rev. L. Swormstedt, his acquaintance ripened into a life long friendship. Having now become established in his call to preach, and proved himself as such, he was prepared for the advanced step which awaited him.

CHAPTER IV.

[1832-34.]

JOINS THE OHIO CONFERENCE—GRANVILLE—ATHENS.

ON September 19, 1832, the Ohio Conference met for its annual session at Dayton, Ohio. In a class of twenty-seven candidates, who joined Conference that year, we find the name of L. L. Hamline. He was appointed as a junior preacher to the Granville circuit, at a reasonable distance from home, Granville being about thirty miles from Zanesville, though the average distance of the appointments on the circuit was probably greater. Three preachers manned the circuit, of whom S. H. Holland was the second junior, and H. S. Farnandis the senior. In the technology of the day it was an old-time "six weeks' circuit." Farnandis was a godly man, of great zeal and tact and respectable ability, but of remarkable humility. He was small of stature, and David Young, of Zanesville, used to say, "he was the greatest little man he ever knew." He was preacher-in-charge of Athens circuit in 1827, when the great revival was experienced, and William Herr, Edward R. Ames (our late Bishop), Joseph M. Trimble, and others were converted. He was skillful to save souls and nurse them when converted. Mr. Hamline felt happy in being with one as his senior who was in such perfect sympathy with his own spiritual aspirations. A friendship sprang up between them which was ardent and life-long. On his death-bed Farnandis sent for Mr. Hamline (then Bishop), and when the latter came and entered the house the dying patriarch burst into tears and exclaimed, "My brother, have you come?" and, throwing his arms around him, clasped him to his heart. Bishop Hamline stayed two weeks, comforting the sick man, preaching to and for him in his sick-room, administering the sacrament, and in various ways relieving and cheering his last hours. When they parted it was till the great reunion in heaven.

A glorious success attended the year. In the town of Newark the work was specially prosperous. We could not better give the keynote to Mr. Hamline's zeal and aspirations than he himself has given in the following letter to his friend, Rev. E. D. Roe, M. D. Roe had left the medical and mercantile professions, as Hamline had the legal, to "preach the kingdom of God." He was a man of true piety, fine culture, and noble aspirations. They had both joined conference this year, and both had entered their new fields of labor. Hamline had just returned from his first visit to his circuit, to which he was to return the same week. His letter has the ring of the heroic days:

"ZANESVILLE, O., *November* 10, 1832.

"REV. E. D. ROE,—Your note reached me at Newark, inviting me in kind and brotherly terms to visit you this Saturday and Sunday. I am not able to do so. As I have just commenced my labors, I can not consistently leave my circuit at this early stage. I am pleased that you enter with comfort upon your labors, and trust that your health, patience, and zeal will wear well. I hardly know what to promise myself. I start to-morrow morning to ride, preach, and, by the grace of God,

seek and feel religion. The *circuit* is *my* home, and if I can
only take my family along, I shall then be able to say, 'All I
require I have—a Savior, a circuit, a family, a living.' Do you
feel well? Are you inspired with an increasing zeal for your
God and Redeemer? Do you not repent this resignation to the
labors of the vineyard? When you sit and listen to the blast
by night and watch the 'scowling cloud,' and know that you
are to ride in 'sleety shower,' and shelter in the half-composed
cabin, among the rude or rustic, does not your soul draw back?
Come on, my dear Edward, and see thy Savior on plain and
mount, and sea and land, with fishermen and 'publicans and
sinners,' rejected by a scornful world; in the Garden, before
Pilate and Herod, and *on the cross.* . . . I'll go through
storms and tempests, floods, and flames to serve this blessed
Savior. If I have a wife, he had a mother. If I have gold and
riches, he had the riches of heaven and earth, and for our
sakes he became poor.

"I feel better. I have half written down the enemy.
Blessed Lord God, give me a glorious victory! I do trust to
see good this year. Our quarterly meeting was more than
ordinary for Newark. Few joined. I left you a line at Strowth-
ers. If possible, meet me somewhere on that part of my circuit. I long to speak with you.

"My poor Eliza has cares pressing upon her in my absence, from which I would be glad to see her delivered."

From his circuit he writes back to his lonely wife
a month later:

"GRANVILLE, *December* 10, 1832.

"MY DEAR ELIZA,—I have passed around the north-east
part of the circuit since last Sabbath (yesterday week), and
through awful roads and high floods, and preached at seven
appointments. I could not reach Granville on Saturday because of the streams; but on Sunday morning several gentlemen started with me and helped me on, so that I got into town
a few minutes before meeting time. Preached at eleven and
half past one. Held a prayer-meeting at candle-light. A good
congregation, and I trust a profitable Sabbath.

. . . "I trust you are better and more happy in the Lord,
your God. O how I long to be a Christian like Fletcher or

Bramwell, and see my dear Eliza as devoted as Cooper or Rowe! The Lord help you."

At Newark the work went forward gloriously. Again he writes to his friend Roe, dated Newark, February 12, 1833:

"Our meeting is glorious. We have had seventy mourners at a time; forty-six have joined. I know not when the meeting will close; probably next Monday. This is the sixth day. The town is shaken. God walks among the people, and they tremble. Universalism reels beneath the blows of truth.

"We have now no helps from abroad; but God helps. I must say I have been blessed in my own soul. I have been called four times to the pulpit, and my fifth appointment comes this evening. I pray God to send us a little help. I can say to no man, *Come* thou. But I put this prayer down for *your* eye: I pray God to send us a little help. Amen."

Mr. Hamline appears evidently rising in strength and "mighty through God." Speaking of his labors on this circuit, a writer who knew him well says:

"One of the best sermons I ever heard, he preached in Granville at one of his ordinary Sabbath appointments. He never lacked the stimulus of a full house, for wherever it was known he was to preach, eager multitudes flocked to hear. On the occasion referred to the text was Gal. vi, 7, 8. The sermon impressed me like some grand edifice of immense magnitude, of faultless proportions, of exquisite workmanship, and so perfectly fortified as to be impregnable at every point. For days it was almost constantly before my mind. I could not help a feeling of wonder that any merely human intellect should originate conceptions so grand, of such marvelous beauty, and then combine them into a whole of such wondrous strength.

"But while I give the preference to this sermon as a whole, it did not produce more manifest present effect than some others preached during that year. I think the most marked impression that I ever witnessed under his preaching was produced by a sermon on the text, 'How shall we escape if we neglect so great salvation?' It was preached at night during a protracted meeting in the town of Newark.

"The church, as usual, was crowded to the utmost, and he held the audience as if spell-bound. As he proceeded the excitement became intensely painful. He seemed as one standing where he could look down into the measureless depths of the gulf of perdition, and contemplate all its indescribable horrors. And he brought us all up to the same stand-point with himself, and then stood there, pointing out to us the unutterable woes of a lost soul. Never, before nor since, was the scene brought before me as such a terrible and present reality. Throughout the congregation not the slightest movement was visible, and the silence was unbroken save by the voice of the preacher, and now and then a deep groan, which seemed to come from the depths of some stricken or sympathizing heart. At length a point was reached where I felt that I could not endure much more. I could not help wishing he would stay his hand.

"Just at the critical moment our minds were turned from the contemplation of this fearful scene of suffering to consider the justice of God, which not only permitted but required such seeming severity in the punishment of sin. This was done in few words, and so skillfully that when in concluding he cried out,

'And let all the people say, *Amen*,' it seemed to me that every one in that congregation, as if moved by one common impulse, joined him in that *'amen.'*"

"He had not," says our informant, "at that time the matured religious experience which he afterward attained, nor the clear views of Christian holiness which so strongly characterized his later ministry; but I doubt whether he was ever more thoroughly in earnest, or more successful in winning souls to Christ, *than during that year.* He was most lovingly associated witht he heavenly minded H. S. Farnandis and the zealous S. H. Holland, and glorious revivals of religion crowned their labors."

It can be easily conceived how such zeal and effort would naturally exhaust the enfeebled normal forces of his system and leave him prostrate. His health broke under the severe pressure, almost to the despairing of life. The house where he lay confined was surrounded by a beautiful grove, and he said, "If I get able, I will go out and inscribe the name of Jesus on every tree." Among the numerous and kind friends who came to see him in his affliction was Bishop M'Ilvaine, of the Protestant Episcopal Church. After a most fraternal interview and prayer, the Bishop took the sick man's hand in leaving, and said, "Bless God, Brother Hamline, there is a strength that never shall decay."

The following year (1833) Mr. Hamline was appointed to the Athens circuit, with the Rev. Jacob Young for his senior colleague. This was grateful. Mr. Young had been his counselor and co-laborer on the "old Ohio circuit" in 1830. "He was," says Herr, "wise in counsel, able in debate, and clear in discourse." He was proverbially called "the wise old Jacob," and was one of the strong men of the conference, for there were giants in those days. Hamline told him "he felt like riding two circuits that year." The year opened with hope, and was prosperous.

At Batemantown, a strong hold of Universalism, there was a great work. The whole moral phase of the place was changed. But some resisted. On one occasion a Universalist challenged Mr. Hamline to prove from the Bible that any soul was ever lost. Hamline quoted Ezek. xxxiii, 13, 14, "When I shall say to the righteous that he shall surely live; if he trust to his own righteousness and commit iniquity, all his righteousness shall not be remembered; but for this iniquity that he hath committed, he shall die for it. Again when I say unto the wicked, thou shalt surely die; if he turn from his sin and do that which is lawful and right, he shall surely live." "But," says the dialectician, "that does not say that he *did* die, but that *if* he turn from his righteousness he shall die." "No," says Mr. Hamline, "it does not. Neither does it say in the next verse that the wicked man *did* turn from his wickedness and live, but only *if* he turn he shall live. The suppositions are exactly equal in both cases." Nothing more was said, and Mr. Hamline rode off. It was his practice never to combat Universalism, but to preach the Gospel fully. If men saw the truth and accepted it, the error would be displaced; if not, nothing was gained by controversy.

But the year had its trials of unexpected severity. In the later winter Mr. Hamline set out for his appointment, fifteen miles away, at a time when the traveling, especially in crossing streams, was perilous, His friends earnestly advised against, but to him engagements knew no compromise. A recent freshet had swollen the streams, which, on a sudden freeze, were covered with ice, so that when the water subsided the ice stood above the water. He came to a bridge, the planks of which had been swept away, and there was no crossing but on the sleepers. He had hitherto been compelled to walk much of the time on the ice along the banks of the stream, leading his horse and holding to the fences. There appears to have been no house or help near, and he must cross here or renounce his journey. Shelving ice was cleaving to the sleepers on both sides, the banks were almost perpendicular, and the stream impassable except by crossing this fragment of a bridge. Having confidence in the sagacity of his horse, and hoping that *possibly* the ice would not fall till he had reached the opposite shore, he solemnly committed himself to the care of God, and started to lead the horse across one of the sleepers. He was certain that should the ice give way the horse would take fright and spring, in which case only providential interposition could preserve him. When *almost at* the other shore the ice fell with a loud crash. He *threw* himself to the shore, and the horse sprang quite over him, his corked hoof striking as near as he could ascertain within one inch of his head.

At dusk he reached another stream which he must cross by ferry. After great difficulty in rousing the ferryman on the opposite shore he at length crossed and reached the place of destination, but in a state of complete exhaustion. He preached, however, sitting in a chair. This effort came near costing him his life. A long sickness ensued, in which, for a time, little hope was entertained of recovery. The effects of that day's adventure he felt through life. His system was not robust, and could not sustain such treatment. But in the sickness that followed his soul was lifted above his infirmity and triumphed in his Savior.

The following letter, written upon his sick-bed, to his loving and faithful wife, is not only an exposition of his thoughts and feelings while on his sick-bed, but of intrinsic doctrinal and practical value:

"MY DEAR ELIZA,—I shall devote a few of my restless moments this evening to you. You know that we are to die, and whether we shall pay the debt of nature with a full warning of what is about to come upon us we know not. Should I die without your presence, and without the privilege of conversing with you, I pray you, as with my dying breath, to be thoroughly convinced of the following truths, namely:

"That there is a God consisting of three persons, the Father, the Son, and the Holy Spirit. That God is omnipotent, omniscient, and omnipresent, holy, just, and merciful; that the Scriptures of the Old and New Testaments are a revelation from God; that Christ has made a vicarious atonement for sin; that man is depraved; that our only hope is through faith in Christ's name; that man is immortal, and accountable for his actions and *feelings;* that sin unrepented of will destroy the soul; that the misery of the wicked will be eternal; that impenitence is the sinner's fault; and that the finally impenitent destroy themselves.

"These truths, my dear Eliza, embrace all the pillars of the Christian's faith, and contain more sound sense and philosophical wisdom than all the aphorisms of all the great men of earth. Let them enter your heart and communicate their spirit to your very soul, and they will exalt you above all the Platos of old, above all the Humes of modern times.

"You will reasonably be surprised that I have not been a

wiser and better man, since my professions proclaim me in possession of this heavenly knowledge. It is difficult to redeem myself from the charge of inconsistency, but it is not difficult to screen these principles from the charge of inefficiency. Whenever I have felt the ruling power of these truths I have been in some degree both wise and good. Not that I have then *felt myself* either, but on the contrary have then been most deeply sensible of my failings and delinquencies ; but now, while I revert to those periods when I have and have not felt the force of them, I can discern a striking contrast in which the former state is the light shade of the picture. Yes, holiness of heart and life, purity of thought and action, are the legitimate offspring of these principles ; and without them all that has the resemblance of moral virtue among men is spurious. It is factitious goodness, unsubstantial as the shadow, unreal as the dream of night, and wasting as the dew of morning.

Let these principles, my dear Eliza, rule your life, and you can not act wrong. Forget and reject them, and you can not act right. O that I had always been ruled by them ! It would have saved me many a pang, it would have brought me many a joy ; it would have brightened the morn of life, and it would cheer the evening of my days ; it would have illuminated the vale of death, and glorified my soul in the world of bliss.

" I have nothing to do but say, *as you value the peace of your soul*, listen to these instructions. May God be your father, may God be the husband of your soul, may he give you the garment of salvation, and cause you to sit in a heavenly place at his right hand ! Adieu, my Eliza ; my *own* Eliza, adieu."

So late as May 23, 1834, we find him sick at his beloved home in Zanesville, to which he had retired from his circuit. At this date he writes to Rev. Jacob Young :

" MY DEAR BROTHER,—Your letter reached me upon my sick-bed, but it seemed doubly welcome. I attempted to preach for Brother Fox on Sunday last, the first attempt since I left Athens, and on Tuesday my ague returned. I am once more under the doctor's care. And now I must give up all hope of seeing you this summer, and can indulge but a faint expectation of reaching conference. Since my return I have been very much afflicted, but had supposed for three or four weeks past my complaints were leaving me, and that I should soon regain my strength. Now I think it most likely that I shall, if I live, wear out a season or two in a feeble state. This is my well day, and I feel comparatively comfortable."

Mr. Hamline seems to have been laid aside mostly for the balance of the conference year.

CHAPTER V.

[1834-36.]

APPOINTED TO CINCINNATI.

A T the session of the Ohio Conference at Circle-
ville, August 20, 1834, Mr. Hamline was ordained deacon, and appointed to Wesley Chapel,
Cincinnati, with Zachariah Connell as a senior colleague. This appointment opened to him a field of
labor and a class of associations more suitable to his
natural gifts, and brought him before the public in a
new and wide relation. Until this time he had never
moved his family from Zanesville. The frail life of
his loving companion would not admit of the rough
usage of the circuit system. She now, however,
consents to move. It was no ordinary trial for one
in feeble and declining health to leave the beautiful
home of her childhood, with its gardens and extensive grounds, its seventy acres of natural grove,
trimmed and cleared of undergrowths, rising back in
elevated and graceful undulations from the banks of
the Muskingum and laid out in drives like a park.
The scene was enchanting. The winding Muskingum lay at their feet, the city of Zanesville was
spread out in full costume, villages on the west en-
livened the landscape, while a rich background of
cultivated farms every-where tinted and softened
the view. As she walked over the extensive lawns
with Jacob Young, catching new views at every

turn, Mrs. Hamline asks, "Do you wonder that I have been reluctant to leave this home?" "It is very fine," replied the stern itinerant, "but is not quite equal to Paradise." Mrs. Hamline was in declining health, too feeble for a safe removal. Her careful husband removed her in her own carriage, a nurse accompanying them in charge of the two children. Unfortunately, the house selected for them was inadequate. As to parsonages, there were none. Short were the intervening months between her removal to Cincinnati and her translation to the heavenly home, for which she had resigned her earthly.

The first weeks in Cincinnati were inauspicious. In a letter to Dr. Roe Mr. Hamline says:

"We reached here in safety, and in time to witness a severe spread of cholera. It commenced on Saturday last, sudden as plague, and in twenty-four hours about twenty were laid low. It ceased as sudddenly as it came. I have felt the wind of the shot, but am not 'killed nor wounded.' The atmospheric influence was as sensible as the shock of an electric battery. Oh, how strange! On Sunday the scene was mournful: the hearses dressed in imposing black, the processions of mourning carriages, and the mourning of the bereaved, deprived almost in an hour of dear and adored friends, made all our hearts ache. Several of our brethren died. We feel, notwithstanding, calm and comfortable. We are keeping house with a few borrowed and purchased articles of furniture."

Mr. Hamline entered upon his duties here with his usual inspiration, checked only by the weight of his domestic trials. The public expectation was high; his fame was spread abroad, his responsibilities great; but for himself his fame, in its human sense, was of no account, and his ambition was high only to please God and fulfill worthily his holy calling. The reader must not judge of his popularity by the standard of domestic arrangements for his reception. That was but an accident due to the infelicities of the age and the imperfect facilities of transportation. But, morally and socially, preacher and people were in a high state of satisfaction. His ministrations called out the people and drew upon other congregations. The intelligent found material for instruction and culture, and the pious and humble soul the pure Word of God earnestly and persuasively delivered.

There is a mystery and mournfulness in the dispensation of Providence during most of his stay with this people. For months together the energies which he longed to bestow upon his needful public work were depleted and exhausted by the sorrows and solicitudes for the waning life of his loving and faithful wife, and for the desolations of his home. Between the harvest field which called him into public life, and the withering griefs for a suffering companion and a darkened home, he seemed like a pendulum vibrating between lights and shadows, life and death. In a letter to his friend, Rev. Jacob Young, January 8, 1835, he says:

"For some weeks my soul has had work at home. My sympathies at present seem almost incapable of diversion. We are afflicted. Mrs. Hamline has been declining ever since Conference, and appears now to be rapidly sinking under the influence of hectic fever. I am watching her day and night with an anxiety which you can better conceive than I describe. God has in mercy relieved me of one mighty burden. She has never enjoyed a clear evidence of her acceptance with God until last evening. Judge with what joy I witnessed her reception of Jesus by faith, and heard her proclaim, 'All is well.' 'I have no fears now.' 'I have no longer any will but the will of God.' Bless God! eternally bless his holy name! that he has heard prayer, and given her her heart's desire.   Let me now be bound forever to *his* cross who hath saved us by his blood. My dear brother, I doubt not but you will give us your prayers, and plead with Jesus to bless us in our afflictions.   I very much fear that we may not honor God in our sufferings."

The decline of Mrs. Hamline was rapid, and her end was peaceful and triumphant.   She had sought the Lord with her husband, but had never attained a clear and assured consciousness of her acceptance with God until, as we have seen, upon her last bed of sickness.   But now all was clear.   She had participated with her husband in his convictions of duty to preach, and though not able to follow with him, she had given him up for this work.   They had walked together in true harmony and love, bearing their common cross in mutual sympathy and prayer. Of the children which God had given them two only were still living, one of whom followed his sainted mother that same year; the other, Dr. L. P. Hamline, still survives.

The feelings of Mr. Hamline in watching the ebbing out of a life dearer than his own to him can not better be given than in his own words, in the following letter to his friend, Dr. E. D. Roe, dated March 3, 1835:

"Yesterday I received yours. . . .   As for us our harps are on the willows and our tents pitched by the Euphrates, while we have scarce the grace to weep when we remember Zion.   I can not tell you all our difficulties by letter.   Should I see you face to face I could talk with you.   Suffice it to say, my colleague is discouraged beyond all measure, and thinks he can do no good in Cincinnati.   This, besides my afflictions, which I shall not relate to you, paralyzes all my efforts and makes me hopeless.

"My dear wife has gradually declined in health since I

wrote to you in autumn, and now lies helpless, emaciated, and much of the time almost speechless by my side. I have watched her night and day with the assiduity and the feelings of a husband. And having said this I need not inform *you* that my strength and flesh are much wasted, that my ministerial efforts have been confined to the pulpit, and that they have been made without any preparation and under every possible embarrassment. Twice in the mean time I have been severely ill, but I have not been kept from my Sabbath appointments but twice, and from my week-day but two or three times. I have found valuable friends and many of them. All that mortals can do is done for us, and more than this, God has been unutterably good to us. Mrs. Hamline is in a state of mind which hushes all our murmurs, though it can not dry our tears. She welcomes all providences, and 'rejoices in tribulation.'

"And now, my dear brother, I trust that these hasty lines will stir up your mind to pray for us in our most severe afflictions, that those sorrows which the world can not relieve may find some cordial in the religion of Jesus Christ. I dare not tell Mrs. Hamline that I write to you. She sleeps. She has spoken much of Sister Roe, and would send much love.

"Affectionately yours," etc.

At the writing of this letter the hour of parting was near. Mrs. Hamline died twenty-four days later, March 27, 1835. When she asked a friend if she was dying, he replied, "It appears very much as though you were." "Then," said she, "sing." They sang her favorite hymn:

> "Jesus protects, my fears begone,
>   What can the Rock of Ages move?
> Safe in thy arms I lay me down,
>   Thine everlasting arms of love.
> While thou art intimately nigh
>   Who, who shall violate my rest?
> Sin, earth, and hell I now defy,
>   I lean upon my Savior's breast."

As the cadence of the last line died away her spirit took its flight. The answer of Dr. Roe to the above letter of Mr. Hamline, dated April 30th, will best describe the generous flow of sympathy to the bereaved partner from a wide circle of friends. We select this from many expressions of loving condolence, because Dr. Roe was received into conference and ordained in the same class with Mr. Hamline. They had been friends before either entered the ministry, and years of fellowship only served to perfect the union of their hearts. The parties have long since all rejoined in heaven. He writes:

"Your kind, desponding letter was received with mingled feelings of pleasure and of pain, and would have been answered before this had I been certain that you were in Cincinnati.

"And now I do not know how to write to you in your most severe affliction. I can say nothing to assuage sorrow arising from the source from whence yours flows. Affection will claim its right and must be allowed its tears. But religion may moderate its sorrow and hallow its grief. He whose servant you are has said, 'My grace is sufficient for thee.' 'As thy day is so shall thy strength be.' My heart cries out in your behalf, 'O Lord, fulfill thy word unto thy servant who is devoted to thy fear.' I would not trifle with your sorrow by saying mourn not, nor by attempting to point you to any source for consolation, but to 'the Rock that is higher than we.' Oh may Divine consolation be poured upon you. She has gone, but *Jesus* was with her. He showed her 'the path of *life*' and led her onward in it to his presence, in which there is 'fullness of joy,' and to him at whose 'right hand there are pleasures for evermore.' Say ye to the righteous, it shall be well with them, for living in the 'patient continuance of well doing and seeking glory, honor, and immortality they shall have everlasting life.' She sleeps, but she sleeps in Jesus, and 'them which sleep in Jesus will God bring with him,' and 'the dead in Christ shall rise *first*.' 'Blessed and holy are they who have part in the first resurrection; on them the second death hath no power.' Suffer me, my dear afflicted brother, to comfort you with these words. I will write no more now. My heart is with you. My prayers are for you. Will you write to me soon?

"I am, truly and affectionately," etc.

The loss of his bosom friend was an overwhelming sorrow. Mr. Hamline was yet young in the ministry, in his third year as a member of Conference, with an important city charge upon his hands, with three sermons to deliver each Sabbath, as the custom then was, with a sickly body, and the new and untried care of two lovely children. His popularity in the city was great, and his usefulness and success seemed to demand for him the quiet home and soothing retirement which had now been ruthlessly broken up. It was a moment of trial of his faith and his manhood strength, and he turns from the sad obsequies with a withered heart and exhausted strength to meet the stern demands of public life. And this, with God's blessing, became a chief means of sustaining him, so that some years later he advises an afflicted friend in a like condition to the same course. He says: "My beloved brother, let me not be thought forward when I urge you to go out at once from your solitary home to the district, and dwell and labor constantly among God's people. Let the zeal of God's house eat up your soul. I think in my distress labor for God was my preservation." It had always been his habit, as one says of him, to spend most of his time among his people.

The affectional nature of Mr. Hamline was attuned to the most delicate sympathy, and while it now became the occasion of a livelier suffering to himself, it also became the generous medium through which, more than ever before, he was "able to comfort them which were in any affliction, by the comfort wherewith he himself was comforted of God." His grief was not a barren grief. Through his sufferings

he found an open channel of access to other suffering hearts, and it is beautiful to witness how true he
is, in all his letters and communications, not only to
humanity, in a delicate appreciation of our social
nature, but to the claims of his ministerial calling to
bring souls to Christ.   His letters of friendship and
sympathy themselves would make a volume.

It was in Cincinnati during these years that Mr.
Hamline's soul was drawn out in special concern for
many who had fallen under the soothing opiate of
the Unitarian theory.   They were attracted by his
preaching and attached to his ministry, but how to
bring them to Christ through a saving faith was the
problem he constantly and prayerfully revolved.   Several of the sermons found in the first volume of his
published works were written for this specific end,
such as his sermons on "Depravity," "The Sufferings of Christ," "Jesus Reviled," "The Wages of
Sin," etc.   Had he been permitted to remain a longer
period in the same place there is little doubt but his
efforts in this direction would have been crowned
with signal success.

It may be proper to say just here that Mr. Hamline seldom wrote out a sermon in full.   The twenty-
four sermons which appear in his published works
(one of them in the second volume) are all the
finished sermons which appear in his manuscript
remains.   The forty-seven sketches and skeletons in
volume second are a full specimen of his habit of preparing briefs for the pulpit.   As he was called upon
to prepare three sermons each week (for it was the
custom then to have three sermons each Sabbath to
each congregation), he appealed to Bishop Morris for

advice. The bishop counseled him that if he could prepare more easily by writing, it would, under his circumstances of affliction and depleted health, be admissible to do so. To a very limited extent he complied with the suggestion, but it was not his habit. Neither was it his practice to write and commit and then deliver the discourse *memoriter.* This his mental habit made wholly impossible. The heads of thought he made familiar to himself before going into the pulpit. If it was an argument which required special care and involved special responsibility, he wrote paragraphs embodying his definitions and more difficult forms of presentation; not for language but simply to familiarize his own mind with the just dimension of the thought. It was marvelous that he could speak extemporaneously with such classic precision and purity, and this probably led some to suppose that he either read his sermons or spoke from memory. But it was a mistake. He spoke equally well, in the same faultless style, from the promptings of the moment, after an approved outline of thought had been matured.

A venerable ministerial friend gave him the following wise counsel: "Do not," he says, "depend on great sermons for your success in the ministry in the city, but visit your people and become acquainted with the children in the families where you go." This advice was carefully followed. It was his practice to take a class-leader with him in his rounds of visiting the classes, and go from house to house. His labor with the children was never forgotten. Long afterward they would say, "He always talked with us about religion, and we love him."

CHAPTER VI.

[1834-38.]

*APPOINTED ASSISTANT EDITOR OF WESTERN CHRIS-
TIAN ADVOCATE.*

M R. HAMLINE'S residence at Cincinnati, as
we have seen, was shadowed with affliction.
A beloved wife and one of the two remaining children had been taken from him, and the only surviving
child had seen a year of sickness. Yet under all he
had been sustained, and had not only succeeded to
a high degree of satisfaction in pulpit and pastoral
labor, but had given much aid to ministerial brethren
abroad. The following year Mr. Hamline was married to Mrs. Melinda Truesdell—a most opportune
and favored union. She was a lady every way fitted
to give character to his ministry and happiness to his
home, as years of self-denying and useful labor have
amply confirmed.

At Columbus, in the summer of 1836, the incumbent pastor, Rev. E. W. Schon, had been compelled
from bodily indisposition, to retire. Schon was, says
Herr, "the *Apollo Belvidere* of the conference, a perfect
Christian gentleman, eminently successful in his ministry, and remarkably popular among all classes of
society." The place was important, and it was not
easy to find a successor to the retiring pastor. Mr.
Hamline, who had now been nearly four years a
member of conference, and nearly two years at Cin-

cinnati, was selected. Hitherto he had served only as junior preacher, and had meekly followed the direction of his senior, but was now put upon his responsibility. The field was open and he was ready. He received his appointment early in June, 1836, and engaged in his new sphere of labor with characteristic ardor and success; but after three months was suddenly called by his Conference to the office of assistant editor of the *Western Christian Advocate* at Cincinnati. The people of Columbus were now universally aroused at this sudden and disastrous turn of their affairs. All classes and professions felt that they had sustained a loss which they were not able to endure. One said, "This is not the Lord's work; this is man's work." But they were powerless to avert the calamity. Nothing was left to them but the humble right of petition, and in this forlorn hope they all united. In their memorial to Mr. Hamline the Church says: "We have great cause to thank God for his having sent you among us." They express their "disappointment" and "astonishment" at the decision of conference by which he was removed from them, assure him of their belief that "the very best interests of Methodism and religion require his return," and then delicately and appreciatively pray that, if he can do so consistently, he will "resign his place in the Book Concern, and stay with them at least another year." The citizens also take it up, and in another memorial to the same effect, say: "We believe that you are peculiarly calculated to call the attention of a large portion of the inhabitants of this place to the great truths of the Christian religion, and the public worship of God;" and they then pray that, "if his services in the Church elsewhere can, without too much sacrifice, be dispensed with, he will make such arrangements as will permit him to remain with them another year." But if these events may illustrate the hold which Mr. Hamline had upon the people of Columbus, they also show that the "callings" of the Church are "without repentance."

But the new position, as editor, could not hush the voice nor dim the light of the preacher. He entered upon his new duties about the middle of September, and for a time abated his usual labors in the pulpit till he became initiated in his editorial work. In a letter to a friend, dated January 4, 1836, he says: "I have probably preached ten times since conference, half of which were since I reached Cincinnati. Our station amounts to a location, but it may be time for me to locate. I am satisfied with my new business. It affords a little excitement and keeps us at work. My colleague is a fine companion, and all things go on charmingly. We are now preaching more to those afar off than to those at hand. To these we have rare opportunities of speaking 'a word in season.'" These last utterances are characteristic. He wrote and edited from the stand-point of the pulpit, and of the work of saving souls. His colleague, the Rev. Dr. Charles Elliott, was a man of like mind, and the two were bosom friends to the close of life.

His labors, however, soon proved too much for his strength, and he was forced to suspend for a time his extra preaching. In reply to a call, April 23, 1837, from a beloved friend, the Rev. E. D. Roe, to come and help him in a protracted meeting, he says: "I have not attempted to preach since early last January. Even now my appointments are filled by my brethren. . . Nothing could be more agreeable to me than to visit you as you propose. I am almost in mind to come if it be only to preach to *you*, under the trees of your door, and scold you for your low spirits, and your hints about locating, *i. e.*, a soldiers' retreat. I would just (as my good Brother Elliott says to me when I am down) 'scourge you powerfully' if you did not rise up and be cheerful, and just as happy as a mortal man could be." He then cites him to the encouraging particulars of his history and condition, and adds: "I believe there is no state below heaven so near to heaven as that of a dutiful traveling minister. Bishop Morris, now here, would be thrown into spasms of delight if he could, by right, go back to what he was ten years ago. He groans beneath a bishop's cross. As to book agents, and editors, etc., I assure you if you groan *seven* times, we seventy times seven. . . . Put your trust in the Lord and go forward. Never leave the work till you are sure God calls you to leave it. Then a blessing will follow you in retirement."

In earlier years Mr. Hamline had suggested to him: "I rather suspect you may be taken for a nobler calling by the Redeemer, whose life was toil and pain, whose death was agonizing and full of shame, whose resurrection was triumphant, and who now sits in glory! O may God direct us to follow him in all things, and may he lead us to his heavenly rest."

The publication of the *Western Christian Advocate* was authorized by act of General Conference in 1832, and the paper was started in 1834, with Rev. T. A.

Morris (afterward Bishop) as editor. In 1836 Mr.
Morris was elected bishop, and Rev. Dr. Elliott was
elected his successor. In September of the same
year, as we have seen, Mr. Hamline was appointed
assistant editor. The paper, therefore, was about two
years and five months old at the time he entered the
office. Journalism in the Methodist Episcopal Church
was at this time in its infancy. The *Christian Advocate*, of New York, the oldest General Conference
weekly, was only ten years old. The whole field,
both in its financial and literary aspects, was new.
The country, too, was new. Contributors were not
abundant, and not well educated in writing for the
public eye. The editorial chair was not one of ease
and rest. It was less difficult, however, to provide
and publish matter, and adjust all to a proper standard, than to train in a corps of contributors who
would please and edify the body of patrons. But
the authorities had well selected their men. Neither
learning, taste, tact, nor piety were wanting to secure
editorial success, and in this Mr. Hamline entered
with the same zeal and holy aspiration that characterized his ministry. We must refer to the columns
and fortunes of the paper for the proof of what we
say. From those columns much will be found valuable as the gems of Jeremy Taylor.

Not the least of the difficulties which embarrassed
the editorship of the infant paper was the antislavery
controversy. This, which had already risen to a fervid heat, had been fanned to an unwonted glow by
the debates and action of the recent General Conference, which had held its session in Cincinnati, May,
1836. It had been the intention of a majority of

the Conference to avoid the discussion, as not seeing how, within their legitimate province as an ecclesiastical assembly, the peace of the Church or the good of the slave could be conserved thereby. But thrice the subject of abolition and slavery was brought before them, and the last time in a manner so extraordinary and outside of all parliamentary usage or courtesy, namely, by a published address to the conference by some of its members, that the agitation could no longer be repressed or avoided. Unhappily the subject was complicated with outside influences, political party movements, and the censure of the indiscretion of certain of the delegates.

When the Conference adjourned the whole country was in the greatest excitement. The frame-work of the Church violently shook, and all thoughtful men trembled for the ark of God. The Rubicon was passed, the war was inevitable, all hope of reconciliation was lost. Six years later came a secession at the North, under the leadership of the Rev. Orange Scott, of the New England Conference, and two years after that the division of the Church, North and South, followed by a division of the Book Room property. Seventeen years later came the secession of the Southern States, with the wail and crash of civil war.

It is not germain to the purpose of this memoir here to dwell upon the general features of this great antislavery, or, as it was commonly called, abolition agitation. On the ethical and civil character of slavery the North were generally agreed. It was a wrong and an outrage upon humanity in every sense and in every aspect of the case. But the Church,

as such, could deal with it only ethically, and what
was the sphere and limit of her jurisdiction, and
what her duty within that jurisdiction were points
upon which diverse opinions obtained.   The complications and difficulties of the subject might well
baffle the feeble efforts of human wisdom, and the
difficulty of preserving brotherly charity and confidence and Church harmony and fellowship seemed
insurmountable.   In the "Pastoral Address" of the
General Conference above alluded to the subject is
specially treated with an earnest dissuasive to uncharitable, unchurchly, and unfraternal discussion.
The Address even proceeds to the extreme of
conservative care and solicitude, and, as the safer
measure, advises "wholly to refrain from this agitating subject, which is now convulsing the country,
and consequently the Church, from end to end."

It was in the din and dust of this battle that Mr.
Hamline took the chair of assistant editor of a
Church paper which was destined and intended for
the families of the "Great West," and large portions of the bordering slave states of Virginia, Kentucky, and Missouri.   It was but natural that ardent
young knights should burn to try their "battle-
blades" in the columns of the *Western Advocate*.
One of these, a personal friend, not without merit
already gained, and hope to his rising star, makes
request, to which Mr. Hamline discreetly replies.
We give only an extract:

"You see, my dear S., that I write to you as a friend in
expectation that you will appreciate my *motives, feelings,
views*, and *position*. In regard to your proposal, I sincerely
believe that the subject to which you allude [the subject of

slavery] ought, as a question of morals and of sacred theology, to be discussed, and *must* and *will* be. But I also think that our relation to the General Conference, and its decision on the subject, should for the present induce us to waive the discussion, for a few months at least. Things are approaching a crisis at which a conservative power must be gathered up, and in the West, if anywhere, not, as I can scarcely hope, to suppress revolution of some sort, but to guide and temper and meliorate it in some degree. Should we begin to discuss this theme now, two sides would immediately appear—pro and con. Must both be heard? This would take the molding of the discussion out of your hands, in which I doubt not it would preserve a meek and Christian temper and attire, and, ere we were aware of it, we should find ourselves in the midst of a tempest, blowing from some quarter very unexpectedly, perhaps descending upon us from heights as inaccessible to our peaceful charms as the fastnesses of the Gauts, and overwhelming as the rush of fires from the volcano. All this we would not deprecate did we not believe that it would result in damage to the Church, and in the end would rather defer than hasten the object at which you would philanthropically aim.

"All this is said on the spur of the occasion, and I will gladly hear from you again on the subject, and I will candidly weigh any remarks you may make on this question.

"By looking back to my address in 1830, you will know how much I was an abolitionist then, and I am as much so now, with this difference, that what was then *doctrine*, and was uttered in the spirit of cold speculation, has become now a fervid sentiment—a feeling painfully intense—so as sometimes to rob me of my slumbers. Yes, my dear S., I *feel* now what I *thought* then, that this nation must speedily be purged or God will spurn it, blot out its name, *and commission his curse to dig its grave.*"

The next generation, who will wonder that slavery ever existed at all, may think the attitude here described was overcautious, but candid men who lived in those times and weighed the issues and relations of things will pronounce it the highest wisdom.

As we have stated, Mr. Hamline entered upon his editorial duties with the same spirit and for the same ends which prompted him to enter the ministry. Of this he never lost sight, and to it every other call was held in abeyance. Indeed, he was ready for any form of work, at home or abroad, for saving souls. A mission to France was then much talked of, and at the General Conference of 1836 Dr. Bascom had brought it before that body, and introduced a resolution, which was adopted, that the Committee on Missions be instructed to inquire into the expediency of sending a deputy to France to ascertain the practicability of establishing regular missions in the principal cities under the auspices of the Methodist Episcopal Church. Dr. Fisk had pointed to France as a promising field of usefulness, and subsequently Dr. Durbin amply confirmed the opinion of Dr. Fisk. The Wesleyan Methodists, of England, had already entered the field. The sympathy between France and America, growing out of our free institutions and our Revolutionary history, greatly stimulated the American Churches. In a letter to Rev. Jacob Young, April 15, 1837, Mr. Hamline says: "My mind has been for many months greatly bent on the subject of missions. Some four months since I began to think much about France, the land of my forefathers. I am now anxious to be sent to that fair but desolate clime to preach Jesus and the resurrection. I am studying the language in all my spare hours, with some hope that I may find my way among that people. I think some of making a formal offer of myself to the Bishops while they sit in New York. If there be no other way for me to go to France I think I might go at my own charge." The Bishops held their meeting and brought before the Missionary Board the subject of the establishment of a mission in France. Bishop Morris writes to Mr. Hamline that should the Board concur in such a measure "you will not fail to be recommended at an early period for the place." But the hopeful anticipations of the Church in this direction were never realized.

From every quarter came calls for help in revival labors and for extra occasions, to which he gave a joyful response to the utmost limit of his time and strength. Every-where his labors were owned of God. The following is an extract from a letter of the Rev. Joshua Soule, Bishop of the Methodist Episcopal Church, then residing at Lebanon, Ohio, dated March 18, 1838. The reader must bear in mind that this was six years before the great separation, and the organization of the Methodist Episcopal Church South. At this time Bishop Soule stood high in the estimation of the Church at large, and, as Rev. Jacob Young afterward said, "as high in the Ohio Conference as in any other on the continent." The letter was addressed to Rev. E. W. Sehon and Rev. L. L. Hamline. He says:

"I am induced, not only by the solicitation of friends, but also by the clearest convictions of my own mind, to invite you to 'come over and help us.' It is, I judge, of special importance that we have your help on next Sabbath day. A strong effort, it is believed, will be made on that day to draw away from our fold those who have received all their religious impressions at our church. Religious influence is manifestly increasing in our village among all classes of society. Many have been happily converted to God since Brother Hamline left us. I believe I have never known so many souls reckon their convictions from the labors of one day, as from the Sabbath on which Brother Hamline preached in our church. His sermons resulted in incalculable good. Brethren, I assure you that the call for your help at this crisis is of no ordinary character. Please, brethren, don't fail to come. I shall wait with no ordinary interest to hear from you. Let me know when we may meet you with a carriage at M. Can you be there on Thursday morning or noon? The 'south-east' corner of my heart will be in reserve for you.

"Yours, with much affection,   J. SOULE."

It was computed that nearly one hundred persons dated their awakening from the sermons of Mr. Hamline on the Sabbath alluded to. His labors were every-where attended with visible results. His sermons were marked for their system, their force of argument, pathetic appeals and vivid description, and above all by the power of the Holy Spirit. His manner was earnest, often impassioned, always dignified and serious, his imagination lively and chaste, combining beauty and strength, with a voice of richness and melody, and his appeals often seemed irresistible. The moment he opened his lips the people intuitively felt they were in the presence of a great mind and a man of God. Many of his visits abroad were specially owned of God. In the year 1841 he visited Ripley, about fifty miles above Cincinnati on the Ohio river. Under his first exhortation the work broke out and twenty professed conversion that evening, and within the week more than one hundred were received into the Church, and many more were hopefully brought to Christ.

While at Ripley he felt strongly impressed to visit Levanna, two or three miles down the river, a place notorious for its poverty, intemperance, and wretchedness. In the eyes of his friends the measure seemed hardly prudent, but Mr. Hamline was resolute. In a small boat he dropped down to Dover, a place opposite Levanna, and immediately began a prayer-meeting. In a letter to his wife he says: "While the prayer-meeting was going on I sent a brother to an old village [Levanna] of ten or twelve decayed houses, opposite Dover, to obtain a room and appoint preaching at half past twelve o'clock. The appointment was made at the home of three cripples, who are most miserable objects. Several went over from Dover, and eight or ten of the villagers, poor-looking objects, came in. I preached on the prodigal son. God was with us." After the sermon the tavern-keeper, who had heard the sermon in concealment, stepped forward with an apology for this meager reception, and asked him to preach in his house, which was agreed to for the next day. At three P. M. he returned to Ripley and preached to the children, and again in the evening. The Sabbath was spent at Levanna. The whole region poured out its families to hear him. With an assistant, whom he had called to his aid, the hours were filled with preaching, prayer, and praise. On Monday the congregation was still increased, and men, women, and children stood in the drenching rain (for no house could contain them) to hear the word of the Lord. A brother, who had come to join the work, says: "I found Brother Hamline standing in the door of a log house (the log tavern) preaching to hundreds in the door yard, like Wesley and Whitefield, to the poor and wretched." Hamline returned to his editorial work on Wednesday, having received fifty persons into the Church, including the tavern-keeper, besides many others at Dover, for the work was carried on in both places.

On another occasion the Rev. M. P. Gaddis was with him, and says: "Mr. Hamline preached from the text, 'Why will ye die?' His soul seemed overwhelmed with a sense of the sinner's danger. Instantly he fell upon his knees in the pulpit, and for several minutes engaged in silent prayer. It was one of the most moving scenes I ever witnessed. Nothing, for some time, was heard but the sobs of the penitent. The speaker arose and resumed his discourse. His face seemed radiant, his soul inspired anew. He pleaded with sinners to come to Christ. At the end of that sermon scores were converted and added to the Church." "At another time," says the same writer, who was present, "he was preaching on Sabbath night from 'How shall I give thee up, Ephraim,' when, in the midst of his discourse, a man arose in the congregation and began to propound infidel questions. The preacher replied courteously, but with such readiness and pungency that the colloquy soon ended, and the objector sat down in confusion. The speaker then opened his batteries and proved himself 'mighty through God to the pulling down of strongholds.' Scores were converted and added to the Church." No man ever excelled Mr. Hamline in power and tact to meet a sudden emergency, which he always did with meekness and dignity.

About six miles from Cincinnati, in the vicinity of Cheviot, was a Universalist neighborhood, with only one Methodist family. Mr. Hamline opened meetings there. Considerable dislike was manifested, and the opposers said, "He would only frighten a few old women and children." But God poured out his Spirit, and men who had despised fell under the power of the word. Some conversions were quite extraordinary. The revival changed the phase of the neighborhood, and a good society was formed.

At Covington, across the river from Cincinnati, the pastor desired to be absent for a few weeks, and applied to Mr. Hamline to supply his pulpit. Mr. Hamline consented on condition that he might hold a protracted meeting, in which the pastor gladly acquiesced. Mr. Hamline entered at once upon the work. A revival broke out, and on the return of the pastor about one hundred had been converted, many of whom were of the best citizens in the place. By this the church was greatly strengthened, and their attachment to Mr. Hamline, thereafter, was strong, so that after the separation of 1844 (to be hereafter noticed), the people, retaining their former love, urgently invited him to come and preach to them again. But the plan of General Conference for the regulation and limitation of evangelical work, in reference to the line of division, was such that Mr. Hamline (then Bishop) felt himself forbidden, and affectionately declined.

It is impossible to give more than a specimen of his common method of labor. The instances of his revival work, and pulpit labors are too numerous to be inserted in our limits. But the following, from the New York *Evangelist*, we can not withhold. We give only an extract. It was in 1842, after his great baptism. The writer says of Mr. Hamline:

" The noblest exhibition of his popular talent, I saw in the Wesley Chapel in Cincinnati one Sabbath evening after the stationed preacher (Rev. J. L. Grover) had finished his discourse. Mr. Hamline, who was in the pulpit, immediately arose and began to exhort the impenitent part of the congregation to come to the altar to be prayed for. He had a cloak on, and as he began to 'warm up' in his exhortation the cloak would slide first from one shoulder and then from the other to be drawn up with a jerk. At last, with a violent motion of one arm, it was thrown off entirely. Meanwhile his heavy features had kindled into a most animated expression, and his neat and perfectly appropriate words were flowing in a torrent. In this way he spoke several minutes, when he suddenly ran down from the pulpit to the altar, never intermitting his speech, and standing there he delivered one of the most thrilling appeals to sinners I have ever heard. An audience of some two thousand people was present, and the effect was soon visible in the scores who hurried up to the altar to be prayed for. The whole mass was in a state of excitement, as was plain from the vociferations, groanings, and prayers which went up in all parts of the house. It required more skepticism than I ever had to doubt the entire sincerity of the man, as I heard the prayer which he poured out in behalf of 'the mourners;' it was so fervent yet so reverent, it pleaded the promises with such appropriateness, and seemed so full of an anguished spirit in behalf of the perishing, that to me it was the 'effectual, fervent prayer of the rightous man.'

"Evidently in Methodist tactics—if I may so name them without disrespect—the exhortation to mourners to come up to the altar, at least in former days, was one of the strongest agencies employed. In many cases more depended on 'the exhortation' than on the 'sermon;' and considering this, I must place that 'exhortation' of Bishop Hamline as the most thrilling I ever heard. In those days when he rode the circuit, and attended camp-meetings as a preacher, he probably had not many, if any, superiors in this difficult work of exhorting. Many men exhort as they would blow a blacksmith's bellows; but to mingle up argument and incident, statement and inference, imagination and fact, in such an appeal as bears down all resistance, is a field for high gifts, and here Mr. Hamline was entirely at home. Ten years ago, when I heard him last, he was one of the most noble preachers of the word in Ohio, and he certainly was a prince among exhorters."

At a camp meeting one evening, during a heavy rain, Mr. Hamline repaired to the church on the edge of the ground where he found a company of eight or ten men who had retreated there to escape the rain, and were lying on the benches. Mr. Hamline immediately began to exhort them with affectionate earnestness and power. The spirit of God fell on the auditors who yielded and sought the Lord. Before morning they were all happily converted to God.

These are but glimpses of his spirit and method of life. The days of his editorial career were days of a wide and varied and wonderful evangelism. And this was worthy of his profession. True Christian influence is not limited and partial. The stream which flows through a deep-cut channel may be limpid and refreshing to the traveler who seeks its cooling waters, but it can not overflow to irrigate and fertilize the adjacent landscape. "Thoroughly furnished unto all good works" is the divine description of a perfect Christian. The influence of such is expansive like the atmosphere and the light of heaven. The qualities of Mr. Hamline's character, and the varied adaptations of genius and culture, were channels through which the inward power of grace found access to different classes of society and conditions of men. Various indices of his popularity in the Church, and beyond the sphere of the pulpit, appear in the course of his editorial life. He never sought place or fame, but often declined both, and always when they at all impeded his one great and loved work of saving souls. His classical taste, his legal acumen, his dignified mien and his unaffected humility he could not conceal. They were patent to all.

They impressed the vulgar and the cultivated mind alike. The student, the statesman, the scholar, the humblest laborer felt that he came within their sphere, was their advocate, and took equal sympathy in their cause. Numerous were his calls to lecture on topics of public interest, to literary societies, and in the province of Christian benevolence. College literary societies every-where solicited the favor of his acceptance of an "honorary membership," evincing that his personal influence had diffused itself widely among the young men. Various were the applications of colleges North and South to fill the professorial chair in belles-lettres or the classics. At the time Mr. Hamline turned his thoughts to the ministry an influential leader in politics declared it had been his intention to bring forward his name as a candidate for Congress, which, had he consented, from the known position of the friends and the party, would probably have secured his election. As late as 1840 his political friends urged him to give his name for the national election. His answer was such as we might suppose the prophet Elijah would have given Ahab or Jehoshaphat, had they tendered him an office of government. (See his reply, Introduction to Vol. 1, p. 21, of his Works).

Variously and widely his influence was felt, and the judgments of all ranks of men must be the verdict as to the adaptations of his gifts. As an advocate or as a counselor at law none of his age surpassed him. But while the legal, political, and literary fields of enterprise lay open before him, he abode in one mind without hesitation or wavering. The Wesleys were not truer to their one calling. Nor was wealth an obstacle in his way. The path lay open before him. It was the opportune hour in the West. But the glitter of earthly riches had no attractions for him. His business was consigned to an agent, and he never "left the Word of God to serve tables," nor "turned aside having loved this present world."

Of learning he was the friend and patron, and every-where he lent his aid in advocacy and money to encourage every worthy enterprise. In Cincinnati he was chairman of the first meeting called to consider the feasibility of establishing a female college in that city, under the patronage of the Methodist Episcopal Church. He was on the committee to draft and report the plan, and also the committee to open the institution. It has long held the rank of a reputable and flourishing college. He was equally active and prominent in the transfer of the property at Delaware, Ohio, to the Methodist Episcopal Church, for the establishment of an institution now called the Ohio Wesleyan University. Notices of his benefactions to literary institutions will appear in another place.

CHAPTER VII.

[1838-44.]

GERMAN APOLOGIST—LADIES' REPOSITORY.

THE German missions in this country were begun in the Autumn of 1835, by Rev. William Nast. The gracious work spread beyond expectation, and two years later it was proposed to start a German weekly newspaper to meet the wants of the people. Nothing less than this would enable the missionaries to cope with their opponents, and reach the people with information necessary to awaken the religious conscience and fortify them against the subtle and ignorant assaults of German neology and a dead formalism. The proposition was made by the Rev. Thomas Dunn, of the Ohio Conference, to raise three thousand dollars by ten-dollar subscriptions to start the paper. The friends of the enterprise were numerous and earnestly advocated the measure. The Church papers liberally engaged to awaken the public mind to the claims of the subject. Conference action followed in its course. But none were more active than Mr. Hamline. A question arose as to the authority of the agents to publish such a paper without the order of General Conference. The bishops were to hold a session at New York, May, 1838, and Mr. Hamline wrote them a strong memorial and argument in favor of the paper. Rev. J. F. Wright, Western Book Agent, was deputed to lay the case before them. They return, through Bishop Morris, their answer: "We agreed to recommend the publication of the German paper at Cincinnati, provided the funds of the Book Concern should not be employed therein." On the first of January, 1839, the specimen number of the German *Apologist* was issued, and as the proposed amount—three thousand dollars—had not been secured, a committee was appointed—Rev. L. L. Hamline and W. H. Raper—to prepare an address to the public to urge immediate attention thereto. The address is full of instructive information, Christian beneficence, and eloquent appeal. In their closing paragraphs they say concerning this enterprise:

"The German *Apologist* is abroad. The New Year gave it birth, and ere this it has probably been cast a foundling at your thresholds. We beseech you, brethren, receive it, nurse it to maturity, that it may be employed, through a long and useful life, as an instrument of mercy to open the eyes of the blind and proclaim liberty to a multitude of captives. Brethren, can we appeal in vain for your aid to consummate an enterprise so noble, so hopeful, so every way desirable? You have done a noble part, and so much the greater pity that all your toil should go for naught, that your works should begin to go to ruin while not yet finished. We deprecate the shame. You have laid out thousands to construct a strong *foundation*, which now stands to be gazed on by the world. Desert not the enterprise. Add a few hundreds more. Half a thousand will complete the enterprise." "This paper," they go on to say, "may be considered our German missionary Bishop. It is to travel over the whole land, to teach and warn, and, by the blessing of God, to convert and build up."

At the next session of the Ohio Conference Mr. Hamline writes from the seat of Conference: "I preached on Sabbath in the Episcopal Church and had a very pleasant time. Last night I exhorted in the Methodist Church, made an appeal in behalf of the *Apologist*, and obtained one hundred and seventy subscribers. I never saw more enthusiasm."

For some time the *Apologist* did not sustain itself, but the zeal of its friends would not let it go down. The Rev. W. H. Gilder says, "One of the editors of the *Advocate* [Hamline] told me that before such an event should be allowed he would take off his coat and sell it." And the writer adds: "When I was informed of the astonishing influence it was exerting I felt very much like giving my coat in with Brother Hamline's."

The work went forward, the paper was sustained, and the missions have prospered. No mission-field has been, and is, more successful or remunerative, or has given better omen of good influence on the generations to come, both in this country and the "Father-land." The Rev. Dr. Nast, the apostle of American German mission work, after the first two years of labor, says: "I travel in five weeks through an extent of nearly three hundred miles, and have about twenty-two preaching places." This might seem like the day of feeble things. But sound conversions were multiplied, strong and educated men were brought to Christ and entered the field, and Churches were every where established. At present the German Methodists of this country and Europe number about 50,000, with over 500 preachers. Their literature is quite extensive, and the *Apologist* finds its way to many thousand families.

The field was one into which many great philanthropic hearts entered. From the beginning Hamline grasped the greatness of the movement and threw his full force into the work. In a recent letter from Dr. Nast to the writer of this memoir, he says: "Without the powerful appeals of the sainted Bishop Hamline the *Apologist* would never have been started, nor the German missions at Cincinnati." In the first German love-feast held in Cincinnati Mr. Hamline was present. To the Germans it was all new, but the Lord was present in gracious power, and Mr. Hamline related his experience, which was rehearsed by an interpreter in the German tongue, much to the joy and comfort of the new society. The experiences of these German converts were exceedingly rich and abiding. Dr. Nast, in his sermon before the Pittsburg Conference, says:

"The honest Dutchman, when he is tempted to go back to the beggarly elements of the world, tells the devil once for all: 'I's been there once, I goes there no more.' One of the chief ministers of the Lord Jesus, the Rev. L. L. Hamline, to whose ardent and eloquent appeals the German Missions owe an everlasting debt of gratitude, said once: 'There is strength in German character which must eventually give it influence. Their mental aptitudes, their habits of secular diligence and carefulness, should enlist concern as well as admiration. Doubtless hereafter they will bear much sway in constituting the authorities which are to control this land, in molding the nation's mind and in fashioning its morals, and in making up the sum total of its weal or its woe. Let them become a leaven of malice, and unless saved by Omnipotence, the Church and the nation are undone. Let them become a leaven of holiness, then liberty, and science, and heaven-born religion may concert their holy and everlasting jubilee."

"So you see," adds Dr. Nast, "the Germans are worthy to be saved not only for their sakes, but for your sake." On the political influence of the German population of this country, he further says:

"Our beloved Hamline says upon this point: 'Self-preservation, which is the first law of nature as well as charity, binds us to save our denizens and such as will soon be fellow citizens. If crude and contaminating elements are perpetually mixing with the proper constituents of the Church and state, and borrow no refinement nor purity from the intimate contact, they will gradually impart their natures to the bodies civil and ecclesiastical. And it is perilous on our part to suffer such a process. What will follow in due time? The very fountains which refreshed the distant regions of Africa and Oregon will themselves become dry, and if they flow at all, will send forth to the nations not healing but poisonous waters'."

The zeal, the extensive knowledge of his times, and the sagacity of Mr. Hamline naturally placed him in the front ranks of Christian enterprise and evangelism with the great men of his day who, like the sages of Issachar, "had understanding of the times, to know what Israel ought to do.".

But Mr. Hamline not only wrote and spoke for the Germans, he contributed of his means as well. To the first German Church edifice in Cincinnati he gave five hundred dollars, with the pledge of one hundred dollars to every church they would build throughout the bounds of their mission work. At this time of his life Mr. Hamline was possessed of only a frugal competence.

In the editorial department a new sphere awaited him—one which gave a wider scope to his literary and classical taste, and the out-reaching of his spiritual life. "Previous to the General Conference of 1840 [we quote from the *Western Christian Advocate* for December, 1854] the subject of publishing such a periodical as the *Ladies' Repository* (a monthly octavo) was discussed in Cincinnati. Samuel Williams, of that city, was the original projector of the scheme. Rev. J. F. Wright, the Book Agent, entered warmly into the subject. Consultations were had by the Editors, Agents, and others. The Book Committee looked upon it with favor. The result was that a memorial was sent to the General Conference of 1840, urging that body to consider the subject and order its publication. The Conference viewed the matter favorably, and the proper authority was given to the Book Agents to proceed with its publication, 'provided the public would give due encouragement.'" Meanwhile, at the said General Conference, Mr. Hamline was solicited to take the editorship of the *Advocate* at New York. "The members seem determined," he writes to a friend, "to make me editor of the *Christian Advocate and Journal*, if I will consent. I shall probably decline. I believe I would rather be a Methodist preacher in the West." The Ohio delegates unanimously nominated him as assistant Editor, with Dr. Elliott, at Cincinnati, and editor of the *Ladies' Repository*, should the same be published. The Western Conferences heartily seconded the nomination. He was so elected by the General Conference, and the public voice approved it. It was a large advance and a new experiment in the developing adaptations of our Church press. There is no comparison between the circumstances of that time and those of the present as to the difficulties of such an enterprise. It had never been tried. There were then comparatively few writers in our Church to take a liberal interest in the support of Church periodical literature, and fewer still familiar with the labor and appreciative of the demands of such an enterprise as was now proposed. The publishing house was poor, and payment for contributions was scarcely known among us. Some feared the whole was in advance of female culture and education, especially as ladies were generally treated to light literature, less religious than what was now proposed, while others augured that the most refined and literary taste, and a high tone of religion would characterize the forthcoming ladies' book. "The expectations of none [we quote as above] were disappointed, though those of most were exceeded, when the first number was issued, January, 1841, under the editorial supervision of Rev. L. L. Hamline. Few men alive possessed equal gifts, as a writer, with Brother Hamline, whether it regards style, pure Christian sentiment, literary taste, or logical acuteness. His great powers, with small assistance at that day, were brought to bear on the *Repository*, the happy effects of which remain till this day impressed on its pages. This was the man that gave character to the *Repository*. He gave it form and fashioned it after a pure model, and the result remains."

The novelty of the movement as a Church enterprise, to be conducted in the spirit of the higher religious culture, and its acknowledged legitimacy and importance as an advance in the right direction, roused the hitherto latent powers of the Church. The preliminary steps were taken with great enthusiasm. Its publication was looked for with intense interest. Great hope, however, was still mingled with many fears. The first number dispelled the furtive doubts of its friends, and the second assured them of a victory already achieved. Prof. G. W. Blair writes of it in the *Richmond Advocate:*

"The pleasure which I realized in reading the first and second numbers of the *Ladies' Repository and Gatherings of the West* was so great, that I felt at once an almost boundless desire for its success and extensive circulation throughout the borders of our beloved Zion.

"If the introductory numbers may be taken as a true index of its future character, it will prove an unspeakable blessing to the Church. I expected much from it, knowing the hands to which it had been committed, but it has exceeded my highest expectations. Some of the finest writers in the Church are contributing to its columns, and these have claimed for it a high place among periodicals of literature and taste. And all is sanctified by the deep vein of piety which runs throughout. No one can read the excellent articles of the Editor, especially that on the 'Nativity,' and that on 'Works of Taste,' without feeling that he is holding converse with a rich, cultivated, and spiritual mind. His intellect will be improved, his taste refined, and his heart made better. There is a grace and harmony in the style, a sweetness in every word, and a mellowness in the spirit, which impart their own nature to the soul. A holy sympathy is begotten in the heart for the writer, and if one is so fortunate as to know that these are but the natural and unforced expressions of the qualities of his heart (as is happily known by all who have made his acquaintance), his pleasure is complete. I consider these articles alone well worth the price of subscription."

Hamline not only wielded a facile pen with Addisonian chasteness, but possessed the true enthusiasm which warmed and animated whatever theme he took. In his hands common events assumed a new interest, not by the illusive dress of fiction, but by the discovery of new and higher relations, while the crowning charm of his writings proceeds from the high moral end for which he wrote, and the in-breathed and living desire to save souls. Preaching or writing he had this one object in view and upper-most. This was no detriment to literary taste or merit, but gave to both a more exalted standard and refinement. Nor was his skill in engaging others to work inferior to his own ability to execute. The class of writers which constellated about him were of a very high order. A large proportion were edu-cated, of both sexes, and with as much variety of talent as perhaps any corps of contributors could boast. Indeed, the public were surprised at the sudden awakening of gifts in a Church which had never competed for fame in literary and religious journalism. No periodical published by the Meth-odist Episcopal Church ever called out a greater amount and variety of literary and religious talent in the sphere of popular journalism than has the *Ladies' Repository*, and none has exerted greater influence in molding and elevating character. "It received," says Dr. Elliott, "its first great impulse and char-acter from the graphic pen of Hamline, its Editor, and it was deeply imbued with the spirit of devotion and of religion." Before the sitting of General Conference in 1844 the *Repository* was fairly estab-lished, and that body "recommended that it be con-tinued, it having more than paid its way."

CHAPTER VIII.

[1842-43.]

THE GREAT CHANGE—ENTIRE SANCTIFICATION.

WE now approach a crisis—we should rather say an epoch—in Mr. Hamline's history ever memorable to-himself, and not less important to the Church. We refer to his entering into the experience of "perfect love," or entire sanctification. Although widely useful and marvelously blest in his pulpit and personal labors, he was often exercised with a painful consciousness of deficiency and a growing conviction of the need of a deeper work of holiness, a more perfect conformity to God. It is a law of the kingdom of heaven to "give" to those who "ask;" to fill those who "hunger and thirst after righteousness;" to bestow the "pearl of great price" on such as "sell all they have" to procure it; to bestow grace on such as are prepared for it, by an exhaustive sense of their need. Conviction and repentance must precede pardon, and conviction of the necessity of entire sanctification, and desire for it, up to the point of total surrender, the giving up all for Christ, must precede the bestowment of the blessing sought. It is thus that the Holy Spirit leads us first to self-knowledge, self-abhorrence, self-renunciation, before Christ to us can be "all in all."

Although Mr. Hamline was in the height of his self-denying labors and his usefulness, fulfilling all known duty, and, we must admit, growing in grace; or to use his own words, "had been attentive to the means of grace in the closet and in the sanctuary;" yet he felt that his devotions had sometimes been formal, lacking vitality; that he was lacking in full confidence in drawing nigh to God; that there was in him a proneness to wander, his tempers being not always equally subdued; that in his heart were the roots of many evils which "springing up troubled him," though kept down while under the reign of grace, and that in this state there was not assured safety. His sense of unfitness and unworthiness at times unmanned him. Once, while walking to church on Sabbath morning with his wife, he stopped short and exclaimed in his agony, "I could prefer strangling and death to such a state." And this was at a time when his popularity was at its height, and his congregations overflowed.

As his spiritual convictions and perceptions became more and more clear and strong, so he increased in prayer and wrestling with God. He says: "I spent several weeks much of the time before God. I felt that without a clean heart I should soon fall." Indeed, prayer was the habit and occupation of his life. As he drew nearer to God, God drew nearer to him, and his soul increased in power and the fruits of the spirit. He saw holiness more in its loveliness and desirableness. He saw the loveliness of the Divine character, of the word and of worship, in a new light. Still his soul was not satisfied. The introspective habit of his mind, and the acute sensibility of his conscience, allowed no half-way measures, and he found no place to rest short of a finished

work. His incisive views of the breadth and spirituality of the law, and of the depravity and deceitful-
ness of his own nature, became the gauge and meas-
urement of that work for which he groaned and lan-
guished. God was preparing him for a great work,
and for "showing him how great things he must
suffer for his name's sake." He had counted the
cost, and joyfully accepted the cross. All was real
as eternity. With him it was a work of destiny.
His being was to be rendered back to God for a new
creation, even to be "sanctified wholly," for which
he now gave himself with a profounder view and
comprehension of the act than he had ever before
attained. His convictions were not general, but specific. Like the woman who had lost the "piece of
silver," he sought a definite good. Like the blind
man who, in the midst of general destitution, asked
only that he "might receive his sight," so with him
all seemed comprehended in the one blessing which
he sought.

In the month of March, 1842, Mr. Hamline went
to New Albany, Indiana, for the purpose of enjoying
religious privileges of worship, and the counsel of
Rev. W. V. Daniels, the pastor of the Church, who
was a godly man and walked in the light of a full
salvation. He reached the place on Saturday, heard
a sermon in the evening on "perfect love," and
after sermon bowed before the altar with others who
were seeking the blessing. Through the Sabbath
his heart was in a deep struggle. On Monday morning he rose early, and wrapping his cloak about him
continued until breakfast to plead for the baptism
of the Holy Ghost. Hastily partaking of a slight

repast, he returned to his chamber and fell upon his knees.

It is worthy of remark that he reached the point of deliverance through a process of thought. Faith is not reasoning, but we come to it by a mental process of which we are more or less conscious. Every act of faith presupposes certain antecedent states of the understanding,

"Through reason's wounds alone your faith can die."

The steps of the reasoning faculty immediately preceding the final act of faith in the present instance were simple, and natural as they were Scriptural. Mr. Hamline himself thus describes:

"While entreating God for a clean heart my mind was led to contemplate '*the image of Christ*' as the single object of desire. To be *Christ-like*, to possess '*all the mind* that was in' the blessed Savior; and this became the burden of my earnest prayer. 'And why do you not take this image?' was suggested, 'for he has taken yours. Look at the crucified Lamb. Why does he there hang and bleed, "his visage so marred more than any man, and his form more than the sons of men?" Is it for himself?' No, O no! He is innocent, immaculate. It is for *me*. There on the cross he bears my sin, and shame, and weakness, and misery and death. And why does he bear them? To give me, in their stead, his purity, and honor, and strength, and bliss, and life. Why then not take this image? Give him your sin, and take his purity. Give him your shame and take his honor. Give him your helplessness and take his strength. Give him your misery and take his bliss. Give him your death and take his life everlasting. Nay, yours he already *has*. There they are bruising him and putting him to death. Nothing remains but that you take his in exchange. Make haste! Now, just now, he freely offers you all, and urges all upon your instant acceptance.

"Suddenly I felt as though a hand omnipotent, not of wrath but of love, were laid upon my brow. That hand, as it pressed upon me, moved downward. It wrought within and without, and wherever it moved it seemed to leave the glorious impress of the Savior's image. For a few minutes the deep of God's love swallowed me up; all its billows rolled over me."

Under this influence he fell to the floor, and in the joyful surprise of the moment cried out in a loud voice. The work was done. The struggle and the outcry were heard in the house, and for a time proved the occasion of a temptation, as if propriety had been transgressed by this liberty among strangers. But the temptation was momentary. The work was clear, the experience undoubted, and from that hour to the close of his mortal life he referred to it as the great epoch of his life. He says:

"My joys now became abundant, but were peculiar. In my happiest hours my joys mingled with such a sense of vileness as I can not describe. Sometimes in my near approaches to my Savior (for I seemed to commune with him almost face to face), with tears pouring almost like rain from my eyes, I used to say, O my blessed Lord, how canst thou thus visit and inhabit a heart so vile!"

But this glorious opening of a new life, though not forfeited, was shadowed, and experience became variable by a not uncommon error—the suppression of a clear and distinct confession. God will be honored by the full acknowledgment of all grace received. And this is not rendered simply by the fruit of a cleansed heart as it appears in the daily life, but with the lips also; "with the *mouth* confession is made unto salvation." The New Testament word for *confession* or *profession* (for the original word is the same) signifies a *verbal agreement* to a given statement, doctrine, or fact. It is of the nature of "setting our seal" publicly to the truth of God. The idea of *language*, written or spoken, enters into the essence of the word. Confession or profession *objectively—*

i. e., of the doctrines and history of Christ—was, in apostolic times, and ever has been, a fundamental test and duty of all Christians. The same *subjectively*— *i. e.*, of the *experiences* of the truth through faith in Christ—is not less fundamentally required. "Go *tell* what great things the Lord hath done for thee, and hath had mercy upon thee," is not limited to the healed demoniac, but expresses a universal obligation. Mr. Hamline confesses, "For some eighteen months I was like Samson shorn, because I did not fully confess God's goodness toward me." This withholding was not from a motive or thought to shun the cross, but from excessive humility and self-distrust. His sense of personal unworthiness was far beyond the common measure, and often proved an occasion of great despondency, timidity, and reserve.

On September 27, 1843, the Ohio Conference met at Chillicothe, and Mr. Hamline was appointed to take charge of the Sabbath morning love-feast. He had been clearly admonished by a humble disciple of hallowed celebrity, that if he retained the blessing he had received he must publicly confess it. In his opening address in love-feast he accordingly spoke distinctly of the great work of grace which had been wrought in him eighteen months before, and that he had come near "making shipwreck," as he phrased it, by withholding confession. When he sat down he found he had not received the special blessing he had expected in the performance of this duty, and feared it was because he had made a mistake and overstated the case. He therefore, true to the honesty and humility of his character, thought he must rise and say that he had been mistaken, and that he was only a seeker. But the thought came to him, "How can it seem strange that you are not blessed when you yourself doubt your own testimony?" Instantly he saw the snare of the temptation and as instantly repelled it. From that moment his faith took hold of Christ, and his doubts were dispelled. Perfect peace, love, and joy filled his soul. Henceforward his lips uttered freely what his heart prompted and his life corroborated, that he was indeed fully saved. In the afternoon of the same Sabbath, by appointment, he was to preach to the conference. A ministerial brother called on him and asked, "What do you propose to preach from?" "I think of preaching from the words, 'Our sufficiency is of God,'" was the reply. The friend rejoined, "Brother Hamline, don't take a new text. The people have come from all parts to hear you preach. The occasion is very important. Take one of your familiar and favorite texts." But Mr. Hamline's thoughts were full of the words he had announced, and he could not change. He followed the leadings of the Spirit and adhered to his first proposal, and that afternoon the Spirit bore witness to the word with overwhelming power, while all rejoiced when they "perceived the grace which was given to him."

A new life now dawned upon him. Not one without clouds, temptations, and sore wrestlings, but one in which over all these he was to have victory. He could now say, as never before:

"Now I have found the ground wherein
Sure my soul's anchor may remain."

With a body afflicted little less than that of Paul with his "thorn in the flesh," with a nervous structure which even in health would be subject to great alternations, and with a life of intense labor and the antagonisms of this "evil world," a perpetually "quiet sea" was not to be expected.   His exquisite sensitiveness often occasioned him sorrow and temptation where a common mind would experience no embarrassment.   On one occasion where the subject of sanctification had obtained prominence, and a revival was in progress, the preacher had not mentioned the great salvation, either in his prayer or sermon.   The heart of Hamline was warm and tender, and he was grieved at this omission.   When he rose to exhort, his earnest words were upon the theme of entire holiness, urging the Church to seek the full salvation. The effort was timely and proved effectual.   But when the meeting was over he suffered much from the apprehension that his zeal had been misguided, and his distress became so great that he found no relief till the next day, when he was advised to resort to special prayer.   Scarcely had he bowed in the attitude of prayer when the cloud burst, and he was filled with joy unspeakable.

At the session of the Ohio Conference, at Hamilton, September 28, 1842, he had succeeded in avoiding a press of conference business, and even of preaching, probably in consideration of his editorial care and the great number of visiting strangers.   This enabled him to enter into the enjoyment of conference with a keen relish.   To his wife he writes:

"I am well and happy.   Conference moves on slowly.   I hope to return more blest than when I went.   Bless the Lord, O my soul.   Be holy.   Friends and foes are all one.   *None are foes.*   Who can harm us if we be followers of that which is good? . . . Yesterday (Sabbath) was one of the best days of my life. I had no preaching to do. Except the bishop's sermon all the appointments were filled with foreign brethren. Many are from Kentucky, North Ohio, and Indiana conferences. There is more religion in our conference than I ever saw before. Many are sanctified. Many others are pressing into the kingdom, and the fruit of this revival in the conference already appears. Ten thousand were added to our Church in this conference last year—an unheard of thing in all the history of Methodism! My mind is kept in peace."

The great baptism amazingly quickened his love for souls, and his ardent zeal to save them. In his diary for November 26, 1842, he says: "I feel as though I had come to the verge of heaven. I have had sad dreams, but am happy now, filled with weeping and praise. I feel like one who has been wrecked at sea and has got into the long-boat. Persons are sinking all around, and he clutches them by the hair. So I see souls are sinking. I feel in a hurry to save them. And it matters not what I eat or what I wear, or who are my companions, for when I have rowed a few miles I shall get home and shall find all my friends there." We have already seen specimens of his habit of labor in this department with his brethren in the pastorate. In one of his excursions, whence he had purposed to return after the Sabbath, he writes to Mrs. Hamline, on Monday: "There seems to be so special a call for me to stay here to-day, that I do not know but I shall yield. . . . If I am not home sooner you may expect me Wednesday evening, but likely to-morrow," and a little farther on he says: "If I can stay till Thursday, say so." Thus his earnest soul was often in a strait betwixt his editorial claims at home and the revival work in the Gospel battle field. In the same letter he says: "Such a day as I had yesterday might be expected to be followed by some conflicts. Satan could not see me as I was yesterday without great wrath. I preach at half-past nine this morning and this evening. I preached three times yesterday without the least inconvenience. . . . Reports are coming in from the people which make me wish to stay. God is wonderfully working. I have a special call here. I am happy! happy! happy! God is doing wonders. It exceeds all."

In a letter to his friend, Rev. C. W. Sears, December 16, 1842, he says:

"Since our conference rose on the 6th or 7th of October, I have by the divine goodness been almost constantly employed in preaching Christ and him crucified, in Ripley, Dover, Levanna, Covington, Shiloh, Cheviot, Aurora, and Warsaw in Kentucky. In these places the word of God has had free course, and more than five hundred have been added to the Lord. For one week I have been resting from these labors and enjoying the peace of home. My breast, which was much affected by preaching more than seventy sermons in two months, with all my editorial duties, is now getting strong again, and to-day I expect to go ten miles into the country and recommence my labors. I have been 'watered also myself.' God has made the labors of the ministry sweet—*unspeakably sweet.*"

In the Fall of 1842, within less than three months, he says: "I have enjoyed the privileges of attending some eight or ten protracted meetings, at each of which there was a glorious display of God's saving power." Does the reader ask how he could, under such circumstances, not only give satisfaction but win reputation as the editor of the *Ladies' Repository?* He answers the question in part: "My labors are heavy. I take my papers often into the country and write *between preachings.*" He was a ready and rapid writer. When his mind was roused and concentrated, and that was as often as duty demanded and health permitted, after the first dictation little was left for critical review. His writings would read as well at the first as at the fortieth edition. Yet all this and more could not have sufficed to sustain his editorial care, had not his ever faithful and highly accomplished wife, herself a writer and a critic, Mrs. Melinda Hamline, relieved his office duties, and substituted much of his editorial work. They perfectly sympathized both in the editorial and evangelical work, and they wrought as "true yoke-fellows."

Some of his letters in these times may suffice to indicate his conflicts and triumphs and his habit of labor. In a letter to his wife, dated Lebanon, Ohio, Wednesday, January 18, 1843, he says:

"I want to see you very much, more than usual. I trust you are near to Jesus. I hope you are not sorrowing. Yesterday was a blessed day to me, until near night, when very heavy clouds came over me. I could hardly keep from starting right home. Brother Elliott preached powerfully last night. Our congregations have been very large, solemn, and affected, but something holds back. Sister Brodie and three others joined last night. She was happy. I have preached eight times since Saturday night and feel no inconvenience. I start for Franklin in two or three hours. This morning I am somewhat burdened, but hoping. My conflicts are mental, the absence of love and joy, no special temptations, much *outward power ;* and know no reason for my conflicts but ' the cup which my Father giveth me.' O may I meekly drink it. Pray, my beloved, as I know you do."

To the same he writes, having reached Franklin, Friday morning, January 20, 1843:

"The meetings here are blessed, especially to the Church. Yesterday morning was one of the best times I ever *saw,* and

the P. M. one of the best in my closet I ever *felt*. I feel
much stronger in Christ. I am struggling for the blessing both
for you and myself. My health is excellent, and my breast
very little affected. Preached twice yesterday. We have sacrament this morning and I shall preach to-night. Leave in the
stage to-morrow morning at 9 o'clock for Hamilton. My return
will depend somewhat on appearances there. Write a letter on
Saturday and direct to Hamilton. Let me know if I am
wanted. I hope to be greatly blessed to-day ; have been up
since 6 o'clock (now half past seven). O may Jesus bless us
exceedingly. I told you, I think, that the day after I came up
the stage upset near Jamison's tavern, and almost killed the
driver and one passenger. I thought we should be destroyed
on the way. It was fearful to travel in the stage on that road."

In the midst of labors beyond his strength, and
which he afterwards admits laid the foundation of
his premature infirmities and his retirement from
public life ; with a popularity which exposed him to
envious criticism; and with the two mightiest social
forces in his hands—the pulpit and the press—one
might well fear for his humility. But to him selfish ambition was unknown. For himself he sought nothing,
desired nothing ; for Christ, every thing. His dead-
ness to the world and his self-abnegation were almost
startling, even to his friends. His views of natural
depravity and the malignity of sin in the light of the
divine law left him in utter amazement at that divine
love which had borne with his life of unbelief so long,
and had multiplied such boundless "grace upon grace"
in his redemption.

Before Mr. Hamline was converted he was acquainted with a young lawyer of respectable parent-
age and position who was indulging freely in the social
glass till habit was fixing its iron rule, and the young
man was on the way to ruin. Mr. Hamline was

moved to interpose an effort for his rescue, and wrote him several anonymous letters. Although the lawyer knew not who was the author of the letters, yet the letters wrought such a powerful effect upon him that he turned from his cups and became a sober man. Afterward, in the height of Mr. Hamline's popularity, the lawyer writes to him, in real respect and friendship, urging upon his attention the duty of preparing an autobiography, suggesting meanwhile that perhaps some "concealed" grief might deter him or be the cause of his unwillingness. To this letter the following characteristic answer was given:

"CINCINNATI, *December* 20, 1843.
"To A. S. C., ESQ.

"*Dear Sir,*—Whether I have written to you before with my own proper signature, I do not recollect. But for circumstances known to you I should never have been covert in my correspondence. I am glad that your friendly letters open the way for frank and full communications. You speak of autobiography. But for one fact I could never discourse, or scarcely think again of self. Except for that one thing I should be the most ultra of all misanthropes. And yet my man-hating would be concentrated self-abhorrence, while I should, without effort, look tolerantly on mankind. And what do you imagine is the isolated fact which renders me often willing to think of self? If you were doomed to bury your chiefest friend, how would you thereafter read over and over the productions of her admired pen? As fruits and evidences of the riches of her mind they would be very precious.

"Now, there is ONE—Jesus the son of God—who is doing a great work amongst sinners upon earth. He is saving them 'by the washing of regeneration.' The enterprise was commenced upon the cross. In every believing heart he has written his law in letters of blood. All the regenerated are examples of the power of his cross, and the efficiency of his Spirit. I am an unworthy receiver of this grace. In my own renewed heart I read those characters which his wounded hand has there graciously inscribed. For *this* I love to look in upon myself. Every motion of my heart—every thing in my whole being, which does not bear the stamp of total—of *ineffable* depravity, is a fruit of my blessed Savior's sufferings and love, and an illustration of his wonder-working *grace*.

"In this connection I can bear to see myself, and to scan my inward life in its most repulsive aspects. In this connection I can review my outward life, for the efficacy of grace is not only evidenced in whatever sanctified affections I may possess, but also in the long journey by which mercy brought me from the Egypt of my bondage to the Canaan of God's love. The artisan's skill should certainly be judged of not merely from the excellence of his mechanical productions, but also from the material out of which he wrought them. He who from dross could produce a single dime, would merit more than he who should coin millions out of pure massive bullion.

"You see now, my dear friend, how only the sight of self can be endured. It is a helper in crucifying pride. It can contribute to cast me down deep into the dust. It can aid my views of Christ. It often helps me to conceive more clearly the *love of Jesus passing knowledge* as displayed toward one so vile. I am this dross. Yet on *me* Jesus lays his hand of pity and of power. He takes '*my* feet out of the pit,' and places them 'upon a rock.' He takes away *my* notes of mourning, and puts into my mouth the song of joy and praise. Casting all my sins behind him—removing them '*far* from me,' he raises me up to 'sit in heavenly places' with his saints.

"The song of the redeemed, even in the heavenly world, regards their lost estate on earth, as well as their beatitudes in paradise. 'Thou wast slain and hast redeemed us to God by thy blood—and made us unto our God kings and priests!' The Savior's love and glory appear not only in their present eminence and bliss, but also in running back to what they once were, and in the redeeming process which sanctified and crowned them. In the connections here expressed, I have use for all my past remembered life. Let its history be graven on my soul forever. I never must—never shall forget it. It must and will remain in everlasting junction with the cross of my Redeemer. No—no—thou *bleeding one*, let neither time nor eternity—nor both with their brief or lengthened cycles—efface from memory the past! O how will the greatest follies and offenses of my life gather a welcome freshness from the future, as seen in the ever growing light of a Savior's cross and passion !

"While I sit in meditation on a theme so mortifying, and yet so salutary—so self-annihilating, and yet so life-giving, connecting all with Christ's most gracious sufferings and doings, my nature is dissolved. To my consciousness existence seems naught but *flames*, and *tears*, for *gratitude* and *penitence* do swallow up my being. And these very meltings are fresh fuel for the flames because themselves are new instances of God's exceeding great compassion. He kindles up this life of ardors or it never could exist. A threefold death is conquered first, that Life may gain dominion afterwards. You speak of some 'concealed' grief. *No, my friend, I have none. There is not a sorrow of my nature but you and all the world may know. But would you know it you must come along with me to Calvary.* All my deep emotions are now kindled at the Mount. My griefs and joys, of any moment, are blended with its scenes. O my friend! be assured that I am born into a new and higher life, which slights, as insignificant, the interests and the sympathies dissevered from the cross. Can you understand this? To know it well is the acme of all wisdom and felicity in time. 'T is climbing up to heaven. It is ascending to where angels would, but can not soar."

CHAPTER IX.

*GENERAL CONFERENCE OF 1844—ELECTION TO THE
EPISCOPACY.*

IN the preceding chapters we have brought down
the manner of life of Mr. Hamline to the fall of
1843.   This was the time to elect delegates to the
General Conference which was to be held the following May.   Mr. Hamline had not expected to be a
delegate to the General Conference of 1844, he having been sent to that of 1840, and it was understood
that others from the Book Room should now take
their turn.   With him it was all satisfactory.   "It
will be a trying session," he said, "involving important interests and great responsibility, and I would
greatly prefer my every-day duties at home."   He
had never sought place or preferment.   His physicians, also, had earnestly advised against his going.
But an occurrence happening in which Mr. Hamline
had meekly submitted to a public and unprovoked
indignity, from the jealousy and rivalry of a senior,
which his ministerial brethren deeply regretted and
strongly resented, it was determined popularly that
he should be elected.   In this, also, there was a
providence.

The conference met September 27, 1843, at Chillicothe.   Toward the offending brother Mr. Hamline
indulged no enmity.   Concerning him he says: "I

have had no hard feelings toward S. at any moment since we left home. Still, I disapprove of his course, and, though I had nearly made up my mind to vote for him, I now hesitate. He is very kind and his ambition is a *disease* of the *heart* which I can overlook, yet I think maturer grace is needed in General Conference. These little occurrences, with the undisturbed tempers with which I met them, greatly encourage me. I cried all day by turns, 'O Lord, give others all the honor, and me all the reproach, only so my heart be cleansed and kept pure.' So I feel now."

The hour of election arrived, and Hamline, with a younger brother, walked abroad conversing delightfully upon the "great salvation" which was now all his theme. When they returned he found himself elected. To his wife he again writes:

"We are getting along tolerably well. The election, which was, most of all, in our way, is now over. Brothers Elliott, Finley, Trimble, Raper, Sehon, Connell, Ferree, and your unworthy husband are the delegates. My election is one of the most unexpected events of my life. I can now scarcely credit it. My position alone [as editor] was, I supposed, an entire bar; but I had left all to God, and I have one satisfaction—a sweet one it is: not more than *one* minute, put it all together, has been spent in talking of General Conference in my company since I reached Chillicothe. I did not know that one person was going to vote for me, nor did one, as I know of, expect me to vote for him. Thank God that he gave me a higher calling, heavenly and blissful, so that I could not find it in my heart to talk of elections or General Conference. You may wonder how, with so much opposition to the Book Room, two editors should be sent. I wonder, also. I feel satisfied that it is of God. This is the best of all. I feel more and more that God is working in me mightily. He blesses me."

On his spiritual experience at the same Conference he further adds:

"I believe God has sanctified me throughout—soul, body, and spirit—and I am willing all the world should know it. He has sprinkled me, and I am clean. 'From all my filthiness and from all my idols he has cleansed me.' This I first confessed in our love-feast last Sabbath morning. At first the enemy thrust sore, and almost devoured me, but the light is increasing. I believe this work was accomplished in New Albany eighteen months ago, and that I have been in bondage ever since by 'hiding his righteousness within my heart.' I shall talk more of this if I live to see you. The Lord strengthens me. 'I live not, but Christ liveth in me.' Adieu, my beloved."

The intervening months till General Conference were spent partly in his usual editorial and evangelical labors, and partly in perilous sickness.

On the 5th of January, 1844, four months before General Conference, he returned home from a protracted meeting, after several days of hard work in preaching, exhorting, and revival labor. The next day was Sabbath, and three city appointments awaited him. About midnight he awoke with violent symptoms of illness, notwithstanding which he arose at his usual early hour to prepare for his Sabbath work. But a ministerial friend calling in, who was himself an experienced physician, perceiving his condition, said, "You must not preach to-day, your pulse is one hundred and twelve," and kindly engaged to see his pulpit supplied. His family physician was called, but no remedies took effect. After a few days a counseling physician was called, and then a third. The decision was that the heart was seriously diseased. Mr. Hamline now relinquished all hope of being able to attend the General Conference, and prepared for easy traveling as a relief of the faintness and partial paralysis from which he suffered. He spoke only in whisper, and much of the time could not endure the presence of any number of persons in the room. But the Ohio delegation were unwilling to release him, and urged that they might have his presence at the General Conference, or at least in the city, where they could consult together. He replied: "I may not commit suicide, and my physicians say that to go there will be death. But at the call of the Church I am willing to go even unto death."

As late as the month of March, six weeks before General Conference, his symptoms left little hope of recovery. March 16th, Dr. Worcester, who had spent six years in Paris as a student making pectoral diseases a specialty, was called in to examine him with the stethoscope. It was decided his heart was seriously diseased. Afterward Brother Schon, who was present at the examination, and had been conversing with the physician, came in. He said: "I told Dr. Worcester that you had been in the habit of preaching five sermons in a day, and he looked astonished at this." Mr. Hamline said: "I am not sorry I did so." Brother Schon said: "But that was living too fast." Mr. Hamline replied: "But it was sweet living, and if I die now I am glad I worked while I could."

On Sabbath, the 17th, he stood looking out at the window, and remarked: "It is pleasant to look out upon these things, upon which, after a little time, I shall look no more with these eyes, or in this manner. The thought of so wonderfully changing

one's mode of living is very exciting. To leave so
many friends behind, to go to meet so many who
have gone before, to leave so many saints who are
struggling on their way, and so many who are not
struggling, and so many sinners to be saved!"   A
little after he said: "Could I to-day be introduced
to a thousand of those who are gone before in Wesley Chapel; could I see Jesus in the pulpit, and the
apostles sitting in the altar, and Wesley and Fletcher
and Fenelon and Guyon and Hester Ann Rogers
and their companions in another circle; and could I
spend the day with them and hear them speak in the
order of love-feast their experiences, the Savior first
uttering words of wisdom; and then hear Abraham
tell of Isaac and of his feelings when he offered him
up, with what wonder should I gaze upon their faces
and listen to their words; that is, if they were men
in the body and had never died.   But I hope soon
to see them and spend, not a day, but an eternity,
with them!"   His wife said: "Your unusual calmness and the manner in which you have regarded
death has, ever since you were ill, made me feel that
your condition was that of serious disease."   He
replied that "calmness does not always precede
death.   Hezekiah was greatly troubled at the thought
of it."   "True," she said, "but he did not live
under the Christian dispensation."   He rejoined:
"I could not ask for fifteen years to be added to
my life nor for five months nor five weeks;" and
his joy increasing in the near hope of heaven, he
said: "I feel as though it would be easy for me to
enter upon the song, 'Worthy is the Lamb.' My
lips feel as though used to it."

In the afternoon he said: "It is a precious Sabbath to me. I feel like Columbus and his crew when they got in sight of land. My soul sings a '*Te Deum.*' But Dr. L. comes in and says it is all a mistake, it is only mountains of fog I see. But as an eagle stirreth up her nest, and hovereth over her young, so the Lord stirreth me up and teacheth me to fly, and I think he will soon burst the cage and let me soar. I feel as though my soul had wings." His disease had been called "fatty degeneration of the heart." "It does not matter," he says, "whether my heart be turning to fat or to stone, physically, nor what ails it, so that it will answer to receive Jesus. This is all I want of it." "Choosing diseases," he adds, "is like going into a flower garden. One can hardly tell which to select, all being so beautiful." At another time he said: "It will be very delightful for me to cast my crown at His feet, and cry, 'worthy is the Lamb.' But I don't know what he will do with me in heaven. I feel as though he would place me away in some corner, so unworthy! But I sometimes think grace has done so much for me that I shall stand out a monument to show what Jesus can do for sinners."

The General Conference of 1844 held its session in the city of New York. It was a time ever memorable in the annals of American Methodism, and sad as it was memorable. It ended in the separation from the Church of fifteen annual conferences, including Indian Mission Conference and Florida Conference, in thirteen slave-holding States, and their subsequent organization under the title of the "Methodist Episcopal Church South." So great an event invests every act or person with historical importance who bore any responsible connection with the doings of the session; and, as no one can claim this honor more than can the subject of this memoir, it becomes due to his name, and to the honor of the grace of God in him, that he should be placed in his true position.

Upon arriving at the seat of the General Conference, the delegates soon found that the great issue between the North and the South, on the subject of slavery in the Church, was upon them. The alarm was great. The hour had come when decisions must be made, as to Church discipline, which would prove a final test of the strength of our connectional union. Like the strong man, when the cry was made, "The Philistines be upon thee," the Church representatives arose in their strength and wisdom and piety to meet the inevitable question. Old men were there, great men, men of renown and experience, fathers of the Chucrh, veterans of a hundred battle-fields. Young men were there, fresh, strong, and versed in the history of the times, upon whom devolved the chief weight and brunt of the militant labor. The writer of this was there, a member, too young to enter into the great agony which made old men weep when they pleaded with and against each other—when like Olin and Bangs, they sobbed out: "Brethren, is this the last time that we shall meet in General Conference?" The North could not give up without, in their judgment, surrendering fundamental moral and ecclesiastical principles. The South claimed the same. And whatever doubts might have been subsequently expressed as to the sincerity of either side, it is certain as history and personal observation can make it, the parties believed and respected and loved one another at the time.

As to Hamline, he had no personal feeling as a party in the great issue. He had come to the conference under the call of the Church, which he accepted as the call of God, to assist as he might, in counsel with his fellow delegates. But above the storm of ecclesiastical debate and excitement his soul dwelt in the serene atmosphere of peace. The conference opened May 1st, at 9 o'clock, and he closes his letter to his wife that morning with the words: "I am now going to see the conference opened. God is with me. I am happy. Not a temptation. Glory to God."

The divisive question came up in a twofold form. The first was that known as the "Harding case." The Rev. F. A. Harding, of the Baltimore Conference, had been duly tried, and suspended from the ministry, for holding slaves. The case was appealed by the defendant to the General Conference, and in this light came up as the order of the day on the eighth day of its session. The trial continued five days, and the action of the Baltimore Conference was sustained by a vote of General Conference of 117 to 56. It is not relevant to the purpose of this memoir to enter upon a statement of the evidences and arguments in the case, which the reader will find in the published journals and speeches of conference, but the importance attached to it was of vast significance. The Discipline strictly forbade "all office" in the Church to those who held slaves, where the laws of the State allowed emancipation, and permitted the emancipated slave to enjoy his freedom; but it allowed preachers to hold slaves where the laws prohibited emancipation and freedom to the liberated slave. The whole question in the Harding case turned upon the single fact as to the laws of Maryland in the case. The decision of the case was understood to be a final test of the sentiments and purpose of General Conference in regard to the intent and application of the disciplinary law, as affecting traveling preachers. It was understood, also, to have an ominous and unmistakable bearing on the decision of the case of Bishop Andrew, yet pending, which we shall notice hereafter. It was received every-where in the South as "the knell of division." By speakers on the conference floor, in private letters, by the weekly papers of the South, in all circles, the tocsin of alarm was sounded. Eight days of the conference passed in this increased and increasing agitation, when Drs. Capers and Olin offered the following preamble and resolution:

"In view of the distracting agitation which has so long prevailed on the subject of slavery and abolition, and especially in the difficulties under which we labor in the present General Conference on account of the relative position of our brethren North and South on this perplexing question; therefore,

"*Resolved*, That a committee of six be appointed to confer with the bishops and report within two days as to the possibility of adopting some plan, and what, for the permanent pacification of the Church."

The resolution passed unanimously, and Wm. Capers, Stephen Olim, Wm. Winans, John Early,

Leonidas L. Hamline, and Phineas Crandall were appointed that committee. A day of fasting and prayer was ordered by the conference. Two days passed and the committee was unable to report. The time was lengthened. The delegates North and South were requested to meet separately to assist in the deliberations. The result proved that no ground of pacification could be found. It was in view of his thorough knowledge of civil and ecclesiastical law, his known practical wisdom, and his pacific spirit that Mr. Hamline was chosen to act in this most delicate, most responsible place.

On the twenty-second day of its session the case of Bishop James O. Andrew was formally brought before the conference by the report of the Committee on Episcopacy. It was admitted by Bishop Andrew that he had come into the possession of slaves, which he then legally held. One was bequeathed to him in trust, another had come to him by inheritance from the mother of a former wife, others his present wife, not he, owned.

Immediately upon the presentation of the case, on motion of Rev. John. A. Collins it was adjourned and made the order of the day for the 22d of May, the day following. It was well to approach so grave a responsibility with calm deliberation. Probably no question in any age or country ever elicited more able debate, more breadth of view, more resolute courage to abide by what was deemed right in principle or expedient in policy, or a broader charity and conciliation.

It was never held that Bishop Andrew had violated any statute of the moral or ecclesiastical code.

The Church had never had occasion to legislate, or frame a rule, on the case. Public sentiment, the common consent of the Church, had hitherto been a sufficient guard. The case, therefore, was not considered judicially. The "impediment" simply lay in the relations of a bishop as a superintendent of the whole Church, in which relations, under the present circumstances, Bishop Andrew must be unacceptable to the larger part. It was not a question of pure ethics, but of expediency in its highest and purest sense. The high antislavery feeling and conscience of the Church in the free States, could not concede to the system of American slavery the implied sanction which such an example of one of her bishops would seem to give. It was certain and inevitable, if General Conference countenanced any legal connection of the episcopacy with slavery, the great majority of the Church in the free States would renounce its jurisdiction, and disruption, division and misrule would overspread the land. They were conscientiously opposed to all voluntary slave-holding, as against the rights of man and the laws of God, and they could not seem to justify it by so important a concession as the South now claimed. A bishop was not, like a common pastor, limited in his residence to conference boundaries, or annual appointments. He could choose his residence anywhere. The case of Bishop Andrew, therefore, could not be considered under the rule on slavery as applying to members of annual conferences. The South had no right to demand a slave-holding bishop, and the North could not concede it. Indeed the public Christian sentiment North, and in a large proportion of the South forbade it. But having openly taken the issue, it became impossible for either party to compromise or recede.

Bishop Andrew had always been considered as a Southern man. As such he was elected to the episcopacy. "I did not support Bishop Andrew's nomination," says Dr. Capers, of South Carolina, "with all my heart, but he was brought forward by the Georgia and North Carolina delegations concurrently [in 1832] at the first instance of Brother Hodges." But when Bishop Andrew saw the gathering storm in 1844, he shrank from the conflict, and shuddered at the thought of being the occasion of strife and division. "When I reached New York," he says, "and found the course which events were likely to take, I resolved to resign, and relieve myself of a burden of care and anxiety which I had long felt too heavy to be borne with comfort, and also to prevent a General Conference debate which might very possibly be protracted and exciting." But knowing the feelings of the South, he resolved to advise with them as to the effect which such a step would have on the peace of the Southern Church. Their advice was, "If I valued the peace and unity of the Southern Methodist Church not to think of resigning: that my cherished object of giving peace to the Church could not be accomplished by my resignation: that my resignation under existing circumstances would be the signal for wide-spread disaffection, and very probably a general secession of a greater portion of the Southern Church." The bishops hitherto had been selected from the Northern Conferences. Dr. Capers would have been elected to the episcopacy in 1832 had he been free from slavery. This he well knew, and when the South finally complained that the practice of thus selecting bishops had the effect to keep them in servility to the North, and was an implied reproach, and demanded that a Southern man should be put forth, Dr. Capers himself wrote and pleaded against it, as a measure calculated to divide the Church. His influence had the effect to ward off the evil for the time. But when the South found, in 1844, that they had a bishop already on hand who was connected with slavery, they instantly determined to fight the battle on that issue. The South would accept nothing as a pacification but "the permanent admission of slavery into the episcopacy," which Bishop Soule himself, it was said, "admitted to be impracticable." Dr. Wm. A. Smith, of Virginia, and two of the Southern papers, had taken the ground beforehand that "if the South was not indulged with a slave-holding bishop in 1844, the slaveholding conferences must set up for themselves, or the Southern ministers must tamely submit to be proscribed and degraded."

On the day for opening the case, the Rev. Alfred Griffith, of the Baltimore Conference, offered a resolution by which Bishop Andrew was "affectionately requested to resign his office as one of the bishops of the Methodist Episcopal Church." For two days the debate was on this resolution. The arguments ran slightly upon the powers of General Conference to act in the case, and chiefly on the nature, justice and propriety of such action as the resolution contemplated. Little advance was made beyond the discovery that the parties were immovably intrenched in their positions. It was seen also that the language was too severe. The thing therein proposed—"resignation"—was more than the offense called for, at least in this stage of the proceedings. The error was natural. The case was new, and the time short for maturing thought. They approached the painful responsibility cautiously, tentatively, respectfully, but firmly. They wished to save the bishop, whom they greatly esteemed, and to save the Church, which they loved more. But the obstacle must be removed. Both sides displayed intrepid fidelity to what they believed to be right in principle and expedient in action.

At the end of two days a substitute for Mr. Griffith's resolution was introduced by the Revs. J. B. Finley and J. M. Trimble, "That it is the sense of this conference that Bishop Andrew desist from the exercise of this office so long as this impediment remains." Five days of debate, in all, had passed, including the Sabbath, when on Monday morning, the twenty-seventh day of the session, Mr. Hamline took the floor. There was (we see him now as we saw him then) a meekness and gentleness in his mien, a deep and seated restfulness in his countenance, a calm deliberation in his manner, and a peculiar blending of majesty and humility in his appearance. Though quiet and unassuming he had already become known to the leading men. The classification of his thoughts was simple: "First. Has the General Conference constitutional power to pass this resolution? Secondly. Is it proper or fitting that we should do it?"

It is impossible to give a summary of his argument, which will convey any adequate idea of its scope and force. The reader will find it in full in the second volume of Bishop Hamline's Works. From the moment he opened his mouth, and his first sounds and sentences fell upon the ear, it was evident enough that he had control of the subject and of the audience. I can not describe the scene better than in the language of Dr. (now Bishop) J. T. Peck: "It was evident that the question, so involved and far reaching was in the hands of a master. His positions were logically perfect, without a word to spare, and yet in rhetoric and oratory, as fine as if intended for popular entertainment. The tones of voice were new to many of us, and they were actually enchanting. All noise in the vast assembly ceased, and he seemed as if alone with God, uttering thoughts and arguments as of inspiration 'True, true, every word of it true,' we would say without speaking, for no one would have dared to speak or move. 'Conclusive, splendid, irresistible.' The last sentence was finished; the speaker quietly resumed his seat. A thousand people drew a long breath; and the great issue was logically settled."

The same day Dr. Wm. A. Smith, of Virginia, rose to speak. He was an able debater, thoroughly informed upon the subject, and thoroughly Southern in his sentiments. Subsequently he was president of Randolph Macon College, and published his lectures to his senior classes on slavery, holding it to be a legitimate and divinely authorized institution, on the same principle of all civil government. Mr. Hamline had so evidently settled the legal and ethical principles of the case that no champion speaker in the opposition could make any advance in his argument until the argument of Hamline should be disposed of. In the opening of his speech Dr. Smith regrets his want of "eloquence," and "persuasion," "so vast," he says, "are the interests involved—so absurd are many of the doctrines stated on this floor—and withal so ingeniously have some of them been defended by the eloquent speaker that has just taken his seat, Brother Hamline, of Ohio." He then proceeds to notice the salient points in Mr. Hamline's argument. Later on he attempts to show that the Northern conferences will not, with comparatively small exception, reject Bishop Andrew, and adds: "Nor will the Ohio Conference refuse the services of Bishop Andrew. Brother Hamline, who preceded me on this subject, may go thus far. His speech, years ago, on the subject of slavery, so strongly characterizing him as an abolitionist (and which I never heard of his retracting), may justify this opinion. He is an eloquent man—a man I am told of great influence—and may draw others after him. But still, sir, I have yet to learn that the Ohio Conference will take this offensive attitude toward the South, and the unity of the Church."

The attempt to mark Mr. Hamline as an agitator and a leader of the abolitionists added nothing to the logic or candor of Dr. Smith's argument, and in the eyes of others was accepted as a strategy to lessen the force of his opponent's argument by impairing his personal influence in the conference. But he had mistaken his man, not only as to his antecedents, but as to his power to defend himself, and his strong intrenchment in the confidence and affections of his brethren. Hamline meekly and courteously heard

the speaker through, though parliamentary law gave
him the right to interrupt him for misrepresentation.
The reply to his opponent is as remarkable for its
Christian humility as it is for its point and precision.
When the speaker was through Hamline arose and
obtained leave to explain, as follows:

" *First.* Dr. Smith says: ' He (Mr. Hamline) brought you
to the conclusion that Bishop Andrew had acted improperly.'
I answer,—I did not name Bishop Andrew, or any other
bishop. I intended to argue, not to accuse ; and, if I carried you to that conclusion, as he says, whether it was by
argument or not, it could not have been my confident assertion, as to Bishop Andrew's conduct.

" *Second.* I argued that a bishop may be displaced at
the *discretion* of the conference, when, in their opinion, it
becomes ' *necessary,*' on account of improper conduct, and, I
might have said, without improper conduct, on his part, so far
as *constitutional restrictions* are concerned.

" *Third.* I never said, as Brother Smith affirms, that the
administrative powers of this conference are ' *absolute.*' I
said they were ' *supreme.*' *Absolute* means *not bound.* This
conference is bound in all its powers, whether legislative,
judicial, or executive, by constitutional restrictions. ' *Supreme*'
means that, while acting within its constitutional limits, its
decisions are *final* and *all-controlling.*

" *Fourth.* As to my use of the word *legislative,* the hyper-
criticism of Brother Smith would apply to the use of the term
judicial with equal force, for properly the conference has
neither the functions of a legislature nor of a court. I used
the term as it is used every five or ten minutes by all
around me. And it is amusing that Brother Smith should
have fallen into the very fashion for which he reproves me.
He said: 'If the conference does this *it acts above law.*'
Now, where there is no legislation there can be no law. I
commend to him, in turn, the report of 1828, which has long
been familiar to me, and of which I most cordially approve ;
yet I presume that he, as well as myself, will continue to use
the only convenient terms, *legislation* and *law,* to distinguish
one class of conference powers from another.

"*Fifth.* As to the assertion that the analogy between bishops and inferior officers will not hold, because this conference is not responsible for its action as removing officers are, I answer,—This conference is responsible to the constitution, and, if it wished to bind itself not to remove a bishop, it could call on the annual conferences to aid it in assuming a constitutional restriction. Not having done so proves that it intends to hold this power, and execute it when necessary.

"*Sixth.* As to the abolition address charged to me, the conference may be surprised to learn that it was a colonization address, and was so acceptable that the Colonization Society in Zanesville published it in pamphlet form. Moreover, a friend of mine forwarded a copy, without my knowledge, to Mr. Gurley, of Washington City, who noticed it with unmerited commendation in the *African Repository*, the official organ of the American Colonization Society, and gave extracts of it to the public. Surely the brother is too magnanimous to have attempted to counteract the force of my argument by misrepresenting and rendering me personally odious. As to my exerting my slender influence for evil ends at home, I must submit to be judged by my own conference, who will know how to estimate the value and the motive of the insinuation."

To this reply no rejoinder could be made, and none was attempted.

During the debate Dr. Winans, a vehement Southern man, one day met Mr. Hamline in the street and said to him: "Mr. Hamline, I wish to do only one thing before this conference closes. I wish to answer your speech." Mr. Hamline replied: "Well, Brother Winans, I don't think there is much in it to answer, but if you really wish to undertake it I will try to give you something to answer." Mr. Winans replied: "Mr. Hamline, I am not afraid of you." "And I am not afraid of you," was the answer. Mr. Winans never attempted an answer to the speech.

It could not be expected that Mr. Hamline's

speech should be well spoken of by his opponents. Dr. Capers, of South Carolina, said of it afterward, in the *Christian Advocate and Journal:* "Read the speeches of Drs. Olin, Hamline, and Durbin—men of noble honors and nobly meriting them—and see what they amount to. . . . Dr. Hamline's genius, put to the rack, found out a new interpretation of the constitution, by which he fortified himself, and strengthened his brethren in the persuasion that they could depose the bishop if they would, and therefore they had a right to do it—an argument which, put in a nutshell, is not very unlike 'might is right.'"

The speech of Mr. Hamline needs no higher tribute to its logic and its effect, than such attempts to parry and paralyze it. Still more inexplicable is the course adopted by Dr. Redford, of the Methodist Episcopal Church, South, in his recent "History of the Organization" of that Church. Professing to give a full and fair statement of the arguments *pro* and *con* of the General Conference of 1844, on Bishop Andrew's case, he omits Mr. Hamline's speech altogether, and simply mentions the fact that he, with others named, spoke to the question. Could he not afford to his readers at least a brief of the argument of Mr. Hamline? Was a statement of the arguments on the case complete without it? Did it comport with historic faithfulness, and with justice to the majority of that General Conference to suppress it? The doctrine of Mr. Hamline's speech relating to the power and jurisdiction of General Conference over a bishop—the doctrine so specially objected to by the South—was fully reiterated subsequently in the Report of the Committee on "Reply to the Protest," and adopted by the General Conference. It is the doctrine of the Methodist Episcopal Church and has been from the days of Coke and Asbury, who specifically took this ground.

On the tenth day of the discussion the bishops, after long consultation, presented a formal address to the conference, in which they "unanimously concurred in the propriety of recommending the postponement of further action in the case of Bishop Andrew till the ensuing General Conference." It was a last and forlorn effort to prevent precipitate action, secure the greatest maturity of thought, to more fully test the sentiments of the entire Church, and, if possible, to effect conciliation. But the measure was not satisfactory to either party. The case, it was judged, admitted of no delay, and the sequel confirmed this opinion. After respectful consideration the "address" was laid on the table.

The debate continued till June 1st—ten days in all—when the resolution of Mr. Finley was adopted by a vote of 111 yeas against 69 nays. The last hope of continued union seemed now gone, and all further efforts were in the direction of some amicable and equitable adjustment of the questions of Church property and jurisdiction in case of separation.

Two days after this decision—June 3d—Dr. Capers introduced a series of resolutions, providing "that we recommend to the annual conferences to suspend the constitutional restrictions which limit the powers of General Conference so far, and so far only, as to allow that the Methodist Episcopal Church in these United States and territories, and the Republic of Texas, shall constitute two General Conferences, to meet quadrennially, the one at some place *South*, and the other North of the line which now divides between the States commonly designated as free States, and those in which slavery exists. That each one of the two conferences thus constituted shall have full powers, under the limitations and restrictions which are now in force and binding on the General Conference, to make rules and regulations for the Church, within their territorial limits respectively, and to elect bishops for the same." The one was to be denominated the "Southern General Conference of the Methodist Episcopal Church," and the other the " Northern General Conference of the Methodist Episcopal Church." The Book Room property and the Missionary Society were to remain intact, and the proceeds of the former to be divided among the annual conferences as heretofore. This is the substance and purport of the plan, which was referred to a committee of nine, to-wit: William Capers, William Winans, T. Crowder, J. Porter, G. Fillmore, P. Akers, L. L. Hamline, J. Davis, and P. P. Sanford. In view of the importance of the case, the committee were allowed to hold their meetings during conference hours. When the committee were in session they asked Mr. Hamline his opinion on the possibility of thus dividing. " Brethren," said he, "my opinion is that you can not divide. The moment you do this you forfeit all the church property now deeded and held in the name of the Methodist Episcopal Church." Mr. Winans said, " Brother Hamline, you have told us what we can not do; will you tell us what we can do?" " Brethren," he replied, "you can secede; nothing else." Mr. Winans replied: "That is true, I see it; but I hope you will not call us seceders." Mr. Hamline replied, "*I* will not."

The committee found the plan submitted to them impracticable, first because it was unconstitutional; secondly, because to pass it in General Conference would cause that body itself to take the initiative step to division. It was, therefore, then and there understood that nothing could be done unless the South took the first step by declaring separation inevitable, in which case the conference might make provision, as far as its power extended, for an equitable division of church property, and the continuance of fraternity. For the present, therefore, they could only return their papers to the conference, which they did in a verbal report.

Two days after the presentation of the above resolutions of Dr. Capers, fifty-one southern delegates united in a "declaration" that the agitation of the subject of slavery and abolition, the frequent action of General Conference on that subject, and especially the recent action had in the case of Bishop Andrew, "must produce a state of things in the South which renders a continuance of the jurisdiction of this General Conference over these conferences inconsistent with the success of the ministry in the slave-holding States." The loud tocsin had now "tolled its last alarm." Immediately, on motion of Dr. Elliott, a second committee of nine was ordered, to whom this declaration of the southern delegates was committed. This committee consisted of Robert Paine, Glezen Fillmore, Peter Akers, Nathan Bangs, Thomas Crowder, T. B. Sargent, William Winans, Leonidas L. Hamline, James Porter.

No act of the General Conference hitherto had embodied the significance and solemnity of the appointment of this committee. Hitherto their measures had been tentative; this was final. Hitherto all movements had proposed the continued unity of Church; this contemplated probable, we might say hopeless, separation. Soon after the committee was constituted J. B. M'Ferrin, of the South, and Tobias Spicer, of the North, offered the following resolution:

" That the committee appointed to take into consideration the communication of the delegates from the Southern conferences be instructed, provided they can not in their judgment devise a plan for an amicable adjustment of the difficulties now existing in the Church, on the subject of slavery, to devise, if possible, a constitutional plan for a mutual and friendly division of the Church."

Mr. Hamline arose and said: "I will not go out with the committee under such instructions." Dr. (now Bishop) J. T. Peck, said: "Let the General Conference beware. This is a proposition to commit this conference to a division of the Church. We are sent here to conserve the Church, not to divide it." Dr. Early replied, and a desultory debate arose. Mr. Hamline thought he could propose an amendment which would be satisfactory, and asked, "will the mover change so as to read: ' That in case no plan of amicable adjustment can be found, the committee be instructed to inquire if there be a constitutional mode for dividing *the funds* of the Church?'" After some hesitation, reluctantly, the amendment was accepted. It will be seen at once that the amendment totally changed the important point of the resolution, but it was all that could be conceded. By an unaccountable mistake, says Bishop Peck, this change in Dr. M'Ferrin's resolution was not made in the minutes, and the resolution went upon the journal in its original, not in its amended form. The next morning, upon the usual reading of the minutes for final correction, Dr. Peck was absent from the city on duty. Mr. Hamline immediately called the attention of Dr. Bangs to the point, and urged him to call the attention of conference to the same. Dr. Bangs felt reluctant to open a controversy, and thought it would make no material difference. Mr. Hamline, feeling that he was a younger member, and a comparative stranger in the conference, shrank from volunteering to arrest the matter against the judgment of seniors, and having expressed his opinion to Dr. Bangs that the phraseology would, in law, be against us, he resigned it to others. The minutes were approved, and the error passed into the journal. All parties, at this time, considered a rupture of some sort inevitable, and anxiously guarded all points where misunderstanding or legal interference might widen the breach. Subsequently, when the division of the Book Room property came before the Supreme Court of the United States, the court took the ground that the General Conference had all the powers of its constituency as in the Church economy prior to 1808; and (it was assumed) as the aggregate body of Methodist preachers might prior to 1808 have resolved themselves into two distinct General Conferences or church organizations, so now the delegated body of the General Conference, representing the total Church as then existing, possesses all the powers of its constituency, where not inhibited by special restrictions

and reservations.   As to the "restrictive rules" of
the constitution, they do not specify or forbid the
division of the Church; hence, it was inferred, the
power to effect such a result vests in General Conference.   The "plan of separation," it was held, was
an ordinance of General Conference authorizing and
providing for, the separation of the South; that it
was of the nature of a compact between contracting
parties; that the single fact of separation was authorized by General Conference, and was complete in
itself, without referring the same to the annual conferences; and that the single point of the division of
Book Room property was, according to the plan,
the only matter dependent on annual conference
concurrence.

In the work, by Dr. E. H. Myers, of the Southern
Church, on "The Disruption of the Methodist Episco-
pal Church," he argues these points in full, and
charges Bishop Hamline, in his speech on Bishop
Andrew's case, with teaching the doctrine that the
General Conference had power to divide the Church.
His argument runs in a line with what has already
been said, but he especially charges that when Mr.
Hamline, in General Conference stated that the legislative supremacy of General Conference "consists
of full powers to make rules and regulations for our
Church," under the given restrictions, he does, by
necessary implication, comprehend the power to
divide the Church, inasmuch as this is not embraced
in the inhibiting rules.   That is, according to the logic
of Dr. Myers and the court, "full power to make
rules and regulations for the Church" comprehends
power to divide or dissolve the Church!   This mode

of arguing calls for no answer. The power to do what is legitimate to conservative legislation, can not imply the equal power to do what is not legitimate to legislation, and which no constitution in Church or state ever made provision for.

The powers of General Conference, be they more or less, being delegated, not primal, the object and intention of the act of investiture must become the gauge and limit of the power invested. To transcend this limit is a fraud and a usurpation. This is not less a principle of law than of ethics. In the intentions of the constituency lay the ethics and legal limitation of the delegating act, beyond which the acts of General Conference had no *jure humano* ground or validity. That the power to divide the Church was not specifically mentioned in the "restrictive rules" is no evidence that it is specifically vested in General Conference. It is evidence only that a power so extraordinary, not to say monstrous, and so contrary to the history and philosophy of all delegated bodies in Church or state, could not be supposed to have entered into the minds of the constituency as a possible future assumption. Nor had the constituency of 1808 itself the moral right thus to divide, without, at least, the concurrent voice of the entire body of the membership. To have assumed it would have been a usurpation and a violation of the tacit but real compact of Church fellowship. The ministry were not the total Church.

The resolution of Dr. M'Ferrin, as it stands upon the Conference Journal gives countenance to the hypothesis that General Conference might have power to divide the Church, and the facts that the confer-

ence ordered it first to go to the committee, and then
passed it into their Journals as legitimate conference
business give a *quasi* indorsement of the hypothesis.
Especially as the committee to whom this resolution
of instruction is said to have been committed actually
brought in their report in the form of the so called
"plan of separation," it might seem that they had
only followed the said instructions.   And all this when
it was known that the committee on Dr. Capers's resolutions had decided that church division under sanction of General Conference was simply impossible!
which the conference had declared from the first.

That the present reading of the Journal is an
error, is sufficiently sustained by the facts, that Bishop
Peck distinctly recollects the case, and his own remonstrance against Dr. M'Ferrin's resolution, as above
given ; that Bishop Hamline, subsequently, often repeated the fact of his prompt refusal to go out with
the committee under such instructions ; that the matter became a subject of written correspondence between Dr. Peck and Bishop Hamline soon after the
publication of the journals of General Conference, Dr.
Peck expressing his surprise at finding the *erratum;*
that the resolution, as in the journal, makes the General Conference contradict itself; for it was their uniform doctrine from the first that General Conference
had no power to divide the Church, whereas this
resolution gives to General Conference the initiative
step, tentatively, to separation ; and finally, it places
Bishop Hamline in direct contradiction to his most
clearly and publicly declared sentiments.   Indeed,
the fundamental error which the General Conference
avoided from the beginning, was that of involving

itself, by sanction or encouragement in any form in the responsibility of either a division of the Church or a separation. This was not from unfriendliness, much less to fix a reproach upon the South for separating, but simply and only from conviction of want of constitutional authority. The utmost good will toward the South prevailed, and bating a few extremists North and South the designs of the Plan might have been amicably carried out.

The day after the appointment of the committee of nine, already noticed (June 6th), the delegates from the South presented to the conference a protest against the action taken in the case of Bishop Andrew. It is called the "Protest of the Minority." In it the action of conference was severely, and, as it was believed, unjustly, reviewed and animadverted. The case was new in the history of the Church. No occasion had ever occurred to equally test the constitutional powers of General Conference in relation to bishops, and the extent of their accountability to that body. The case being without precedent, their action must determine the meaning of law and the genius of our episcopal government, and establish a precedent for future time. Upon the reading of the protest, therefore, Dr. Simpson (now Bishop) rose and offered a resolution,

"That the conference appoint Brothers Olin, Durbin, and Hamline a committee to prepare a statement of the facts connected with the proceedings in the case of Bishop Andrew, and that they have liberty to examine the protest just presented by the Southern brethren."

The design in appointing the committee was to

present the facts and principles involved in the case on which the majority had acted, as an answer to the protest and a vindication of General Conference. It is entitled, "Reply to the Protest."

The election of Mr. Hamline to the episcopacy the day following made it necessary that he should retire from the committee, and Dr. George Peck was appointed in his place. The matter is mentioned here as another indication of the rank Mr. Hamline held in the confidence and confidential business of the Church.

Three days after the appointment of the second committee of nine—June 8th—they reported to conference. Mr. Hamline took no part in the debate which ensued, having been, as we have seen, elected bishop the day previous. But during the debate he arose twice to explain the action of the committee. He himself took what may be called middle ground as to the parties—*i. e.*, he opposed *in toto* all committal of General Conference to the division or separation of the Church, but in case the South found it necessary to separate and erect a distinct Church organization, he was wholly in favor of giving them their *pro rata* share of the church property. This was the ground on which the report of the committee and the final action of General Conference on that report were based. But this seemed to some a *quasi* approval and encouragement of division, and to obviate this impression, while the matter was under discussion, Mr. Hamline arose and explained. He says:

"When the first committee met they had before them a paper [the resolutions of Dr. Capers] which proposed a new form or division of the Church. The committee thought there were difficulties in the way of such a proposition. One provision (of Dr. Capers's resolutions) was to send it to the annual conferences. But that was unconstitutional and revolutionary in its character; and when their votes came back, the General Conference would have no more authority than they had now. Why, then, send it? The Book Concern is chartered in behalf of the general Methodist Episcopal Church in the United States; and if they did separate until only one State remained, still Methodism would remain the same, and it would still be the Methodist Episcopal Church in the United States.

"But if they sent out to the annual conferences to alter one restrictive article [as in the report now before the house] it would be constitutional, and [thus confer power] to divide the Book Concern so that they might be honest men and ministers. The resolution [before us] goes on to make provision, if the annual conferences concur, for the security and efficiency of the Southern conferences; for the Methodist Church would embrace them in its fraternal arms, tendering to them fraternal feelings and the temporalities to which they are entitled. And the committee thought that it could not be objected to on the ground of constitutionality. He, for one, would wish to have his name recorded affirming them to be brethren, if they found they must separate. God forbid that they should go as an arm torn out of the body, leaving the point of junction all gory and ghastly! But let them go as brethren 'beloved of the Lord,' and let us hear their voice responsive, claiming us as brethren. Let us go and preach Jesus to them, and let them come and preach Jesus to us."

The comprehensiveness of this explanation, its spirit, its fidelity to the law and fellowship of the Church, can not be fully appreciated without a general grasp of the circumstances and posture of the debate. The gist of the controversy lay in the unfoldings of these few statements. The reader will understand that the power of General Conference to divide the Church into two separate, yet co-equal parts, was conceded to be constitutionally and legally impossible. The South might "*separate*" by its own voluntary act, upon its own responsibility, and become an independency, but the Church could not divide itself. The report of the committee of nine said nothing about division, but only of separation, in the event that the South should find it necessary, as a condition of their retaining their pastoral relation to master and slave, and in that case provided for their proportion of the Church property. In order to this latter, one constitutional provision, which limited the appropriation of the dividends of the Book Room funds, must be altered. This law reads thus: "The General Conference shall not appropriate the produce of the Book Concern nor of the chartered fund, to any purpose other than for the benefit of the traveling, supernumerary, superannuated, and worn-out preachers, their wives, widows, and children." To this the report of committee proposes to add—"and to such other purposes as may be determined upon by the vote of two-thirds of the members of the General Conference." This change was considered sufficient to enable a future General Conference to award the South its equitable share. It will be perceived that this change would be a prudential guard upon the misappropriation of the funds independently of any relation it might bear to the question of separation. But suspicions were awakened, and for a time the debate was arrested at this point. Mr. Hamline again arose and explained:

"They (the committee) had carefully avoided presenting any resolution which should embrace the idea of a separation or division. The constitutional article which was referred to the annual conferences had not necessarily any connection with division. It was thought as complaints were abroad respecting the present mode of appropriating the proceeds of the Book Concern, it would be for the general good that the power to appropriate such proceeds should be put in the power of a two-thirds vote, instead of that of a mere majority, thus making it more difficult to make a wrong appropriation. And the *occasion* of this report was taken hold of by the committee, to make it more difficult to misappropriate the funds, in which they believed they should serve both the particular object of the report and the general good of the Methodist Episcopal Church."

After this statement little more was said, and the report was adopted. If the reader has surveyed the breadth and variety of the debate he will be surprised at the brevity and clearness of Mr. Hamline's statements. He spoke only from the stand-point of first principles, and what was fundamental to the question, and his modesty adventured only so far as represented the convictions of the committee.

CHAPTER X.

[1844-45]

ORDINATION—VISITATION OF CONFERENCES FOR TWO YEARS.

MR. HAMLINE'S duties, as delegate were now ended. A single glance over his course at General Conference seems due, and will suffice to show the extraordinary history and characteristic qualities of the man. He had come to the conference a comparative stranger; he left it with a name and influence as widely known and felt as the bounds of the Church. He had used no arts, taken no measures, to bring himself into notice. What was done by him was meekly performed as a duty growing out of his position, and what was done to him by the conference was done spontaneously. It was the impromptu voice of the Church. His whole demeanor was quiet, humble, and retiring, without thought or consciousness of acquiring fame or influence, and when elected to the episcopacy he was both surprised and humbled. As a human call he would have at once declined the honor, but the circumstances of the case were so extraordinary, and the exercises of his mind so strongly corroborative of the hand of God in all, that he bowed in humble submission. The office had sought him, not he the office. The thought of his fitness for the episcopacy had burst upon the conference like the sudden

blaze of a meteor when he stood before them, fourteen days before the final adjournment, and delivered
his incomparable speech on the case of Bishop Andrew. In private intercourse, and in committees, he
had already been felt and appreciated, and his name
was getting into the leading circles. But it was on
that day and in that speech that he first stood before
the public in his full proportions. Every subsequent event only confirmed and enlarged the impressions then made. The fame of that hour never declined. He proved himself master of the situation,
and he held it. We find him on all the most responsible committees. When in committee his
opinion was sought, and when he spoke in conference, his words were received with marked attention.
Still he was the same, unchanged, humble man, content if he might only walk with God.

Eleven days after this speech, June 7th, the conference proceeded to elect two bishops. The result
showed that Leonidas L. Hamline and Edmund S.
Janes were elected. The next day (Saturday), by
motion of Dr. S. Luckey, the time for ordination of
the bishops elect was fixed for the ensuing Monday
at eleven o'clock. The hour arrived, and the business of conference was suspended. The bishops
elect were invited to chairs in front of the altar,
Hamline sitting between Brothers Pickering and
Fillmore, and Janes between Brothers L. Pierce and
Capers. The collect and epistles were read by
Bishop Waugh, the Gospel by Bishop Morris, and
the questions and prayers by Bishops Soule and
Hedding. Brother Hamline was presented by Brothers Pickering and Fillmore, and Brother Janes by

Brothers Pierce and Capers. The imposition of hands was by the four bishops, Soule, Hedding, Waugh, and Morris. Thus the two newly elected bishops were solemnly set apart for their great work. Two purer, worthier men were never consecrated for the holy office. They have both an honorable record, were beloved and revered in the Church, and have entered into rest.

Of the occasion of his episcopal consecration Mr. Hamline thus speaks in a letter to his wife, dated Monday, June 10, 1844, at twelve o'clock noon:

"Yesterday was a day of holy delights. I preached my first sermon for five and a half months, in the Sands Street Church (Brooklyn), from the text, 'If we walk in the light,' etc. It was a precious season. Preaching seemed to bring to my soul a world of gushing emotions, such as I can not describe. This morning Brother Janes and myself were consecrated to the episcopal office at Green Street Church (in the presence of a great crowd), and were conducted to our places in the altar. My emotions were so overpowering that it was with difficulty that I could answer the questions, or make the responses. I wept and wept till I knew not what to do, and brethren around me joined in weeping. But O they were tears which, vile as I am, I believe were bottled up in heaven. It was a holy and delightful morning, one of the most solemnly joyful I ever had on earth. I feel fully that God has called me to the office of a bishop. In my heart he has set his seal to the commission in a way I hope never to forget. I feel that I am his in deed and in truth. O, may I grow in the grace which now purifies, strengthens, and saves me."

The General Conference adjourned at a quarter after twelve o'clock, the night following, to meet in Pittsburg, May 1848. Bishop Hamline thus writes to his wife, Tuesday, June 11, six A. M:

"I sat in conference until 11 o'clock last night, making about ten hours of constant sitting through the day, without much weariness, or rather with *simple* weariness without sickness. I slept soundly and feel well and blest this morning. I feel *cleansed* wonderfully. The bishops meet this morning at 8 o'clock. The New York Annual Conference sits to-morrow in Brooklyn. I shall, if God permit, attend it diligently, to learn my business, for you know I never was in a stationing room. . . Much as I love you, and delightful as it would be to see you, thes Lord gives me perfect patience and holy resignation. *Wednesday morning.*—I feel, my dear wife, that God's mercies are so great and so many that you will not be afflicted when I say that I go to the Troy Conference next Monday, thence to New Hampshire Conference, thence to Black River, thence to Oneida, thence to Genesee, thence to Michigan, and finish my first year's work in October, from which I shall have rest until next July, when I go to Pittsburg, Erie, North Ohio, Ohio, Indiana, and North Indiana. The next year, Rock River, Iowa, Illinois, Missouri, Arkansas, and Indian mission. The fourth year, Troy again I shall have six. months' rest yearly, unless some other superintendent fail. Traveling is my health. I expect to improve by every mile of travel. I can now walk rapidly two miles, and feel an unusual vigor of body and soul. . . . I know I need not ask your prayers. I am perfectly (almost miraculously, it seems to me) free from the least temptation except to unbelief. Oh, what hath God wrought! I am dead, and my life is hid with Christ in God. Don't feel any concern about me. I never had less concern about myself in a temporal point of view. The Lord is with me. I go in his strength and under his wing. I feel no loneliness. I never wanted to see you more, yet am perfectly content as it is."

In this spirit he entered upon the vast care and labor of his office. He felt that his call was of God, for he had never sought or desired it. This his friends well knew. He himself declared "he would rather be a drayman than a bishop." This he said, not from disrespect of the office, but from a sense of its labors and responsibility. His state of health, also, was understood to be a formidable impediment. He had come to General Conference, as we have seen, according to the statement of his physicians, at the peril of life, under medical protest against his preaching or entering into conference business.   But he had considered his election as delegate in the light of a providential order, and when elected bishop he felt the same providential and spiritual call to assent.   To him the will of God was supreme law and supreme delight.   He contemplated the episcopacy from the spiritual stand-point, and entered upon it with the single aim to the salvation of souls and the sanctification of the Church.   His past life had been a preparatory discipline, and his great baptism in 1842, the qualification of power for this strange and unexpected work.   Not the least of his evidences and his consolations, was the common and hearty approval of the Church at large.   The stay at Dr. Palmer's while in New York had been a grateful cordial to his spirit, and also a special favor to his physical health.   From the numerous congratulations of his friends I may be pardoned for giving the reader one—all our limits will afford—from a hero in the Ohio Conference, the venerable Jacob Young, D. D.   He had known Bishop Hamline from his earlier life, was his first senior colleague on the circuit, and was a life-long admirer and friend.   In a letter dated Cincinnati, Ohio, July 3, 1844, he says:

"We are at this time far apart, and it is not likely that we shall meet very soon in this world.   But neither time nor distance can cool the ardor of my friendship.   We have passed through many changes since the Savior first united our hearts. You were living in Zanesville with your beloved Eliza, and I in Marietta with my beloved Ruth.   Some time after our first acquaintance, our lot was cast together on old Ohio Circuit, where we became true yoke-fellows.   You have passed through a variety of changes since those happy days that we spent together on Short Creek hills, and, to say all in a few words, you are now a bishop of the Methodist Episcopal Church. Well, my dear brother, I have had but one opinion of you since we first met in Wellsburg till this day. I need not tell you what that opinion is, but I will say, I am thankful to Almighty God that you are a bishop. It has been my wish and expectation for some years that you would be called to fill that office. Though the cross is heavy, and the station responsible, grace will sustain you if you rely on the Savior, and if my feeble prayers will be of any avail, you will always have them. You will stand in need of both moral and natural courage. I pray that God may give you good health; I am sure he will give you favor in the eyes of all good people. . . .

"My heart was in agony while Bishop Andrew's case was before the Conference, but at present I am calm and happy. I love many of the Southern brethren, but I love the Church too well to have a slave-holding bishop. I have with my dim eyes read your speech over and over, and will say in truth I I can not take one exception to any line or word in it. I think you have taken a correct view of the constitution of the Methodist Episcopal Church. . . . I would not take such liberty with any other bishop, but I know you love the Savior and love the Church, and, though you are my bishop, and I am happy to receive you in your true character, yet, when I write to you, you seem more like a son than a superintendent. I believe you will be sustained by God and the Church. Be strong in the Lord and in the power of his might. And now, my dear brother, I commend you to God and the Word of his grace, which is able to save you and to give you an inheritance with all the sanctified."

In a memorandum later made, he records: "At the General Conference in 1844, most unexpectedly to myself (and to nearly all, I believe) I was elected to the superintendency. A translation in the chariot of Elijah would not have overtaken me much more unexpectedly. My struggles were peculiar, and yet I found evidence that I was *called to this ministry.* On the 12th of June I first occupied the chair in the

New York Conference, at Bishop Hedding's request. My soul all the while overflowed with unutterable baptisms of the Spirit, such as I can never describe. As business proceeded my soul cried out to God in behalf of his ministers." "Bishop Hamline being present," says Dr. Bond, "was introduced by Bishop Hedding. In the course of proceedings Bishop Hamline took the chair, which he seemed to fill with great dignity and ease, and much to the satisfaction of the conference."

After four days he left for the Troy Conference at Poultney, Vermont, of which he records:

"I commenced my first conference June 19th. The Lord was with me and gave me blessings. I was ill—very ill—for two days; but my worthy friends, Rev. J. T. Peck and lady, nursed me with the greatest care and kindness, so that I was able to attend to the ordination."

His attack, here referred to, was sudden and violent, so much so that at one time Dr. Peck exclaimed: "The Bishop is dying!" The Troy Conference closed the 28th of June, and after twelve days of rest he reached the seat of the New Hampshire Conference, at Portsmouth. He arrived there four days before the opening of the session, and not finding at first the deep congeniality and sympathy of feeling on the doctrine of holiness, which had sustained him during the previous weeks, his heart sank into partial discouragement. "But," he says, "the preachers are coming in, and I am told that some of them are warm and sunny and fiery, and can weep and shout. Oh, I bless God for religion and for Methodism. But when Methodism affects the dignity and silence and stiffness and corpse-like aspect of formalism, it makes me weep. I want to see it the warm, breathing thing it was in the days of Abbott, and not a statue. Thank God, I feel his life in me this morning." The session proved a pleasant and profitable one. He says: "It is said by the brethren that they have never witnessed so much spirituality and devotion in any former session of their conference. It is all through, so far, a sort of love-feast. . . . I find no great difficulty in my business, only to keep my heart right. Whatever I do without the sensible power of grace is foolishly done, and I am ashamed of it; but when I feel Christ with me all seems to be done as it should be." As to his health he says: "I am as well now as I have been at any time since leaving the West."

On Sabbath he attended love-feast at eight in the morning, heard two sermons and attended to two ordinations, "equal to one sermon." The day was an ovation throughout. In the morning Rev. M. Sorin, of Philadelphia, "preached an excellent sermon," and in the afternoon Dr. Olin. Of the latter he says: "It was one of the grandest exhibitions of intellect I ever witnessed, and as pious as it was majestic. He preached from the witness of the Spirit and the doctrine of perfect love to a vast number, I presume, who despise both. I doubt not that Dr. Olin is the greatest man on the continent, and simple as great." His text was John xiv, 1. "My text," says Bishop Hamline, "and my leading propositions: 1. The belief of God the Father and Judge troubles the heart. 2. Believing in Jesus is the only method of relief from that trouble. I often think it strange," he adds, "that in all my hearing and reading I never lighted on that division of the text, it seemed so obvious and so important; but it was my supposition that I *alone* had it, except some one had borrowed it from me.   But he made so much better use of the divisions than I could that I freely relinquish it to him."

Bishop Hamline had avoided preaching, not from positive inability, but to give his system time to rally and re-establish itself after the shock at Poultney. His spells of physical strength were transient and at irregular intervals.   On his journey from Plattsburg to Potsdam, to attend the Black River Conference at its session of July 31st, he notes that he "suffered much, but was helped of the Lord and blessed by the company of his dear wife, who ministered to both his soul and body."   His kind host, Rev. T. Seymore, pleaded against his going, but he ventured, bolstered up in the stage in a recumbent posture.

August 21st he presided at the Oneida Conference, Ithaca, New York.   He says: "The Lord was with us and his ministers were blessed.   This is a model conference.   Many enjoy perfect love, and the people, like their ministers, press into the liberty." At Genesee Conference, Vienna, (now Phelps) New York, September 11th, he makes this entry: "Here I found much talent and piety, but fear that Count Zinzendorf has taken some of the young men captive. May the Lord make us a pure people in heart and life and doctrine."   He alludes to the doctrine, which some had imbibed, that justification and sanctification were identical, or, at least, simultaneous, after which no distinct stage of Christian life was to be expected, but a gradual growth in grace. This sentiment was distinctly repudiated by the Wesleys, and Bishop Hamline regarded it, as they did, as directly antagonistic to Scripture and experience, and mourned over it as the greatest calamity of the Church wherever it obtained. At this conference, though so feeble that most of his meals were brought to his bed, the bishop attended the five o'clock morning prayer-meetings, and labored in the conference sessions and out of them for the spiritual good of the preachers. There were many warm and earnest hearts among the latter, some witnesses of perfect love, and his visit was a public blessing. At the close the conference passed a resolution warmly expressive of their high appreciation of his services, and of their feelings of affection and confidence. In October 2d we find him at the Michigan Conference, at Cold Water, Michigan. He says: "It was a devout season, and perfect love was very much the theme. The conference adjourned on Wednesday, and we started for Fort Wayne, the seat of the North Indiana Conference, Bishop Waugh presiding." October 29th he reached home, in Cincinnati, "comfortable," he says, "health improved and blessed of the Lord." Thus ended his first tour of episcopal visitation of conferences, which every-where left impressions of spiritual religion upon the Churches never to be forgotten, while his method of presiding and his administration gave equal satisfaction.

On the Sabbath following his return home he preached, and of the Church which he served he says: "I have found war and wickedness here. Let me keep my garments clean and live in peace. Trials bear on me. If God be for me who can be against me? I have been *carried* hitherto, and if I go I must be carried by the arms of my Father's love; and, if *borne* on, none can check me, and I shall not turn aside."

We next find him at Springfield, Ohio, December 22d. He says: "Preached this morning to a large congregation, and though I had not those fervors which are so agreeable in ministering, I believe the word preached will not return void. Since I left Cincinnati, on the 12th inst., I have preached three times in Xenia, where the Church was stirred up and one entered the state of perfect love, and five times here, where there is now a great hungering and thirsting after righteousness, I believe, amongst this people."

January 1, 1845, Bishop Hamline is still at Springfield, where he renews his covenant with God in language and spirit which the Church universal might well adopt: "A new year! I dedicate it to thee, Father, Son, and Holy Ghost! May I and mine be wholly thine! Let me have grace to employ *every moment* of life from this hour for thee. If thou pleasest, let this year end my pilgrimage; if otherwise, let its commencement end my unbelief, my coldness in thy service. O that this may be such a year as I have hoped to see on earth, or such as I long to see in heaven! Let what may come, I give myself to thee, soul, body, and spirit, without reserve, to be forever thine. I seal my vows before heaven and in thy sight, O thou all glorious God! I am forever thine. Amen and amen!"

He adds, touching his labors in that place:

"The Lord is at work in Springfield. His ministers are athirst for perfect love. Their families are pursuing it. Several members are exceedingly stirred up, and three or four have already attained this great blessing."

In a letter of the same date to his venerable friend, Rev. Jacob Young, he says:

"The Lord is pouring out his spirit in Springfield, where I have spent a week, and have been able to preach six times. This I never expected to do again. The work is principally in the Church, where it is most needed for the present. . . I have enjoyed here much of the presence of Jesus. My soul exults in the perfect love of God. There is a glorious fullness to me in Christ. I trust the Church will be stirred up on that subject. O, for a shaking among the followers of the Lamb!"

Again, January 5th, he says: "I am at peace, and see that God is moving on many pious hearts in this town. Let me labor, and then die and soar to him whom my soul loveth. I have peace."

At Zanesville, April 27th, we find this entry: "Here the Lord works on the hearts of his people. I have visited Columbus, Newark, Irville, and some other places, and found the preachers faithful and the people blest."

"July 9, 1845. Closed the Pittsburg Conference at Beaver. Had a blessed season. This is a large and pious body of ministers. They go out in the spirit of their Master."

"July 30th. Closed the Erie Conference at New Castle. A spiritual season. The Lord is pleased to put his strength in me that I may serve him. My soul often dwells above. My life is hid with Christ. Eternal things come near, and earth is all forgotten. Blessed be God!"

"August 3d. Spent in Ravenna, and Sabbath, 10th, in Tiffin, Ohio, and on the 13th commenced the North Ohio Conference at Marion. About one hundred and twenty preachers present, talented, devoted men. A good session. Parted with my dear brethren feeling that it was good to be here."

It is to be much regretted that more full notices have not been preserved of his wonderful influence on annual conferences. A writer in the *Western Advocate* thus refers to the special encouragement given on the subject of holiness by Bishop Hamline's labors:

"The North Indiana Annual Conference closed its session on Monday, 29th of September, 1845, after a most delightful and harmonious sitting of five days. Your presence at the conference, and editorial remarks, preclude the necessity of additional communications touching the general spirit actuating the members, and the harmony and dispatch with which business was accomplished. One feature of this conference, however, is worthy of peculiar notice—the anxiety generally prevalent among the preachers on the subject of perfection. While many profess, others are earnestly seeking this essential and indispensable requisite for a traveling preacher, having been greatly encouraged in seeking its attainment, by the example and exhortations of Bishop Hamline, whose spiritual and business qualifications, as a superintendent, are probably unsurpassed."

His eye was ever watchful of the devotional and charitable spirit of the conference. Often at the appearance of uncharitableness or levity, he would arrest business, and, in his own inimitable way, address the brethren briefly, calling them lovingly to watchfulness and prayer, and then propose a brief season of prayer, calling on the brother aggrieved, or perhaps the one offending, to pray. He was commonly successful, but few could follow his example here.

CHAPTER XI.

[1845-48.]

DIFFICULTIES OF EPISCOPAL ADMINISTRATION.

WE have already referred to the steps by which the General Conference of 1844 cautiously and anxiously strove to maintain the unity and integrity of the Methodist Episcopal Church, and by which they were at last compelled to anticipate separation as probable, if not inevitable. The Southern delegates strenuously and solidly maintained that the action of the conference in the cases of Mr. Harding and Bishop Andrew were so against the laws and public sentiment at the South, and would awaken so violent a prejudice and opposition to the Methodist Episcopal Church, that no ministers acting under her authority and government could be allowed access to the master and the slave, or be tolerated on the soil; and that said action, therefore, would practically destroy their influence, and annul their ministry. Nothing, therefore, remained to them, as they averred, but the dread alternative of abandoning the South or erecting themselves into a new organization, independent of the rule and government of the Methodist Episcopal Church. It is only necessary to say that the Northern delegates confided in the sincerity of their Southern brethren, and admitted that experience might prove such an alternative necessary. Of this the Southern brethren alone could be the judges, but the necessity must be real, and beyond the control of either party. Whatever might have been the feelings of some individual members of General Conference, known as extremists, and whatever subsequent years may have developed, it is certain and beyond dispute, and to the everlasting honor of that body, that it was pervaded by a disposition and purpose to do justice, and conciliate, and preserve fellowship. But when the question came down from General Conference to the annual conferences, and fell in among the existing political and Church parties, and above all, when the press took up the gauntlet, and extreme Southern politics entered the arena, the gathering clouds thickened and the elements of commotion intensified, till the raging storm swept over all the land. To trim and guide the ship before this storm was a task eminently committed to the bishops. Prudent, wise, and godly men were given for that emergency. The memories of Hedding, Waugh, Morris, Hamline, and Janes are a legacy to the Church beyond price, for all time, and a savor of peace.

In order to meet the threatened exigency a plan was devised whereby it was hoped that fraternity might be preserved should a separation take place. This plan was called popularly, "The Plan of Separation," but in the archives of the Church it is known as the "Report of the Committee of Nine on the Declaration of the fifty-one Southern delegates to the General Conference of the Methodist Episcopal Church, adopted June 8, 1844." Two objects were to be secured, first, to provide and define terms on which the geographical line of distinction between the two organizations should be determined; secondly, an amicable and equitable division of the Church property. Fifteen annual conferences, lying within thirteen different States, it was supposed would unite in the separation, should it occur. The Church property had been created by the joint patronage and concurrence of North and South, and hence, if separation became inevitable, a division would be just. The boundary line between the two organizations was not to be determined by State lines between slave and free States, but by conference limits, leaving the societies and conferences contiguous to this border, on the south, free to adhere to the Church South, by a vote of the majority. On this latter the following provision was made, to-wit:

"Should the annual conferences in the slave-holding States find it necessary to unite in a distinct ecclesiastical connection, the following rule shall be observed with regard to the Northern boundary of such connection: All the societies, stations, and conferences, adhering to the Church in the South, by a vote of the majority of the members of said societies, stations, and conferences, shall remain under the unmolested pastoral care of the Southern Church; and the ministers of the Methodist Episcopal Church shall in no wise attempt to organize Churches, or societies, within the limits of the Church South, nor shall they attempt to exercise any pastoral oversight therein; it being understood that the ministry of the South, reciprocally observe the same rule in relation to stations, societies, and conferences, adhering by vote of a majority, to the Methodist Episcopal Church; provided, also, that this rule shall apply only to societies, stations, and conferences bordering on the line of division, and not to interior charges, which shall in all cases be left to the care of that Church within whose territory they are situated."

As to the division of property, first it was proposed to submit to the annual conferences the ques-

tion of altering a rule in the constitution of the
Church (the "sixth restrictive rule"), by which the
proceeds of the Book Concern are to be appropriated "for the benefit of the traveling, supernumerary,
superannuated, and worn-out preachers, their wives,
widows, and children," so as to read in addition, "and
to such other purposes as may be determined upon
by the votes of two-thirds of the members of the
General Conference." On this point, and in order to
this change, a vote of three-fourths of all the annual
conferences and two-thirds of the General Conference was necessary. Had this obtained, commissioners from North and South were to divide the
Book Room property, so that the capital and produce awarded to the Southern Church "shall have
the same proportion to the whole property of the said
Concern, that the traveling preachers in the Southern
Church shall bear to all the traveling ministers of the
Methodist Episcopal Church; the division to be made
on the basis of the forthcoming Minutes."

Immediately, upon the adjournment of General
Conference, the Southern delegates held a meeting
in New York, and assuming that they possessed the
right to decide, as representatives of the South, that
the necessity of separation already existed, issued a
call to the Southern conferences for a delegated convention, to be held at Louisville, Kentucky, May 1,
1845, for the purpose of organizing a Methodist Episcopal Church, South, independent of the jurisdiction
of the Methodist Episcopal Church. Thus the movement of actual separation was inaugurated.

It seems necessary to have inserted thus much of
the doings and documents of General Conference, in

order to put the reader into position to appreciate the difficulties of administration of the Methodist episcopacy in the years that immediately followed. When submitted to them the annual conferences did not concur in the proposition to alter the constitutional rule, and did not, therefore, indorse the separation of the Southern conferences. There was hence no power in the Church to divide property, and the case went up to the United States Court. But the ecclesiastical question involved was different. The General Conference had a right to instruct the bishops, who were officially bound to obey. The provisional plan of procedure, above mentioned, on the contingency of the necessity of separation, was in force, in so far as it was an official order, binding on the bishops to follow, in all matters ecclesiastical. As might be expected the country was filled with exciting controversy, apprehension, and alarm, and all parties anxiously watched the final event of things. Men trembled for the union of the nation not less than for that of the Church. In a letter to Rev. Jacob Young, dated January 1, 1845, Bishop Hamline says:

"I ventured to you the opinion last January, that within ten years this confederation would be dissolved. You thought not. It seems to me you will now consent that possibly the *prophecy* (forgive the word) will be fulfilled. May be the whole South will not go: but if South Carolina is not out of the Republic in nine years I shall be surprised. 'The Lord on high is mightier than the voice of many waters; yea than the mighty waves of the sea.' This is cause of holy thankfulness and praise."

In another letter to Rev. J. B. Finley, February 17, 1845, he says:

"The times are full of promise of revolution, not only in Church, but in state; and one is naturally reminded by all the

aspects of that Scripture, 'He shall overturn and overturn.'
In the midst of all we are assured that the Church shall only
be purified by all the fires through which she may pass. I do
not believe that Methodism has finished her work, or is about
to be laid aside as unfit to work out the good for which she was
originally raised up. And in all that is now going on or is
threatened, I expect to witness the deliverances and defenses
of an all-controlling Providence in her behalf."

In a letter to Rev. W. H. Raper, April 4, 1845,
he further states:

"I thought you would be interested in learning that our
dear Brother Goode reached Cincinnati Wednesday morning
from the Indian Mission Conference [a contested ground between North and South], and spent an hour with me before I
left home. As some of his communications were strictly confidential, I can not speak of them even to *you*, from whom I do
not feel careful to conceal *any* of my own secrets. But I will
say generally that his communications lead me exceedingly to
fear that the secession of the South is not only inevitable from
the state of feeling there, but that it will involve more of stub-
born hostility to the North and to the Methodist Episcopal
Church than I expected. Oh, this acrimony among Christians
and Christian ministers, the disciples and apostles of Jesus
Christ! I am sick at heart as I consider its prevalence and its
effects. I trust our hearts will be kept free. I would choose to
love my enemy with his dagger in my heart, and kiss the hand
which stabs, rather than possess the feelings of suspicion, jealousy, and uncharitableness, which I fear now occupy some
bosoms in the Church of God. Am I in *this* uncharitable? I
fear I may be; for, while charity is the most desirable of all
graces, as being the fruit and the fragance of all, it is at the
same time the most difficult of them all to acquire and to retain. How easy it is to offend against charity !"

These predictions (for they deserve the name) of
political secession of the South, and the dismemberment of the Union, discover an insight into, and
appreciation of, present circumstances and the true
logic of events worthy the mind of a great statesman and a faithful watchman upon the walls of Zion.

He dated the revolt of the South only six years too early. In his General Conference counsel and influence, in 1844, especially in his unanswerable speech on the Bishop Andrew case, Mr. Hamline had drawn down upon him the displeasure of the South, and all who sympathized in their views. Thenceforward he was regarded as their most troublesome opponent, and one who had done their plan of separation irreparable injury. His speech was never answered, and the spirit in which it was given was never questioned, but it was, nevertheless, impossible to prevent assaults upon his personal standing and influence. Herein he felt the unkindness of their smiting. In his diary, April 18, 1845, he says: "I have had some severe trials about the Church. Though my own condition has been what many would call a trying one, I have cared little for myself. My General Conference speech is charged by the South and its friends as being a grievous evil. I can not see it in this light, and until I can I shall rejoice that it was delivered. If the South secede, they must answer it. The leaders in this business of secession will have heavy accounts to settle with the Great Judge. If not the present, some future generation will have woe enough as the result of this madness. I am not sure that the *agents* will not be the *victims* also."

The time drew nigh for the Louisville Convention, above noticed, to meet. The subject had been debated through the public prints, and otherwise, on both sides, with a warmth of party feeling which left no reasonable hope of reconciliation. Various of the Southern delegates, *en route* to the convention,

stopped over at Cincinnati. In a letter of Bishop
Morris to Bishop Hamline, dated Cincinnati, April
29, 1845, he thus lifts the veil upon the times:

"Many delegates of the Louisville Convention left Cincinnati this morning, after a visit of two or three days. Most of
them are from Virginia, North Carolina, and South Carolina.
They found more sympathy here than they had expected.
The tone of the Northern *Advocates* had led them to conclude
they would scarcely receive the common civilities of life anywhere north of the Ohio River. But their feelings were evidently softened by the kindness shown them here. Every man
who does not wish to see our Church violently sundered should
avoid whatever is calculated to irritate feelings. This is no time
for the friends of peace to discuss either slavery or abolition,
but simply the question, What can be done to restore confidence, peace, and order, and save the connection at large from
ruin. May the Lord pity and spare the Methodist Episcopal
Church for Christ's sake, and for the souls of the people in and
out of her."

Mr. Hamline's rising star at the General Conference, climaxed by his election to the episcopacy,
had, as we have noticed, placed him, unwittingly, in
the front of the contest. This, to him, was a sore
trial. He had only acted from conscience of duty,
and had volunteered nothing. He had spoken evil
of none, had been discourteous to none. Truthfully
could he say: "I am a man of peace; but when I
speak they are for war." His sensitive nature, and,
above all, his high sense of Christian propriety,
caused the current mode of controversy to become
a source of surprise and suffering. In a letter to
Dr. and Mrs. Palmer, New York, dated May 19,
1845 (the day of the adjournment of the Louisville
Convention), he says:

"Returning from a six weeks' tour of severe labor, I met
at Cincinnati the notice of Brother L.'s charge that I was the

writer of an *editorial* in Dr. Elliott's paper abusing Bishop Andrew—an article that I had no more to do with than Bishop Andrew himself—being, as appears on subsequent inquiry, one hundred miles off when it was written and published. I send you the *Advocate* which contradicts the charge. Think of this. The charge originated with two *Methodist preachers* in Cincinnati, as far as can be learned. On the ground of that charge I have been held up in the Louisville Convention to the execration of all listeners each day for three weeks. The publication of the charge is in the Southern Church papers, and will doubtless go through all the press, and *never* will be *contradicted* except in Northern papers. Now, I say once more, pray for me. This is a trial of no ordinary magnitude. I now cease to afflict you with my complaints and ask you to help me to surrender them up to God."

Bishop Hamline was not mistaken in his supposition that the slander would pass unrecalled and uncontradicted in the South. The editor of the *Richmond Christian Advocate*—Rev. L. M. Lee—had directed the article to be published in his paper as Bishop Hamline's. And when Dr. Elliott, in whose paper it had first appeared, had testified from knowledge that Bishop Hamline was not the author, still Dr. Lee refused to correct his error unless Bishop Hamline should disavow it over his own name. This was carrying the matter beyond the laws of courtesy and honor, and Bishop Hamline, in self-respect, declined further controversy.

Again, in a letter to Bishop Morris, June 14th, Bishop Hamline thus alludes to the times and to the doings of his enemies:

"With you, I am disappointed. I am so in regard to editors. They have a stern sense of duty, and are *immovably fixed*. But some of them are my very best personal friends and highly valued—*true* in their *aim*, however mistaken in their means. I am willing to bear the reputation of being their

15

confidants in matters which have not my concurrence, but my disapproval, rather than occasion another note of *discord* among brethren. I can not see what I have done to divide the Church. I made a speech in which I did not name slavery, abolition, the North, the South, Bishop Andrew, Baltimore, Harding, or any thing else, except the powers of General Conference and those of the superintendents, and thought it would be faultless in one respect, namely, it would be modest and no slander. But it has turned out the worst speech of the fifty, and I give up. I have been in Cincinnati about twelve weeks in fourteen months, and have never written a private letter to Cincinnati on Church difficulties, or a line or a word touching them; but they say I have written nearly all the editorials in the *Western Christian Advocate*, and much of the *correspondence!* Thank God I have had a happy year, and oceans of comfort flow *to* and *over* my soul this day! I am prepared to suffer all that can befall me from the smallest wound to a martyred life, if God give me grace as hitherto, for he has been a 'shield to me, and the lifter up of my head.' "

The Louisville Convention, to which allusion has been made, met May 1, 1845, and adjourned May 19th, having accomplished the organization of the "Methodist Episcopal Church, South." The Methodist Episcopal Church was passing the "narrows" in rough weather, and her timbers creaked and her rigging rattled in the tempest. On Saturday, May 17th, said convention adopted their plan of organization and declared their connection with the Methodist Episcopal Church *dissolved.* The wisdom of men now seemed baffled to determine the path of duty, justice, and expediency. Two Methodist Episcopal Churches in the United States, dividing between them a hitherto common territory, with the boundary line between them not fully settled, and the conditions of settlement variously interpreted. Nevertheless, had a spirit of mutual conciliation and confidence obtained

the difficulties of fraternity might have been obvi-
ated. Up to May, 1845, the leading pacificators had
sought and proposed various plans of compromise
and union. Like wrecked mariners, they clung to
the last to each floating plank of hope. But after
the Louisville Convention the hope of union vanished, and the work of settling the border line began.
Here, it might be supposed, mutual safety and the
common dictates of Christianity would have led to
good will and conciliation. Bishop Andrew writes
to the *Southern Christian Advocate:* "The time and
the occasion for war are past. Henceforth betake
yourselves to the work of peace and Scriptural improvement." Excellent advice! Would that it might
have been accepted! But it were too much to hope
from human nature, and the irrepressible elements
which had been set free. All attempts at conciliation, all plans of compromise had not only failed
hitherto, but had aggravated the spirit of division.
"Your appeals for union," says Dr. Capers, "after
what has taken place, and on such grounds as are
proposed, are little better than a persecution of us.
We can never belong again to the jurisdiction of the
same General Conference. It would destroy us to
attempt it. The whole country would conspire to
cast us out; and our people, especially the slaves,
what would become of them?" The truth was,
neither North nor South could recede. Separation
was inevitable. Dr. Olin well said, the Southern
Methodists "must keep themselves in communication
with their people. They are in contact with the public mind. They know the field of their labors as
others can not know it. They, not we, are account-

able to God for the truth of their declarations on the subject. They affirm that the action of the late General Conference has placed them in such relation to the laws and public sentiment of the Southern community as is wholly incompatible with the discharge of their ministerial duties, and they declare with great unanimity that they can not, under existing circumstances, continue their connection with us." Under these circumstances separation, with fraternal feeling and sympathy, was all that remained for us. Still it was believed by the North generally, and by very many in the South (as the subsequent action of quarterly conferences and societies proved), that the separation was not necessary, and, at best, premature. These opinions augmented the obstacles to fraternal union and amicable division. And this state of things happened at a time of year when the sessions of annual conferences began, and episcopal ministration could not be delayed. The bishops tried to convene their Board for counsel, but the duties of the hour, from the imminence of the annual conferences, prevented a full attendance. Each bishop seemed about to be forced into the field to exercise his functions and administer law, with the positive requirements of Discipline to guide him on the one hand, and on the other a provisional plan of administration quite variant, put into his hands by the authority of General Conference. As officers of General Conference, the bishops were called to obey the instructions of that body, but the complications of the points involved gave rise to various opinions North and South. The question of jurisdiction was fundamental. The Discipline drew one line; the action of the Louisville

Convention, on the assumed basis of the authority of General Conference by the "Plan of Separation," drew quite another. The so-called "Plan" provided that "all the societies, stations, and conferences, adhering to the Church in the South *by a vote of the majority of the members of said societies, stations, and conferences*, shall remain under the unmolested pastoral care of the Southern Church." This assumed that they were under the care and within the jurisdiction of the Methodist Episcopal Church until by a majority vote they should otherwise determine. The Louisville Convention, however, partially reversed this order, and determined that "those societies and stations on the border, within the limits of conferences represented in this convention, be constructively understood as adhering to the South, *unless they see proper to take action on the subject;* and in all such cases we consider the pastor of the society or station as the proper person to preside in the meeting." This reversed the natural order, threw the *onus probandi* on the Methodist Episcopal Church, requiring her to prove her right of jurisdiction over members who had always belonged to her communion and had never signified a wish to be released. It was a violation of the "Plan" and an absurdity *per se*, and increased the embarrassment of the hour.

The question whether the Southern organization had been effected in strict accordance with the specifications and intent of the "Plan of Separation," and whether therefore our bishops should recognize the legitimacy of the measure and abstain from going South, was loudly and widely contested. Again, it was not formally settled whether sympathy with the

South, and personal aid and encouragement rendered in their organization, would work a present disqualification of a bishop for presiding in a Northern annual conference, for if the "Plan of Separation" was authorized by General Conference, and the separation was in strict accordance with its provisions and intent, it would seem that sympathy with the separation would be also authorized and loyal. On the other hand, when the Southern organization was effected it became a distinct and independent Church, and no bishop could, in ecclesiastical or civil law, be recognized as having legitimate jurisdiction in both bodies. These and other questions belonged properly and legally to General Conference to settle, but were left, through the exigency of circumstances, to be determined administratively by the bishops. A proposition was made and initiatory steps taken for an extra session of General Conference, but the effort failed.

Chapter XII.

DIFFICULTIES OF EPISCOPAL ADMINISTRATION— CONTINUED.

IT seemed necessary, as already stated, that the bishops should hold an extra session of their Board to adjust their administration to the new and extraordinary action of the Louisville Convention. The Pittsburg Conference, meanwhile, was about gathering for its annual session. Bishop Hamline, who was to preside, had not time to adjourn the conference, and the circumstances were too important and critical to leave the presidency to one of their own body. The following extract from a letter of Bishop Hamline to Bishops Hedding and Waugh, in reply to their proposition for another meeting of their Board will give his appreciation and judgment of the present posture of affairs.

"*June* 25, 1845.

"DEAR BRETHREN,—Your letter was duly received and forwarded to Bishop Morris. He will do me the favor to explain the reasons of my absence. I regret that I can not be with you, so as to be aided by your counsels in the duties which lie instantly before me.

"What points you will discuss I can only conjecture. Probably an early question will be, 'Is there a separation?' With hesitation (from the fact that some whose opinions weigh much with me think otherwise) I deem the 'Methodist Episcopal Church, South,' fully organized. It seems to me that its General Conference meets next May, not to form an organization, but under an organization already formed, which has provided for holding said conference, has dictated its ratio of representation, has appointed its time of meeting, and, by the adoption of a discipline, imposed on it its duties, clothed it with its powers, and limited its action in all respects. Furthermore, it is evident to me that nine-tenths or more of the people in the separated conferences approve of, or assent to the organization. To view the organization as complete seems to me not only in harmony with facts, but also of safe tendency. The Louisville Convention affirms its entire separation in its resolutions, announces it to the people in its pastoral address, and insists on it in many forms, protesting against all 'entangling alliance' with the Methodist Episcopal Church in tones of deep and solemn earnestness. . . .

"But if you say the Methodist Episcopal Church, South, is organized, you will probably form a new plan of episcopal visitation ; and though as last year, the bishops have all an equal disciplinary right to visit all or any part of the work (a right of which none can be divested but by 'the Committee of Nine,' or the General Conference), yet, for the promotion of peace, I suppose each bishop will go where his visits are likely to be acceptable and produce happy results. If any of us can certainly determine whether he can serve the Methodist Episcopal Church, South, would it not be better to regard that fact ? If so, adhering as I do to the Methodist Episcopal Church, I so far beg your indulgence as to ask a release from obligation to labor in conferences represented in the Louisville Convention, three of which are embraced in my circuit next year. . . . To conclude, if any thing is expressed dogmatically in this letter, let me assure you it is not a flow of temper, but a lack of that grace of utterance which I admire in others, but could never well compass myself. I feared you would claim some expression of views, or I should have chosen silence, and speaking at all I was forced to speak thus from a belief that any mingling of the work of the two Churches now will prolong war and not restore peace. True policy seems to require that our herdsmen and their flocks turn at present to the right and to the left and feed apart till strifes are forgotten and wounds healed. May Infinite wisdom guide for Christ's sake.

The "Committee of Nine" above alluded to was the committee which, according to the Discipline at that time, had power to suspend a bishop for cause, in the interim of General Conference. The reference to the equal right of bishops "to visit all or any part of the work," and the suggestion that for the promotion of peace "each bishop should go where his visits are likely to be acceptable and produce happy results," are delicate allusions to the case of Bishop Soule, whose anomalous position will soon be noticed, and which, at this time, gave the Board of Bishops no little perplexity. The letter of Bishop Hamline, it will be seen, completely covers the main features of the whole ground, and as a specimen of legal opinion, cautiously and meekly advanced, is a model.

The bishops met in New York, pursuant to call, July 3, 1845. Bishop Hamline was accounted as present, "he having given his opinion by letter." After reviewing the action of the Louisville Convention, they fully state in a preamble the fact of the separation of the Southern conferences, and their organization into an independent Church, and condense their decisions in the following resolutions:

"*Resolved*, That acting as we do under the authority of the General Conference of the Methodist Episcopal Church, and amenable to said General Conference, we would not consider ourselves justified in presiding in said conferences [to-wit: those within the new Southern organization], conformably to the plan of visitation agreed upon at the close of the late General Conference, and published in the journals of the Church.

"*Resolved*, That the secretary be instructed to publish the resolution just adopted, relating to the superintendents presiding at those conference, represented in the Louisville Convention."

As Bishops Morris and Janes were assigned, in the plan heretofore fixed, to visit and preside in various of these now separated conferences, they also publish, over their own signatures the following notice, to-wit: " In view of the opinion of our colleagues, as above expressed, we hereby give notice to the conferences South, in our respective districts, that we respectfully decline attending said conferences." Thus our bishops withdrew all juridical connection with and superintendency over the Southern and separated conferences. By the highest executive authority in the Methodist Episcopal Church (the highest which the case admitted till the next session of General Conference), the final separation was recognized. The greatness and the responsibility of this act the reader will in some degree estimate when he remembers, that it was solely the prerogative of General Conference to recognize the separation, but in the exigency of the hour the bishops were forced (yet upon their responsibility) to declare it under the " Plan of Separation," and so far as might regulate their episcopal jurisdiction. They had nothing to do with the legality of the separation, but only with the fact, and its necessary and determinate bearing on the question of jurisdiction. The ensuing General Conference must settle all other points, and they must also review this episcopal decision. In this act fifteen annual conferences were treated as separated from the Methodist Episcopal Church, including nearly four hundred and fifty thousand members and fourteen hundred preachers, not to speak of the amount of church property involved. Many considered it would work the ruin of the Methodist Episcopal Church. This meeting of the Episcopal Board, fourteen days after the Louisville Convention, is a notable illustration of the efficiency and promptness of our episcopal government and the ability and fidelity of our bishops. It will be remembered that in the new plan of episcopal visitation made necessary by the action of the Louisville Convention, and in which the bishops withdrew, their jurisdiction from the South, the positions of Bishops Andrew and Soule are left unexplained. As to the former, as we have seen, the late General Conference had advised "that he desist from the exercise of his office while the impediment [of his connection with slavery] remains." But as this was advisory, not mandatory, they also voted that, "whether he be assigned work by the Board of Bishops is to be determined by his own decision and action," by which the bishops understood that "the responsibility of the exercise of the functions of his office rested exclusively on himself." Accordingly, Bishop Andrew, making no statement to the Board of Bishops that he desired work, was left off the published plan of 1844; but a provisional plan was made, by which, should he at any time signify his purpose to take work, he was assigned his usual round of service.

The case of Bishop Soule was different. He had continued his usual official service since the recent General Conference. The recent meeting of the bishops had not released him from the plan of 1844, by which he had, for the year 1845, three annual conferences to attend in the North, besides others in the South. But his attendance at the Louisville Convention, his strong sympathy with and approval of the acts of that convention, his consent to preside over its deliberations, and his avowed and published intention to join the Church South at their General Conference

in 1846, had placed him in an offensive light before
the Methodist public in the North.   As yet he had
attended no Northern conference since the above convention, and hence had met with no practical test of
his unacceptability with them.   But the public prints
and other indices of public sentiment left him not without apprehension of trouble.   The venerable Bishop,
though an experienced diplomatist, began to feel the
toils of the net of his own spreading drawing around
him.   "The prudent man foreseeth the evil and hideth
himself," and he now seeks release from his Northern
conferences under high and magnanimous motives.
The following letter of Bishop Morris to Bishop Hamline, July 21, 1845, explains his dilemma:

"I received this morning a long letter from Bishop Soule.
As it is contrary to his principles to choose work not regularly
assigned him, or decline that to which he has been regularly
assigned, our new arrangement has embarrassed him much,
in that no action was taken as to his appointments.   Yet he
makes all easy by requesting me to attend Rock River, Iowa,
and Illinois Conferences for him, that he may be at liberty to
attend the destitute conferences South-west, to which I have
consented.   Though he does not name it in his letter to me it
is probable, as I otherwise learn, that he may stop at Ohio Conference, a few days, on his way to Kentucky conferences, which
may be of advantage in settling semi-border cases between the
conferences."

This last suggestion was, indeed, charitable.   But
Bishop Soule had now passed beyond the province of
mediator, having committed himself wholly to one
side, and to the inevitable policy which that committal implied.

Meanwhile the hour had come for Church administration to grapple with the stern reality of things.
"Pittsburgh Conference," says Bishop Hamline, "sits

on the 2d of July. It is a border conference, with free and slave territory, the first that has sat since the secession. Delicate questions and interests are before us. I expected Bishop Morris to be with and aid me, but he is called away. Pray for me. O for wisdom which is from above." The session was held, and at its close he writes: "July 9, 1845. Closed the Pittsburg Conference at Beaver; had a blessed season. This is a large and pious body of ministers. They go out in the spirit of their master." In a letter to Rev. Jacob Young, July 16th, he says: "Our conference has passed off delightfully. It was an orderly, devout, and happy season as far as I can learn, and is said to have been the shortest and most harmonious session the conference has had since its formation. About two hundred preachers were stationed. We closed on Wednesday noon. I have heard not a word about secession, and I think that the Virginia work is so manned that all will be quiet among them."

His next conference was Erie, of which he makes this note: "July 30th. Closed the Erie Conference at New Castle. A spiritual season. The Lord is pleased to put his strength in me that I may serve him. My soul often dwells above. My life is hid with Christ. Eternal things come near, and earth is all forgotten. Blessed be God!" The North Ohio Conference followed, of which he records: "August 13th, commenced the North Ohio Conference at Marion. About one hundred and twenty preachers present, talented, devoted men. A good session. Parted with my dear brethren feeling that it was good to be here. The Lord blesses still."

The annual session of the Ohio Conference drew near. Bishop Hamline was to preside. "I look forward," he says, "with trembling to the Ohio Conference." On the 3d of September the members convened. Bishop Soule was also present as a visiting bishop. The embarrassment caused at his presence was great. On the one hand, Bishop Hamline felt bound in courtesy to invite Bishop Soule, at some period of the session, to occupy the chair. However imprudent and faulty the conduct of the latter in his course adopted at the Louisville Convention, and in the expression of his strong Southern proclivities, he stood unimpeached and unreproved by the proper authority, and it was not the prerogative of Bishop Hamline, as presiding bishop, to adjudge the case, as the withholding of the accustomed courtesy from a visiting bishop would, under these circumstances, seem to imply. He could not thus seem to pass judgment on his senior. On the other hand, the conference, embracing some of the strongest men in the connection, venerable for their years, their experience, and their wisdom, determined they would not act under the presidency of one whom they regarded as having violated the spirit of the "Plan of Separation," the intention of General Conference, and the dignity and duty of his office as a superintendent and shepherd of the whole flock. They had determined not to act under his presidency in one, even the smallest particular, for even that would recognize the legitimacy of his jurisdiction and the legality of his previous course.

Before the opening of the conference on the first day of its session, three brethren—Raper, Wright, and Marlay—men of rank and influence waited upon Bishop Soule, and endeavored to dissuade him, for the peace of the conference, from occupying the chair. Bishop Soule replied to them, "that a principle was involved and he should feel it his duty to occupy the chair."

The mission of peace proved unsuccessful. On the morning of the opening session the preachers assembled early in the yard, but declined entering the church till they knew who should preside. Bishop Soule passes them and enters the church. The preachers propose to retire and leave the conference with insufficient numbers to transact business. But Finley comes and assures them Bishop Soule will not preside. They enter. Bishop Soule conducts the opening services. Immediately, before any action could be had, or motion made, the Rev. Jacob Young arose and proposed to offer a resolution. An effort was made to defer the motion till some other matters should be disposed of. Finley sprang to his feet and solemnly protested against any act of conference before the proposed resolution was disposed of. After a little the opposition was withdrawn, and the following preamble and resolution were offered:

"*Whereas*, Bishops Soule and Andrew did preside at the convention at Louisville, in May last, composed of delegates from the Southern conferences; and *whereas*, said convention did resolve the said conferences into a separate and distinct ecclesiastical connection, solemnly declaring that they were no longer under the jurisdiction of the Methodist Episcopal Church; and *whereas*, Bishops Soule and Andrew did pledge their adherence to the Church South; and in view of the Southern organization, and the course of said bishops, at a meeting of the bishops in New York, Bishops Morris and Janes declined presiding in the Southern conferences; therefore,

"*Resolved*, That, although the conferences composing the Methodist Episcopal Church will treat the bishops of the Church South with due courtesy and respect, yet it would be, in the estimation of this conference, inexpedient and highly improper for them to preside in said conferences."

Bishop Soule observed that he took the chair by request and could not resign it but at the request of the bishop who invited him; but that the resolution was one which he could not put. Many voices called for Bishop Hamline to take the chair. The latter remarked that Bishop Soule was in the chair and that it would be disorderly for another to put the question to vote. Upon this Bishop Soule offered Bishop Hamline the chair, which he declined, calling on David Young, and then Jacob Young to preside, but both declined. After some delay Rev. James Quinn consented to take the chair. A desultory debate followed, and the house was evidently getting into confusion. The chairman had no power to control the elements. In a short time things had reached the ultimate limit of delay, when Bishop Hamline stepped forward crying "order! order!" and waving his hand to the chairman to retire, he took command. In a moment the conference came to order, when he thus addressed them:

"The confusion which is arising promises to be so great, that I feel solemnly bound to interpose, and will cheerfully assume the responsibility of doing my utmost to conduct the conference through this crisis.

"The Southern conferences have met, by their delegates, in Louisville, and undisturbed have organized a Church, declaring themselves separated from the jurisdiction of the Methodist Episcopal Church. I trust that while we will not invade their rights, we may innocently seek to enjoy our own. If they expect us to leave them free, we will expect them to

leave us free and undisturbed. I trust we will show our brethren of the South that we know how to respect their rights
and secure our own. I am an officer of the Methodist Episcopal Church, and for the time preside over this conference.
All I can legally do, or rightfully sacrifice, to direct the business
of the conference in a calm and devout manner I will cheerfully attempt. I would sooner have my right hand wither
than not feebly reach it forth, when the peace of the conference is threatened, and exert myself to avert the evil. These
remarks are not intended to apply to Bishop Soule, but those
which follow are.

"I have extended to him, as a visiting bishop, the usual
courtesies; but if this is to break up the peace of the conference, and interrupt its business, it will cost *you* too much. I
can not claim to practice courtesies of mere ceremony at the
expense of the Church. I now wish to know if Bishop Soule
can occupy this chair without inflicting on you what you
deem a grievance. The resolutions before you will decide that
point. I shall, therefore, put the motion for the previous
question, without allowing further debate, and, if carried, the
main question will promptly follow."

The motions were then put, and the conference
voted the resolution, one hundred and forty-five to
seven. The case was thus finally settled. Bishop
Soule could not be acceptable as a bishop of the
Methodist Episcopal Church, the action of the Louisville Convention could not be indorsed, and the two
organizations were separate and independent of each
other. Bishop Soule had already stated to the Southern Convention "that he felt himself bound in good
faith to carry out the plan of episcopal visitations as
settled by the bishops in New York" [1844], and published in the official papers of the Church, till the
session of the General Conference of the Methodist
Episcopal Church, South [*i. e.* till May, 1846], after
which, he says, "I shall feel myself fully authorized,
according to the Plan of Separation adopted by the

General Conference of 1844, to unite myself with the Methodist Episcopal Church, South." And this he might have done had he not attended the Louisville Convention, and had prudently kept aloof from all party sympathy. But the experiment failed. He could not serve officially in both organizations. The Ohio Conference having declared his status (for they expressed the sentiment of the North), he had no further reason to tarry with them. "It was not long," says Dr. Cyrus Brooks (an eye-witness) "until the lofty form of Bishop Soule was seen moving toward the door, with his portfolio under his arm and his hat in his hand. He disappeared and was seen among us no more."

Dr. Brooks thus describes Bishop Hamline as he came forward to resume the chair: "The critical moment had arrived, and it seemed that the next instant must bring hopeless confusion. Just at that instant Bishop Hamline stepped upon the platform. I can never forget his appearance. Twenty years have not dimmed the recollection of it in the least. It was full of animation, yet calm, commanding, majestic. No human movement ever so impressed me with the idea of irresistible power. It was power, too, wielded with consummate skill, and for a most beneficent end. I have seen him in some of his happiest moments, in some of the loftiest flights of his sublime eloquence, but I never saw him appear to so good advantage as then. He seemed to me almost more than man."

It is not easy for any one who is not conversant with the general circumstances and principles involved to appreciate the delicate and difficult position of

Bishop Hamline, nor is it easily conceivable how he could have conducted with greater moderation and sagacity. It was an act great in its bearings and results. It settled the point, not judicially but practically, that a bishop, committed to the Southern organization, even assuming said organization to be in harmony with the Plan of Separation, could not consistently and acceptably serve the Methodist Episcopal Church, for no bishop could hold executive superintendency over two separate and independent Churches. But it reached further. The act of Bishop Soule was a bold strategic movement to force on the conference a practical indorsement of the legality of the doings of the Louisville Convention. Had the Ohio Conference accepted the presidency of Bishop Soule, even to the extent of allowing the roll of the previous session to be read, they would have conceded his right to preside, and hence, by implication, and, so far as their opinion could go, have legitimated all his previous course at the Louisville Convention, and the acts and aims of the convention itself as being in harmony with the Plan of Separation, and hence authorized by General Conference. And this appears to have been the "principle involved" which Bishop Soule wished to test. If the Ohio Conference submitted to his presidency by courtesy, other conferences might concede it as a right. At least, the precedent would embarrass other conferences in resistance. As it was, the Gordian knot was completely cut, and the threatening troubles avoided. Bishop Soule had forecast the possibility of rejection, and had, as we have seen in his letter to Bishop Morris above, arranged for release from his Northern conferences. Dr. Trotter, in a letter to the *Western Advocate*, June 11, 1845, had already sagaciously penetrated the policy. He says:

"Bishop Soule well knows the North, as a body, and a respectable portion of the South, have resisted and are resisting such an idea [as the unity of the two organizations], and that the Methodist Episcopal Church intends to remain one and indivisible. And has he not discernment to see that the last step of his [in presiding in the Louisville Convention] is a sort of popular, declamatory trial of the issue? *If he come to us legally, and passes to them legally, then the whole is legal.*"

His course had been publicly discussed and condemned at the North, and by various societies and quarterly conferences in the slave holding States. This was known to Bishop Soule. But it was a final and practical test that he persistently sought and amply obtained.

The day after the close of the session Bishop Hamline made the following entry in his diary:

"*Cincinnati, September 14, 1845.*—Yesterday closed the Ohio Conference held here. Bishop Soule came (the Lord be judge between him and me), and the conference refused to sit under his presidency. I had to interpose with great firmness, or see my beloved Ohio Conference thrown into utter confusion. I believe the Lord helped me, and an explosion was avoided. Little did I think such trials awaited me when, eighteen months ago, I lay sick on the borders of heaven. O Lord, if I have done less or more or otherwise in this trying scene of labor than was right, forgive me, for Christ's sake! And forgive him or them who mistakenly or maliciously have troubled our Zion here! I fly to thee for refuge. Amen."

Twelve days after the conference had adjourned, September 26th, Bishop Morris thus writes him:

"Your kind letter from Cincinnati has been received. You had truly a stormy time. Had I been in your stead I should have invited Bishop Soule to the chair as you did. But had I been in Bishop Soule's place I should, under the circumstances, have respectfully declined the acceptance of it. Upon the whole, I doubt if any one could have passed through the scene of excitement and confusion better than you did. The appointments in the Ohio Conference, as a whole, appear to me to be well made. I feel thankful that under such trying circumstances you have been enabled to regard the Plan of Separation according to our instructions from General Conference. Had a majority of the annual conferences pronounced the Plan unconstitutional before the conferences South availed themselves of its provisions, that might have been our justification for suspending the operation till General Conference of 1848; but, as no such action was taken, we seem to be bound to carry out the Plan in good faith, which, by the grace of God, I am also aiming to do."

CHAPTER XIII.

[1845-48.]

DIFFICULTIES OF EPISCOPAL ADMINISTRATION— CONTINUED.

IN the preceding pages we have seen how the
relations of the Southern bishops to the Methodist
Episcopal Church was practically decided. But there
were other questions, relating to the settlement
of the border line, as affecting societies and pastor-
ates, which were still open. The separation of the
Southern conferences drew a line between the Methodist Episcopal Church and the Methodist Episcopal
Church, South, of about twelve hundred miles in
extent. Strong Northern conferences, bordering on
this line, penetrated more or less south of it into
Virginia, Kentucky, and Missouri, as the Baltimore,
Pittsburg, Ohio, and Illinois Conferences. The
boundary of conferences was not originally determined by State lines, and the Plan of Separation
made no recognition of State lines in fixing the
dividing line between the Northern and Southern
organizations. But societies and conferences within
the slave States, along the border, could determine
their relation North or South by a majority vote.
Societies not on the border, though but one pastoral
remove from it, were to remain intact. It was soon
found that, though the societies within slave States,
belonging to conferences north of the line, were as

antislavery as their Northern brethren, yet, owing to the extreme pressure of Southern sentiments, and the homogeneous interests and sympathy of all the slave States, the tendency of things was to establish the line between the free and slave territories. It is easy to perceive that herein a wide door was opened for difference and conflict of opinion to the embarrassment of Church administration and the injury of the Church, not to say the scandal of the Christian religion. Back of all other questions, as already intimated, lay the institution of slavery, and, despite all remonstrance of prudent men, the simple issues which were before the General Conference of 1844, the conciliatory spirit and catholic motives which swayed that body, were unhappily lost sight of, the issue was taken upon the abstract principle of slavery, and its factual legitimacy as it existed in the United States, and the effort was made to despoil the Methodist Episcopal Church of all its territory within the slave States.

The Rev. B. T. Crouch, in a letter to the *Western Advocate*, thus states the case: "I can not hide it from myself that the position, circumstances, and interests of the Kentucky Conference, in relation to the matters that are now agonizing the Methodist family, are unavoidably Southern. Any efforts, therefore, that do not tend to remove the necessity of a Southern organization, but only to throw difficulties in the way of such an alternative and to disaffect the Kentucky Conference, or any part of it, with the South, can not fail to produce the result of dividing our hitherto delightful and harmonious conference, just to the extent that these efforts may be available to any certain end." What is here said of the Kentucky Conference simply applies to all portions of Northern conferences which lay within slave-holding States.

But the Plan of Separation, not being interpreted, and hence not adhered to, by the Southern bishops and conferences harmoniously with those of the Methodist Episcopal Church, "confusion worse confounded" followed. Many presiding elder districts and portions of districts, with strong pastoral charges, within bordering slave States, belonged to the Methodist Episcopal Church, to which they were strongly attached, and with which they could not readily dissolve their connection. Many large and respectable minorities of Churches which had voted to attach to the Southern organization, held out for a time in hopes of receiving a preacher from the North. These cases excited great sympathy in the Northern Churches, and greatly increased the agitation of the people and the perplexity of the bishops. But the "Plan of Separation" was a standing order of General Conference, binding on the bishops as executive officers, whatever might be their private opinion. "I exceedingly regret the state of things at Cincinnati,"* writes the venerable Bishop Hedding to

* The case of Cincinnati alluded to is as follows: The Rev. G. W. Maley, city missionary, by appointment of Ohio Conference, having formed a society in 1845, to the number of several scores, they voted to go South, and were accordingly recognized by Bishop Andrew, in violation of the Plan of Separation, at the Tennessee Conference, October 22, 1845, by a vote of ninety-eight members, and attached to the Covington District. It was called "Soule Chapel," in honor of the Bishop. Dr. E. W. Sehon and G. W. Maley withdrew from the Ohio Conference and served them 1845–6; Dr. C. B. Parsons in 1847, Rev. H. H. Kavanaugh (now

Bishop Hamline, in 1846. "I also feel much for the brethren at St. Louis, at Covington, and all others similarly circumstanced. But what is to be done I hardly know, as the General Conference has tied our hands. But this subject will come up for deliberation at our meeting (should such a one take place), and then we shall understand each other in regard to our future acting." On the same subject, and the severe animadversions of the Church press, the same year Bishop Morris writes to Bishop Hamline:

"Recently some of these Church papers appear to have become a sort of self-constituted tribunal, to regulate bishops and General Conference, and woe be to the man who dares to dissent from any opinion which they utter. One editor has made a formal and official proclamation that if the next General Conference do not change the "Plan" so as to provide for the minority ministers and preachers of Missouri and Kentucky, etc., he will renounce with them the jurisdiction of said General Conference, and aid them in forming an independent conference. This is nullification in earnest! If I had assumed such an attitude of hostility to the General Conference when I was editor nothing short of an humble confession and a public recantation would have saved me from being deposed; nor could I have complained that the sentence

Southern Bishop), in 1848-9, Richard Deering in 1850, Dr. J. H. Linn in 1851-2, and Dr. L. D. Huston in 1853-4, when the Church disbanded. Though their congregations were large (says a friend who furnishes most of these items) the membership averaged only about two hundred and fifty. Most of the members were from Wesley Chapel, a few from other charges.

This was a measure which the bishops of the Methodist Episcopal Church greatly deplored, and never practiced within the territory of the Church South. They persistently refused to send preachers to minorities where the majority voted to attach to the Church South, or to societies made up of minorities from different Churches. In all cases they closely adhered to the "Plan of Separation," for which they were often severely censured by the unthinking popular voice.

was unjust. I am sometimes led to wonder what will be the end of all these things! But the subject is so melancholy that I have to recede from it, and seek relief by committing the Church and myself to God's own keeping. Perhaps you will conclude I feel depressed in spirit or I would not inflict such gloomy reflections upon a friend in a familiar correspondence. I am not, however, conscious of any more want of cheerfulness than I have suffered ever since May, 1844, when our Church difficulties first assumed an alarming aspect."

The agitation connected with fixing the border lines began soon after the Louisville Convention, May, 1845, and was inflated with new life after the first General Conference of the Church South, May, 1846. This was the signal to the border Churches for final, prompt, determinate action, and their choice might have been peacefully made without injury to fraternal relations had the societies been influenced by peace-making leaders, and left to their calm, deliberate judgment without foreign interference. But, unhappily, from the first the subject was taken up popularly by outside and political managers. Extensive slave-owners would naturally look at the question with reference to its ultimate probable influence on the institution of slavery, and professional men, wealthy men, and politicians would as naturally fall in the current of extreme Southern leaders. These considerations presented a formidable array against the freedom and purely spiritual motives of choice. Terror became, not unfrequently, a determining agency. The Kanawha District of the Ohio Conference lay wholly in Virginia, and, while it was believed on good authority that the majority of the people, left to themselves, were as antislavery in their opinions, and as much attached to the Methodist Episcopal Church, as the other portions of the Ohio Conference, yet lying within a slave State, and being stimulated by individuals of an intenser Southern feeling, combined with much misrepresentation and misapprehension of the feelings and policy of the Methodist Episcopal Church, the district became the theater of great commotion. At the session of the Ohio Conference, September, 3, 1845, above noticed, the Kanawha District was manned, as usual, with preachers from Ohio. No action of the societies on the district had as yet resisted the old *régime*, or intimated a wish for the new one. But unfriendly and hostile elements were now awakened.

In addition to the political elements already alluded to, the rejection of Bishop Soule by the Ohio Conference had awakened a strong Southern resistance. Bishop Soule had also published a letter, August 22, 1845, "to the preachers and border societies of the Kentucky and Missouri Conferences, and of the conferences bordering on them," calling on them without delay to decide to which Church they would attach themselves, North or South. These "other conferences" probably referred to those north of the line, as the Baltimore, Philadelphia, Ohio, Indiana, Illinois, for he says this call "will apply to border societies on either side of the line." Up to this time, says Dr. Elliott, editor of the *Western Christian Advocate*, "we are well informed that the great body of our members in Kentucky, Missouri, North Arkansas, and Western Virginia are very much opposed to the doings of the Louisville Convention, and to their severance from the Methodist Episcopal Church." Dr. Bond, editor of the *Chris-*

tian Advocate, New York, also says of the Virginia Churches generally, April, 1845, "An abiding attachment to the union of the Church universally prevails; or the few exceptions which exist are so inconsiderable as not to threaten any disturbance of the general peace." As late as April, 1846, the Baltimore Conference say that "very few of their Church members in the slave-holding portions of Virginia are willing to unite with the Methodist Episcopal Church, South."

But the fall of 1845 witnessed the "beginning of sorrows," and returning to the Kanawha District, we can not better convey to the reader an idea of the state of things at this date than by extracts from a letter of the Presiding Elder, Rev. John Stewart, to Bishop Hamline, dated October 12. 1845:

"BISHOP L. L. HAMLINE.—*My Dear Brother:*—I have attended, at the time appointed to hold my first Quarterly Meeting for the present year, at Parkersburg. The preacher had left, not so much from his own choice as the choice of his friends, and his enemies. His enemies were intent to effect his degradation. The citizens held an indignation meeting; appointed a committee of three, to wait on Brother Dillon [the pastor], and let him know that it was the wish of the people that he should leave the State forthwith. George Neal waited on him as foreman, and delivered the message. Dillon asked for time to deliberate, before he should give an answer. Neal reports to the meeting Dillon's answer. They give him till Saturday to leave, and appointed a committee of sixty (though the *Gazette* states a committee of forty) to remove him from the State, should he not remove of his own accord. He stayed till Saturday morning; then Brother Woodbridge of Marietta, came after him, and after the friends of the old Church had held a meeting, they unanimously advised him to leave till the excitement should abate. He was loath to submit. Those same friends had held a meeting before, and had as unanimously advised him to stay, and they would stand by him and support him. However, he left,

having behaved while he stayed as a minister should. It is
now thought that a reaction has taken place. It is said that
many who took a part in this opposition to Dillon are ashamed.
I hoped to have found him in Parkersburg, but he was instructed by his friends not to return till they sent for him. I
think the proper time has not yet come. I went over on Saturday morning, visited many of the families. Some of them are
for staying and some for going. Brother Cook accompanied
me, and all gave me a friendly reception. As I informed them
that I had come to hold my first Quarterly Meeting, the Southerners professed to lament that the meeting-house doors were
closed against all preachers belonging to the Ohio Conference,
and I was of course included, and the resolution must not be
rescinded, even should Sehon* come, if he came as a preacher
of the Ohio Conference. This was the language of the champion,
George Neal. He said that he had consulted many on that
side of the question that day, and they all said that they were
sorry to treat me as they must treat me to carry out their object.
The Methodists of the old Church I am inclined to think are in
the majority. It is so stated by several with whom I have conversed. I saw a minute statement made out by some one and
published in the Marietta *Gazette.* From that it is plain that
the majority remain. But their house of worship is locked up.
There is no preacher sent to them from the South. This they
had confidently expected. But when the news came that
Bishop Soule could not send them a preacher [from the Southern Church] they quailed and said they had been too fast, and
gave some intimations that they would open the house. But
soon they changed their minds, and said the house should not
be opened.

"They now say that in Kentucky a number of preachers,
sufficient to supply the Kanawha District, are reserved for that
purpose. Also that majorities in Wayne, Guyandotte, and
Port [Point?] Pleasant circuits [of the same district] had declared themselves for the Southern Church. . . . If they
will stoop to take every advantage without regard to truth, as
mere politicians, they will probably take Western Virginia.

---

*Rev. E. W. Sehon, an intense Southerner, then Bible Agent,
who afterward left the Ohio Conference and joined the Methodist
Episcopal Church South.

The leading men have the wealth, the negroes, and they generally endeavor to make the people believe that all in Ohio are abolitionists, and when that is fully believed the victory is gained. Our hands, in part, are tied. We can not expose the evil of slavery as we once did; and though the majority of the people in Western Virginia are as much abolitionists as the Ohioans, yet it does not seem so to them."

By the Plan of Separation no society, not on the line, could change its relation, and the bishops on either side were forbidden to send preachers to any Church beyond their own line. The Little Kanawha circuit lay one hundred and fifty miles north of the border, with five intervening circuits. "In all this distance there did not adhere, by a majority vote, a single society to the South." Notwithstanding this, preachers from the South, by Bishop Andrew's authority, entered the field, and organized societies out of fragmentary minorities "stretching across three circuits and as many counties." A year later the presiding elder reports "no circuit, station or society has voted to go over" to the Southern Church. "All have voted to stay where they are." Still out of three large circuits, embracing as many large counties, a Southern preacher formed a circuit out of fragments of minorities, contrary to the "Plan."

To facilitate the Southern work agents were employed to canvass societies, false reports were circulated to disparage and bring into odium the preachers of the district. One they publicly maligned as a negro whom the Ohio Conference had palmed upon them, stating that thus "the Ohio Conference had imposed abolitionists and negro preachers upon them." This was asserted in a public meeting. "The Southerners and the mobites," says Stewart, "sanctioned in

the strongest terms all that was said." The treatment of Bishop Soule at the Ohio Conference was
highly resented, he being considered as "almost a
god at Parkersburg."

We have ventured so much as a specimen of the
spirit and methods employed and indulged in various
places in settling the border line. In all these trials
and sufferings our bishops administered according to
the "Plan of Separation," construing it always in
the interests of peace and fraternity. But this generation can appreciate little of episcopal embarrassments and Church afflictions of these times. In the
midst of all, and throughout, the bishops were the
balancing, conservative power of the Church. Whether
or not they could have conducted affairs with greater
success if they had been left to their own united
wisdom and discretion, untrammeled by any General Conference order, we will not presume an opinion;
but having a most clear and solemnly enacted order
of procedure given them by General Conference, to
which the bishops North and South stood equally
committed, obedience to that, as executive officers,
was not only a first official duty, but an indispensable
condition of law and order and unity in the Church.
Never did constitutional law and the love of it endure
such a strain and test in the Methodist Episcopal
Church. The people, the Church editors, even the
annual conferences, could not be trusted as guides
and counselors. Nullification, as Bishop Morris calls it,
was openly advised, not considering that such an example of insubordination to law would shake the
foundations of the Church and spread misrule and
disorder every-where. "If the foundations are de-

stroyed, what can the righteous do?" In another letter to Bishop Hamline, December 22, 1846, Bishop Morris says:

"Still I think it will be best for us to adhere to the plan of amicable separation, though it should be departed from in one or two instances by others. If some brethren should break over the line from either side, and not be held to strict account by their conferences, that would not involve our administration, provided they do it against our instruction. For myself I do not intend ever to indorse or practice the doctrine of nullification as set up by some advocates and some conferences, because I believe that doctrine, carried out practically, would ruin Methodism and destroy souls by thousands. The barrier of the Plan once broken down, the scenes transpiring in Parkersburg, Maysville, Cincinnati, St. Louis, etc., would become common from New York to Mobile. If it be said the nullification contended for by editors, correspondents, and conferences, has reference to only one act of General Conference, I answer, that is sufficient to settle the principle, and when settled it will be applied just as local interest or party prejudice may direct. I do not wish to turn *croaker*, but can not avoid indulging serious fears that, unless the spirit of violence and recklessness now so rife be checked, the Methodist Episcopal Church is doomed to a second division. The fearful issue is already forming. 'Who have withdrawn from the connection this year?' '*None*,' says the bishop. But 'A., B., & C. have seceded,' says the *Advocate*, and joined the 'Schismatics.' Well, what next? '*Resolved*, That we approve the editorial course of Drs. B. and E.,' says the conference, by a *rising vote*, and consequently that the administration of the bishops be condemned. '*Resolved*, 2. That the action of the General Conference respecting the Plan (under which the bishops act), is a *nullity*, and should not be regarded.' 'But we must regard it and do regard it, so far as our administration is concerned,' say the bishops. '*Resolved*, 3. That the bishops of the Methodist Episcopal Church be requested to visit Kentucky and Missouri, and hold conference with the minority preachers.' 'We can't do it,' say the bishops. 'There is a day of reckoning for you in 1848 (say the ultraists), and we will see that the bishops are censured; that the terms of the compact of 1844 are dissolved; that the South get no part of the Book funds, and that her territory be invaded by sending missionaries, etc.' 'Then you will have to seek somebody else to carry out your measures,' says ————, for if all this is to be done, or the half of it, he will quietly resign and get out of your way. Thus chafed with abolitionism and a train of innovations on one side, and goaded by nullification, with its ruinous train of evils, on the other, there may come up a point in the history of our difficulties, beyond which men of peace will think forbearance ceases to be a virtue. Already some of our best members are going to other Churches to seek relief from contention. The decrease of Church members is fearful, but not half so fearful to me as the *breakers ahead.* I have tried to imagine I was viewing the dark side, and turned to see the light side of the cloud, but can not find it. On the contrary, the storm increases, both in extent and violence, and the roaring thereof mingles with the terrific sound of the breakers just before, and I shudder in anticipation of feeling the dreadful shock. 'Save, Lord, we perish.' "

The "abolitionism" above referred to was the measure urged in various quarters to make non-slaveholding under all possible circumstances a condition of membership, which would have excluded the Baltimore Conference and various sections along the line of separation. But worse than that, it would have riven the Methodist Episcopal Church through its heart from one end of the country to the other.

We have noticed the organization of a society in Cincinnati, of members withdrawn from other Methodist societies. The appointment of a preacher to this society by Bishop Andrew was against the Plan of Separation. Bishop Hamline had addressed a letter to Bishop Hedding, as senior bishop, for advice, and the answer of the latter will indicate the perplexity and trial of the hour:

"JANUARY 2, 1846.

"DEAR BROTHER,—Yours of the 22d ult. is before me. I am sorry Bishop Andrew appoints preachers to Cincinnati. I fear it will produce great evil. I suspect he has done the same thing by appointing a preacher to a place on the eastern shore of Virginia, within the bounds of the Philadelphia Conference. When I shall be fully informed of the facts, if I find them to be as I suppose, I shall write to Bishop Andrew, requesting him to withdraw his preacher, whom he had placed within our bounds, contrary to the 'Plan of Separation.' You ask, 'Can you give me any advice?' I advise you to take the same course in relation to those appointments in Cincinnati which I propose taking to the one above named. Deal plainly with him. If this course is continued it will destroy the last feeling of friendship between the Methodist Episcopal Church and the Church South. I do not know that I can give any other advice till we meet with and consult our colleagues, or till the General Conference.

"Affectionately yours,   E. HEDDING."

We have already referred to the disturbances in the Kanawha District (Va.), Ohio Conference. The following letter of instruction, from Bishop Hamline, a few months later, to the pastor of Guyandotte Circuit, in that district, illustrates the tone and spirit of his administration:

" CINCINNATI, *February* 20, 1846.

" From all I can learn, I think it probable that the next General Conference will form an annual conference of Northwestern Virginia. I did not suppose any preachers would be sent from the South into the Ohio Conference after the stations for the year were made out in the Ohio and the bordering conferences. I consider it a violation of the Plan if any such are sent into Kanawha District. And if that be the case, I wish all the Ohio preachers to pursue their work, preaching to all who will hear them, and in the spirit of their Master saving all the souls they can.

" There were no border appointments in the Ohio Conference that declined receiving a preacher from their own conference at its last session, and none such applied by a majority vote for preachers from Kentucky or any other conference South. Our preachers were sent there for the year, and we desire them to pursue their work, not disputing with any, but with much prayer and mighty faith doing and suffering, remembering it is enough if the disciple be as his Master.

"You will keep the charge of Guyandotte Circuit through the year, as long as people will receive your ministrations, whoever may come from the South with instructions to supersede you. If *all* withdraw from the Methodist Episcopal Church, you may consider yourself released, and return to Ohio. The districts are under our jurisdiction for the year, and we can not surrender the field in an irregular manner. When the year runs out the question may remain whether the Plan requires us to yield up the territory which has once aquiescingly adhered to the Methodist Episcopal Church.

"The resolutions of your Quarterly Meeting Conference seem decided, and will encourage you in your duty. We will not forget to remember you, and plead for God's aid to enable you to be wise as a serpent and harmless as a dove. Live near the throne. Say but little about the difficulty, but talk much of Jesus. Get all the people to pray without ceasing. Speak evil of none on the other side. Like Micah, the prophet, plead with God till you can say, "I am full of power by the Spirit of the Lord.' Then you shall go forth like a mighty man. The Lord bless you, my brother, and teach your hands to war and your fingers to fight, so that 'a bow of steel shall be broken in your hands.'"

To a friend to whom he apologizes for the delay of writing, he says: "The great agitation kept up on Church difficulties has added much to the busy engagements which were inevitably connected with my relation to the Church, and I have deferred my letter till now." But he adds: "I trust you are finding great spoils for your soul and for your Savior in your private devotions and public ministrations. There seems to me nothing more to be desired for us than to get by faith, and communicate by prayer and exhortation, the good things of Christ's kingdom."

Bishop Morris, in a letter to Bishop Hamline, March 19, 1846, thus gives us a hint of the times:

"So far as I can judge from present appearances Church difficulties growing out of "separation" have but just commenced. There is evinced in the Church papers a determined spirit of hostility between the contending parties, which seems to me to threaten mutual destruction, not of parties, as such, but of most that is desirable in each. Yet I do not believe that such a course is approved by the great body of our brethren, preachers or members, North or South, and if about one score of would-be-thought great men on each side of the line of separation, were sanctified wholly and taken to heaven, I believe all the balance would very soon become friendly, attend to their appropriate work, glory not save in the cross of Christ, and we should hear but little more of the whole matter. But forty men setting up to be leaders, and intent on party measures, are sufficient to keep a million of Church members and preachers in a state of agitation for years. I can not contemplate the scene but with shame mortification, and sorrow. Most sincerely do I pity those who "bite and devour one another," lest they be "consumed one of another." If I had any hope that I could succeed, I would aspire to the office of "peace-maker;" but alas! whoever names "peace" pulls down on himself the indignation of both parties; he is looked upon with contempt as one destitute of principle, of courage, and independence, if not of moral honesty. Well, there is one thing I can do, and by the grace of God will not neglect, that is, to pray for all such brethren. Oh, that I could pray in faith."

The first General Conference of the Methodist Episcopal Church, South held its session in Petersburg, Virginia, May, 1846. Much of the odium cast upon the Methodist Episcopal Church and her bishops bore personally upon Bishop Hamline, solely because his unanswered arguments in debate, in 1844, his great influence in the councils of the Church, and his intrepid integrity and energy of administration had placed him in the fore-front of the controversy, and presented a troublesome obstacle in the way of violent partisan opponents. To him it was simply a source of sorrow and trial. His soul fled from strife and contention as the affrighted bird to its mountain, and his public position had come unsought in the course of conscientious duty. He thus speaks in his diary, May 11th:

"The Methodist Episcopal Church, South, is in session at Petersburg. Bishops Soule and Andrew are their presidents. Each has, in leaving the Methodist Episcopal Church, shot a Parthian arrow; the one complaining of the loose views of the Methodist Episcopal Church on the subject of episcopal authority, the other characterizing the Northerners as wildly and waywardly fanatic. All these things make not for peace. Denunciation is too common in these days. 'Things that I knew not are laid to my charge.' Unholy accusations from unholy lips (alas, that I must say *lying* lips, for that is proven) might vex me were it not that the Lord turns the edge of their sword, and their weapons hurt me not. I desire to 'bless them that curse' me. I do bless them in the name of the Lord."

On their selection of bishops he says, in a letter to a friend, May 15th:

"News has just reached us that Dr. Capers and Dr. Paine are elected bishops of the Methodist Episcopal Church South. Of course, the question of slave-holding bishops is *thoroughly* settled among them, three out of four being *thorough* slave-holders. The news was quite unexpected here, as all supposed that the Rev. Mr. Bascom would be one, and many expected Rev. E. W. Sehon would be another of their bishops. The business of their conference seems in rapid progress, but many disaffections will spring up amongst them in Kentucky, and other northern regions from this selection of bishops."

As an illustration of the embarrassment and confusion experienced from want of harmony of action between the bishops North and South, the following very pertinent and pungent remarks of Rev. Dr. J. T. Mitchell, in a letter to Bishop Hamline, February 18, 1847, may be given:

"The prospect for a settlement of the difficulties on the border is very discouraging. Indeed, we are in a state of open hostilities, if not of declared war, in the Kanawha District. When in company with Bishop Soule last month I took the liberty to express my regret that he should have made any appointment in that district, when the previous appointments of Bishop Morris to the same territory were before him, remarking that if the acts of a bishop on one side were not recognized and respected by the bishops on the other side, it would be impossible to define the line of separation; that I thought when an appointment had been made and announced, and conflicting claims to the territory were set up, it was at least due to the bishop who had made the appointment, that these claims should be laid before him, and his decision on them be had, before any other steps were taken.

"The Bishop was thoughtful a moment and replied, 'That might have been done.' But it was not done, nor is it probable that the error will be corrected.

"I rejoice that in the midst of all your mind dwells in 'the region of peace.' This is an inestimable privilege, and blessed be God; it is secured to all who will have it, in 'the Prince of peace.'"

The reader will keep in mind that the Southern bishops and the Southern Church were as much obligated to keep to the letter and spirit of the "Plan of Separation" as were those of the North, for it was an agreement to which both parties had solemnly subscribed, and upon which the Southern Church grounded all their claims to legitimacy, and to a division of the funds of the Church.

Chapter XIV.

[1845-48.]

DIFFICULTIES OF EPISCOPAL ADMINISTRATION— CONTINUED.

THE troubles already alluded to, and the public complaints and controversies growing out of them, necessitated a meeting of the bishops for the purpose of defining and publishing their construction of the "Plan of Separation." They met in Philadelphia, March 3, 1847, the venerable Bishop Hedding presiding. The following are the chief points determined as principles governing, and to govern in future, their official acts:

"1. That the Plan of Separation provides for taking the votes by conferences, stations, and societies, and not by circuits, in fixing their Church relations.

"2. That in our administration under said Plan of Separation we consider the period of taking the vote of conferences, stations, and societies is limited: for conferences to the time of the next session after the organization of the Methodist Episcopal Church, South, and for stations and societies to the time of the first session of their respective annual conferences, subsequent to said organization.

"3. That in our administration we will, under the Plan of Separation aforesaid, consider the first vote, regularly and fairly taken after the organization of the Methodist Episcopal Church, South, by any border station or society south of the line of separation, as final in fixing its relation to the Methodist Episcopal Church, or to the Methodist Episcopal Church, South.

"4. That we can send no preacher to any station or society south of the line of separation which, subsequent to the organization of the Methodist Episcopal Church, South, has once received a preacher from said Church without a remonstrance from the majority of its members.

"5. That when a border station or society, north of the line of separation, has once received a preacher from the Methodist Episcopal Church—subsequent to the organization of the Methodist Episcopal Church, South—without remonstrance from a majority of said station or society, it fixes finally the relation of said station or society to the Methodist Episcopal Church, even if it were to be admitted that the Plan of Separation allows stations or societies north of said line to vote on the subject of Church relationship.

"6. WHEREAS, The Discipline says: 'Virginia Conference shall be bounded on the east by the Chesapeake Bay and the Atlantic Ocean,' and 'Philadelphia Conference shall include the eastern shore of Maryland and Virginia'—the Chesapeake Bay, an arm of the Ocean, being between them—therefore,

"*Resolved*, that in our administration we will regard the 'eastern shore of Maryland and Virginia' as not being border work in the sense of the Plan of Separation.

"7. That from the information before us, after mature consultation, we agree in the opinion that the Kanawha District, Ohio Conference, under the Plan of Separation, belongs to the Methodist Episcopal Church, and that we will govern our administration accordingly.

"8.—That our administration within the bounds of King George, Westmoreland, Lancaster, and Warrenton Circuits, Baltimore Conference, be governed by the principle laid down in our first resolution, and that we feel obliged to furnish preachers to said circuits as heretofore, if it be practicable.

"9. That as our immediate duties do not require us to speak publicly of other parts of our border work, where difficulties exist, we deem it unnecessary to make known our opinions concerning them at present."

In his diary Bishop Hamline makes this entry:

"*Wednesday*, 3.—Bishops' meeting in progress. Offered a resolution which will serve to make the line of separation a fixed, not a movable line, as our Southern brethren intend, and it was unanimously agreed to. It was agreed also that circuits have no privilege of voting.

"*Friday*, 5.—Bishops closed their meeting. I offered two

resolutions, asserting that Kanawha District, Ohio Conference, and King George, Westmoreland, Lancaster, and Warrenton Circuits, Baltimore Conference, still belong to our work and are to be supplied by us. Carried unanimously. It was also agreed, *nem. con.*, that the Plan of Separation had been violated in Cincinnati (Soule Chapel), and on the Peninsula (Philadelphia Conference), as well as in Kanawha and the above circuits."

The resolutions offered by Bishop Hamline here referred to are the resolutions 5, 6, 7, and 8 in the published list, and are of marked importance in their line of policy.

At the Baltimore Conference, March 14, 1847, Bishop Hamline preached in the morning of the Sabbath, and enters upon his diary:

"Many preachers were present, and I tried to discharge my duty by urging on all the doctrine of entire sanctification and exhorting them to seek it. O that I had more of it in my own heart. Yet the Lord has done great things for me, indeed. Since March, 1842, I have enjoyed new states of grace which I was till then a stranger to. It is on this ground alone that I am able to say, 'Cast down, but not destroyed.' I should have been destroyed root and branch but for the strength which God has given me. I have often, under the provocations connected with the disunion of the Church, found that nothing could support me but grace, abundant grace. Men have in this matter laid to my charge things which I knew not, and these have been published in religious journals without the least shadow of authority, and when proven false have not been retracted, but were permitted to go to the world as solemn and well-attested truth. I can by grace forgive and forget. And I pray God to save the agents of so unwarrantable a mischief. Two of these agents have, I doubt not, been actuated by a spirit of deep, diabolical malice; but so much the more do I pray, 'Lord, forgive them.'"

The deepening shadows of care were upon him at these border conferences, and the stern perplexities of administration, added to incessant labor for the spiritual elevation of the preachers and Churches, drew heavily upon his slender resources of strength. Still, through grace, he was able to make this entry in his diary:

WASHINGTON, D. C., *Saturday, March* 20, 1847.

"Closed the Baltimore Conference. It is said to have been the shortest, most harmonious, and devout session they have had for many years. I anticipated great difficulty. The Lord has opened our way. It has fatigued me beyond measure, but thanks be to God."

The next day he preached in M'Kendree Chapel, President Polk, Secretary Buchanan, and other officers of government present. "Tried to deal faithfully with all," he writes; "but O for power in preaching! I mourn."

The Philadelphia Conference was to meet in Wilmington, Delaware, March 31st. As this also was a "border conference" much difficulty had been already experienced from that portion of its territory lying within Virginia. Bishop Hamline, who had arrived at Wilmington, writes to Mrs. Hamline, and thus refers to his apprehended trouble:

" O for help here ! I dread this conference more than I did Baltimore. I learn that the difficulties in this conference, in Accomac and Northampton, are growing worse and worse. The Methodists are determined to stay in the Philadelphia Conference, and the mobites (citizens) are determined they shall not. The former say they want preachers this year that ' are not afraid to die.' This looks like the ' perilous times,' and surely ' a man's foes are those of his own household.' The time is at hand and hasteth greatly. I desire to be prepared, and have my family (and the Church) prepared, for all these things. I think God, who has so wonderfully wrought hitherto, will help us. There are fearful sights and great signs. I will join you, my beloved wife, in humble endeavors that we may be found worthy to stand before the Son of Man."

A little later, April 14th, in a letter to his old friend, Rev. Jacob Young, he writes:

"Worn down as I am by the labors of the Baltimore and Philadelphia Conferences I take up my pen to extricate myself from embarrassments relative to our long continued, confiding, and to me most pleasant and profitable correspondence.

"We closed the Baltimore Conference the Saturday week after it commenced, having enjoyed great harmony in conference, and gotten through much earlier and with less difficulty than usual. Border difficulties may be anticipated in Warrenton, King George, Westmoreland, and Lancaster Circuits, Virginia; but these we must leave to the control of Providence, commending the four preachers sent to them to the prayers of the Church and the protection of Almighty God. In the Philadelphia Conference the preachers sent to Accomac and Northampton will have to meet most formidable difficulties; and in the former, the 'citizen mind,' as Dr. Capers calls it, arrayed against the 'Methodist mind,' may kindle flames which nothing but the blood of several victims can quench. The violence of the excitement in Accomac exceeds all I have known in connection with our border difficulties."

The apprehensions here expressed of trouble in that part of the Baltimore Conference which projected into Virginia were well grounded and too fearfully realized. The session of the Baltimore Conference, just referred to, was their first, after the date of the first General Conference of the Church South. Up to 1846 the Churches of King George, Westmoreland and Lancaster Circuits had expressed themselves in favor of retaining their connection with the Methodist Episcopal Church, but when the preachers from the Baltimore Conference returned to these circuits that year, they found them supplied by the Southern bishops from the Virginia Conference. Many received the Baltimore preachers cordially as personal friends, but sorrowed that they could not receive them as "Baltimore Conference men, or as Northern men." Few places were open for them to preach, and in some they were exposed to personal danger, from which their friends could not shield them. They could do little else than make a reconnoissance, and after a time were recalled for other fields of labor. In 1847 the above circuits were dropped from the Minutes of the Baltimore Conference, and from the scattering societies still adhering to said conference, they constructed a circuit under the name of "Northern Neck," including the Southern section of country lying between the Rappahannock and Potomac rivers. To the preachers sent there, Bishop Hamline gave instructions according to the information laid before him, and in harmony with the pastoral address of the conference wherein they state that the Baltimore Conference could not voluntarily withdraw its jurisdiction from any circuit or station within its territory. After personal survey of the ground, the preacher in charge of "Northern Neck" writes to Bishop Waugh for further instruction, which he forwards to Bishop Hamline, as the proper adviser. The whole affair appeared dubious. The next year the circuit was "left to be supplied," and the year following, dropped from the Minutes. On Warrenton Circuit one of the Churches, where the society had voted by majority to remain in the Methodist Episcopal Church, the house of worship was forcibly entered and new locks attached to the doors, and the Baltimore preacher excluded. A suit at law was commenced for the recovery of the church, but in 1849 the field was abandoned and the circuit dropped from the Minutes. At Leesburg a similar state of things occurred, and in 1849 it also was abandoned and left off the Minutes. It was not for territory that the Baltimore Conference strove, but for the maintenance of the pastoral relation over a people whom they had brought to Christ, and who had, when left to their own choice, asked for their continued oversight. They felt bound also in good faith to execute the plan of General Conference respecting territorial lines, as a solemn agreement between North and South and binding upon both.

The Philadelphia Conference had still greater trouble with her Virginia territory. In the counties of Accomac and Northampton, lying east of the Chesapeake Bay, by which it is separated from the rest of Virginia, the excitement and violence transcended all precedent. The preacher in charge of Northampton Circuit was seized in the pulpit and forcibly taken out of the church. The court was in session at Eastville, the county seat, and on Monday, with several Methodist friends, he repaired thither to seek redress and protection. Again the mob met him, then and there, drove him from the seat of justice, and warned him to leave the county. Considering his life in danger, he retired.*

---

* The pastor himself, the Rev. V. Gray, thus narrates the affair: He had been advised, before entering the church that he would meet with difficulty, but his friends thought best not to interfere, unless serious violence should be offered to his person. He says: "I went into the pulpit, and while selecting the lesson to read the mob entered the house. The foremost of the mob came up within a short distance of the pulpit, and addressed me in language to this import. 'Mr. Gray, we command you to submit the pulpit.' I answered, 'I can not do it, sir.' Several of them then came near the pulpit. I asked them for their authority for such a course of conduct, but they showed me none. Several brethren entered into

In Accomac County a public meeting was held at the court-house April 21, 1846, "to take into consideration the serious evils to be apprehended from the adherence of the Methodists of this county to the Philadelphia Conference, and to urge upon them the necessity of connecting themselves with the Methodist Episcopal Church, South." The meeting was called to order by the judge of Northampton County, from whose bench the mob had driven Rev. Mr. Gray, above mentioned. The meeting adopted the report of their committee, in which they " respectfully ask the members of the Methodist Episcopal Church in this county to take into consideration,

conversation with them, on the impropriety of their conduct, telling them they were violating the laws of the State. They said 'they did not regard the law.' I asked them what I had done to deserve such treatment, but all they would say was, 'You are a Northern man, and we do not intend to let a Northern preacher preach here.' After they had been in the church some time, one said, 'Well, if I had been foreman of the committee I would have had hold of him long ago.' One of them then came into the pulpit and took hold of my arm, while some cried, 'Put him over the top of the pulpit.' Several of them reached over the pulpit, but could not get hold of me. While the one in the pulpit had me by the arm another got upon the bench, and reaching over, caught me by the coat collar and cravat, and choked me considerably, also pulled my hair. Two or three others came into the pulpit and forced me out of it. They then let me go, and asked if I were not going out of the church. I told them I was not. They then seized hold of me again, and forced me out of the church. During this struggle they tore my coat. After I had gone to my carriage they told me not to come back or the consequences would be serious. On Monday I went to Eastville, where the court was in session, to seek redress. But while I was in the court-house I was met by the mob, and told that I must leave Eastville in fifteen minutes. I intimated that was a short time to get my horse and carriage. So they gave me an hour, and told me I must leave the county. Thus I have been driven away without redress or protection."

and to restore peace and a feeling of security to this community by severing their connection with the Methodist Episcopal Church North, and uniting with the Methodist Episcopal Church South." A committee was then appointed "to address the people and the Methodist societies in Accomac," pursuant to the sentiments and purposes of the meeting. The Methodists present had already been informed by the honorable chairman they were not to vote. The address was published in the *Richmond Christian Advocate*, and was extravagantly commended and eulogized by its editor, Dr. Lee, who says: "With the present race of Methodists Methodism must die out of Accomac, if they now persist in their adherence to a Church so justly chargeable with abolitionism." Into the controversy men of all ranks, outside the Church, entered. The point urged was, not that any man or conference had committed overt acts of impropriety, but, that the public influence of the position of a society, in its adherence to the Methodist Episcopal Church, was against the peace of society in the slave States, by silently encouraging discontent among the slaves, and practically approving and abetting what they now called an abolition Church. The matter of choosing between the North and the South was now fully taken up by the populace, backed by the peculiar, local politics of the extreme South, leaving only the empty name of freedom of choice to the Methodist societies. Preachers were, in various instances, prudently advised to leave the county. The press was assailed as well. The opposition of the South to the *Christian Advocate* published at New York appeared immediately after the Gen-

eral Conference of 1844. Both it and its editor, Rev.
Dr. Bond, were repudiated and proscribed in un-
measured terms, although from first to last no fact
of history is better established than that Dr. Bond
unfalteringly maintained the conservative disciplinary
ground, to which the united Church had hitherto
strenuously held.   But "at the court of Accomac
County, March 29, 1847, the grand jury returned into
court with a presentment against the 'New York
Christian Advocate and Journal,'" because "it advises,
and is calculated and intended to persuade, persons
of color, within this commonwealth, to make insur-
rection or rebel, and denies the right of property in
their slaves, and inculcates the duty of resistance to
such right, contrary to the statute in such cases made
and provided."   The intended effect of this was to
prohibit the circulation of this paper in that county,
"postmasters not being permitted, under penalty of
the law to give it out from their offices."   This had
its influence for a time.   The same had been done to
the *Western Christian Advocate,* by the grand jury of
Wood County, Virginia, April, 1846.   A cowardly
assault upon religious freedom and the liberty of
the press!

Similar troubles were experienced in Kentucky
and Missouri, which we need not particularize, as we
are not writing a history of the disorder of the times,
but lifting the curtain upon the sad picture only so far
as may illustrate the embarrassment of episcopal administration.   It was not the least of the sources of
embarrassment to the chief executives of the Methodist Episcopal Church that a warm controversy was
early opened at the North on the constitutionality of

the Plan of Separation. A division of opinion at this point, among prominent individuals and annual conferences, necessarily made the decisions of the bishops unsavory to the opposing party, and caused them to feel wounded in the house of their friends. By the best minds, however, both the constitutionality of the "Plan" and the action of the bishops were sustained. The General Conference had simply assumed it might be necessary for the Southern brethren to separate, as their leaders solemnly asseverated it would be, in order to retain their pastoral relation, and have access to master and slave. Yet if they separated it would be their own act, done and committed on their own responsibility. Of the necessity of this act they alone could judge, and the judgment and the manner of reaching it were committed to them. If they separated on this principle, in the true spirit of the " Plan," they would do it, indeed, upon their own responsibility, but it would not necessarily destroy fraternity. Then, in such a case, the General Conference agreed to submit to the annual conferences, for their action, such an alteration of one of the constitutional restrictions of the Discipline, as would allow the South their *pro rata* share of the Church property. The "Plan" itself was thus grounded in the highest equity and courtesy of Christian brotherhood, and reverence for constitutional government. The General Conference proposed nothing at variance with either; and standing as we do upon the more elevated ground of history, more favorable, in its retrospection, to correct observation and just judgment, the present age and posterity will award to that body, that it acted both with constitutionality and Christian urbanity.   And this was the ground which Bishop Hamline took at the first and sustained to the last.   If the General Conference erred at all, it might, with more plausibility be considered to be, not in trusting too far the prudence and integrity of the great body of the Church North and South when left to their own Christian convictions, but in not counting fully upon the influence of a few extreme leaders, and, more than all, the pressure of outside and ultra Southern politics which was brought to bear on the case.

It has been already noticed that the bishops were pressed for opinions and decision upon the two questions of ecclesiastical division and jurisdiction, and the division of Church property in favor of the South. On the latter, the subject had been constitutionally laid before the annual conferences for their concurrence, and they had failed to secure the legal vote necessary to authorize the measure.   What now to do was the vexed question.   If the General Conference could have divided the Book Room property, and given to the Southern organization its *pro rata* share, the question would have been simplified, and its session of 1848 might have determined the case. But as the matter now stood the wisdom of the Church seemed baffled.   The following letter of Bishop Hamline to Bishop Morris on the subject is worthy of historic preservation.   It evinces, also, the characteristic modesty, carefulness, and thoroughness of the author .

"WILMINGTON, IND., *November* 18, 1847.

"REV. BISHOP MORRIS,—*Dear Brother :* Two or three times I mentioned to you my doubts whether the General Conference has authority to divide the funds of the Book Concern without the concurrence of the annual conferences by the usual 'three-fourths' vote. Since I have had leisure I have thought more on the subject, and am in still greater difficulty to reach any other conclusion. True, the Discipline, in its sixth restriction, mentions only the 'produce' of the Book Concern. But it seems to me that our whole capital is the accumulated produce of the Book Concern ; and that to divide this principal would be in fact dispersing the amassed or treasured produce in direct violation of the restriction.

"This was the opinion of many brethren, both from the North and the South, in the last General Conference. The fourth resolution in the ' Report of the Committee of Nine,' indicated my opinion ; and I believe every member of the committee concurred with me then ; or at least I heard from no one a contrary hint. I think we have contemplated the concurrence of the annual conferences as indispensable to give validity to those resolutions of the report (succeeding the fourth) which relate to the division of Church. Looking at the remarks in debate on the report, you will see that Bishops Capers and Paine, as well as others, clearly held that opinion, and that some even went much further, and held that the whole Plan of Separation was of no force unless approved by the three-fourths vote of all the annual conferences. (See pp. 223–226, of Debates of 1844.) We all supposed at that time that the annual conferences would concur, and but for that conflict which was commenced through the press almost immediately, it is probable they would. They *did not*, however, if we may trust report, and now the question is, whether the General Conference can divide the funds, not only without their concurrence, but in the face of their *non*-concurrence either by formal vote or by declining to vote.

"I do not argue that they can not, but frankly avow that as my opinion ; and repeat it to you that if you see otherwise, my mind may, if practicable, get clear of the difficulty. I should be obliged to you for your views, and if they differ from the above, for your reasons, that I may have an opportunity to ponder them. You will perceive that I am somewhat committed to this doctrine of General Conference inability, by the ' Report of the Committee of Nine;' and yet I do not believe any man should be tenacious of error. If my views were then

incorrect, I, convinced of them, shall renounce them. If they
seem to me correct, I suppose it would not only be wrong to
give them up, but even bad policy to do so. It is better to
maintain the constitution of the Church than to suffer the most
pressing exigency to draw us into an obliquity from its rules ;
and to meet the existing exigency in any case we must turn to
such measures as harmonize with our restrictions. I am at a
loss what these should be. But time may show.

"If it be not too great a trouble, I would be glad to have
your views (for my private use strictly) in writing. When I
reach the city, through *my* haste or *your* absence, I may not
have opportunity for a full conversation on this subject ; add to
which I am of so poor a memory that I can not distinctly
enough recollect what you might say, for after and mature
meditation. If you will write me a letter and explain your
views on this subject, I will weigh them carefully, and then be
better prepared to converse with you afterwards.

"I think this question may in the end become of considerable moment. I find many are anxious to settle this matter
peaceably with the South, but are at a loss as to the method. I
I would not wonder if the whole question should, before the
General Conference, be resolved into a 'How?' I am not sure
but it is of sufficient importance to be a theme of correspondence with all our colleagues to obtain, if practicable, harmony
amongst us all. I would *suggest* this, and submit it to your
judgment."

Bishop Morris differed with Bishop Hamline on
the question of the constitutional power of General
Conference to divide the Book Concern property, and
his views and the strength of the argument on that
side are clearly given in his answer to the above letter, dated January 3, 1848, which it seems proper to
give to the reader. He says:

"In regard to the authority of the General Conference to
divide the Book Fund with the South without the concurrence
of the annual conferences, your views are such as I understood
to be entertained by a large majority, both in 1844 and since,
while I knew full well that mine were those of a feeble minority, for which reason I have never felt much zeal in recom-

mending them, believing it would be lost labor. I would not wish to come in collision with the constitutional scruples of so many respectable brethren in any public manner. Still I have my opinion, and have occasionally ventured to express it to a friend. I have no copy of the debates on the subject. If I had not heard them I might have felt curiosity or interest enough to buy and read them. But my opinion rests on other grounds than the expressed opinions of brethren in General Conference while arguing the case. I found my opinion first on the language of the sixth restriction, 'They shall not appropriate it to any purpose other than for the benefit of the traveling, supernumerary, superannuated, and worn-out preachers, their wives, widows, and children.' To these objects, then, the proceeds may be, nay, must be, appropriated. I am not willing they should be applied to any other. Nor do the Southern conferences propose to apply their dividends to any other objects than those specified in restriction sixth. 2. I found my opinion on the action of the General Conference of 1844. When separation was anticipated, the General Conference esteemed it their duty 'to meet the emergency with Christian kindness and the strictest equity.' This latter clause, 'strictest equity,' evidently refers to the division of property, subsequently described, and is a clear recognition of the Southern claim to be used in case of separation. The objection that the brethren South separated without cause avails nothing, seeing we agreed 'That should the annual conferences in the slaveholding States find it necessary to unite in a distinct ecclesiastic connection,' etc. No *mode* of finding that necessity was prescribed; they selected their own mode, and say they have found it, and have therefore become a distinct body. Nothing was required of the annual conferences to make the division 'of the capital and produce of the Methodist Book Concern' so soon as the South organized, but to concur in altering the sixth restriction. The failure to obtain that concurrence by the three-fourths majority prevented the commissioners from estimating, and the agents from transferring the funds till further orders, but should not finally deprive the South of their just claims. If that method of meeting their claims be impracticable, we should adopt some other. If the brethren South, each individual for himself, had withdrawn from the communion of the Methodist Episcopal Church, as did O'Kelly and his follow-

ers, the Methodist Protestants of 1828, or the self-styled 'True
Wesleyans' of 1842, I would unhesitatingly admit they had no
claim. We never proposed to provide for such cases. But all
the superannuated preachers, wives, widows, and children of
thirteen conferences, having just claims on the Book Concern,
were transferred in a body, without any act of their own, or
any wish on their part to leave the Church. Surely their claims
should be met with 'strictest equity.' If their claims be with-
held on any alleged constitutional ground, the natural conclusion of mankind will be either that the constitution of the
Methodist Episcopal Church is wrong, or that it is badly administered, either of which would operate against us. If in this
matter we have sworn to our own hurt, we ought not to change.
Our lay brethren where I have been are generally in favor of
allowing the claim and ending the dispute. The preachers,
too, appear to lean more that way than heretofore. As to what
will be done, I am alternately hoping and despairing. Were
it not for my belief in an overruling Providence I should be
still more discouraged with the prospect. If the question of
claim must needs go back to the annual conferences, we shall
be agitated four years longer, and then be just where we are.
To think of obtaining the concurrence of three-fourths of the
preachers is hopeless. As an individual I am persuaded that
allowing the claim at once would be a less evil than to reject
or refer it back."

The bishops and the whole Church were anxious
to effect an amicable and just settlement of the claims
of the South on the Book Room property. These
great questions agitating the Church could not fail to
act injuriously upon the spiritual prosperity of North
and South. "I can not avoid the fear," says Bishop
Morris, "that Methodism will never resume its
wonted prosperity till the matters now in dispute
between the North and the South are amicably settled
so as to terminate the controversy. May the Lord
hasten that important event in his time."

CHAPTER XV.

[September, 1845, to April, 1847.]

VISITATION OF CONFERENCES AND EVANGELICAL WORK.

WE resume the thread of our narrative, which was interrupted at the date of September 14, 1845, two weeks after his rencounter with Bishop Soule at the Ohio Conference. (See Chapter xii.)

Bishop Hamline's next appointment was at the session of the North Indiana Conference, Lafayette, Indiana, September 24th, of which he says:

" This is one of the most interesting annual conferences I have yet visited. Here I find very holy men. Nearly all our business was done on Saturday noon. Two days and a half would have finished it but for ordinations. Read out the appointments Monday morning, and rode to Crawfordsville. Spent the Sabbath, October 5th, in Indianapolis, and reached this place (Madison, Indiana) to attend the Indiana Conference with Bishop Morris. This is the first annual conference I have been permitted to attend throughout its session with another bishop since my election to office, and from my small experience I expected to find myself in many mistakes. But I am surprised to find how few and unimportant I have committed. I believe it is because God has helped me."

Bishop Hamline closes the year, as usual, with abundant labors. His one absorbing object was to awaken the ministry and the Churches to the higher claims of their holy calling, and to reach out a hand of rescue to the perishing. His summer months were spent in attending annual conferences, and his win-ters in visiting the Churches. At Gallipolis, Ohio, November 16, 1845, he records:

"In consequence of the death of Brother Ferree, the Presiding Elder of this (Portsmouth) district, I have been in this neighborhood some three weeks attending quarterly meetings and doing what I could. This is a barren place at present, but when God shall build up Zion he shall appear in his glory. Come, Lord Jesus."

January 22, 1846, he writes from Lawrenceburg, Indiana, where were four distilleries named after four evangelical Churches in that place, the Baptist, Methodist, Episcopalian, and Presbyterian. He says:

"This is a day of his power here. The Methodist Church has been noted in this place for its wealth, its backsliding, its internal strife, and its inconsistencies. But, blessed be God, a change has come over them. We came here on New-Year's to spend two or three days, and have been with them twenty-two days. More than seventy have joined the Church; but the greatest blessing is, more than a hundred Church members have been converted—truly converted; for I believe there was not a sinner in town more removed from justification than many of them were. Your little 'Way of Holiness' is leading many of them into liberty."

Again, February 27th, he says:

"I have spent the last three months thus: In Athens, with my dear friends, and Brother Jacob Young, one week; four weeks in Lawrenceburg in a glorious revival, preaching twenty-two sermons, with other labors; one week at Aurora and on Cheviot Circuit; some days in Portsmouth, Ohio; and several in this city (Cincinnati) and vicinity, preaching the word and writing. I have had some blessed seasons. Glorious revivals are breaking out in almost every part of the North-west. Eleven hundred accessions to the Church are reported in one week by the *Western Christian Advocate*. In Cincinnati, where 'grievous wolves have entered in not sparing the flock,' the Lord is doing wonders. Wesley Chapel is all alive under the ministry of the Rev. J. M. Trimble, and many are getting the blessing of perfect love. Glory be to God!"

To Rev. J. Young he says:

"I have been shut up with sickness almost three weeks, and in the midst of sickness I have to confess that my faith has been for me unusually weak, and, of course, my strength and comfort feeble. It has been a season of spiritual barren- ness. This shows, as you say, how liable we are to change in this world of sorrow. The last time I wrote you I was on the mountain top, and it seemed as though I never could come down. But alas! I have descended into the valley; may learn some lessons there! It is a school for such proud worms as we are, always forgetting."

"*Cincinnati, May 9, 1846*—This day closes the forty- ninth year of my life. What a waste of years is behind me! I am an old man, but have done little for my Lord. I often wish to die. Holy joys so swell my bosom that I long, as Paul did, to depart and be with Christ. But I chide the longing. In view of my wasted years, I should long and struggle to live and labor and suffer for Christ. O for ten or fifteen years, if that might be, of hard labor for God and his well-beloved Son. I have been absent nearly nine weeks in Xenia, London, Columbus, Reynoldsburg, Lura, Hebron, Jackson, Rushville, Zanesville, Brownville, New Carlisle, Mt. Vernon, Utica, New- ark, Charleston, Sharonville, and Lockland. Preached some thirty-five times in those places. Often filled with holy joy. Glory to God!"

But the time drew near that he should resume his wonted summer work in visiting the annual con- ferences, and after a few days' respite we find him on his way. In a letter to Mrs. Phoebe Palmer, of New York, dated June 15, 1846, he writes:

"Having started on our way to the conferences, I write to solicit your special supplications on my labors this year. . . . For two years, I am constrained to acknowledge, God has helped me. If prayer be continued for me, I still have hope. I am now on my way to the Pittsburg Conference as a visitor (Bishop Morris presiding), and on the 9th or 10th of July start for Galena, Illinois, a long journey to the Rock River Conference. My conferences are as follows: At Galena, August 12th ; Iowa Conference (at Bloomington, Iowa), September 2d ; Illinois Conference, at Paris, Illinois, September 23d ; and Indiana Conference, at Connersville, Indiana, October 7th. At these times plead with God for us.

" Deep impressions were made at the conferences last year on the subject of perfect love. As one minister after another has written to me, and announced 'liberty' from sin, and stated that he left conference resolved never to rest without the blessing I have sunk in deep humility before God. O, may he use us still as his instruments!

"I say *us*, for I deem Mrs. Hamline's labors are, if any thing, more fully blest than my own. We enjoy the presence and holy smile of the all-seeing God. My soul trembles often under the weight of his love. He draws me by the sweet violence of faith and love after and near him. I feel like giving him glory.

"For two years I trust God has shown me favor, and good has been done, but now the third has come, and I have fears. I fear that my hands will slacken, and that 'giants in the land' will make me afraid. Pray for us!"

To Dr. and Mrs. Palmer he writes on steamboat, July 17, 1846:

"I write on this jarring boat to solicit your special prayers in our behalf. We have just spent three weeks in traveling through the country toward Uniontown, Pennsylvania, to attend Bishop Morris's conference. We make all this journey, Providence permitting, in a private carriage, through a region proverbially sickly, over the corduroy bridges of Indiana, and through swales, forests, and prairies of Illinois, Wisconsin, and Iowa, for the purpose of visiting the societies and preaching the Gospel of the Kingdom. Do follow us with your earnest prayers, and especially at the conferences let us not be forgotten.

"The work of holiness is progressing in the West. A large number of the ministers have professed the blessing the last winter. On one circuit alone one hundred members obtained the blessing. The conferences last year were seasons of refreshing to my own soul, and it seems, by God's grace, to many of the brethren. A leading brother in North Indiana, somewhat skeptical, of great influence, especially in the higher circles, obtained the blessing at New Year's, and preached on the subject with great power. Nine of his station obtained the blessing in a few days. He writes that at conference he resolved to rest no more till he had tested the doctrine by a thorough effort to seek the blessing. On our present journey we met with a sister whose husband (a member of the North Indiana Conference) experienced the blessing at conference. Of this we had not before heard. Thanks be to God if our conferences, so often dreaded by the preachers as seasons of backsliding, can be attended by such results.

"Mrs. Hamline is as well as usual at this season of the year. I have urged her to spend the summer in New York; but she *will* go with me. It will try her strength to the utmost. Yet, in truth, I need her. I find her conversation with the preachers often does more good than all my exhortations in the conference. A remarkable power also attends her prayers. Under them souls have been directly and powerfully sanctified. Pray earnestly for her, also, and that Satan may not hinder us, for there are many adversaries."

The journey before them might well induce anxious thought for Mrs. Hamline, as here expressed. The hotel accommodations for travelers over the prairies were yet in their primitive, Western, romantic stage. One day, after traveling sixty miles, often out of sight of human dwellings, they stopped at the only place in the region for lodgings, worn down with fatigue. The wife and only woman of the house had recently died. Five stalwart men held the fort. None to cook a meal of victuals, and no victuals to cook. The bed was constructed of sticks laid across four rude crotches, and the dressing of the bed of an ash color from long use without washing. The men slept upon the floor with portmanteaus for pillars. Four other travelers had met at the same place at the same time for hospitalities, and still other preachers afterward came straying in. The man of the house was kind, but powerless. The guests retired after such supper as their scanty lunch bag afforded, and the next morning resumed their journey to some more hopeful inn, in search of breakfast.

The Illinois Conference this year was at Paris, Illinois, September 23d. Dr. Elliott, who was there, writes:

"The manner in which Bishop Hamline conducted the business of conference greatly contributed to expediting it, and promoting the kindest feelings one toward another. The frequent exhortations of the Bishop to prayer and devotion and the promotion of holiness had the most salutary effect upon the minds of the preachers. They prayed more than usual. They watched their words and governed their spirit and endeavored to profit by the godly advice given. All the preachers were delighted beyond measure with this first visit of their new bishop."

The beginning of 1847 finds Bishop Hamline at Staten Island, with "Father Henry Boehm, for many years the traveling companion of Bishop Asbury." The two months following are spent in New York, New Jersey, and Pennsylvania. In New York his society in the family of Dr. and Mrs. Palmer was delightful and refreshing. He says:

"NEW YORK, *January 5th.*—At Dr. Palmer's. I enjoy precious privileges in the society of this holy family. Intimate acquaintance changes approval into admiration of God's grace in them. I know two persons at least who live up to their profession. Jesus can make his disciples wonderfully like himself. In these I find a proof. Grace has been here with her plummet and line. The stones are all shaped and polished ready for the temple. They will be used by the great Builder as his wisdom pleases. The polisher knows where. My soul is helped.

"*Thursday, 7th.*—I have met at Dr. Palmer's and conversed with two brethren whom I greatly desired to see, President Mahan and Professor Upham. They seem to me to be exceedingly devoted Christians. I deem them both sanctified men, and pioneers in spreading holiness in the Congregational Church.

"*Saturday, 9th.*—Spent this week in New York. Sat for a portrait at the solicitation of Dr. Palmer. If we get to heaven it seems a waste to be pictured on earth. Shall we not live forever? How will such a sinner as I have been look, washed and glorified in heaven!"

In one place he says:

"Methodism trembles in this region. The subject of perfect love is strange in the ears of many. Spiritual death prevails, of course. Methodist preachers shall answer for it at the bar of God. He that stands up at the altar and repeats the usual answers to the solemn questions in the conference examination, and then makes light of the doctrine of perfect love, is fit for almost any thing but the pulpit. According to Mr. Wesley, he is either a dishonest man or he has lost his memory."

At another time when, at family prayer, freedom was indulged in historic and sometimes curious questions on the Bible lesson, he remarks:

"It is unfavorable to devotion to me. I lose all the ardor of devotion by such a method. In family prayer I wish to leave my dictionary, whether English, Greek, or Hebrew, out of sight; and also my geography, natural history, metaphysics, and all else but God. Just then I would be as Moses in the cleft of the rock—able to think of nothing but the overwhelming presence and glory of God."

In another place he says:

"A great dearth prevails here. Preacher is smooth, polished. He needs perfect love. The people need it. They are as near death as they well can be, yet live. In the language of the Word, 'are ready to die!'"

In a letter to Rev. Edward D. Roe, January 23, 1847, he says:

"You are now, by the providence of God, restored to the delightful labors of the ministry, and I am in no worse health, perhaps somewhat better. God's ways are not as our thoughts, thanks to his name!

"I saw you seventeen years ago, a merchant. How rapidly time has run! It seems scarcely so long since, in company with my now sainted wife, I rode from Washington, six miles, and you with us, on the 'little bay;' but it is seventeen years last or will be next September. What a large breach in one's life is seventeen years! Well, my dear brother, we do not regret it, only that we have not been more diligent and lived nearer to Jesus.

'But he forgives our follies past.'

"I have been able to preach from three to five times a week this winter. My labors have been in New York and New Jersey, where I now am, and tending toward Pennsylvania, and so on toward the Baltimore Conference, which sits in four or five weeks. I have two petitions to present: 1. That you will give me your prayers, especially in regard to my labors this spring, that God will conduct me safely through embarrassing scenes in connection with our border difficulties; and, 2. That, if it be not a disagreeable task, you will favor me with a few lines, friendly and affectionate, for Christ's sake, and let me hear a word about the grace of God toward you and in you, in your return to the pleasant work of preaching Christ and him crucified.

"I am happy to say that Christ is precious to me, and that, through much tribulation, I hope to enter into the kingdom of heaven."

He reached Philadelphia, January 29th, where he spent eight or nine days. He says:

"*Sunday, January 31st.*—Preached in the morning at Union; had comfort and some freedom. At night tried in 'Old St. George's.' A great crowd. I find if any 'running after' comes upon me I am discouraged, and, also, if there is a great falling of. Agur's prayer about riches seems to meet my views of a congregation: 'Give me neither a crowd nor empty seats;' but I should always leave this to God. I have comfort to-day, and feel that I am on my journey home. 'Home!' precious word.

"*Thursday, 4th.*—Had at Brother H.'s a pious meeting. Mrs. Cookman there. What a monument of God's sanctifying grace! She said: 'I should have died of grief before now, but for that perfect love which enabled me, and does enable me now, to say, Thy will be done.'"

Mrs. Cookman was the wife of the late lamented Rev. George G. Cookman, who was lost at sea, in 1841, in the ill-fated steamship *President*, from which and its passengers and crew no information has ever been obtained. Cookman was one of our most eminent pulpit orators, twice elected chaplain to Congress, a godly man and greatly beloved.

"*Friday*, 5.— Preached this evening in Warton-street Church. A good congregation. By mistake walked about three miles before preaching. Expounded, and rather a dull time. Lord, give me far holier and mightier labors in thy blessed cause!

"*Saturday*, 6.—I pant for God this day. Many precious friends call to see us. God is merciful to this family (Mr. Boswell's). His wife is panting after God, the living God. May she be filled with righteousness!

"*Sunday*, 7.—Preached in Trinity Church in the morning, and in Eighth-street Church at night. One of my happiest days. O how full has my unworthy soul been of God, the living God! It is near unto heaven to spend such a morning in this way in God's house. O may there be fruit of my labor!

"CAMDEN, N. J., *Monday*, 8.—Have started on a three weeks' tour. Lord go with me. Preached this evening to a crowded house. Tried to be faithful. Reproved cold and wandering professors. May the work take effect. Lord, save!

" *Tuesday*. 9.—Great mercies to-day. In private and in communing with saints Christ was in me the hope of glory. Truly could I say, 'The best of all is, God is with us.' Not able to attend meeting at night, but filled unutterably full of glory and of God. Death looks sweet. I long to depart and be with Christ."

From Camden he passed on to Burlington and Mount Holly and Pemberton, preaching at each place.

Of his stay at the latter place he thus records:

"*Monday*, 15.—A good day to my poor soul; deep, precious peace. Prayer-meeting in the basement at 6 A. M. Sisters' prayer-meeting at 2 P. M.; Mrs. Hamline attends. Speaking-meeting at night, and all the churches at the altar. Glory be to God for his goodness.

"*Tuesday*, 16.—Not so joyful a day as yesterday. Prayer-meeting at 6 A. M. Many out. Preaching at night, large auditory, very serious. Our Baptist brethren push the battle. Lord bless them abundantly, and bless thy needy Methodist children also.

"*Wednesday*, 17.—A precious prayer-meeting at 6 A. M., preaching at 10 A. M., and a better season I have scarcely had or seen in my life. O glorious baptism of the Spirit! Thou waterest thy heritage, O Lord. This morning our bow abode in strength, for God himself was with us truly.

"*Thursday*, 18.—Prayer-meeting at six o'clock, preaching at nine. Much worn down. 'The flesh is weak.' Have had a good season, however. The Lord has verily been present with me here. O what seasons of refreshing! Never shall I forget them. My chamber at Brother A.'s has been a 'Bethel indeed.'

"NEWTOWN, PA., *Sunday*, 21.—Came on Thursday from Pemberton to Mount Holly, and put up with Brother James, whose godly wife so resembles her sanctifying Lord that it brings to mind the saying, 'For he who sanctifieth and they who are sanctified are all of one.' Friday came through Burlington and Trenton to this place to dedicate the new church, thirty-six by fifty. Dreadful weather to-day. Prayer-meeting in the morning (best dedication), preaching and prayer-meeting P. M., at old house; dedication sermon at night in the new house. A good congregation for such a fearful storm. It was a blessed day for my soul until night, when I was worn out; spirits flagged, poor preaching, and felt ashamed to render to Christ so poor, *poor* a service. Fear I did not get the right subject. I rejoice I have 'an Advocate with the Father.' Jesus, forgive and save!

"*Wednesday*, 24.—Preached twice to-day with great comfort. God was in the midst of us. Young Brother Cookman preached at night. Small congregations. As the weather prevented collections for the Church on Sabbath, they were received to-day, and amounted to two hundred and seventy-five dollars, leaving the new church about one hundred and fifty dollars in debt. This is a good day.

"*Thursday*, 25.—A pleasant day. Brother Hand preached at night. Theme, 'Christ and his Government.' My soul rejoiced. A solemn season. The Lord is near this people. Weather has been rather unfavorable most of the time."

It was during this visit that Bishop Hamline became acquainted with that beloved and distinguished man of God, the late Rev. Alfred Cookman, mentioned above, son of the Rev. George G. Cookman, already referred to. Alfred Cookman was the pastor of the Attleborough Circuit, Pennsylvania, and through a pious mother's counsels had been led by the Holy Spirit to see his need of entire consecration and the full baptism of the Spirit. Under deep convictions he was earnestly seeking the Divine anointing. He says:

"While thus exercised in mind, Bishop Hamline, accompanied by his devoted wife, came to Newtown, one of the principal appointments on the circuit, that he might dedicate a church we had been erecting for the worship of God. Remaining about a week he not only preached again and again, and always with the unction of the Holy One, but took occasion to converse with me pointedly respecting my religious experience. His gentle yet dignified bearing, devotional spirit, beautiful Christian example, unctuous manner, divinely illuminated face, apostolic labor and fatherly counsels, made the profoundest impression on my mind and heart. I heard him as one sent from God, and certainly he was. His influence so hallowed and blessed has not only remained with me ever since, but even seems to increase. O how I bless and praise God for the life and labors of the beloved Bishop Hamline."

It was while engaged with the bishop and his wife in prayer that Cookman received the witness. He says: "The great work of heart purity was wrought, and the evidence was as direct and indubitable as the witness of sonship vouchsafed at the time of my adoption into the family of heaven." In a letter to Mrs. Hamline he further says:

"It was after a sermon which fell from his precious lips, preached in the afternoon, that I carefully and intelligently consecrated all I had and hoped for to God. The entire consecration, with faith in Jesus, brought peace—deep, full, sacred, blessed peace—but it was not until the following day, when you and I were praying together, that the witness came, clearly, strongly, and satisfactorily, that I was wholly sanctified through the power of the Holy Ghost. With me, in that epochal time in my history, my heart turned toward you with an unutterable interest and love. May our kind, heavenly Father visit and bless you with abounding consolations. You must soon realize the joy of reunion with the glorified, and, more than this, the beatific vision of Jesus. Oh, may I not hope to be associated with you and dear Bishop Hamline in the many-mansioned home."

"DOYLESTOWN, PA., *Friday*, 26.—Rode fourteen miles to this place this P. M. Preached this night to about one hundred souls. Methodism low as to numbers, but a good chapel and an attentive congregation. Put up with Judge Smith; not a member, but an afflicted, and, I judge, a serious family. Not a lively season in public.

"NEWTOWN, PA., *Saturday*, 27.—Rode from Doylestown this morning in a dreadful storm. One of my worst journeys on a small scale. We were in a one-horse sleigh, snow half gone, rain and wind in our faces. I worked hard to hold an umbrella braced against the storm, and we reached fourteen miles in three hours.

"*Sunday*, 28.—Preached twice; not warm in my affections. Not one of my best Sabbaths. Let me bless God for the past, and trust him for the future.

"PHILADELPHIA, *March* 1.—Came to the city and put up with my dear friends, the Boswells. A pleasant home. The Lord bless us here for Christ's sake. Absent three weeks; preached seventeen times."

His business at Philadelphia was to attend a meeting of the bishops, and especially to settle upon principles of administration by which they would be governed in relation . to the Methodist Episcopal Church South, according to the Plan of Separation. Of the doings of this meeting we have given account in a previous chapter. From Philadelphia he passed on to Baltimore, where he says:

"*Sunday*, 7.—Preached in the morning at Light Street; a good time. P. M., went three-quarters of a mile on foot to a German love-feast. Weary and sick. Preached at night at Charles Street. Splendid Church; not much like the manger or the cross.

"WASHINGTON CITY D., C., *Tuesday*, 9.—One-fourth of a century since I was here. Baltimore Conference commences to-morrow. Lord, help me and help thy ministers."

In a letter written from this place to Mrs. Hamline he says:

"*March* 10, 1847.—Opened the conference myself. Bishop Morris present. Read the fourth chapter of 2 Corinthians, and sang a hymn. Prayer by Bishop Morris, Brother Gere, and Brother Guest. A good time. Addressed them five minutes on the importance of order, diligence, and devotion, the last above all. It was a pleasant session. . . . Brethren are generally very kind. I feel thankful and promise my heavenly Father more gratitude and fidelity.

"*March* 11.—Conference progressed rapidly. Last year it sat seventeen or eighteen days, this year I hope it may adjourn in nine days. If the Lord will aid (and his servant seeking he will aid) we may close on Friday the 19th.

"*Saturday*, 13.—Nearly half the business of conference is finished unless some unforeseen difficulties arise. Lord, help! I feel firmly resolved to urge holiness of heart on Christ's members. I will die rather than give it up. God help me to be faithful!

"WASHINGTON, D. C., *Saturday*, 20.—Closed the Baltimore Conference. It is said to have been the shortest, most harmonious and devout session they have had for many years. I anticipated great difficulty. The Lord has opened our way. It has fatigued me beyond measure; but thanks be to God!"

In his closing address to the conference the Bishop urged upon them the necessity and obligation of class-meetings, Sabbath-school labor, parental discipline and instruction, the missionary enterprise, and personal holiness. On this latter theme, says the reporter, "He read several extracts from the writings of Mr. Wesley. He referred to the London Conference, held forty years before, which insisted that no one should hold an office in the Church unless he believed in total depravity, the atonement of Christ and his divinity, justification by faith, entire holiness, as understood by the Methodists. These were cardinal doctrines of the Church." The parting hour was solemn and affecting. As a true fellow-laborer he spoke of the crosses and triumphs of their itinerant life, and their parting hour was at once solemn and exultant.

"*Sunday*, 21.—Preached this morning with much effort (being exhausted) in M'Kendree Chapel. President Polk and family, and Secretary Buchanan, and other officers of the government present. Tried to deal faithfully with all; but O for power in preaching! I mourn."

On the 22d he reached Baltimore greatly enfeebled, and on the 24th records: "My dear Mrs. Hamline left me this morning for Tarrytown, New York, to see Leonidas [their only child], who is sick. I, too, am sick. Lord go with her and stay with me, and bless the sick. How perfectly has the conference worn me out." A few days, however, restores him so that he is "nearly as well as ever," and he thus writes: "Sunday, 28th.—O happy day! Preached in the morning at High Street, to Mr. Cole's ragged Sunday-school. A heavenly season. How sweet it is to preach in the strength of the Holy Ghost!

Lord, thou wast with the people. P. M. at Washington Temperance Sabbath-school. It is a high day to my soul. Glory!" In writing to his wife he says of his sermon at High Street in the morning. "Preached on 'the mercies of God.' My voice was weak, but my heart was strong. It was a very feeling time among the people." Of his afternoon sermon at Washington Temperance Hall, he says: " A large congregation was assembled. I preached forty minutes on 'the best robe' with unusual liberty."

" *Monday morning.*—Feel well, except my cold, and much better in mind. I have been much afflicted at times since you left me, that I am so unmindful of God's goodness, and especially one act of his goodness, namely, in bestowing upon me yourself as a help to escape from sin and ruin, and in a wonderful manner to reach heaven. . . . If others have angels for 'ministering spirits,' so have I, with one addition, that God was pleased to give me, also, one to minister to me visibly and personally ; and when we reach the place of purity and repose I expect to make the full acknowledgment of it before God and the holy angels. What a history will it unfold !"

On the same evening he preached to "the most crowded congregation he ever had of colored people, in Sharp Street. Had a very precious season."

The next day, March 30th, we find him at Wilmington, Delaware, the seat of the Philadelphia Conference that year; and the day following, Wednesday, March 31st, the conference was opened by Bishop Morris, who had accompanied Bishop Hamline. At half past ten conference business was suspended to hear a sermon from one of its members, Rev. David Dailey—Text, "We preach Christ crucified." Says the Bishop :

"One among the best sermons I have ever heard, overwhelming in its clear and forcible exhibitions of truth. How strange the taste of the people! Here is a man of whom I never heard until I reached this place, and little known beyond his own conference ; yet there are men whose fame as orators is on both shores of the Atlantic, and after whom there is a rush of 'crazy crowds,' who probably have not in all the sermons they ever preached delivered so much real oratory as this humble man gave us in one sermon. The conference understand it, call for his sermon to be published, and it would do them honor if it could travel and be read in two hemispheres. It is worthy to be placed beside Wesley's.

"*Sunday, April* 4.—Preached at half past ten o'clock, and ordained fifteen elders. Lord, I will record thy goodness. Thou hast helped me in deed and in truth. Thou gavest me to speak thy word. I feel thy love still all flaming within me. I yield my body unto God a living sacrifice forever! Amen."

Writing to Mrs. Hamline of the same morning service, he says :

"Christ is truly with me to-day. One of the sweetest seasons my Lord and Savior has ever given me is to-day. And the fire which has burned gently in the morning, and waxed brighter and stronger till the close of the ordination, is a heat of joy and strength unspeakable now. Well may you, my beloved helper in the way, exhort me with the encouraging words of your precious letters, which came as messages from heaven, with a power of refreshing and strengthening unspeakable to my poor soul. Doubtless, while I was trying to preach, 'I beseech you, therefore, brethren, by the mercies of God,' etc., your heart, if not your lips, was pleading for me and for the cause in earnest struggles. The Lord did not, I am sure, turn away his ear or his heart from your faith and desire. Thank him, when you read this, at least as earnestly as you prayed.

"*Monday morning,* 7 *o'clock.*—I had some wakefulness in the night and a wonderful nearness to Christ. I had, indeed, upon my pillow more than ever before,

'The solemn awe which dares not move, And all the silent heaven of love.'

I did not know but the 'heavenly atmosphere' would stop my breathing, and that in it my soul would float away to the bosom of my God. But no, I am here ; yet how sweet the morning !

Its heavenly perfumes are all around me ; the air is loaded with odors unearthly. Penitence, faith, glowing love, O how sweet !"

To his son Leonidas, with whom in his sickness at Tarrytown his mother is watching, he writes :

" MY DEAR SON, —May the God of your fathers bless you ! Seek the Lord and you shall live. Were you and mother here, both of you in the same spirit, how much it would add to my joy ! Read the Bible, talk of Jesus, pray, and never rest without religion. Death and judgment are always near."

Conference was progressing pleasantly. " A much better spirit prevails in the conference," he says, "than I expected. Many, very many are hungering after righteousness. It is one of the best conferences as to order. I have not had occasion to say a word on the subject for four days. This shows that there is a spirit of devotion abroad. How often we are disappointed." Disappointed he was indeed! In a former chapter we have seen how much he apprehended of perplexity and trial from the border disturbances, crying out, "O for help here! I dread this conference more than I did Baltimore." But though God had smoothed his way and lifted him above his anticipated trouble in a marvelous manner in both conferences, yet was he not wholly without anxiety. He writes :

" WILMINGTON, *April* 5.—Conference was harmonious to-day. Business progressed rapidly. I had strength and comfort. A long communication has come from the citizens of Accomac County, Virginia. They would warn us from sending preachers to that region. But we must send them. The Methodists want them, and we are not at liberty to deny our people pastors. This interference of the citizens with the Church affairs of their pious neighbors is extraordinary. I have known nothing like it in America. Where is our boasted liberty of conscience? That question, in connection with the times, awakes my fears. '*O tempora!*'

"PHILADELPHIA, *April* 8.—Conference closed at nine o'clock last evening. A short address. Solemn close. The Lord has been gracious to me. I am much fatigued, but hope to escape sickness."

Immediately he repairs to Tarrytown to the bedside of his sick son.

"TARRYTOWN, *April* 9.—Preached here at eleven o'clock, having left Philadelphia yesterday afternoon, and reached New York at ten o'clock. Find Mrs. Hamline improved in health. Leonidas very feeble, but getting better. Thanks be to God for all his mercies! Praise his holy name!

"*April* 10.—Made up the minutes for the Book Room. Had a laborious day; little time for meditation. In the evening Mr. Lyon returned with our excellent friend Mrs. Palmer. The Lord gives us great privileges. How wonderful his gifts and blessings!

"*Sunday*, 11.—Heard Mr. C. in the morning; felt well, but faint in body. Did not think I *could* preach in the afternoon; but at three o'clock *tried*, more because I *desired* to preach than from any special sense of duty. It was a comfortable exercise, in which I took pleasure, and if any change an increase of strength."

Chapter XVI.

VISITING CONFERENCES—EVANGELICAL WORK.

AT the bishops' meeting in March 3, 1847, the subject of providing a president for the Liberia Annual Conference was up; the present superintendent, Rev. J. B. Benham, having given notice of his purpose to return to the United States on account of ill health. As the conference would be thus left without a president at its next session it became imperative that one should be sent. None of the bishops were in condition to go. Bishop Hamline did not announce openly his willingness to go, but with prudent reserve enters upon his diary:

"*March* 5, 1847.—The subject of visiting Liberia Conference was up. All against going. Got a resolution passed not to object. Lord, shall I go? Teach me."

Under date of April 11th, 1847, we find this in Bishop Hamline's diary:

"I am thinking a little of Africa. It seems to me if I die soon it would be agreeable for me to try African soil, and offer same little sacrifice to Christ before I go to meet him face to face. How little I have done and suffered for my Savior! May I find guidance from his hand, and wisdom in regard to this visit to Liberia! I feel somehow drawn that way."

In his perplexity he thus writes in a letter to his venerable and honored friend, Rev. Jacob Young, for advice, dated, Tarrytown, April 14th, 1847:

"I wish to consult you, *confidentially*, on a matter of some importance to me, and possibly to the Church. While the bishops were holding their meeting in Philadelphia a paper reached us from Brother Pitman, secretary, etc., inclosing a letter from Brother Benham, superintendent of the Liberia Missions, urging a visit from one of the bishops to Africa to attend their next conference in January, to ordain the eight men elected to orders there, expressing great surprise that in seven years no bishop has visited their conference, and hinting that the Wesleyans at Sierra Leone, and the Protestant Episcopalians south of them, are urging our colored preachers to join them and receive ordination at their hands. The paper was read, and the secretary asked our counsel what should be done. The bishops passed a resolution that we did not see it to be our duty to visit Liberia, and recommended that the eight elected men be brought over two by two, ordained, and sent back to Africa. Not perfectly assured that this was right, I proposed a resolution, 'That though we could not recommend any one of our number to visit Liberia, yet if either felt it his duty to go, we would not disapprove of it.' This is the most favorable resolution they were willing to pass. Now for the facts:

"1. If the eight men come over, two by two, for ordination, it will cost from twelve hundred dollars to sixteen hundred dollars; our journey there about two hundred and fifty dollars to three hundred dollars.

"2. If one does not go, I fear brethren will find fault with us, and say we are afraid, and missionary funds are lavished on our fears.

"3. The climate is proving more and more fatal to whites. One of our late missionaries (Hoyt) has returned, and the talk is of surrendering up the field wholly to the blacks.

"4. If any one goes, I must, as evidently none else feels it to be his duty. All decline promptly, and discourage me.

"5. If I go, I can only attend conference and come directly back (having ordained the missionaries), and perhaps my brethren would think worse of my going than of my staying here, unless I delay there long enough to visit the several stations and explore the country. Now I want your advice. Dr. Bond and others say I shall die if I go to be there but a week. Now, if ready, it is a pleasant thing to die; but if I throw away my life, I shall not be ready to die. I can not tell whether it would be suicide or not. Write as soon as you can. Ask God for wisdom, and counsel me this once."

April 16th, he records:

"A fast unto the Lord. A precious season, felt drawn toward him. A fresh application of the blood of atonement. Had Africa in view to-day. Suspect I have not a warrant to go there. Had my colleagues encouraged me, or had I any thing that looked like a call to go, how freely would I start! The Missionary Board, I understand, have invited two of the missionaries over to be ordained. If so, my way is scarcely open to go. May be the next General Conference will direct some one of us to go. If so, well."

Thoughts, interviews and councils were had, and the time drew near that a decision must be made. But as yet no clear providential indications appeared. Wednesday, October 6th, he records:

"I think much of going to Africa. Can not give it up. I have written letters which will probably decide me. They say I will die. That I shall, whether I go or stay, at no distant day. Africa needs a visit from one of the Methodist bishops."

In a letter to Mrs. Hamline April 19th, he says: "Brother Jacob Young sends me a *long*, good letter. Says I must *not go* to Liberia."

October 27, 1847, the Board of Managers of the Missionary Society passed a resolution, "That we approve of one of our bishops visiting our missionary stations at Liberia, Africa, should he come to the conclusion that it is his duty to do so, and that we will appropriate funds to defray his expenses." This was done by the Board without any knowledge on their part that either of the bishops had thoughts in this direction. Bishop Hamline had engaged Bishop Janes to present such a resolution, and the matter had been committed to Rev. George Lane, who framed and offered it. It was done to test the senti-

ment of the Board, and none but the above three
had any knowledge of Mr. Hamline's feelings. An
important obstacle was now removed by this favorable disposition of the Board, and Bishop Hamline confidentially communicated with Rev. Dr. Pitman, corresponding secretary, and a few others. A
limited talk was had in a private circle, but no one
was authorized to speak openly. The call was urgent.
About eight preachers in Liberia were eligible to
elder's and deacon's orders, and there was no presiding
elder who could, according to the provisions of the
Discipline, preside at conference, ordain, and make the
appointments, consequently no conference could be
legally held, or ordinations given, or appointments
made. The appointment of a superintendent rested
with Bishop Hamline, and no bishop was, as their
correspondence shows, able to advise as to his going,
or the person to appoint as a superintendent of the
mission. Bishop Waugh asks, October 16th, "What
can be done? I am without knowledge of a suitable
person to take charge of this most interesting, important (and if properly managed), most promising
field of labor. Please give me your knowledge,
opinion, and advice on all the aspects of the case as
they present themselves to you." Bishop Hedding
also writes Bishop Hamline, October 18th : "It may
be that Brother Benham [the present superintendent
of the mission] will not come to this country, or, if
he come, he may go back before the conference
meets, or possibly you may see cause to send out
another president from this country to meet the conference in January." If all contingencies failed he
named the person he would send. Bishop Janes

considers it "entirely optional with Bishop Hamline to dismiss the present incumbent from the superintendency of the mission, whenever he judges it best to do so." But he has no candidate to recommend in his place. Meanwhile Bishop Hamline opens the secret working of his heart in his diary.

"*November* 15.—Spent this day in writing. Have my mind on Africa. Read some in Cox's Remains. He died like a hero. Nearly alone, in barbarous Africa, in a room where the rains made it look as though 'tubs of water had been poured on the floor,' in unutterable triumph he breathed out his soul to God. Where are the thousands to 'fall' like him before Africa be given up! Lord supply them by thy spirit.

"*Wednesday,* 17.—I am in trouble to find so many men willing to go to China, and so few to Africa. Ought not some of them to look after their motives? A Chinese mission is more genteel, and has in it more of literary honor."

The difficulty of obtaining missionaries for Africa well deserves this admonitory question. Yet heroic men like Coker and Ashmun and Carey and Seys have toiled and fallen there. Fourteen years before Bishop Hamline proposed to go it was the "dying grief" of Cox, first missionary there from the Methodist Episcopal Church, that help was so tardy in coming. The example of Miss Sophronia Farrington, the first female missionary the Methodist Episcopal Church ever sent into a foreign field, is worthy the best ages of the martyrs, and that of young Dr. Wesley A. Johnson must be ranked in the same class. He served as assistant to the governor, Rev. J. J. Matthias, and saved his life. After six years of great activity and usefulness, having laid upon the altar of God talents and education of the first order, he returned in 1844 to die. A proposition to go to Liberia was indeed like leading a "forlorn hope," but the Church is now entering the African field in every direction. Bishop Hamline continues his diary:

"*Monday, December* 6.—Think much about Africa. Am waiting for news from the Liberian packet. Now think, if it sails by the 1st of January, I shall go, especially if Brother Benham, the superintendent, returns in her. May the infinitely wise God direct me!

"*Wednesday, December* 22.—Give up going to Africa. So I am persuaded it is the will of God. The packet can not sail by January 1st, and I dare not start later than that. I had begun to set my heart on going, but now I expect never to see Africa."

This whole matter, which was real to him, and in the eyes of all was a question of life and death, evinces the readiness of his mind to undertake any service for Christ to which he might be called. For nine months the subject had been before his mind with growing convictions and desire. The probabilities, for a time, seemed to turn in favor of his going, and he promptly acquiesced, but when a change in the time of sailing, as first advertised, was made, it became little less than blank suicide to go, and he declined. No act of his life was more unselfish or heroic than this willingness to visit Africa with his state of health.

In his diary for January 1, 1848, we find this entry:

"The last three weeks before December, 1848, were spent at the house of M. Brooks, Esq. It was a rest season, as I supposed, preparatory to visiting Liberia, as I had determined to take the voyage if the packet sailed by January 1st, as she was advertised."

We left Bishop Hamline at Tarrytown, April 11th, with his wife and sick son, now convalescing. From thence he went to New York, to Dr. Palmer's, "a pleasant, profitable place to sojourn." He writes: "In the pure, Christian fellowship of this household let us be richly, richly blest." From New York he came to Philadelphia, April 19th. "We now fly, not travel." Thus he writes to his wife: "At present, who needs our prayers and tears and affectionate counsel more than our dear Leonidas? I feel continually as if I were preparing an answer for the judgment, as to how I have warned and counseled him. The Lord help me to be more faithful to him. I will try to remember him much and often and fervently in prayer."

April 21st we find him at Salem, New Jersey, the seat of the New Jersey Conference, now convened for its annual session. "Conference opened with a short prayer-meeting. Session passed through pleasantly. About one hundred and fifty preachers here. Salem is a pleasant place for its session. Have a retired place to lodge. All right."

The sickness of his son bore heavily upon his heart, and it is a beautiful comment on his fatherly and Christian qualities that in the midst of great cares and the pressure of conference duties he could turn aside to give vent to his feelings in a letter like the following:

"SALEM, *April* 21, 1847.

"MY DEAR SON,—Though pressed with business at conference time, I desire greatly to write you a line this morning before I go to the church. It is so critical a time with you now that I can neither suppress nor conceal my great anxiety on your account. I have been thinking what a happy life mine would be, above what it now is, if at your age I had been acquainted with the Methodists, and from seventeen years old had lived a Christian. It seems to me, were the city of New

York mine in fee simple, I would give it all away in one moment for the privilege of knowing and remembering that my whole life, from seventeen to thirty years old, had been given to Christ. I was at seventeen under deep religious impressions, but my Calvinistic parents could not tell me how to be saved. I became stupid, and then they thought me converted; and for three or four years I thought so too, and studied Greek and Latin, expecting to be a minister in the Congregational Church, and prayed and talked in meetings; and some were convicted and converted under my little talks. But I gradually became convinced that I was not converted, and finally gave it all up, and went to studying law, and took license as a lawyer in 1827 at Lancaster, Ohio.

"But soon after, in 1828, your little sister, Eliza Jane Price, two and a half years old, our little idol, was taken sick and died, and with her your dear mother, and I buried all our earthly hopes and projects. We were then spending the Summer near Buffalo, New York, and in a Methodist family and neighborhood; and among them, while under this bereavement, your parents were converted to God, truly and gloriously. Then I knew that my former state was not religion.

"I began to talk to the people, and they got convicted and converted, and in a year I was licensed to preach without asking for license, and since 1829 have been trying to labor a little in the Lord's vineyard. I was above thirty years old, if I remember, when licensed. Now, if I had been among the Methodists, as you are, at seventeen, I presume I should have commenced preaching at twenty-one or earlier, and here would have been ten years saved; and in them, by God's blessing, thousands of souls might have been saved by my feeble instrumentality. These ten years haunt me often, not to wound my conscience with guilt, but to wound my love and affections with great grief, that I should have used my Savior so cruelly. Oh, I would give a world if I had it that I could blot them out! And then these years were wasted, and my Christian character has not that staidness, and I have not that power to do good that I *should* have had if I had been a Christian from the age of seventeen. I am not half as well qualified for usefulness now on account of my ten years lost.

"My beloved son, will you not let your father's errors warn you? I expect in all eternity to be grieved (or something as

near it as heaven will permit) at those ten years lost. Sometimes I feel almost afraid to go to heaven and see my Savior
on account of them, and the poor, unfaithful service I have
rendered since, on account of habits of mind then formed.

" Now, my beloved son, when I think of your losing ten
years to come (and under Methodist training, too), it fills me
with distress; and I fear, in addition to that, you will lose your
soul. I had not your privileges. I heard nothing of Methodism. When, at thirty years old, I got to know what it was,
it wrought on me. When you get to be thirty Methodism will not be to you, as it was to me, a startling discovery,
suddenly rousing you, and newly opening to you hopes and
ways and prospects that you never before understood. What
was by God's grace salvation to me will have been already
tried in vain on you. That which was a new medium to my
soul will be an old one to you, tried thirty years in vain. O,
my son, now let the remedy be effectual! Come into the
Church with the simple resolve, as Adams said: 'Sink or
swim, stand or fall, live or die, I go for serving God.' I write
in great anxiety, and must now break off and commit you to
God's gracious love and care."

It should be remarked that the duties of his
episcopal office, calling him abroad in extensive traveling and incessant labor, and his precarious health,
demanding the constant presence and care of his
faithful wife, completely broke up his family life,
which increased his solicitude for his son. The latter, now in the course of his education, was thus left
without a home. This fact aggravated his anxie-
ties for both the health and spiritual welfare of
his son, who said "he never had had a home since
he left Zanesville," in 1836. Itinerant preachers and
their families well know what this care and privation
mean.

On conference business he records:

"*Thursday*, 22d.—Business goes on rapidly; slow in the
stationing room.

"*Saturday, 24th.*—A week of toil, but health and comfort. Bishop Janes has helped me, but he leaves this evening. Conference business forward, but in stationing backward. Feel Christ's presence, but O for more!

"*Sunday, 25th.*—A good day. Tried to be faithful. Lord forgive my failures; but thanks to thy name for comforts large and plentiful."

In a letter to his wife he says:

"The close of the P. M. services was followed by a voluntary general class. One old preacher (Father Neill, whom you saw at Burlington) commenced it by springing up and telling his experience with shouts; then Father Vannest followed; then Father Boehm, of Staten Island; and then an old local elder by the name of Jaquett. It was a glorious time. The whole house was on fire; and if the New Jersey preachers don't believe in perfect love, they believe in shouting. I think there is a good and rising spirit in conference. But alas! many of our preachers get *happy* rather than *holy*, and think more about it. I am well."

"*Monday, 26th.*—Hard work to-day. Fear I have exhorted the conference too little. In the midst of hard labor I forget. O blessed Jesus, fill me with the Holy Ghost! Amen.

"SALEM, *Tuesday, 27th.*—At 10 o'clock P. M. closed conference. Much worn down, but well and comfortable. O Lord, help me to be more faithful! Go with thy servants. Comfort them. Some of these preachers have hard work. They will not be crucified. O may the God of the harvest go with them!"

The New York Conference held its session in Allen Street, New York, May 12th. He immediately returns to the city, to Dr. Palmer's, where his wife and sick son were:

"NEW YORK, *Friday, 30th.*—At Dr. Palmer's. Reached here from Philadelphia at 3 o'clock. Found my son very sick. Expected to meet him nearly well, as letters to Salem had so announced. Disappointment. It is our lot, but good for us. 'If ye endure chastening, God dealeth with you as with sons.'

"*May 1st.*—Son no better; very ill. I give him, blessed Jesus, to thee. Save his soul. Had a long interview with P. P. Sandford, Presiding Elder of New York District. I perceive there will be work enough on hand here. Lord, help thy servant, for Christ's sake.

"*Sunday, 2d.*—Preached at half-past 10 o'clock A. M., in Vestry Street, and at 3 P. M. in Second Street Church. Rain and small congregations. Enjoyed the morning; P. M. less. Very weary. Spent the evening at home. L. very sick; suffering much.

"*Monday, 3d.*—General Missionary Committee at 9 A. M. Called out at 12 o'clock to see my son, who was seized with convulsions. Spent the afternoon in the sick chamber. At 2 o'clock he had another dreadful convulsion—thought him dying. This evening little hope. Lord, help! Nature groans in me.

"*Tuesday, 4th.*—Able to go to missionary rooms this morning and afternoon. L. better. Hope for his recovery. Sick to-day. Head much distressed. Nervous system disordered. Lord, I give all to thee—all! Committee finished its business.

Wednesday, 5th.—Spent the day in much relaxation, which I exceedingly needed. Have had toils and watchings. Feel low in spiritual things. L. still better, and a good prospect. I have never asked his recovery, but on condition that it is God's will, and he sees that my son will glorify him.

"*Thursday, 6th.*—Walked about the city. Some relieved of my hard labor. Mind and body may spring up again in liveliness. Refreshing sleep does much for me. My habits are almost too regular in regard to sleep, as they can not be violated.

"*Sunday, 9th.*—This is my last day of fifty years. A half century gone. It sickens me to look back, but it comforts me to gaze at the cross. Sin and salvation, guilt and grace! What couplings! yet they go together. I have enough of each for both penitence and praise. Blessed God! Thou knowest that this weeping, rejoicing heart feels both. Glory be to God!

"*May 10th.*—This day I am fifty years old. One half century have I lived in this world. As to any good my life has done, how vain it all looks. I can not review the past in connection with myself, but I am pained at my very heart. I must fly from all to Christ. Lord, help me to fly! I desire to yield a different service to my Redeemer for any time to come which he permits me to stay below.

"If I may stay and labor ten or five years, and in these could be 'full of faith and of the Holy Ghost,' and exactly faithful to the solemn trust committed to me, may be I should redeem time, of which there is great need.

"Fifty years—one-half century! O how these years are fled! Lord, pardon afresh all their transgressions. Sprinkle me to-day with atoning blood. Create in me a clean heart, O God, and renew a right spirit within me! Help me, for the honor of thy name. 'Teach my hands to war and my fingers to fight' in thy good cause. Hold thou me up, O Lord, that by thy strength I may toil, and by thy wisdom may do good to souls, and be the means of rendering praise to thy holy name in Zion! What little time remains to me on earth may I spend to thine honor and glory, through Jesus Christ our Lord. Amen!

"*Monday, 17th.*—New York Conference has been in progress since last Wednesday. Nearly three hundred preachers in connection with it. Business has so far gone on rapidly, but many difficulties threaten us ahead. This body is too large. If a constitutional restriction had limited our number to one hundred it would have been better for the Church. These large conferences embarrass the business in the conference, and the stationing is at a disadvantage of from ten to twenty per cent.

"*Thursday, 27th.*—Conference closed this day at half-past 9 A. M. Have never seen so much business transacted in one annual conference. The conference sat fourteen days, and most of the time had three sessions per day. . . Mrs. Hamline was taken sick during the conference, and continues quite ill. Between public duties and private griefs I have been unusually burdened. But the Lord has fulfilled his word. 'As thy day so shall thy strength be.' I have endured beyond all my hopes."

The Bishop's private family sufferings were at this time indeed great. The terrible convulsions of his sick son, above mentioned, had so shocked the nerves and prostrated the health of Mrs. Hamline that the consequences threatened were alarming. With his own life held by a slender tenure, he was now walking in the "shadow of death."

Bishop Hamline stayed in the city till the 23d inst., watching his sick family, preaching on Sabbaths, and attending official duties. On that day he left for Hillsdale, New York, Dr. and Mrs. Palmer accompanying him to the boat. Of them he says:

"Such friends I have not found; such a family for Christian order and steady, consistent piety I have never before seen. Whatever may be demurred to the doctrine of Christian perfection, here is an example of it. I have been in this family within one year more than to have stayed in it three full months. I have never yet heard an unadvised, uncharitable, undevout word, or witnessed an improper act. What Wesley says of Fletcher can be safely said of them. Truly they are Christ's, and have 'put on the Lord Jesus.' What Sister Palmer is in her writings, she is in her heart and life.'

His next official call was to the Maine Conference, which met at Saco, July 30th. "Conference," he says, "opened by Bishop Hedding. He is in good health, his mind vigorous as in his prime, and probably he was never more useful to the Church than just at this time. The members of the conference seem as his children, and he is truly a patriarch in the midst of them. How venerable his position and character! May the Lord continue him among us for many years to come." The session passed on pleasantly, perfect harmony and order prevailed, meetings spiritual. "The love-feast Sabbath morning one of the best," says Bishop Hamline, "I ever attended, and probably more than half that spoke professed perfect love. A great interest prevails. I have been received as a friend, brother, and minister." Conference adjourned Wednesday, 7th, and Bishop Hamline returned to Hillsdale. The following Sabbath was spent sixteen miles from Hillsdale, and returning, he preached in Barrington Monday evening. On Tuesday he reached his temporary home, and preached to a "parlor congregation" for the benefit of the aged Brother Foster and his wife, now unable to go to church, and administered the sacrament. "It was a pleasant season," he says, "and I think not unprofitable." A few days' rest and we find him at Binghamton, three hundred miles away, to attend the Oneida Conference, *via* Albany, Cayuga, and Ithaca.

"BINGHAMTON, N. Y., *July* 22.—Left Ithaca at six A. M., and reached here [fifty miles] at 7 P. M. [by stage]. Weary. Learn that conference has gone on pleasantly and rapidly. Bishop Morris and wife well. Am quartered near the Methodist church in a comfortable way.

"*Friday*, 21.—Oneida Conference has about one hundred and sixty members. Much talent. Several visitors here—Drs. Olin, Peck, and Dempster. The latter urges the theological school on the attention and patronage of the conference. Is defeated." The same day he writes to Mrs. Hamline : "I feel greatly refreshed to-day ; visited from on high more than usual. I was enabled to speak a few words at the close of conference. Met a great many brethren who seemed full of comfort, and my own heart had a holy day in communion with them and with my Savior. I am glad that I am here.

"*Sunday*, 25.—Bishop Morris preached at eight A. M., and ordained the deacons. I attempted it at ten, and ordained the elders (ten). Dr. Olin preached at two P. M., stirringly. What a man! His eloquence is all out of the ordinary course, yet he has no eccentricity, only greatness. Could I preach as he does I would almost desire never to stop. He will leave no proper memorial of his greatness. He can write, but then his thoughts lie on the paper like the cinders around the volcano, affording no conception of the scenes of the eruption. He is a holy man. For the second time he informed me that he enjoyed the perfect love of God. This was a good day to my soul.

"*Wednesday*, 28.—Conference asks a division into Oneida and Wyoming Conferences. It has elected eight delegates, who will go for nullifying all the last General Conference action on the subject of separation. The elements are gathering.

"*Thursday*, 29. — Conference adjourned at five P. M. Preachers generally satisfied with appointments. The close of an annual conference is sublimely affecting. O thou God of Israel, go with thy servants and give them victory."

During the interval of nearly four weeks between the sessions of the Oneida and Genesee Conferences he was constantly traveling, preaching, and mingling in families and in social worship with the Churches in Tompkins, Tioga, and Seneca Counties. At Ithaca he was obliged to leave Mrs. Hamline for a while, she having been taken sick, and his appointments having been mostly thrown out in advance. To Mrs. Hamline he writes back from Candor, August 5th:

"Your sweet letter helped me. I have had better times here than ever before. God has wonderfully blessed me. I pray much for you, and feel that God hears me. God bless thee, beloved, and sanctify us wholly, soul, body, and spirit. I will talk to you when I see you about God's wonders to my soul. My temptations seem to vanish like vapor before the sun. O! Christ is precious. Almost all the time my peace is like a river. Farewell, with ever-during love in Christ."

In another letter to the same, August 7th, he says:

"We owe more than ten thousand talents, and have nothing to pay; but to the humble forgiveness is so grateful! Where we really and truly forgive, do we not marvelously pity, and, if it be suitable, even love? When God forgives us, he makes a change in us which renders it fitting for him to love us. How, then, must he love us! This thought, a fresh one, makes my heart gush out in streams of holy gratitude. But there is this to be added: we are forgiven in Christ and through his death, and it seems to me God's thoughts and feelings in regard to Christ and his death run over to and on us and embrace us as part and parcel of the wonder. 'As the Father hath loved me, so have I loved you;' Christ and his redeemed became one to the Father's affections. Glory to God! The Lord restore and bless and keep thee!"

"OWEGO, *Sunday* 8.—Preached twice in the large Methodist church here. Not a very satisfactory day's labor. Quite ill this evening; faint and feeble. My work is well-nigh done.

"ITHACA, *Monday*, 9.—Had a sick night at Owego. Found very kind friends who watched me and assisted me, or it might have been my last night on earth. By the mercy of God was able to ride to this place to-day, and found my dear wife some better."

His route thereafter lay through Trumansburg, Jacksonville, Townsendville, Lodi, Ovid, Penn Yan to Geneva, the place of his next conference. Writing to his old friend, Rev. Jacob Young, August 16th, he says:

"I have this year attended my own conferences, namely, the Baltimore, Philadelphia, New Jersey, and New York, and have also visited the Maine Conference with Bishop Hedding and the Oneida Conference with Bishop Morris. I am now on my way to the Genesee Conference with Bishop Morris. From thence I propose to go with him to Michigan, and then to Ohio. I shall have been absent almost a year, and shall have stayed at home only four weeks in eighteen months, having been laboring in the pulpit and at conferences steadily without any rest all that time except four weeks. After I get around to Ohio I propose to spend some weeks in the winter in reading, praying, and writing, and hope the brethren will not think me indolent if I do so."

"GENEVA, N. Y., *August* 23.—Three years ago I was here also, in poor health. God has preserved me. I hope for a baptism while here. I need it greatly. Come, Savior, to my heart. May it be a profitable season to us.

"*Wednesday*, 25.—Genesee Conference opened at nine A. M., and all the session taken up in miscellaneous business. I feel revived these two days past. Thanks be to God!

"*Thursday*, 26.—I am much revived. I have tried confession, and am blessed. I feel Christ unusually near me. I am blessed! O I am blessed!

"*Friday*, 27.—Conference proceeded rapidly to-day. About one hundred and thirty elders were examined at one sitting, and of only two hours. Great harmony prevails, and so far the session is pleasant. 'The best of all is, God is with us.'

"*Saturday*, 28.—Conference agreed on division, if General Conference please. That is right. Brother E. Bowen, of Oneida Conference, preached, on 'Be ye perfect,' a most excellent sermon. Many rejoiced. Blessed be God!

"*Sunday*, 29.—Preached this day at three o'clock. Trust some good may have been done. Bishop Morris preached at ten A. M. a delightful sermon. Deacons were ordained by me at the close of sermon, and elders by Bishop Morris at three P. M. Our love-feast in the morning was one of the very best. The Lord has been merciful to us to-day. I trust his ministers are rising in zeal and purity. Oh, may the baptism come speedily! Lord, revive us, shine upon us, and we will praise thee.

"*Tuesday*, 31.—Conference progresses rapidly. The spirit is good, delightful; no harsh words or looks of displeasure. Several preachers here are very devout. The missionary anniversary last evening was remarkably interesting. Henry Hickok was informed after the services commenced that he was appointed to China, and, being introduced as the appointee, made a short, excellent address; and, after remarks by Dr. Levings, more than three hundred dollars were contributed. Robert S. Maclay is also appointed for China.

"*Thursday, August* 2.—Conference closed at half past ten A. M. A short session for Genesee. It asks a division by the Genesee River. This is well. The body is too large to do business comfortably."

Bishop Hamline, as he notices in his diary, put up with the writer of this memoir, during conference. Mrs. Hamline was with him. It was one of the most delightful and memorable weeks of our family social life. Great blessings came to us through their means, and great regrets were felt at parting. This is not a place to dwell upon particulars, the blessed fruits of which abide to this day. The reference which the Bishop makes to his Sabbath sermon, and to his influence on the conference, gives no adequate idea of the reality. His administration was indeed sanctified to us, and left a savor which long remained. His sermon on the Sabbath is not yet forgotten. Tears and shouts and feelings too deep for expression by either tears or shouts, responded to the blessed and searching words of his lips. We have never heard it excelled. The plan of his discourse—on "Ye are my witnesses"—is given in his Works, volume 2., "Sketches and Skeletons."

From Geneva Bishop Hamline passed on to Buffalo and Detroit, preaching in both places, and reaching Ypsilanti in time for the conference.

At Detroit he preached morning and evening— "had a good love-feast in the morning." Many gave witness of perfect love. Good Sabbath."

"*Monday* 13.—Looked about Detroit. Find it teeming with Germans. Three mammoth Roman churches, one about eighty by one hundred and eighty feet. Two Methodist Episcopal churches, about forty-two by sixty-five feet. Preached this evening to thirty Germans.

"YPSILANTI, MICH., *September* 15.—Michigan Conference commenced its session to-day. About seventy members present, a goodly company. Conference opened with prayer by several brethren. Some fervor in devotion.

"*Saturday*, 18.—Conference has got along better for a day or two. This is a Northern people. Their house is large, and they sit to prayer, and turn round and gaze at the choir like an exhibition in singing, '*O tempora!*'"

In a letter to Mrs. Hamline, September 18th, he says:

"I have had pleasant communion with Bishop Morris and the brethren. The town is much crowded, will be more to-day. I hope for a good Sabbath to-morrow. Feel determined to *try* to do my duty. Find a few men read sermons here. A brother read one last night (or night before), and it was a Maffitt affair, except taste and elocution, having angels with their 'sunny pinions,' and 'rosy clouds,' and many such like matters all through it. O for men filled with the Holy Ghost to *preach* Christ crucified!"

Sabbath 19th, was a "precious day." He says:

"At two o'clock I tried to preach thirty-five minutes, from Romans xii, 1, and we wound up in a storm. . . After tea poor, sad Dr. T. (my host) scolded about the shouting. He won't say Bishop Hamline intended to make them shout, but he thinks 'Tippett' did, and he is indignant. He says they have not so much of the 'animal' up this way. Bishop Morris hits him on one side, and Pittman gives it to him without mercy. I think we shall get a shout under Pittman's sermon to-night, and may it come in *thunder*."

Bishop Hamline leaves Ypsilanti, Wednesday, 19th, for Detroit, where he preaches the same evening, and is rejoined next day by Bishop Morris. Crossing the lake by night they took canal boat at Toledo for Cincinnati. Spending the Sabbath at Defiance, they reached Cincinnati, September 29th. He says:

"I have now been absent from Cincinnati, since the 16th of November, 1846, more than ten months. This is itinerating largely. I have enjoyed and suffered, have labored and been perplexed. What is before? May I accomplish as an hireling my day, and be received to rest everlasting!

"*Friday, October* 1.—Rest from toil. Home. I need rest. During my absence I have presided in the most difficult conferences. Stationed a large number of preachers, ordained many deacons and elders, sat up at night, felt great perplexities, and preached a great number of sermons. I need rest."

He preached once on Sunday, and says of him-self on Monday, 4th.

" Very busy to-day in little arrangements for winter and its toils. I can not afford to rest long. Why should I ? My Mas-ter calls me to many labors. I must be up and doing. The day of labor will pass away.

" *Tuesday* 5.—Busy, busy. Much news from the [Mexican] war. One or two thousand Americans killed and wounded ! What scenes the battle-field must present ! But a nation is drunken with the triumph of our arms.

" WILMINGTON, IND., *Friday* 8.—Reached here this even-ing on a lumber wagon from the river, riding on the reach and a board, and holding my trunk. Found my friends well.

" AURORA, IND., *Sunday* 10.—Preached and held class in Wilmington at eleven A. M., and preached here in the evening. A good day for these cold times. The class-meeting at Wil-mington exhausted me, there being some seventy present. But I asked help of the leaders and obtained it. It seems as though there were a little movement on the minds of the people here and at Wilmington.

" CINCINNATI, *Tuesday* 12.—Reached here at eleven o'clock last night, and found my dear family, and Brother T.'s fam-ily well. This little trip was on the whole pleasant and prof-itable."

The next day he reaches Columbus, Ohio, "weary and sick, thankful to have reached there at all. The journey required five hours in the cars, and six in the stage. The last were painful, being crowded." He expected to be in Zanesville, but failed.

" *October* 14.—Expected to be in Zanesville to-night, but was too unwell to proceed. Had to lie over one day. Spent it at Mr. M.'s tavern, very still, and resting much in bed. I long to be Christ-like in all circumstances.

" ZANESVILLE, *October* 15.—Reached Mr. Lippitt's at five o'clock. Brothers Dustin, Warnock, and Moorhead called dur-ing the evening, and also Brother Brush. May the Lord bless this place ! Here, just by, my dead lie buried !

" ZANESVILLE, *October* 16.—Was taken unexpectedly ill in

the night with fearful distress (like dying) and faintness indescribable. Sent to town for medicine, and received all the
attentions the family could bestow.

Monday, October 18.—A little relieved. What confusion of
thought sickness makes! I scarcely think at all, or rather I
have ' broken fragments of scattered thought.' I desire to be
ready to die *before* death comes."

Under the same date he writes to Mrs. Hamline:

"I reached Zanesville on Friday without inconvenience,
but was taken with one of my spells during the night, but did
not faint. . . . I love, but I have not served as I ought.
These distressing turns might carry me off. I have to remember that I was truly converted on the 5th of October, 1828, in
Villanova, New York. I was wholly sanctified in New Albany,
Indiana, in March, 1842. I have enjoyed great peace with God,
and commend his blessed religion to all. Should I die, I think
through Jesus's blood I shall rest with the sanctified in glory.
But of this I have no hope but through the blood of the cross.
No hope besides.

> 'To the dear fountain of thy blood,
>   Incarnate God, I fly.'

"*Saturday,* 23.—Have been sick through the week. Have
walked out two or three times into the grove, but was the worse
for it. Have thought I might die here and go into the tomb
close by. Had several visits from dear Christian friends and
enjoyed them. But 'none but Jesus can do helpless sinners
good.'

"*Sunday, October* 24.—This is the second Sabbath I miss
labor. It is of the Lord. I can do but little, and other men
are here who can labor, I sincerely believe, to better profit than
I can. If I go out again, Lord go with me!

"*Monday, October* 25.—Have been able to walk out to-day,
and the tokens are of convalescence. By a careful diet, and
watchful guarding against cold and damp, hope to improve.
God is good, healing our diseases.

"*Sunday, October* 31.—Preached this morning in Putnam
at quarterly meeting. Had not been in the church for fourteen
years. A good and attentive congregation. Not so much plain
Methodism as twenty years ago. Is the fine gold changed? O
Lord, thou knowest!

"XENIA, *Saturday, November* 6.—Reached here at six
A. M., after riding all night and from twelve o'clock yesterday
(noon). Stood it quite as well as I could have hoped. Spent
a pleasant day in rest.

"*Sunday, November* 7.—Preached at eleven A. M. and
seven P. M. A tolerable season. Trust some one may get
good. Lord, arm thy word with power! Let the Spirit descend
and water the seed! Sanctify the people through thy truth;
thy word is truth!

On the 9th of November he returned home to Cincinnati, and "found all well." Two days more and
he is at Wilmington, Indiana, where he hopes to rest
a little. "I need retirement," he says; "an opportunity to read, pray, write, meditate, get nearer to
Christ. Lord, help me, for Christ's sake!" Sunday,
14th, he preached at Wilmington at eleven A. M.,
and again at 3 P. M., to the children. Monday was
spent in writing, and thinking of Africa, of which
we have already made mention. On Sunday, 21st,
he preached at Wilmington in the morning and at
Aurora in the evening. Of the latter he says: "I
think a protracted meeting here would be likely to
be attended with a glorious revival. People talk
about religion in the streets." He was detained here
by a fall which injured his shoulder, but on Friday,
26th, he reached Madison, where he attended two services on Saturday and preached twice on the Sabbath.
On Monday he preached to the children on "the best
robe," and at night attended love-feast, and exhorted.
On Tuesday, 30th, evening, he preached to the Germans. "Took tea at Brother Richey's, and had several
prayers. This praying in company, he says, does not
come so easy and natural as it did three years ago.
I fear I am not so wholly bent on suffering shame for
Christ's sake as I have been. Lord, increase my faith

greatly for Christ's sake." December 2d, he preached at Mt. Auburn, Cincinnati, and on Sabbath preached with "unexpected peace, joy and help. Souls seemed precious." Here he remained five days with sensible profit to his jaded system. Here again, for the sick and infirm, he "preached and administered the Lord's-supper to a dozen persons." In a letter to his friends in New York, he gives the bugle blast of hopeful victory to the Churches. He says:

"A few glorious revivals are breaking out around us. One, under the labors of Brother Sears, is attended with uncommon tokens of God's power to save. Nothing in this region has equaled it for some time. We have a strong hope that God is about to appear in his glory and build up Zion. The congregations are getting larger and more solemn, and it seems as though there was 'a sound in the tops of the mulberry trees.' O how glorious it will be to see sinners flocking to Christ and saints cleansed and filled with the Spirit! The Lord in mercy hasten it!"

An idea of his method of private visitation is thus given:

"*Friday*, 10.—This has been a good day. My heart waxes warm. Called on Sister Strobridge, whose pious husband went to rest two years ago last month. She is a good woman. This evening has been pleasant. Spent it in social conversation and prayer. God was present. Under my dear wife's prayer, felt that God came down in power. O that I had her power with God, and could prevail as I feel she does! Lord, I thank thee for this gift."

On Sunday, 12th, Montgomery, he preached and ordained two preachers, and on Tuesday returned to Cincinnati, where on the Sabbath he preached. "Rather a cold time of it," he says. "The people seemed cold." But he records on Monday, 20th:

"This has been a glorious day. Christ was with me all the day long. Why yesterday was so barren I know not. Had grace for comfort abounded yesterday as to day, it seems to me I could have preached, 'Thy will be done.'

"*Wednesday*, 22.—This evening, in conversation and prayer, with the family and my dear wife, I had some new views of faith, and urging them helped me, if not others. One thing suggested was, that our thoughts and words must flow in the channel of faith, or we resist the Spirit, who would work by faith. We must not think or say, 'I dare not,' but 'Lord, I believe.'

"SALEM, *Saturday*, 25.—Came out to-day with Brother Sears to spend a few days with the people at Salem. Preached at eleven o'clock to a small congregation. A very pleasant hour. Brother Calhoun labored at night.

"*Sunday*, 26.—Preached at eleven. A moderate congregation. Brother Sears at night. We want power. There is great backsliding among us. We want faith, zeal, spiritual life, crucifixion to the world. We want discipline.

"*Monday*, 27.—This morning preached and administered baptism and the Lord's-supper. Very small congregation, but a comfortable time. Christ was precious. This evening Brother Sears preached an excellent sermon to a few, and meeting closed. Better success than Jesus often had."

From Salem he returned to Cincinnati, whence, after two days not idly spent, he left for Lexington, Indiana, to dedicate a church, and closes the record of the year thus:

"LEXINGTON, IND., *Friday*, 31.—Came to-day from Madison much jolted and weary, with aching bones, but faith in Christ. Put up with Judge White. Did not go to meeting to-night. Felt too wayworn to venture out. The year closes. Adieu! How many will not see the close of another. Perhaps myself among them.

'Prepare me, Lord, for thy right hand,
Then come the joyful day.'

"May I go on understanding and remembering, 'This is the victory that overcometh the world, even our faith.'"

CHAPTER XVII.

EVANGELICAL LABORS—SOCIAL RELIGIOUS FIDELITY—
TRIALS ABOUT POPULAR PREACHING—
VIEWS OF MILLENNIUM.

"LEXINGTON, IND., *January* 1, 1848.—The new year has come. Here I am with a new history commencing. I can not but strongly hope it will be the best year of my life. I cry unto thee, my God, and implore great grace for its duties and conflicts. I feel that I have more faith—that faith which is 'of the operation of God,' and stands in the power of God—than ever I had before. I think, unless my heart deceives me, that God has wrought a strong faith in me within three weeks. And as it seems to me that he is the 'author' of it, he will also be the supporter and the finisher of it. Looking back on the past year, what cause have I for humiliation, for penitence, for mourning. But the 'bridegroom' comes to my soul. I rejoice!"

On Sabbath, January 2d, he dedicated the new church at Lexington, and ordained two deacons, "a good, I might say, a glorious day."

"*Tuesday*, 4.—Preached in weakness last evening. To-day my soul mounts. My heart is near to bursting this morning. The fire burns! burns!! What flames of love! How can I contain it? Blessed Jesus, thou knowest how I love thee, how I trust in thee. Much as thou givest me of thyself, I want still more of thee, still

'I thirst for the life-giving God,
The God that on Calvary died!'

Hope whispers, 'I shall have enough of thee, blessed Lord, by and by,' for the 'mansions' are being prepared. Let me honor thee here and then go home. Amen!"

23

His spiritual exercises seemed specially to tend in the direction of strengthening his faith.   He says:

"My peace is like a river. My faith never seemed so strong. I am going to school to Christ, and he is teaching me much about faith which I never learned. Never did the words, 'Lord, I will believe,' exert such an influence on me as now. Jesus, blessed Lord, let me not forget to ascribe this to thee, to thy teaching, and to the power of the Holy Ghost who enables me to *be* taught."

On January 9th, we find him again home at Cincinnati, preaching on Sabbath in Morris Chapel.   He writes:

"What a field is Morris Chapel to those who should feel inclined to build up a Church in holiness! I know none like it, save Christie Chapel, which is nearly of the same spirit, and has about the same number of sanctified souls.

"*Thursday*, 20.—Preached to-night at Wesley Chapel. Had a glorious time, and some twenty mourners were at the altar. Several were converted. God is at work truly."

On Friday, 21st, he came to Xenia, and thence to South Charleston, Ohio, where on the 23d, he preached a dedicatory sermon.

"Tried to preach Christ crucified. Blessed be God! he was not far from me. Here, where twenty years ago life civilized began to be, is a beautiful church edifice forty-four by sixty-two, of brick, with spacious basement, lecture room and class-rooms, and some seven hundred were crowded into it to-day.

"*Tuesday*, 25.—Well does my soul prove this day ' that the word of God is quick and powerful, piercing even to the dividing asunder of soul and spirit.' In reading the first four chapters of the Hebrews, familiar as they were to me, worlds of light seemed to open to my understanding, and scarcely could my being endure the power which visited me, while reading those wonderful revelations of God's mercy. ' Glory to God in the highest, on earth peace, good will toward men.' Amen and amen!"

In a letter to Mrs. Hamline he says:

"A revival has commenced in Charleston. One was converted each evening during my stay, after the dedication. I labored too hard, preaching, exhorting, and talking to the Church and mourners. Came down to-day in a buggy, refreshed by the ride, but worse for wear. I am in perfect health except exhaustion. You need have no concern, for if I am unwell I am on the railroad, and you can soon reach me. I am not sorry you did not come, and think you ought often to let me take my journeys alone, when Providence opens the way by giving you a home so comfortable and so profitable to the soul. You are feeble and should not forget it. I have enjoyed much, very much of the presence of Christ. Peace, peace! I hear that fifty mourners are at the altar in Brother Inskip's charge, Dayton, and a work is breaking out at Lebanon; a revival in Bellbrook, a wonderful time in Springfield."

Bishop Hamline next visits Xenia, where "the revival was glorious," and Yellow Springs, where he received a great and unspeakable baptism, reaching Cincinnati February 1st, "to spend two or three days, and then start again." But, "unexpectedly," he left the next day for Lebanon, where he preached; the day following he rode twenty miles to Bellbrook, and preached, and, returned the ensuing day to Lebanon, and preached in the evening.

He says: "Went to the church with a full heart, and thought to preach with great power. Was disappointed. I find that I do not always preach best for the people when I feel best. I scarcely ever did. I go into the pulpit with more feeling, and preach with less power."

Saturday, January 5th, he rode to Centerville, Ohio. On Sabbath he says: "Felt as though I could not preach. I remembered how poorly I preached on Friday evening. . . . Yet I went into the pulpit under heavy trials, took 'perfect love' for my theme, the clouds vanished, and seldom have I enjoyed a better season in the pulpit. The lesson taught me is, 'never trust to frames, but preach, depending on God for the increase.'" Passing on to Olive Branch, where was "the promise of a glorious revival," he preached twice, and returned to Cincinnati, where he remained about three weeks, preaching and laboring in the meetings and elsewhere, performing the usual duties of his office, and writing. He says:

"Am trying to prepare a sermon for publication, and find it not easy to turn from travel and miscellaneous duties to the pen. Mr. Wesley's great strength (given him of God) is not seen by those who read his works, but lose sight of his circumstances. Amazing man! traveling and often preaching three times a day, lodging in all manner of ways, and mixing with old, young, and children in a very unretired manner, yet writing works that will render him immortal! God gave him to the Church and taught him to fight.

"*Wednesday*, 8.—Am nearly through with my sermon on Rom. x, 10, written for Brother Miller's book, 'Experience of German Preachers.' I pray God's blessing on my feeble efforts. I write with great labor and difficulty, on account of a tendency to paralysis. Have been, by turns, three weeks writing this short sermon. Have had other writing to do."

As illustrating the tenderness of his conscience in the manner of social conversation and intercourse, the following letter is worthy of consideration. At the General Conference of Baltimore, in 1840, Mr. Hamline, then editor, had been, by special request, a guest of the excellent family of A. G. Cole, Esq., for whom he had entertained a sincere regard and spiritual concern. Fearing, upon a later review of his life, that he had failed to do all his duty to them, he thus writes, under date of January 11, 1848:

"A. G. C., Esq. *Dear Sir*,—The close of the year is apt to bring fresh to our memories the occurrences of the foregoing twelve months. Among these are the scenes of my visit to Baltimore, and, with others, my visit and conversations with Mr. C. and his family. And I feel a desire in reviewing that visit to write and make a humble confession. For it strikes me with great force that there was a great lack of both zeal and wisdom in the ordering of my conversation while with you. Yet, while I confess, I fear I shall mend nothing by my short letter; for I am finding my whole life to be a scene of growing blunders in my efforts to do a little good to others and borrow much good from them. But I feel a solicitude for Mr. C. and his family which I can not repress, and, perhaps, ought not to conceal. Permit me to urge on your attention (I would hope and pray without seeming to obtrude) the rapid flight of time, and the amount of labor which remains to be done preparatory to the close of life, on the part of those who have deferred religion and its duties until the vigor of youth and even of manhood begins to yield to the touches of age."

Later he learned that soon after the receipt of this letter Mr. Cole died suddenly after a short illness. In dying he exclaimed, "I never meant to die without religion; I always meant to be a Christian." Bishop Hamline had been faithful to converse with him upon the subject of religion, and Mr. Cole's mind had been much exercised during the visit.

March 22d, he says: "Have finished my sermon on 'confessing and believing.' It is now hard work to write. My pectoral difficulty, whatever it is, is wonderfully aggravated by it."

From March 15th to May 1st, his time was constantly employed in traveling to visit the Churches, preaching almost daily, attending private social meetings, visiting families, conversing with whomsoever he found disposed to be led to Christ, or to clearer knowledge of God, writing to friends abroad, and attending to the necessary functions of his office. Cincinnati was his home, from whence he made ex-

cursions, returning often to attend to necessary official correspondences and other duties, but giving
himself no rest.   He says, in a letter to Rev. Wm.
Reddy, April 1st:

"My connection with foreign missions has kept me more
at home than I anticipated, as it was necessary for me to be
where I might get letters seasonably; yet three-fourths of my
time has been spent in excursions in the vicinity of the city
(Cincinnati), and now and then one hundred and one hundred
and fifty miles out.   I am now moving toward Cincinnati on
such an excursion, expecting to reach the city in two weeks.   I
then propose to prepare for General Conference."

At Rushville, Ohio, he meets the family of his
late venerated friend and senior.   He can not pass
them by and thus speaks:

"Spent the last twenty-four hours with the pious family of
that departed saint, Henry S. Farnandis.   I was his colleague
1832-3 on Granville Circuit.   He taught and helped me.   What
a man!   Christian!   minister!   He loved God with all his
heart.   Three years ago I met him here on his death-bed.
What a dying saint he was!   How full, how holy were his
triumphs!   Oh, may my last end be like his.   His family
walk in his footsteps.   They will honor the memory of the
sainted husband and father, and the Church and the God
whom he served."

At Zanesville he preached twice, but the second
time with much difficulty from "feeble health."
He says:

"My disease, whether of the heart or what, is serious, and
this morning disarmed me of all power.   I feel almost unable
to kneel in closet prayer from suffocation; but I will 'cleave'
and trust, drag myself, when I can not fly, after Christ."

In a letter to a friend, he writes:

"The work of holiness is spreading in the West, and there
have been some notable cases of God's ministers receiving it,
who have been, until recently, opposed to the doctrine, and

'mad' at its advocates. A great revival is spreading through the West in connection with the faithful preaching of this doctrine. The Church is rising, and where every thing was gloomy and unpromising there is now the freshness of opening spring. One presiding elder writes me that more than two thousand backsliders have been reclaimed on his district the last winter. He thinks backsliding had become universal, and went around the district preaching about little else. A wonderful waking up succeeded, and the revival following exceeds almost all I have heard of since that of Pentecost."

Reflecting at one time on his own ministry, he remarked:

"I believe I could preach more 'popularly,' but what would become of my conscience? It was given out once by my friends that I could be eloquent: so aiming, doubtless I could get more hearers; but I should feel a curse and blight upon my soul. Lord, help me to be more willing than I am to be vile before the people. It tries me to think the Methodists should be told, 'Your bishop can't preach much;' but they may need to be humbled as well as I. Lord, help! sanctify! bless!"

Wesley said, concerning the style of his sermons, "My style is from choice, not necessity. I could write floridly, but I dare not; because I seek the honor that cometh of God only. I dare no more write in a *fine style* than wear a fine coat." And in this respect John Wesley has had no truer son in the Methodist family than the subject of this memoir. Still his sermons were models of chasteness, terseness, and beauty, the natural and unlabored product of his culture and mental movements.

As the period of active labors and most vigorous manhood of Bishop Hamline was that in which his published and private communications more frequently recur to the millennium and the second coming of Christ, it seems proper in this place to insert a few paragraphs, which may suffice to suggest his views, and his testimony of faith and love for the Savior's second appearing. His views of the millennium were not wrought into a perfect theory, not dogmatic as to the relative order of prophetic events. He does not appear to have been established in the pre-millenial coming of Christ, though he did not oppose or deny it. The points relating to the millennium, on which his faith took more the form of dogma, were: 1. That it is to be a period when Christ shall reign "really" and "solely" upon the earth, whether in visible presence or spiritually. 2. That it is to be a state of society "bordering on perfection." 3. That great tribulations, causing a falling away of many, especially of nominal and worldly-minded professors, shall precede it. 4. That a great and daring prevalence of wickedness and corruption should prevail as a sign of its near approach; also powerful and marked revivals of pure religion, by which the distinction between the godly and the ungodly shall more openly appear. 5. That the millennium was near at hand.

Writing on Palestine, Syria, and adjacent regions in 1840, he says:

"We judge, as we have already hinted, that this is one of the most inviting fields for Methodist missionaries on the face of the earth. Long before the return of the Jews shall usher in the full gathering of the Gentiles, we trust it will be occupied by good and true men, who will be prepared to fulfill the pleasure of the Lord in reaping his harvest. At present it is testified that the Druzes are accessible to the missionary, who would be welcomed and received with open arms in nearly all the highland villages of Lebanon. The bigoted priests have little influence over them. Excommunication for reading the Bible, or hearing it read, would not deter or terrify them. Though they are exceedingly ignorant, degraded, and deceitful, yet they wait for the gospel, and in them may be fulfilled that saying, 'The last shall be first'—the most diseased and miserable shall be first to seek and find the Physician of souls.

"Not only Palestine, but the Mediterranean regions generally should, at present, attract the observing eye, and anxious meditations of the Church of Christ. The important signs of these times are connected with the Mohammedan delusion. The various expositions of the prophecies harmonize in regard to the approaching overthrow of this mighty and long-continued system of falsehood—a system which, next to that of the synagogue, is the most obstinate heresy on earth, and has extended its curse and blight and woe over a vastly larger portion of mankind. And when these expectations of faith are fulfilled, as they surely will be, the ground should already be occupied. No *interregnum* between the rejection of the delusion and the application of its antidote, Christianity, should be permitted, lest, instead of truth, error come in the place of error.

"We believe, as Methodists (for an honest Methodist can not believe otherwise), that the gospel is held and preached in its purity by our own Church. And we feel a deep solicitude that in every region which prophecy points out as the scene of approaching revolutions for the destruction of error and the conquests of truth the Methodists should be in the van of the armies of Israel—should be the first to assail the intrenchments of the enemy—the first to wrest from him his strongholds, to seize his posts, and take possession of his forsaken territory. And it is most certain that the prophecies, unfolding to us the series of revolutions, whether past or future, which are most intimately connected with the millennium, point us to the Mediterranean. The three anti-Christian spiritual powers—Judaism, Mohammedanism, and Popery, which, aside from paganism, present the strongest barriers to the universal diffusion of the gospel, are principally located on its shores. There, on seven hills, have arisen out of the sea the 'beast' and the false prophet. There, 'Babylon the great' is to fall, and the man of sin is to suffer. Indeed, as far as we can learn, these regions have been, since paradise was formed, the theater of the most important revolutions which Providence has wrought, to forward the designs of love toward man— the scene where paradise was *lost*—regained—and, perhaps, where—by new, and strange, and overwhelming struggles and changes, the kingdom of God is to come in its full power and glory. At this moment the most gigantic power on earth is rousing itself to battle against the disciples of Mohammed, and we have good reason to apprehend that one of the most sanguinary struggles ever witnessed on earth will occur within the next ten years between the proud Autocrat and the Ottoman Porte: 'Then the *waters will be dried* up, and the way of the King of the East will be prepared.' "

In a letter to a friend concerning his work in great revivals in 1842, he says:

" In this region nothing has ever been witnessed like the present revivals of God's work. Whether the millennium or the judgment is coming I know not, nor am anxious; but God has come forth in his power among the people. Great sins rest upon the nation, and I am looking for great wonders and for woes from heaven. But in the midst of all, as a minister of Jesus, I hear nothing but ' Go ye and preach the gospel.' "

At another time he says:

" I do not know that the judgment is near, but I believe that fearful events are just at hand, and we should be prepared for them. But above all, death is near; our days are passing away, and we shall soon be in the grave, in heaven or in hell. O, that the blessed Jesus may prepare us for our final state!"

Learning from a minister in one place "that a fearful declension prevails, that vice is increasing, and is alarming," he writes:

" The millennium is not come yet. A dark night is to precede that glorious day. The prophets do not lie, and we shall yet have interpreted to us: ' I saw three unclean spirits like frogs.' (Rev. xvi, 13.) Lord help thy people to watch! I feel the need of refreshings in my own soul."

" The times are perilous, and omens of events of tremendous import, just at hand, multiply daily. Sin is becoming more bold and flagitious. It cares no longer for concealment, but reveals itself in every form of which it was heretofore ashamed. Religion is still bashful, but her foe is become bold and impudent."

In a letter to his son, 1842, he says:

"Great revivals of religion are going on all over America, and the millennium, I doubt not, is near at hand. Should you live to be old, I think you would see it. But many great and fearful events will transpire before it fully arrives. The wicked will become worse, and the good more pious than ever. Millions of the former will be cut off by earthquakes, plagues, and other fearful dispensations."

Speaking of the great revivals of 1842, he says:

"Is the millennium come? Surely it is not distant. We are in sight of its holy and happy scenes. The light of a new day streaks the heavens, and the Sun of righteousness is about to be more fully unveiled to a dark and perishing world. Come, Lord Jesus—come quickly!"

Again:

"'But after all do you not think that the day of Christ is at hand?' If you mean the day of judgment, it is doubtless at hand. And it has been for eighteen hundred years. It is even nearer now than ever. It may come to-morrow. But to be plain, we do not gather either from prophecy or observation, that it will come for many years. The only marks of its approach which we are authorized to look for are 'the signs of the times.'"

To a friend he writes, January, 1861:

"You ask what of the 'signs of the times!' 'One thing I know,' said the sage '*I know nothing.*' So of *the signs* I know little; but the times themselves are becoming unveiled, and soon the veils will be so lifted up that the *prophetic* will be the *historic*. I never seemed to myself less capable of interpreting the language of symbols than now, for I am as a man approaching a distant city of which he could form some idea as he saw in the distance where the spires of churches and the outlines of its suburbs could be traced with a clear and unconfused vision; but when he came near and entered its busy streets, all distinct views were lost, and his senses half buried in the bustle and noise. I do feel that we are on the precincts of the city—that we are touching the waves of the tumultuous *Sea* of *wrath* which the 'vials of woe' are to fill with God's fiery vengeance.—Mingled with the increasing indignation of

Jehovah, are those pourings out of his spirit, which will increase more and more, and marvelously distinguish the people of God and the *yielding* among sinners from the obstinately impenitent and incorrigibly unbelieving."

The following remarks on Isaiah ii, 1–5, are in agreement with his constant teaching. He says:

"The chapter read in your hearing this evening is a prediction of that joyful state. And what may we gather from the language of the seer? He tells us of that approaching period, that then the earth shall be full of the knowledge of the Lord; and that the influence of this knowledge shall be most beneficent and grateful. It shall transform the earth into a mountain of holiness, in which there shall be nothing to hurt or to destroy. He predicts a state of purity and blessedness so unlike what mortals have beheld that it is scarcely possible for our minds to conceive it. But we should strive to conceive, and derive from it the chief and all-absorbing motive to zeal and diligence in the cause of missions. What is this millennium? I will not say it is a period in which Christ shall visibly and personally reign on the earth. But I will say it is a period in which he will *spiritually* and *solely* reign, maintaining dominion over all human affections. The millennium has, in my opinion, been unwarrantably viewed as a state of very partial improvement. I believe, and I see no reason why we, holding the doctrine of sanctification as we do, should *not* believe, that it is a state bordering on perfection. Look at the language of the chapter before us."

The reader will find Bishop Hamline's views more fully stated in his admirable essays on the millennium, given in Volume II of his Works, pp. 351, 445. It is clear from these that he accepts the view of the spiritual reign of the Church, not dogmatically, but as the more probable. His views are cautionary on points not fully determined in Scripture, and evangelically liberal, but always practical and positive on what is clearly revealed. His sympathies were deeply committed to the hastening of the Lord's coming.

Chapter XVIII.

GENERAL CONFERENCE OF 1848.

THE General Conference of 1848 opened its session in Pittsburg, Pennsylvania, May 1st. To Bishop Hamline, aside from the great and perplexing questions which invested the session with uncommon importance and difficulty, the spiritual associations of the occasion were of special interest. A pleasing incident, a reminiscence of early life, greeted his first appearing. We have already seen that when a youth, on his return from the South, where he had spent a time for his health, he passed a Sabbath at Pittsburg. At that time he was supposed to be converted (though he himself in later years thought otherwise), and through the influence of parents and others contemplated the ministry. We have also seen that on the Sabbath above named he preached in Dr. Herron's (First Presbyterian) church. More than twenty years had passed. Dr. Herron was still living, at the time of the conference, and pastor of the same Church. Upon hearing that Bishop Hamline had arrived he called at his lodgings early before breakfast. While a member of the family went to his room to announce the call, the doctor stood at the foot of the stairs. Bishop Hamline immediately descended, and the venerable doctor received him in his open arms. At once he was engaged to preach for him the ensuing Sabbath.   Bishop Hamline thus speaks of his first Sabbath:

"PITTSBURG, *Monday, May* 1.—Preached yesterday for Dr. Herron. Had a comfortable season. Heard Norval Wilson in the morning. A good discourse. Have had comfort. This morning Bishop Hedding opened General Conference at nine o'clock by reading a chapter, calling on Bishops Waugh and Morris to pray, choosing secretaries, and then briefly addressing conference. It was a pleasant morning, but many are gone. Lord, help thy servants to be true to themselves, the Discipline, the Church, and, above all, to God. Clouds hang over us, but God can disperse them.

"*Wednesday*, 3.—General Conference has now been in session three days. The sessions have been pleasant and devout. Presided for the first time to-day. The Lord did not forsake me, but it is a trial to preside in the conference before so many colleagues. The Lord help us to be united, discreet, and devout in discussing the important questions which must come before us. 'Except the Lord build the house, they labor in vain who build it. Except the Lord keep the city the watchman waketh in vain.'

"*Sunday*, 7.—Preached at half-past ten at Liberty-street. A large congregation and happy time. Thank God for his great goodness! In the evening heard Dr. Dixon. A great sermon, truly great. Its style simple, its thoughts sublime and moving. My soul rejoiced. God, I trust, has sent this messenger to the American Wesleyan Church.

"*Tuesday*, 9.—General Conference proceeds slowly. God has helped me, wonderfully helped me. I desire to make a new covenant with my God. Heard Dr. Dixon preach to the conference at half-past ten, A. M. A sermon long to be remembered. I dwelt on high. Dined with him and the bishops.

"*Sunday*, 14.—Preached this morning at Beaver Street, Alleghany City, on Christ's intercession. A house full of solemn, attentive listeners. It has been a good day to my soul. I am thankful for the privilege of refreshing my spirit in God's own sanctuary. O that with a larger measure of the Spirit I could plead, both with God in prayer and with man in exhortation and 'prevail.' Lord, wilt thou not help me for the honor of thy name? Christ shall have the glory.

"*Saturday*, 20.—A weary week. The business of the conference fatigues me, and differences of opinion on questions of moment disturb me for a day or two, and for a season my communion with God seems restrained. This last is peculiarly distressing. Lord, why hidest thou thy face from me? 'Return, O holy Dove, return.'

"*Sunday*, 21.—O Lord thou hast returned indeed and in truth, and I hasten to record thine unmerited goodness. This morning the Sun of righteousness gradually arose with healing in his beams. My appointment to preach was at St. Andrew's Protestant Episcopal Church (Dr. Preston's). Little did I think to enjoy such a heaven on earth there. O how precious to my soul was the truth I preached! How wonderfully did God sharpen my appetite and cause me to feast on the honey of his word! Now my soul is strengthened, now I am in the green pastures, and bursting fountains and flowing streams of comfort surround me on all hands. 'Bless the Lord, O my soul, and forget not all his benefits.'

"*Sunday*, 28.—Preached this morning at half-past ten for Dr. Reddle, Third Presbyterian Church. The preaching of the cross is sweet indeed, while the heart bears the cross and its adorable victim. The last week has been spent in the land of Beulah, and this morning Christ was in me the hope of glory. O what enjoyments I have had for some days past! Jesus, my adorable Redeemer, how canst thou take so vile a worm to thy heart!

'O for this love let rocks and hills
Their lasting silence break.' "

The four preceding years had witnessed the separation of the South from the North; the erection of a new Methodist Episcopal organization, consisting of fifteen annual conferences in thirteen States, including Texas; great agitation throughout the country, especially along the line of separation; disagreement between the General Conferences of the old and new organizations; disagreement of administration of the Southern bishops with those of the Methodist Episcopal Church; an active litigation respecting the

division of church property; and a most unhappy
controversy, leading to strong party feeling, every-
where disturbing the quiet of our Zion. They were
also, by the presence of the venerable Dr. Lovick
Pierce, fraternal delegate of the Methodist Episcopal
Church, South, called upon to determine whether
they could fraternize with the Southern brethren under existing circumstances. Our bishops had striven
to maintain fraternity with the bishops South, upon
the Plan of Separation, but complained that their
honorable endeavors had not been reciprocated. It
is not relevant to the purpose of this biography to
notice these general points farther than they may
bear upon the official conduct of Bishop Hamline,
and illustrate the infelicity of the times. He took
his share of individual responsibility in episcopal administration over the Churches which were disturbed
and often rent by the unhappy agitations, and also
in counseling and instructing pastors and presiding
elders. He fully bore his part in the councils of the
bishops, where the policy of administration was
settled. In various particulars that policy was shaped
by his own motion and advice. He was repeatedly
solicited by other bishops for advice in special cases.
He sought no prominence, and he shunned no obligations. He had been modest in demeanor, meek
in spirit, but prompt and resolute in action. In the
height of party sympathy and excitement the bishops
had been threatened with complaints at this General
Conference, but they had steadily held the reins of
constitutional administration and stood together in
counsel. As Bishop Hamline, by his office, was
excluded from all participation in the business of con-

ference except that of chairman, in common with his colleagues, we have little to record of him personally in this connection. Yet, as they were individually accountable to General Conference for their administration for the previous four years, and as what they did in joint counsel and agreement they were liable for personally, the action of General Conference on the great points of difference between the North and South, as it touched the administration of the bishops, touched also their individual history. Early in the session these points came up in connection with the ill-fated fortunes of the "Plan of Separation," and the so-called "Property Question." The time had come for final advice and action. By request of several delegates the bishops had prepared a paper, setting forth their judgment as to the proper method of procedure in settling the "Property Question" with the South. The paper was presented to the conference by Dr. Holdich. It assumed that the General Conference had no power to divide the Book Room property, but that as a suit at law had been talked of by the Southern commissioners, should such suit be commenced, "it would change the form of this difficulty, rendering it a mere business transaction, so as to throw it within the constitutional control of General Conference, and enable them to effect a settlement by arbitration under the legal sanction of the court. If such a suit should not be commenced, they then, in such a case, advised that the question be again submitted to the annual conferences to so alter the sixth restrictive rule of the constitution as to empower the General Conference to divide the funds."

The paper betrays Bishop Hamline's mode of

stating points, and was honorable to the Board of
Bishops and the Church.   It did not pass the conference, but the substitute offered by Drs. Curry and
Simpson (the latter now bishop), which finally passed,
was based in all essential points upon that submitted
by the bishops.   The only difference was that the
bishops assumed that it was necessary that a suit at
law be first commenced by the Southern Church, in
order to throw the question, as a mere business
transaction, within the constitutional control of General Conference, while the paper of Drs. Curry and
Simpson assumed this as possibly an unsettled point
in law.   This seemed more cautious and was adopted,
but the result proved that the bishops were right.

As to the "Plan of Separation," the same General
Conference declared that it "was intended to meet
a necessity which it was alleged might arise, and was
given as a peace-offering to secure harmony on our
Southern border;" that it was made dependent on
certain fundamental conditions which had not been
met; and that "it is hereby declared *null and void.*"
Of the Southern organization they say, " In view of the
whole of which [we have stated] we claim and affirm
that the Southern organization was consummated
in direct contravention of the plan proposed to meet
the results of separation, thus reducing it to a nullity
by the violation of its great and fundamental condition."   "And further, from information officially
given by the bishops of the Methodist Episcopal
Church in answer to a call upon them by the General Conference for a statement of facts in the prem-
ises, that in numerous instances the Plan proposed in
the event of a separation has been openly violated

by the Southern Church, and hence that the peace upon the border and elsewhere, which it was designed to promote, has not been secured." They further declare "that it was clearly and necessarily implied that the friendship and fidelity of the parties should be evinced by voluntarily keeping inviolate the principles and ordinances of the Plan, pending the settlement of the important conditions upon which its validity and binding force depended."

The General Conference further declares the act of organizing a Southern Church was by the act and on the sole responsibility of the Southern brethren themselves; that the plan for the adjustment of relations between the Methodist Episcopal Church and her separating members and ministers was in anticipation of a separation, "when such separation should, by their own act and deed, if at all, occur;" that it was "impossible to point to any act of the General Conference of the Methodist Episcopal Church erecting or authorizing said Church, nor has the General Conference, or any individual, or any number of individuals, any right, constitutional or otherwise, to extend official sanction to any act tending directly or indirectly to the dismemberment of the Church."

Of the administration of the bishops, they say: "The bishops of the Methodist Episcopal Church resolved 'as far as their administration was concerned,' to adhere to the Plan strictly, which, for the sake of the magnanimous Christian example it exhibits, and in view of the right of the General Conference alone to assert the facts of the infraction and consequent destruction of the Plan, we are happy to find they have scrupulously done." This was a noble tribute to episcopal fidelity to constitutional law.

As to their characters and administration, the committee on episcopacy reported, and the report was adopted, as follows :

"The committee have carefully inquired into the administration and moral conduct of the bishops for the four past years, and would recommend to the conference the adoption of the following resolution :

"'*Resolved*, That the administration of the bishops is hereby approved, and that their characters pass.'"

The General Conference further declare that, "In the light of four years, history, we are fully convinced that the act [of providing the Plan of Separation] implied a degree of faith in man not justified by the facts, and under all the circumstances of the case it was not adapted to secure its intended results." Yet, they say, "we can not for a moment question the liberality in which it had its origin." Officially, all that could be done was now done, by way of vindicating the Church administration, and defining its present and future relation to the Church South. In declaring the Plan null and void, the way was open to send ministers to and extend jurisdiction over, minorities of societies in slave territory who adhered to the Methodist Episcopal Church, which the General Conference now resolved to do, but which the bishops had hitherto been restricted from doing by the Plan of Separation. However indiscreet may have been individual conduct among subordinate officers or private individuals, the Church administration had contracted no spot upon its garments. The indorsement of the bishops by General Conference was, to them, like entering a quiet harbor after furious storms, and it has passed into permanent history, to the future honor of the Church.

Bishop Capers, of South Carolina, spoke truly in relation to the Plan of Separation when he said, "It was a peace measure, an act of brotherly justice on the part of the majority holding the power of General Conference toward the minority, to guard them against the consequences of certain acts then just performed. . . . It was enacted in a solemn and Christian manner, with much deliberation, prayer and patience, as the best which, in their circumstances, could be done for the relief of the Church in the slave-holding States." And if it could have gone before the Churches and the annual conferences in the same spirit and with the same enlightened and catholic views, in which it was enacted, undisturbed by controversy, the violence of party spirit, and sectional jealousy, the fraternal bonds between North and South might have been preserved, and the questions of property and ecclesiastical jurisdiction settled with better satisfaction on all sides, and less expense, and no loss to the cause of vital religion.

It is not relevant to our purpose to trace the details of these events further. Later than 1848 nothing occurred, relative to the purpose of this biography, which developed any new principle of administration, or brought the subject of this memoir before the Church in any new light. The highest strain and test had been brought to bear on the constitutional government of the Methodist Episcopal Church, and the Church had outridden the storm. Although Bishop Hamline continued, throughout the active years of his episcopacy, to bear his part in the perplexities and responsibilities growing out of the jurisdiction of the Methodist Episcopal Church over societies and conferences in the slave-holding States, it is remarkable that he records so little of his connection therewith; and it is to be regretted as well, on account of the historic and juridical value of such notes and comments as he might have made. But his heart dwelt aloof from strife, and he sought peace.

In a letter of Bishops Waugh and Janes to Bishop Hamline, dated March 12th, 1851, they say: "Peace is more general in the border of the [Baltimore] conference than at the time you were its president in 1847. Still there are ceaseless and strong efforts in different parts of the border to make inroads into our work. The most of the charges, however, are in quiet, and in more or less prosperity."

To return to the Pittsburg General Conference. The business being completed, Bishop Hamline delivered an animated address to the conference, in which he congratulated them on the harmony and good feeling that had characterized the session, nothing remaining now to be done but to go forth and exemplify their religion. "Before another session, in 1852," he said, "several of this body will, in all probability, have departed from the Church below to the Church triumphant. We will meet up yonder! O blessed thought! Our hearts beat higher in prospect of the coming glories." He exhorted them to be faithful, and to seek after that perfect holiness which is the privilege of the Christian, and all important to the success of their ministry. The motion to adjourn was then put and carried. Bishop Hamline the same day makes this entry:

" PITTSBURG, *June* 1.—Conference closed this day at half-past 1, P. M. This is a short session of the General Conference, and it has been most remarkable for its calm good-nature. In four weeks and four days there have not been half a dozen unkind words spoken on the floor. A most delightful influence has been shed forth on the assembly. Its measures are mostly such as I believe God will approve. Many difficult and trying questions have been settled by votes remarkably harmonious, where no approach toward harmony was anticipated. The close, in a few words of exhortation, prayer, etc., was a feeling time, and may God's most holy blessing be on his departing servants, the members and the bishops! Here have been aged fathers whom we shall see no more on earth. But, O blessed thought! we shall see them, we trust, in heaven. I praise thee, O my blessed Lord, for thy goodness to me, a poor worm! In an especial manner thou hast blessed me. My soul has been visited and made strong. I go now in thy strength.

> ' Myself, my residue of days,
> I consecrate to thee.' "

CHAPTER XIX.

[June 1 to December, 1848.]

ADDRESS ON MESMERISM—CONFERENCE VISITA-TIONS—EVANGELIZING.

AFTER the adjournment of General Conference of 1848, Bishop Hamline spent a few days in Pittsburg, when he passed on to Cumberland, Md., arriving there Monday, June 8th, greatly fatigued. Here he officiated in laying the corner-stone of a church, On Saturday, 10th, he reached New York, "perfectly exhausted." Monday following, feeling "wonderfully refreshed," he departs for Troy, New York, where in the evening he finds himself "at Brother Hillman's with Dr. (now Bishop) J. T. Peck and wife." His severe travel and labor, so soon after General Conference, bore upon him heavily. He says: "I am not so strong as when General Conference commenced. I can not preach much till I improve." On Wednesday, 14th, the Troy Conference opened its session in the city of Troy. Of the first day he says: "Had a delightful session this morning. The Lord was present. Three prayers at opening. Felt well, very well, this noon. God was pleased to meet and bless me greatly in the conference room. It does seem very wonderful how he blesses me in conference." Two days after he writes to Mrs. Hamline :

"My health is perfectly restored. I never felt better in my life than for two days past. My health came back to me suddenly, and as by a charm. All my unpleasant symptoms left me in an hour. Now, at 10 o'clock (night), having just dismissed my presiding elders, I feel almost as fresh as morning. Your letter greatly encourages me. Brother Peck can not come. This conference is three times as needy as Pittsburg. Some twenty of their active men will fail in health, character, and by location this year. I never saw a conference so stripped. What to do for them I know not. In some districts nearly one-third of the appointments seem unsupplied."

Unusual care pressed him at this conference. He anticipated "half a dozen trials." One, a leading and popular preacher and presiding elder, was "arrested for preaching Zinzendorfism." It was thought a majority of the conference would sustain him. "Thus," he says, "what other conferences condemn as heresy, this conference is likely to approve." A sermon of the accused was read before the conference. "He is fully heretical." "But," he says, "the case was finished by the accused coming forward and presenting a paper, stating that as his preaching the doctrine produced excitement, he would cease to inculcate it either in public or in private. The conference accepted the paper and dropped the trial. I called on the brethren to kneel and give thanks to God, and we had a good time."

The session lasted twelve days. Two members were expelled. On Monday, June 19th, he writes:

"Yesterday preached at 10.30 A. M. in State Street Church, from Hebrews ii, 16. A solemn season. Crowded, serious congregation. Trust good may appear to have been done in the *great day*. Heard three good sermons at 3, 6 and 8. Not a lively day, but peace was mine. This conference is, I fear, infected with error. One brother of age and influence is arrested! O Lord have mercy. ' Look down and behold and visit.' I want more *spiritual life*. I want more *of Christ.* I want more power from on high. Lord, be pleased to enlarge me. I breathe after thee. Awake to my help. ' My soul thirsteth for God—*for the living God.*' "

A little later he writes to Mrs. Hamline:

"Here I am, with no hope of getting through until Monday. But we ought to be very cheerful and not indulge one thought of regret, since my health is perfectly good, and, saving one or two days, in which I felt much fatigued, I am as fresh as rest could make me. I never passed through a conference so calmly before. Last night I was weary from sitting, and from being at the missionary meeting the night before until eleven o'clock. But I dismissed my presiding elders last night at eight, lay down and slept until four without waking, and am as fresh as morning now; never felt better. My stationing is done except one little review, and all the business accomplished but three trials.

"I have had a delightful morning. The death of Christ for me and mine, and a dying world, never more deeply affected me than now. When I awoke this morning the thought came rushing in upon me, ' Jesus died for me, my wife, my child, my friends, my foes ;' and the truth seemed so amazing that I thought, Can this be so? Am I not in a dream? Christ—God in flesh—*die* for me! I roused myself to see if I was awake. I then said to myself, ' I can never think of any thing again in time or eternity but this one thing; Jesus—God in flesh—died for me and for mortals.' O what a truth is that! It burns into my very soul. ' None but Jesus will I know, and Jesus crucified.' "

The case of Rev. Ezra Sprague was not a little perplexing. He was arraigned for the practice of mesmerism. The novelty of the case left the conference without a precedent by which to guide its action, and occasioned a diversity of opinion as to the criminality of the offense. The defense set up was that the conference did not know what mesmerism is, and, therefore, were incompetent to render judgment. The fallacy was likely to prove successful, and Bishop

Hamline was waited on privately and requested to charge the conference before the vote was taken. This he declined to do, but the brethren proposed to move the conference to request it, which afterward they did unanimously by a rising vote. The Bishop says:

"I retired to my chamber and hastily sketched the leading thoughts I should wish to utter, if I spoke at all, and followed the sketch from memory as nearly as I could. Soon after the final adjournment I endeavored to correct the sketch, inserting as I then could, the extempore explanations and amplifications of the address. I wrote the notes beforehand as I did, so that, if possible, I might avoid what would injure the interests of both the accused and the Church. I afterward endeavored to conform it to that, because the case was appealed, and because a letter from Brother Sprague convinced me he had misunderstood, or soon forgotten, the tenor of my remarks.

"The 'precedent' referred to in the first paragraph of the address, occurred in 1847, in a conference where I assisted Bishop Hedding to preside. As we sat in the altar, the conference seemed disposed to vote some slight censure on a brother who had been found guilty of 'unchristian conduct.' Bishop Hedding, who was in the chair, spoke to me nearly in these words: 'That will not do. *They have found him guilty of unchristian conduct, and now merely censure him. Do you think it will do for me to speak at this point?*' I answered, 'It may be hazardous, and besides the motion may not carry.' Perceiving soon that the motion was likely to prevail, he said, '*They will do wrong, and I must speak*'—which he did in a few words— and the motion was immediately changed to some comparatively severe penalty, I think suspension."

With this precedent to authorize, and the unanimous request of conference to incite, Bishop Hamline made the following address to the conference:

"The conference has invited to a difficult task which the chair is poorly prepared to fulfill. But as there is at least one precedent, it may not be reasonable for me to decline all remark.

"Your first duty will be to decide by vote, whether any of these specifications are sustained. This requires a careful consideration of the positive and rebutting testimony bearing on each allegation. Your chief effort should be to *recollect* this testimony and apply it discreetly in determining whether or not these allegations are true.

"Several of the specifications are of an ordinary character, such as conference experience must have made you familiar with. The first three are of this character. They are plain, and nothing has intervened, in the progress of the investigation to render them obscure or perplexed. They may, therefore, be passed without special notice.

"But one specification—that which refers to mesmerism—is somewhat novel, and moreover has become involved by the course of argument. A point of considerable interest and difficulty has been raised, and pressed with admirable skill on the conference. It claims, therefore, deliberate consideration. I refer to the position taken by the defense, which I understand to be in substance (not in words) as follows: 'If you sustain this specification, you can not make it support the charge of immorality, for how can you say the practice of mesmerism is *immoral* unless you *know what mesmerism is ?*' This you will perceive is an abstract question, and may be properly noticed by the chair.

"The conference, I presume, *does not* know, and *can not* know what mesmerism *is*, but it may know, from the testimony, what it *claims* to be—or rather what it claims to *do ;* and it is a question of vital importance whether its *claims* do not impart to it a moral character. May not its pretensions alone without regard to its nature, enable you to determine its moral merit or demerit ? Is not the following the true doctrine ? 'You must first know what mesmerism *claims* to be or to *achieve* before you can pronounce the practice of it immoral.' This may sound like the proposition presented in the argument, but they widely differ. One refers to the *nature*, the other to the *claims* of mesmerism.

"As to its nature, it may be nothing but a name or fancy, as many affirm. Or it may be a simple mode of inducing sound sleep, and sometimes, that peculiar sleep called somnambulism, in which view it may be innocent, because such sleep infers no more than belongs to human powers or susceptibilities. But if mesmerism be more than this—say, a newly developed force, or power, which on Christian principles must be accounted superhuman—if it be a science whose manipulations, states, and resolved volitions both mysteriously control and empower the mesmerized to a degree transcending mere human experience, if not the experience of angels, can we hope to understand its nature? Who can explain it. To say it is composed of electric fluid, or 'magnetic currents,' explains nothing and proves nothing. I suppose the conference knows just as much about the nature of mesmerism as the professional mesmerizer—as much as the accused himself knows.

"But if you can not know what it *is*, there is evidence before you as to what it *claims*. That evidence shows that it claims to be a powerful agent, operating the most astonishing results. Are these professed results (as wrought, not by divine inspiration, but by mesmerism), in harmony with the claims of Christianity? The name mesmerism, or 'animal magnetism,' is of no moment. If its feats were denominated 'witchcraft,' 'conjuring,' they would be neither more nor less reprehensible. And if they were called 'witchcraft' would they pass for sound morality? Would it be said you must know what witchcraft *is*, or you can not pronounce it immoral? Perhaps the Jews knew not its nature, though they punished it, and punished it because like ancient magic and sorcery, it professed to work wonders, and profanely imitated miracles, so that the people exclaimed, these are the 'great power of God.' But witchcraft, severely as it was punished, was no more blameworthy than mesmerism; if it made no higher pretensions and assumed to work no higher wonders, on what principle could it be more blameworthy? Mesmerism is not divine inspiration, and if it is said to be 'above the angels' surely its claims are as lofty as those of witchcraft, and as much in rivalry with the miracles wrought by prophets, by apostles, and by the Son of God. And if so, then to vindicate and practice it is to war against Christianity, which Theism may approve, but Christianity must condemn. For what is its tendency but to reduce the prophetic, apostolic, and even Messianic functions to a level with mesmerism?

"But there are functions superior to the prophetic and apostolic, and properly divine. And you will of course inquire if these are trenched upon by the claims of mesmerism. Among the divine functions referred to is that which endows men with supernatural gifts. To *be* a prophet implies no power equal to that which *inspires* a prophet. Does the evidence before you prove that mesmerism goes the length of claiming this last—this incommunicable prerogative of God-head—that it claims to manipulate men into seers, and those generally irreligious men? It is for you to decide whether the parol and written evidence under this specification shows that mesmerism, as vindicated by the accused, claims not only to *be* a prophet, but also to *make* prophets by imparting to others superhuman power—for instance, the power of vision called 'clairvoyance,' which like Jesus discerns 'what is in man,' or like omniscience searches the bowels of the earth, sees hell and heaven naked and open, and reports from inspection who of our friends are in this or in that world. Should you find the accused vindicates mesmerism in these its loftiest claims, and professes practically to achieve, or empower others to achieve these—miracles I will call them—you will then say, in voting on the charge whether this demerits reprehension. You will decide whether claims which, if universally accredited, would put an end to Christianity on earth by destroying all convincing proofs of its divinity, and thus rendering it the theme of just ridicule, may be advocated even by the ministers of Christ without any violation of sound Christian morals.

"In conclusion, if you sustain the specification, you are not bound by technical rules to abide by this charge. You can substitute another caption. This charge expresses the opinion of the prosecutor, and to change it will be no injurious surprise to the accused, because the moral character of his acts when proved, can not be determined by testimony which he would need warning and time to produce, but must be decided on Scriptural grounds, after fair discussion. The specifications warn the accused what testimony he will need. Not so with the general charge, which even at this late hour you can adjust to the specifications. May Infinite wisdom enlighten you, and guide you to just decisions."

It is hardly necessary to say that when the case went to conference for final decision the brother was expelled. He appealed to General Conference of 1852, and they confirmed the decision of the Troy

Conference by a vote of one hundred and ten to thirty-seven.

The Troy Conference lasted twelve days, and on Monday, 26th, he thus records:

"Conference just closed sweetly. Brethren think they never had so good a conference, though it was the hardest they ever had. I am sure the Lord has been with them. O bless his name forever."

Bishop Hamline left Troy the same day the conference closed, for New York, thence, *via* Pittsburg to Wheeling, Virginia, where he arrived July 1st, to attend the Pittsburg Conference. He records:

"WHEELING, VA., *July* 1.—Reached my home for the conference this morning, (Sister List's.) Was brought safely on my way from New York, and reached Pittsburg on Thursday evening, and found all well. Left Pittsburg Friday evening, and, after a restless night, reached here at six o'clock this morning. Lord, help me to seek thee here, and have fresh blessings sealed on my heart. Refresh me from thy presence. I can not, O Lord, do thy work but in thy strength and wisdom. Grant me these at this conference for Christ's sake. Amen."

His labors here, as usual, were abundant and greatly blessed to the ministers and people. On Wednesday, 12th, he records:

"Conference has closed, having done up an immense amount of business in seven working days. It was a peaceful, good session. God was with us. O may it be the beginning of better days for Pittsburg! They need better days. Secret societies do injury among them."

His next engagement was at the Erie Conference, Ashtabula, Ohio, July 26th, 1848. On his way he preached four times, dedicating one church and reached his destination Saturday, 22d. On the following day he listened to "a good hortatory discourse. Fear," he says, "the dull (choir) singing helped me to be dull. O that Methodists would be Methodists! Tried to preach at 3, P. M. A large and attentive audience. Same dull choir singing. Had a little more life than in the morning, yet short, O how short! of what I ought to have."

Conference opened the 26th, but he records nothing before the Sabbath:

"*Sunday*, 30.—Love-feast in the morning in the Methodist Episcopal Church, and six deacons ordained; the seventh objected to, as teaching that the Bible sanctions slavery. At half-past ten A. M. preached in the Presbyterian church to a crowded house and a multitude outside, and ordained six elders.

"God was pleased to bless me to-day and make the word sweet to me, and I trust some of the serious congregation were edified. O Lord, revive thy work! Let thy ministers feel thy power, and be the channels of thy power to a cold-hearted Church and a perishing race of sinners. Praised be God that Christ is mine; is made unto me 'wisdom, righteousness, sanctification, and redemption!' 'I the chief of sinners am, but Jesus died for me.'

"*Tuesday, August* 1.—Erie Conference closed this morning at half-past eleven A. M. It has been a good conference. God has given us peace, brotherly love, and a good measure of his blessed presence, which led us to exclaim, 'The best of all is, God is with us!' Five days and a half to a conference. Religion helps on our work."

From Ashtabula he journeyed to Mansfield, Ohio, the seat of the North Ohio Conference, preaching along the way and laboring privately, in which he was heartily joined by his faithful wife and fellow helper.

"MANSFIELD, *Sunday*, 13.—This Sabbath has been a most precious day to my soul. In the morning I preached with a feeble intellect, and was greatly surprised and somewhat embarrassed to find so little power and freedom of thought, while my heart was so uplifted and comforted. Praised be God for the comfort! and as to my want of power to preach, two good results may follow: 1. It may be that I shall be convinced more than ever that low and high states of joy do not necessarily control my power to proclaim the Gospel, but God's good pleasure and blessed will. 2. I am humbled, and that is important. Many not of our Church were present. The ex-governor sat just before me. I doubt not but he and many others thought that the General Conference acted wildly when it chose me for the oversight of the Church. This humiliation, however (and I was conscious of it), did not disturb my joy in Christ. The fire of his love burned in on my soul, and I was happy still. This assured me of a great conquest over nature. Grace does reign. O God, I praise thee!

"*Monday*, 21.—Conference has progressed rapidly to this time, but Freemasonry and Odd-fellowship have arrested it. Oh, how can brethren allow the peace of the Church to be thus violated! The Lord will judge in these matters! Preached in the morning on Christian fellowship. Some, I trust, may have been blessed. Ordained sixteen deacons and seven elders. The love-feast was excellent. The Lord yet blesses me, and my peace is as a river. O Lord, I will praise thee!

"*Wednesday*, 23.—Conference closed at twelve M. Have enjoyed and suffered much during its session. Masonry and Old-fellowship, a bane in the midst of us, have done us much evil here. Oh, may Methodist ministers be men of one work!"

The days intervening till his next conference were spent in sickness, with much physical suffering and mental trials. As the time for his next official duties drew near the burden of his soul increased:

"I cry unto thee, my God, my Rock! 'Hear me, O Lord for my spirit faileth.' Strengthen me for Christ's sake. Amen!

"INDIANAPOLIS, *September* 1.—Had no great comfort to-day. Lord bless me for conference duties. Oh, how shall I appear before the conference unless thou bless me! Come, Holy Spirit, and diffuse thy quickening grace through all my wounded nature.

"GREENCASTLE, IND., *Sunday*, 3.—O my God and Savior, thou hast met me again in mercy, in unfathomable mercy! My soul, but not my lips, shouts inwardly to thy praise. Thou hast helped me this day. Glory be to thy name forever! What a change hast thou made in me by my spirit! 'Thou hast changed for me my mourning into rejoicing.' Thou hast made me full of joy with thy countenance. Glory be to the Father, and to the Son, and to the Holy Ghost!"

The Indiana Conference convened at Greencastle, Ind., September 5th. On that day he records:

"Conference commenced to-day, and proceeded piously and rapidly with its business. Had comfort in its morning devotions. This is a body of young, talented, and pious ministers. The Lord grant us a pious session for Christ's sake!"

To Mrs. Hamline he writes:

"*September* 4.—Yesterday was a pleasant day without and especially within. The Lord made my heart the 'burning bush' and dwelt within me. I am in perfect health. Have a most delightful place near the church. Pray for me and the conference.

"*Monday morning*, 11.—Had a good Sabbath. A love-feast and sacrament in the morning, and twelve deacons ordained. A good season in preaching.' On the whole a precious Sabbath. Thanks be unto God for his great goodness toward me.

" INDIANAPOLIS, *Monday evening*, 11.—Closed the conference at half-past three P. M., and rode in an open buggy forty miles, reaching here at a late hour. I am not so exhausted by all the labor and riding but that I can bless my God for his goodness. This is the shortest session I have seen for the amount of business. A discussion, too, on college matters of one whole session. A good conference withal, and spiritual. Thanks be to God for all his goodness! O Lord, help, and I will praise thee."

From Indianapolis Bishop Hamline passed on to Lawrenceburg, and thence to Newark, Ohio, preaching as opportunity opened, and resting. The Ohio Conference held its session at Newark, September 27th. October 1st he records:

"Our conference has progressed pleasantly. A good spirit prevails. God has done much for us. This day has been unutterably glorious to my own soul, and, I trust, to the souls of the preachers. O blessed Savior, what hast thou wrought!"

At the close of the conference he says:

"An interesting, religious session. The Lord helped me, and I desire to record his goodness. Never have I been more consciously blessed than in conducting the business of this conference. O Lord, I will praise thee."

After the Ohio Conference Bishop Hamline returned to Cincinnati *via* Zanesville, Rushville (to visit the afflicted family of his old friend, Rev. H. S. Farnandis), Aurora, Wilmington, working with his accustomed diligence.

"CINCINNATI, *October* 20.—Have had a meeting with Bishop Morris, who returned in safety from his long North-west tour. Thus we have finished our work in the conferences in great peace."

The third day following he left for Xenia, Ohio, where he says:

"Here I think to rest, except on Sabbaths, for five weeks to come. I need rest. Since the General Conference I have been unremittingly employed. To relax will be all important. Sometimes it seemed to me I must fail in my summer work; but God helped me, and I have, by his aid and mercy, got through. O Lord, I will praise thee."

But his time was still employed on the Sabbath preaching, and on other days writing letters to friends, especially to the afflicted and on official business, and laboring privately for the salvation of souls. His active soul could not be at rest. His Sabbaths were generally spent abroad, his week-days at Xenia. During these days he made a visit to Cincinnati (December 11th to 14th) where he became the honored instrument of the conversion of a young lawyer, Mr. John M. Leavitt, now Rev. Dr. Leavitt, President of the Lehigh University, Pennsylvania. Mr. Leavitt was an educated man, an eloquent and successful advocate, with a flattering future opening before him. Mrs. Hamline had conversed with his wife, who had become the subject of deep and powerful conviction. On Mr. Leavitt's return from Church one day his wife met him, and proposed to begin a Christian life if he would join her. He asked twenty minutes to consider and reply, and meanwhile sought an interview with Bishop Hamline, who asked him, "Do you believe in the depravity of the heart?" "I never doubted it," was the reply. "Do you feel that you are accountable to God?" He answered, "I never thought upon the subject." After suitable instructions the Bishop prayed with him. The result was he decided to be a Christian. In the evening he called for a second interview with the Bishop, and when about to leave he suddenly paused, put his hand to his forehead, and said, "But stop; I had forgotten one thing. To-morrow morning I have a suit, and I expect to win by using sophistry. What can I do?" Bishop Hamline assured him he could not do it and maintain his purpose to give himself to Christ. "I told him," he says, "he must not wound his conscience, cost what it might." They parted. The Bishop spent that night in prayer; the lawyer also prayed. Nothing more was said. Next morning came the final test. "This morning I trembled for him," says Bishop Hamline. But Mr. Leavitt was decided. He saw his associate in business, committed the cause to him, and turned from the court to his office, locked himself in and gave the morning to prayer. Before the hour of noon the Lord spoke the word of pardon and peace. He was "powerfully saved," and returned to his house "justified." The day following his wife also was converted. The human agency of his great change, Dr. Leavitt says, in a letter to the writer of this memoir, "was wholly that of Bishop Hamline." Thenceforward their spiritual relations and feelings toward each other were those of father and son, as the facts in the case and their future correspondence beautifully show. The event of the conversion of these two persons is thus noticed by Bishop Hamline:

"*Tuesday, December* 12.—This afternoon Mrs. Leavitt, the daughter of Mr. Brooks, experienced religion, or was reclaimed, as the case may be. At four o'clock both of the young converts gave me their names for probation, and I administered to them the sacrament of the Lord's-supper at the death-bed of their happy sister, Mrs. Sears. O what a season! God was there! Such triumphs as this dying saint exhibits are enough to inspire louder songs in heaven. And her raptures at the sight of these new-born souls were inexpressible. These two or three days of wonders my soul can not forget. Praise God forever, even forever and ever. Amen.

"*Thursday,* 14.—This morning left Mr. Brooks, and am ready to start to Marietta. Mrs. Sears [daughter of Mr. Brooks] still alive and full of holy triumph. Mr. and Mrs. Leavitt pressing on their way. What a change! Scarcely have I seen its equal. He says he can never practice law. May the Spirit *guide* him."

And the Spirit did guide him. He renounced the profession of law, gave himself to the ministry, and the year following—1849—was received into the Ohio Conference.

In a letter to his son, dated Cincinnati, January 28, 1850, Bishop Hamline, after referring to great revivals in that region, says:

"Mr. Leavitt, the young lawyer and his wife, are devoting themselves with a wonderful zeal in this good cause. They go out to protracted meetings on his circuit near the city, and after preaching labor together at the altar with great success. Her zeal is equal to his. His seems equal to Wesley's."

Dr. Leavitt has always maintained a high rank in character and usefulness in the spiritual Church of God. We resume the diary:

"POINT HARMER, 16.—Preached here at two this morning. Found Jacob Young absent. His family well. Here are the friends who helped me to Christ. Mother Kent, eighty-two years old, is still in her senses, and understanding clear. O Lord, I praise thee for this privilege.

"*Sunday*, 17.—Preached at half-past ten in Marietta, at two P. M.; visited and addressed the Sabbath-school, and preached at half-past six P. M., at Point Harmer. A precious day to my own soul, but fear no mighty works were done among the people. O my God, help me to be meek, patient, and humble. Thou knowest all my trials. In all these matters, O my God, I cast myself, as well as my work, upon thee, through Jesus Christ.

"ZANESVILLE, 21.—Reached here on Tuesday. Have had much perplexity. I have had a specimen of the morals of Universalism. 'Cursed is the man that trusteth in man.' The Bible is true.

"PITTSBURG, *Monday*, 25.—Reached here on Saturday. Preached on Sabbath at Liberty Street, and to-day dedicated the new Smithfield Church. Brother Kenny preached at three P. M., and Birkett at night.

"*Friday, December* 29.—Preached last evening in basement of Smithfield Street Church. A good time. Hope some good was done. The Lord be praised, who only doeth it."

Bishop Hamline was always tenderly moved toward the aged, the little children, and the afflicted. His heart was the seat of great sympathies by which he strove to draw all to Christ. To his friend, Rev. C. W. Sears, whose wife above mentioned had just departed this life, he writes, December 28th:

"By all means, my brother, see that the rod and the staff of the almighty Comforter be your support, as they have been. Nature can do nothing for you now. Reason—philosophy—can do nothing. The 'Comforter' can do all. The Spirit loves to work where and when nature fails. But you know his efficacy, and all you need is to entertain by faith the heavenly guest. You will, of course, and I perceive do, intend to be comforted. That is right; for such intention harmonizes with the Spirit's aim and office in our hearts. It is co operating with the Comforter. For if he would comfort us, and we volunteer difficulties and hinderances in his way, he will be grieved. He strives to comfort, and we should strive with him to be comforted.

"Blessed be God for such consolations. First the death of the departed is a coronation, which must needs come after such conquests and triumphs as angels may wonder to behold. *Here* is consolation ; yet its influence to console us depends on the work of the divine Comforter himself in our hearts, without which we can not derive from the joy of friends in death the delights and assuagings which triumphant dying ought to afford. All our comfort, therefore, in such sad bereavements, must be from the Holy Spirit."

To another he writes, same date:

"It often falls to our lot to grieve and rejoice at the same event. Yet it seems to me that your case is unusual, in having so deep a grief and joy flow in your heart from one single fountain. Christians must suffer; for through much tribulation we must 'enter into the kingdom of heaven.' But we have two advantages. Our sufferings are relieved and often sweetened by religion, while we feel the pressure of them; and then it is scarcely doubtful that greater tribulations would not overtake us in the sinner's path. If it be hard through much tribulation to enter into the kingdom of heaven, how much harder it must be, through still greater tribulation, to enter into the kingdom of darkness; to crown a life of trouble with an eternal retribution of anguish and despair.

"You and yours are afflicted; but the sorrow must be little in comparison with the joy. You have buried one child; but three or four other children, who were dead, have been raised to life. The deceased child has only been raised from a lower to a higher and perfect life, and with her advancement your other children have been raised up to sit together in the heavenly place vacated by their sainted sister. How wonderful and glorious are all these changes! The advancement and coronation of one whose death you mourn has drawn after it, as a connected sequence, if not in some sense as an effect, the resurrection of the dead in your family circle. Sometimes a profligate child dies in despair, and his brethren sin on. A worldly sinner dies in his purple, and his brethren press on after his fatal example. That is affliction. For a serious parent, to see one child die in despair or blaspheming God, and his brethren pass on unmoved to the same infernal destiny, is indeed heart-rending. But your case is wonderfully different. The dead are gone with halleluiahs to heaven, and the surviving turned by her death-bed jubilations toward heaven."

Chapter XX.

[1849.]

NEW YEAR'S COVENANT--ABUNDANT IN LABORS.

WHEN Bishop Hamline left Xenia, Ohio, of which we have already given notice, he passed on, in moderate stages, to Pennsylvania, intending to spend the winter in that State. At Washington, Penn., he thus begins the new year:

" *January* 1, 1849.—Here I am, commencing another year. Yesterday I tried solemnly to dedicate my life, family, and estate to God more fully than I had ever done. O my God, accept me for Christ's sake! The cholera is abroad fearfully, and in New Orleans is a mighty destroyer. But I would act from love, not from servile fear.

> 'Here Lord I give myself away,
> 'T is all that I can do.' "

Writing to his wife, January 1st, he says:

" Yesterday was a comfortable day, more especially last evening. Crowded houses, and Christ was with us. I have tried to make a new covenant with God, my blessed Savior, for the new year, and feel that I am blessed in my deed."

His first public duty for the ensuing season was at the session of the Providence Conference, April 4th. The three intervening months, the most severe for travel and exposure, he spent in visiting the Churches. Twenty different towns were visited, thirty sermons preached, much private labor bestowed, official and private correspondences to maintain, sickness and infirmity at times baffling his plans, but in all

26

and through all the zeal of the Lord impelling him forward. Much of his travel was by stage, sometimes all night. From Greensburg to M'Connellstown, he says: "Traveled through the night and all the next day, in a coach. Among the company was Dr. M'Calla, a venerable minister of the Presbyterian Church, with whom we took sweet counsel. He wept and we all wept while we talked about Jesus." They reached their destination the evening following, and Bishop Hamline preached "to a moderate assembly, but had comfort in so doing." At Mercersburg he says of the German Reformed Theological Seminary, "Dr. N. at its head has become a great man. Great in a way that any man of considerable art and learning can (by pursuing it) become great. He is great in theological eccentricities. Preached twice on Sabbath, and had some of these people and professors out to hear me. Felt Christ's presence. Spent Monday in visiting, conversing, and praying with several aged members of the Church."

At Carlisle he meets Dr. J. T. Peck (now Bishop Peck), president of the college. Here, he says:

"We had a precious season with the friends of Christ. We stayed more than a week with Dr. Peck, and got both soul and body refreshed, as both were worn down by labor and exertion. I had preached almost every night the previous week, and had a slight touch of my old complaint in consequence, so that I preached only twice while there."

At Lancaster, February 23d, he says:

"LANCASTER, *Friday* 23.—Reached here yesterday at four P. M., and met Brother Urie at the cars. Took lodgings in his very pleasant family, and found a '*pilgrim's rest.*' Am quite unwell. Rested poorly last night, considering how pleasant a room and how downy a bed I had. My system is somehow disordered. My hard labor three weeks ago hurt me. I can do little now but preach on Sabbath. God reigns. I received about forty letters at M., and have them half answered. This hard writing tries me. So do the distresses of some of our sick ministers make me sick. Lord, pity them! Brother Brenton of Fort Wayne, young and strong, is stricken down with paralysis. What shall I do? Well may Bishop Waugh talk of 'stronger nerves.' They who think it a fine thing to be a bishop might discover a more desirable field after trying it awhile. A *circuit* would begin to look lovely after a season. Lord, give us supporting grace!"

To Rev. H. Hickok, missionary to China, he writes:

"Your last letter excited peculiar interest in my mind. It was an encouraging letter. I shall have much more hope of China, if it turns out that the Gospel *must* be '*preached*' to the people. That is what Christ sent his ministers to do, and the promise, 'Lo I am with you,' etc., is not, in my opinion, to be claimed, except by those who go and 'preach.' Literature is an accomplishment much to be desired; but its office is not to convert the world. A tolerable effort has been made already in that mode, without even the shadow of success. If the labors of our missionaries are to flow in such a direction, we shall soon learn the difference between original and derived Methodism—between God's ordinance and human substitutes therefor. And in this I do not intend, for a moment, to set aside literature, or to suggest that any of the converted tribes or nations shall or ought to be without literature. Religion will create letters where they are not, and new create where they are, as in China. But Christianity in its life or being must go before Christianity in its ornaments, or its indirect, but sure fruits."

From Lancaster he passed on to Philadelphia, and thence to New York, preaching and working as he went. At Dr. Palmer's he found, as always, a congenial home, and most salutary medical care with rest. The Sabbaths of the 18th and 25th of February were spent in Newark and Paterson, New

Jersey. At the former place "had a pleasant visit at Dr. Kidder's. An amiable family. Methodism is becoming strong here," he records. At Paterson, where Brothers Monroe and Morrell were stationed, he says:

"Had a moderate time in preaching. A very stormy day. Fear little good was done. My poor health was in my way. The scenery of the Passaic here is exceedingly picturesque, and entertained me more than did the Falls of Niagara. In bad taste, perhaps, but so it was.

"*Wednesday*, 28.—Have received a gracious visit from my Lord. He was near in my chamber devotions. Felt a delightful recumbency of soul upon him. O what a season of restlessness I have had! Lord, thou biddest the cup pass from me. I record thy goodness. After breakfast had a singularly profitable conversation with Sister P. on the way of faith and my own sinful misgivings and unbelief—a throwing away of my shield as it were. I greatly hunger and thirst after thee, O God, my Rock and my salvation! After a season of prayer, in which Mrs. P. and Mrs. H. wrestled earnestly, I withdrew with strength in my soul. Now, O Lord, wilt thou not seal me wholly and forever thine! cleansed by thy Spirit, through faith in Christ Jesus! Then will I teach transgressors thy ways."

The Providence Conference was to meet at Province-town, Cape Cod, April 4th. *En route* to the place he spent the previous Sabbath at Boston, not able to preach, but "administered the Lord's-supper at Russell Street Church." April 2d he reached the seat of conference. At seven o'clock the next Monday morning he 'read off the appointments.' "A conference of one hundred and twenty preachers," he says, "finished in four days is new; but the brethren talked but little and worked hard. I labored with all my powers. Preached twice on Sabbath, and ordained five deacons and nine elders. Did not enjoy the conference, but some did."

While in New England, in one of the cities, he says in a letter to Mrs. Hamline :

"Methodism is certainly dull here, but we shall do no good by speaking of it. Heard a sermon *read*, and it reminded me of *school-boy days.* Yet they call it good preaching. Not a soul kneels in prayer. I thought of Garrick's reply to the question, 'Why is it that you speak *fiction* and make all the people weep, while I preach truth and they all go to sleep?' 'Because you utter truth as though it were fiction, and I speak *fiction* as though it were *truth.*'"

Again he returns to New York to attend the meeting of the bishops. Preached three times while here, and Monday, 23d, left for Springfield, Massachusetts, to attend the New England Conference, which convened April 25th. The session lasted five days and a half. "It was pleasant," he writes. "No deaths or difficult cases in either this or the Providence Conference the last year."

The New Hampshire Conference held its session this year at Lancaster, May 9th. His route to this place from Springfield was to Lebanon one hundred and eighty miles by cars, thence to Littleton, forty miles by railroad, and thence, the last twenty miles, to Lancaster in stage. This last stage of the route is a fit illustration of the not unfrequent perquisites of the episcopal office. Bishop Hamline writes:

"We had two stages to Littleton, where we spent last night, and reached there at nine o'clock. The road was not so bad as I expected, and we went on about three and a half miles an hour. I had a comfortable bed, and room with fire in it, and Brother Clarke to lodge with me ; awoke at three o'clock and got up a little after four, and had a long time at prayers, and much comfort. We took breakfast and started on two crowded stages, one with four and the other with six horses, and drove twenty miles over a dreadful road *without a change* of horses,

reaching here a little before one P. M.   One coach broke down,
and but for providential mercy, some must have been injured.
The axle broke and some on the top were thrown over on the
horses, and others were clinging hold as they could.   The
driver was thrown off, and yet stopped the horses.   The coach
did not upset.   We waited half an hour for our mates to be
remounted on a wagon, borrowed near by."

Second day of conference, he says:

"I am well this morning.   Heard the conference sermon
last night, written and talented, but not in good taste ; would
do well for a Congregational minister in a theological and religious point of view.   A great want of men here.   Preachers
can hardly stand up to sing, and can not kneel to pray.   Here
is degeneracy both in spirit and form from Methodism.   No
altar here in the Methodist church.   They left it out for more
seats to rent.   I asked them what they do in revivals ?   They
said they had never had one since the church was built.   No
wonder."

In the same letter to Mrs. Hamline, May 10th,
he writes:

"This is my birthday.   Fifty-two years clean gone forever.
What years !   May they make an end of sin.   Within twenty
feet of my east window a stream gurgles along beautifully, with
a constant bass, or semi-bass, provoking me to praise.   I feel
peace.   I will try to be faithful."

At the close of the third day of conference, he
says: "We had a remarkably pleasant day in conference.   Business is going on rapidly and delightfully."   The day following (Saturday), he writes: "I
think we shall close on Monday, P. M.   I have not
hurried any, but business seems to melt away remarkably.   A good spirit prevails, I think.   Little
exhortations seem to do good."   The last remark
is characteristic.   No man ever excelled him in point,
precision, and spiritual unction of his "little exhorta-

tions," as he calls them. In a few minutes he would often change the whole phase and spirit of a conference to devotion and a reverent attention to business. The Bishop left Lancaster at Monday noon, the conference having sat four and a half days. He retraced his steps to Lebanon, and thence to New York, where he arrived at Dr. Palmer's, Thursday, the 17th. "A safe journey. 'The Lord is my shepherd.'" His business in the city was to review the new Hymn Book, in company with the other bishops, pursuant to the order of General Conference of 1848. Much of their time was spent, in this work, at the Rev. Dr. Kidder's, Newark, New Jersey. Monday, 21st, he writes:

"*Monday*, 21.—My labors press heavily on my strength. Had to be excused to-day and get out in the open air. The examination of the Hymn Book is heavy business. Lord, help thy servants! And when the work is finished may thousands exult to sing thy praises in its evangelical lines. Preached on Sabbath morning in Seventh-street. Was feeble in body, but comfortable in soul. This evening the New York Monthly Meeting for the Promotion of Holiness was held in the Allen Street Church close by. Mrs. Hamline and the family are there. The Lord bless his people, and made his Church holy, for Christ's sake!"

His labors were wearing him down. Seldom did he undertake preaching, or any other work, but with depleted strength. His life was a wonder to those who knew him. The following letter to his old friend, Rev. L. Swormstedt, dated New York, May 25th, 1849, gives only one aspect of his incessant activity. His friends watched his precarious life with great solicitude. He says:

"I am but poorly. My left side is much of the time like the foot 'asleep,' if you know what that is. My work this spring has been severe. If you have a map of the States, just run your pencil from New York to Provincetown, on Cape Cod, and back to New York, thence to Springfield, Massachusetts, and to Lancaster, New Hampshire, near the Canada line, and back to New York, and you will see what journeys I have taken to reach my conferences and get back twice to meet the bishops. It has kept me constantly engaged, almost without a day's rest, for nearly two months; and I know not which is the hardest, sitting in conferences and cabinets, traveling day and night, or working with the bishops. We have just finished the Hymn Book, and to-morrow I start to the Troy Conference; thence, right back almost to where the New Hampshire sat, to the Vermont Conference, and then incline westward to the Oneida and Michigan, if I live."

With Bishop Hamline, a call to preach implied the entire devotion of the life and talent and being to the one work. All other calls and claims must be set aside for this. The secularizing of the mind of the minister in business, or the diversion of his aims and activities to other professions while holding official pastoral relations to the Church, he justly regarded as a perversion of his calling, and the connivance at it a ruinous policy to the Church. The following extract of a letter to Rev. Jacob Young, at this time, is worthy to be pondered and preserved. He says:

"Let me say, then, that if you could pass over our whole work, and learn its condition as I do in the stationing rooms of the annual conferences, I have the fullest conviction that you would see eye to eye with me on this subject; but, in the haste of letter communication, I must sum up all by saying, if the practice of giving to students of our colleges, and to professors and school-teachers, regular appointments in our work be not withstood, in twenty years from this time we shall not have half a dozen men in some conferences, who are not teaching schools or academies on their stations, or attending colleges or academies, or are professors in theological seminaries or universities, or are employed as merchants, or saddlers, or doc-

tors, or lawyers, or in some other lucrative avocation where
they have their pastoral charge! I wish my dear Brother Young
could see and hear what I have seen and heard this year. I
am sure if he had, he would be as cautious of encouraging a
Methodist traveling preacher to go to college (without locating)
as he would of opening a 'crevasse' in the Mississippi, nay,
more so. Here I leave it; but if I live to see you, will tell you
much more. *Verbum sat sapienti.*

"I love you, my dear old first friend—father—more than I
can express, but I love Zion more; and for her sake let me
exhort you to exhort the young men who have vowed to do so,
to 'give themselves wholly to God and his work.'"

The Troy Conference met at Sandy Hill, New
York, May 30th. Bishop Hamline writes: "Bishop
Hedding is here. Conference goes heavily. Preached
yesterday in the grove to about two thousand souls.
This is a delightful spot; but in the midst of conference business I have little enjoyment. Ministers are
wanting to fill the work. Lord, pity thy Zion."

The Vermont Conference followed that of Troy,
in his plan of visitation, and held its session this year
at Peacham. At Montpelier, on his way to Peacham,
he spent two nights, "preaching on Friday to about
twenty-five persons, at the seat of government, in the
midst of a society of one hundred Methodists! Put
up with a good Brother Scott, who thinks Methodism
is sinking in Vermont." Here (at Peacham), on yesterday, he says, "I preached twice. Once to the
children, and had a good time, though I saw a love-
feast in the morning with no door-keepers, which is
here a uniform practice!" He thought it well that
himself and Mrs. Hamline were in the White and
Green Mountains during the hot season, in view of
their feeble health. "But," he adds, "my dear
brother, we shall none of us die till our Heavenly

27

Father sees best, and then he can easily find the instrument."

The Vermont Conference opened June 20th. He says: "It is a very small village and the preachers have to go three miles and more to lodge. Conference met to day (Wednesday), and we had a pleasant, prayerful season. We hope to close on Monday." They closed on Friday evening. "Three days," he says, "is the shortest conference I have yet had."

The interval till his next conference was needed for rest, but Church calls, and an ever impelling love for perishing men, urged him on in long journeys, frequent preaching, visitation of Churches, and private labor. The general route of travel may be indicated by the chief places he visited—Burlington, Vermont, Troy, Hillsdale, back to Troy, Schenectady, Utica, Sanquoit, Brooklyn (about twenty miles from the latter place), Norwich, to Oxford. Here the Oneida Conference opened its session July 25th. His record of the session is brief, but significant.

"OXFORD, *Wednesday, August* 1.—Closed to-day the Oneida Conference at half-past 12 P. M., one among the best conference sessions I ever witnessed. God was with his ministers. There was among them a great hungering and thirsting after righteousness. O that all our conferences could be thus! Bless the Lord, O my soul, and forget not all his benefits!"

The East Genesee Conference convened at Elmira, N. Y., August 22d. To this time and place Bishop Hamline journeyed leisurely, preaching at every halting place, and having reached Elmira, says of the week preceding: "A good week, and a good Sabbath. The Lord be praised. Amen!" Of the conference session he simply records: "Closed confer-

ence this evening at 5 o'clock. A rapid work.
Appointments well received. But I have had poor
health and poor comfort. Not so spiritual a conference as Oneida. Had pleasant lodgings at Brother
Huntley's." But the reader must not infer from
this that either the Bishop was defective in his labors, or that the conference was inappreciative of
them. The writer of this memoir was there. Blessed
were the fruits of his administration and his godly
counsels. His addresses to the conference were
sweet and heavenly, and his influence long remained,
and with many will never be forgotten. The overwork and gathering infirmity of the Bishop began
seriously to make their mark. To this he thus confesses :

" DETROIT, *Monday, September* 3.—Preached once yesterday with difficulty. Body feeble. Lord help me for Christ's
sake ! My trials this year are peculiar. O for an overcoming
faith. Lord, I fly to thee ! Help me to fly."

The Michigan Conference began at Adrian,
September 5th, and on Sabbath, 9th, he " preached
in the morning, and ordained ten elders, besides
eleven deacons in love-feast." " Have had some
light and comfort," he writes. " The conference is
not lively in its spiritual state, though some of the
brethren are much devoted. The Michigan Conference needs in these regions a very devoted ministry.
Great efforts are being made in behalf of education.
The Lord grant that the good may be obtained without any associated evil."

The Ohio Conference sat in Dayton, Ohio, September 26th. Bishop Waugh presided, but Bishop
Hamline attended to proffer any aid which the fail-

ing health of Bishop Waugh might require. He briefly records :

"Reached here last Friday. Conference is progressing lively. A good spirit. Bishop Waugh in good health. This is a noble body of men. Ordained eight elders and preached on Sabbath in Wesley Chapel."

Speaking of the venerable Wm. H. Raper, he says:

"Brother Raper is indeed gone, body and mind. What a wreck! But his soul is filled with God. He electrified the conference to-day, asking for a superannuated relation. 'If I die soon,' he says, 'I am ready—look for me, away up in heaven.' This was said with peculiar emphasis."

With the close of his conferences closed also his public labors for the season. Tired nature could endure the strain no longer. For six years he had worked with strength daily, and we may almost say, supernaturally, given. His friends, and especially his medical advisers (men highly competent to judge), had beheld his wonderful career with astonishment, gratitude, and apprehension. Few, very few, of the myriads who had hung upon his lips with such wonder and delight, ever conceived or imagined the physical pain which his efforts cost. His diary during the months following gives forth the tones of honest complaint :

"My health is impaired. My disease in the chest seems to be progressing. I can now hardly write or do any thing. My frame shakes with some strange inward pectoral commotion, as though my heart were clogged. I can not expect to do much more but to lie down and die. O that I may die in Christ !

'Happy, if with my latest breath,
    I may but gasp his name ;
Preach him to all, and cry in death,
    Behold, behold the Lamb ! ' "

"*Sunday*, 7.—A storm without, but peace within. God bears to my heart this day the blessings of the Sabbath. It is now 11 o'clock A. M. My dear wife has gone to the sanctuary. I find a sanctuary here. I have the Bible, the Hymn Book, Carvosso, Baxter's Dying Thoughts, Bridge's Exposition of the 119th Psalm, and Wesley's Sermons lying before me. I have the Holy Spirit. I have Christ.

"*Sunday* (Xenia), *November* 4.—This morning, for the first time in six weeks, reached the sanctuary, and heard Dr. Elliott. It was pleasant, O Lord, to tread thy courts. 'O Lord of hosts, blessed is the man that trusteth in thee.'"

The preachers' meeting of Cincinnati "respectfully and affectionately invited" him to make that place his residence, and "assist, as he was able, in the different charges." To this he replies:

"I appreciate the expression of your wishes that I should aid the work in Cincinnati for a season. My plans, however, would take me westward and northward, though at present the prospect of executing them is discouraging. Yet I must carry them out if Providence permit. The rural parts of our work are more needy than the cities; besides which, my familiarity with the pulpits of Cincinnati for sixteen years renders it proper, on Wesleyan principles, that I labor chiefly in other fields. Be assured if supplications for your success can avail, I will strive to remember your several charges. I shall probably be compelled to pause in the city occasionally for a week or two, and if health permit, would cheerfully render my feeble services."

His spiritual birthday comes, and he remembers it with joy:

"*October* 5.—Twenty-one years this day since I lay prostrate on the hearth of a dear Methodist brother's sitting-room, crying for mercy. That night, I believe, my heart was changed, and the next morning I obtained the witness of the spirit that I was adopted into the family of Christ. O that I had been faithful all these following years."

As the weeks rolled by he records the great goodness and faithfulness of God in the support and

triumph given him in his affliction and confinement.
Coming back to Cincinnati, and to his friend, Mr.
Brooks, the great congeniality of his family life became a joy and solace to his spirit.   On the 17th of
December he renewed in a formal and solemn manner his consecration to God, which was a great
means of strength and peace to his soul.   On the
last day of the year he thus records:

"*Monday*, 31.—On this last evening of the year I have
read over my diary for the last two years.   What a record of
God's mercy and of my unfaithfulness.   And now I am soon
to bid farewell to another year of mercies.   I have been
spared amid the dangers of long journeys, exposure to cold
and storms, feeble health, the terrors of cholera, and overwhelming labors amid them all.   My dear wife has been
spared, and all my family.   Many dear friends have died, but
all of them, I believe, in the Lord.

"I believe the effort I made to consecrate myself afresh to
my Savior on the 17th instant was a blessing to my soul.   That
hour I would join with this—this closing period of the year;
and now, blessed Jesus, I renewedly take thee for my portion,
thy commandments for my guide, thy doctrines for my wisdom, thy promises for my stay and support, thy Spirit for my
comforter, and thy heaven for my home for evermore.   O seal
me thine abode!

'Let all I am in thee be lost,
Let all be lost in God.' "

Chapter XXI.

[1850-51.]

DECIDES AGAINST MEDICAL ADVICE—LAST EFFORTS—
HEALTH FAILS—RETIRES.

THE careful reader will have perceived in the
records of the past two-years, especially the last,
the gathering symptoms of decline in Bishop Hamline's health. "I am as a wonder unto many," says
David, "but thou art my strong refuge." Already
he had outlived all expectation of friends, and all that
the admonitory counsels of physicians had authorized
him to expect. But he was raised up for a special
purpose, as the envoy extraordinary of the Lord to
the Churches, and the strength of God was his refuge
and support. His physical sufferings seemed to be
a part of his marvelous calling, as if the power of
Christ was to be specially magnified in his weakness.
The case has few parallels in history, and to himself
Bishop Hamline was a mystery through all those
years. The failing strength of the venerable Bishops
Hedding and Waugh devolved the greater work on
the other bishops, and Bishop Hamline was led
beyond himself in efforts to sustain his proportion of
the common burden. But if his sun dipped low in
the West, and the shadows of care and infirmity
were lengthened, his soul dwelt in light and peace,
and the tenor of his experience was triumphant.

January 8, 1850, he writes:

"My peace since the New Year commenced has been almost uninterrupted. Have been confined mostly to the house, but my room has been truly a Bethel. Sometimes the presence of Christ has been such in its manifestations that I could realize

> 'The speechless awe that dares not move,
> And all the silent heaven of love.'

"*Tuesday*, 29.—Reached God's house yesterday. Exhorted five minutes, and closed with a few words of prayer. It was with great difficulty that I staid in the house for faintness. I have enjoyed Christ for a few days. O how precious such enjoyment. God is pouring out his Spirit marvelously. The Church is moved, and is moving forward. Several are sanctified daily. Praise God!"

In the month of January, 1850, the state of his health was thoroughly investigated by two able physicians, and their report was respectfully introduced by the following letter from one of them:

"Rev. Bishop Hamline, *Dear Sir*,—I inclose you the written opinion of Dr. Lawson and myself in regard to your present difficulties and course advised for their amelioration.

"It is an unpleasant duty that has devolved upon us, and for myself I desire to say that it is peculiarly painful, knowing, as I do, the weighty interests of the Church deposited in your hands, as well as your anxiety to be laboring diligently in your high and holy calling. But neither the Church nor any private circle of friends will hesitate in urging you to a course which promises a restoration of your health, in a reasonable time, and full ability on your part to be active the residue of your life.

"You will plainly understand that we do not expect your complete restoration; *i. e.*, that the heart will assume its normal proportions, but that, from the course recommended, your system generally will obtain such restoration as will enable you to labor, to a great extent, to the end of life. But with the present feebleness of the heart's action, if labor is persisted in, you must not expect recovery; but, on the other hand, a train of symptoms of a very disastrous character. Your contemplated labor in the North-west, next summer and autumn, we think, will add peculiarly to your difficulties, and, if you are able to pass through them, will most likely be the end of your active life. If there be no alternative but for your proportional attendance at the ensuing conferences, it will be far better for you to preside at some in the spring, and the rest of your share in the fall. "Very respectfully, etc.

"CORNELIUS G. COMEGYS."

This judicious advice, so respectfully and affectionately tendered, was followed by the joint opinion of the physicians, dated January 29, 1850, as follows:

"To BISHOP HAMLINE, *Rev. Sir,*—Having carefully considered the condition of your system, we are of the opinion that your bad health is dependent upon an enlargement of the heart. Having arrived at this conclusion we feel obliged to say that great care is necessary on your part to prevent the unhappy consequences usually resulting from an indifference to such an organic affection.

" The well-being of every portion of the system is dependent upon the soundness and perfect working of the central organ of circulation ; and when it is not in a condition to perform its functions properly, it becomes one so afflicted to place himself in a condition most favorable to a restoration of its powers.

"Your present condition is one of great nervous exhaustion, the result of the active labors you have undergone, associated with the important defect of structure alluded to. We think the nervous depression can not easily be restored, unless a cessation of the duties of your office is adopted for a time, as those labors connected with your affection will continually tend to produce the worst results.

"We are therefore united, in view of your future health and usefulness of office, in recommending you to leave the United States for some foreign residence, where you may enjoy · the best facilities for a relaxation of mental and bodily toil.

"Very respectfully, your obedient servants,

"L. M. LAWSON, M. D.

CORNELIUS G. COMEGYS, M. D."

Dr. Comegys had affectionately cautioned him the previous autumn.   He says:

"This winter you ought to spend in Southern Europe. I feel great earnestness in this suggestion. You could leave New York early in October, in a steamer that would speedily carry you out of official cares, which will weigh you down sooner than you think, unless mitigated. Do not, I entreat you, disregard this humble advice. I give it *understandingly* and in the fear of the Lord. Do write me a line saying whether you are likely to do this.

" Praying the Lord to have you in his holy keeping, and spare you for many years, I remain," etc.

The following extracts from Bishop Hamline's diary will show how he received the advice of his physicians, and why he was restrained from folowing it:

"*Friday, February* 1.—A day of days to my soul! Was baptized in the morning in my room while, as is customary with us, myself and dear wife were holding our morning prayer-meeting in our chamber. Filled with joy and with the Holy Ghost, I went to Ninth Street to witness the work of God there. I was enabled to speak to them ten minutes. I suppose near fifty believers and unbelievers were at the altar. Several were sanctified powerfully. It seemed to me that the atmosphere of the house was sensibly embued with odors from God's throne. Oh, in what an ocean of purity and bliss this soul did plunge and bathe! I retired feeling that one half step, as it were, separated me from the heavenly glory. At Brother Thomas's, where I dined, I suffered much for want of breath; thought at one time I might be going directly home. All was well. The doctors, Lawson and Comegys, have written out an opinion that my disease is still of the heart, and has increased, and that a voyage to Europe is necessary. They urge it. My work prevents, and I can not go. I thought to lay it before my colleagues, but it would greatly embarrass them, and I will be silent, attend my conferences, if able, and, if not able, and should die, let me die as near my post as I can get. For me 'to die is gain.' Yes, blessed Jesus, thanks to thy name and humiliation and groans and blood, unworthy as thou knowest I am, for me 'to die is gain.'

"*Sunday*, 17.—I have rather improved in health for the last ten days. Have many blessings to be thankful for. Hear that my son L. is attentive to religion, and hopes by his teachers that it is a radical change. If so, what a mercy! The last two weeks have brought me unusual inward struggles and trials. I have a measure of deliverance. I desire a deeper conformity to God's will. How can I live without it?

"*Sunday, March* 10.—For nearly two weeks I have been confined mostly to my bed. My sickness has been a more aggravated disease of the heart. I have suffered distress, faintings, with inward pains and sinking like death. In all this sickness I have had no sensible emotions of any sort. My state was simply resignation. My language was, 'not my will, but thine, O Lord, be done!' I resign all to God. I know: 1. That I am very unworthy; 2. That I am converted; 3. That God has wrought a deeper work than ever within eight years; and finally, I believe he will receive me to his presence. I trust if my work is done, which seems most likely (and I am content if that be his pleasure), that he will give me peace in death. As to my labors, 'I am not meet to be called' Christ's minister, and I am thoroughly ashamed of every effort I have made for twenty years to preach Christ. When I try to think how his Gospel should be preached, with what holy zeal and ardor, discretion and ability, I can but turn away with loathing from all my efforts. Yet, O blessed God and Savior, thou knowest that thou hast been with me. I abhor myself, but praise thee!"

During his confinement his emotional joys were variable, but his faith was abiding. "Had I health now," he says, "I don't know that I would labor as I used to, for I used to labor too hard; but I would preach, would labor, would do all I could for my Savior." Being very ill one night, he says: "May be I will get off to-night. I am very vile, very unworthy, but my Savior is worthy. He gives me faith—faith. He enables me to trust."

The annual meeting of the bishops, for the arrangement of their plan of work, was held in Philadelphia, March 20th. Before breaking up they addressed a fraternal letter to Bishop Hamline:

"We are now about to separate, and before doing so we take occasion to express to our afflicted absent colleague, Bishop Hamline, our strong fraternal affection and confidence, and our deep sympathy with him in his sufferings and privations. We have daily remembered him in our devotions, and united in interceding for the renewal of his health and strength, and for his religious peace and consolation. Most thankful shall we be if it please the Lord to restore him to health and to our councils. And we assure you, dear brother, you will continue to have an interest in our intercessions at the throne of the heavenly grace, and that you will ever be cherished in our affections and sympathies. . . . We now commend you to God and the riches of his grace. May grace, mercy, and peace be multiplied unto you continually. With Christian salutations to Sister Hamline, we remain your affectionate and sympathizing brothers in Christ.

"E. HEDDING,   B. WAUGH,

T. A. MORRIS,   E. S. JANES."

In conformity to the suggestion of Bishop Hamline, the bishops had agreed upon "an alternate plan" of visitation of conferences, by which, if he should be able he could take his part in the work, or, if otherwise, his work could be distributed among themselves. The work assigned him, on condition of his being able to perform it, was in the West as far as Iowa and Missouri. The attempt to meet it was hazardous in the extreme, though in a more invigorating climate it would be less so. He submitted the case to his venerable friend and counselor, Rev. David Young, who frankly said, "I would not go." "But," said Bishop Hamline, "if you would rather die than remit your work, what would you do?" "Then," said the stern veteran, "I would go." To his friend Rev. L. Swormstedt, he writes, May 10th: "If not much worse I will go to my conferences. It seems to me easier to die than to be all the year idle."

His route lay mostly across a country which was traveled at that time by stage or private conveyance, exposing him to heat and rain and malarious atmosphere, besides the uncomfortable lodgings, and often fare, also, inevitable to a newly and sparsely settled country. In his own private carriage, accompanied only by his wife, he journeyed on, attending the Wisconsin Conference at Beloit, June 26th, and the Rock River Conference at Plainfield, Illinois, July 17th. The first effect of the excitement of labor and riding in the fresh air was exhilarating, and seemed to be an omen of good. The hopes of watchful, anxious friends for a moment revived. His ever faithful physician, Dr. Comegys, penetrating deeper into causes and symptoms, thus writes to him, July 8, 1850:

"REV. AND DEAR SIR,—I need not say how gladly I received intelligence of your health and prosperity. We are continually your debtors, under God, for Christian counsel and example, and we fail not in remembering you before the throne of grace. May our Lord Jesus Christ still stand by you, as though there were not another object of his care in the universe. . . .

"But I must not give you so much to read; allow me, however, to say something in conclusion about your health.

"Though better, you are *sorely diseased; that I well know.* The excitement of official duties and the exhilarations of travel have, to a good extent, invigorated you; but most respectfully and most earnestly let me urge you to make all your arrangements to leave the country as soon as your official duties will allow. From your letters, as well as from a slight conversation with Brother Swormstedt, I insist on this. I doubt not but that you could forego the Indiana Conference; even if no bishop be there, you have, at least, some very experienced and aged ministers upon whom the presidency can devolve. And then, if you take the same work you have this year, you can be absent till June and do your part."

But no prudential counsel which contemplated rest could check the ardent spirit of the Bishop. His love of spiritual work, and his high sense of official responsibility knew no restraint but the last necessity, which, at this time, had not quite arrived.

At the Iowa Conference, held at Fairfield, August 17th, "he was so enfeebled that his brethren supported and fanned him during the ordination of deacons, under a tree, being unable to endure the confined air of the church, while the elders came to his lodgings and received ordination." Yet he preached one sermon here—the last for the year. The Missouri Conference, held in the town of Pleasant Green, Missouri, August 28th, he was wholly unable to attend, and forwarded the papers on special business, with the following letter:

" *To the Members of the Missouri Annual Conference:*

" BELOVED BRETHREN,—Having attempted, contrary to the advice and protestation of my physicians, to prosecute my summer labors as usual, and save my colleagues, who are also feeble, extra labors on my account, I find myself at this point unable to visit your conference, and forward the inclosed papers to be presented to the president of the body. You will please elect a president from among the presiding elders, as the Discipline directs.

" Regretting exceedingly that I can not visit you and enjoy your Christian society and fellowship, and learn in person how your work prospers, yet perfectly assured that there is no prospect of my reaching you if I start, and that to attempt it in the circumstances would be unwise, if not morally wrong, I close by humble and earnest entreaties to the Head of the Church that he will bless you individually with that 'perfect love' which 'casteth out all fear,' and that, the business of the conference being accomplished under his blessed guidance, you may go to your work as Paul went, in the fullness of the blessing of the Gospel of Christ. May he grant it for Christ's sake!"

His last conference for the season was the Illinois, at Bloomington, September 18th, of which, he says, "I presided about five hours in all." After the session of the Illinois Conference, he writes, "I was not able to travel, and seated myself here (at Peoria, Illinois), with no very definite purpose except to rest a little. But as I find the situation pleasant, and have an excellent boarding-house, I may stay through autumn; and perhaps longer. I have had a year of trials," he adds, "but since I paused here I have found in some degree deliverance." To another he writes, October 13th: "I have preached just twelve times in twelve and a half months. I can hear one sermon on the Sabbath and exhort two or three minutes after the sermon. Can pray two or three minutes in the family. I can ride two hours at a time, and keep á horse and buggy for the purpose. Mental labor and business excitement almost take my life. Yet I weigh within ten or twelve pounds as when you saw me, and, except a livid complexion, or hue, look well. I am improving, take no medicine but a little aconite. Jesus reigns. Praise and pray."

The failure of his health left little hope for the future, and his disheartened, yet faithful, physician again writes with great tenderness, dated Cincinnati, October, 17, 1850:

"REV. AND DEAR SIR,—I duly received yours . . . I read the second, dated, I think, at the seat of the Illinois Conference. I prepared a notice which appeared as 'editorial' in the *Advo-*

cate. Dr. Lawson was absent at the moment. I felt as though it was due to you, that the Church should know how precarious your health is, that you might thus more constantly have their sympathy and prayers.

"I have been in hopes you would follow Dr. Lawson's advice, and mine, by leaving for the longest possible time, not only your work, but the country. I think *now*, however, that your exhaustation is too great to allow it. I need not say how deeply we sympathize with you in this trying season ; for it is trying to have a soul blest with divine love, and expanded by an order to engage largely in the work of the Lord, and yet with a poor afflicted body wholly inadequate to the work. After the resurrection, we shall have bodies fully adequate to all the wants of the soul. What a wonderful machinery it will be, moving every-where through Jehovah's dominions, executing the will of the spirit. . . . Pray for us. We cordially unite in Christian love to you and Sister Hamline.

"Your humble brother in Christ,

"C. G. COMEGYS."

November 6th, Bishop Hamline writes:

" My health had improved a little during the early part of October, but for two weeks I have lost ground, and am now nearly as low down as ever—not quite. My mind has been much oppressed at times from the fact that I could not discharge my duties, and this produced a state unfriendly to religious enjoyment. At other times I have had great peace, and since I became settled feel much better. Now I am drinking as it were from the fountain head. Mrs. Hamline is tolerable in health, and struggling for the kingdom."

To another he writes, November 12th:

" I am deprived of most of the means of grace, but my peace is often like a river. Yesterday (Sabbath) I was shut up in my room all day, but had a heavenly time with Christ my Lord. I hope, indeed, soon to meet you in heaven. The millennium will come, but 'troublous times' go before it. May we be prepared."

As to the ensuing summer's work he had little ground of expectation that he should be able to meet it, but clung to the forlorn hope. In writing to Bishop Hamline, December, 1850, Bishop Janes, as secretary of the Board of Bishops, thus lovingly speaks:

"At the meeting of the bishops last March, fearing, from the representations we then had of Bishop Hamline's health, that possibly he might not be able to attend his conferences next year, or that, at least, it might be desirable for him to have rest and freedom from care for the year, we then made out a provisional plan of episcopal visitations. This plan will only require the alteration of the time of two or three of the conferences one week, and will not burden either of your colleagues. I am to publish the changes in the times of holding those conferences when Bishop Hedding judges it proper. I presume in a few weeks.

" You need, therefore, have no concern about your conferences for the coming season. I am confident that I speak the feelings and sentiments of all your colleagues, when I say we wish you to make your health the first subject of your care and attention. Your work will not be left to suffer, and none of your colleagues will suffer for their attention to it. You may, therefore, dismiss all anxiety on that subject. I hope you will be without anxiety on any subject. 'The Lord reigneth, let the earth rejoice.' All wisdom, goodness, and power are his. He loves Zion infinitely more than we can. He bought the Church with his blood; he will preserve it by his power."

Such loving words of assurance and comfort, spoken from the source of Church authority in the matter, might seem to have been sufficient to allay all solicitude and determine the unsettled plans for the future.

His heavy personal cares abated nothing from his solicitude for the Church, whether in the department of her revivals or her literature. Writing to the publishers of the American edition of the Works of Arminius, January, 1851, he says:

"I am gratified at the prospect of a republication of the complete works of James Arminius. 'The Life and Times of

Arminius'—an article which appeared in the *Biblical Reposi-tory*, from the pen of Professor Stuart, some twenty years ago—awakened in me a desire of access to those sources of information which so modified his views of the Leyden Divine. It has seemed to me since then, that the state of theological literature and of the American Churches *demands* this repub-lication. I trust you may find encouragement to proceed with the enterprise."

At Peoria, Illinois, Bishop Hamline passed the win-ter, making rest and convalescence his chief earthly care. His temporary home was pleasant, his life fru-gal and simple, his habits regular and sanitary. But his zeal to save souls could not be quenched or re-strained. Within his narrow limits he still labored for that end. His house was a Bethel, and many there, in their family and private meetings, found peace with God. February 4, 1851, he says: "I have peace that passeth all understanding. I am hoping to sing the song of the redeemed, unworthy as I am, sinner as I am." Later he says: "If I die tell the people that I had heaven before I died. And the greater sinner I am the more let them praise God." Referring to letters received, he says, February 27th, "Friends seem to be changing their prayers for me; they pray less for my life. I take it as evidence that I may be going home. Jesus is very near to me to-day."

To a friend who had recently experienced entire sanctification he said: "There are two gates of the heart which ought always to be watched. At one of these Christ enters, at the other Satan enters. One is faith; this should be always opened. The other is unbelief; this is the only one at which Satan can enter. He may knock loudly at others, at pride, worldliness, etc., but can not enter while unbelief is kept closed." March 25th he writes: "There are glorious revivals around us, and the report of conversions and sanctifications in the weekly papers, with the daily reports from our own sanctuary at Peoria, where God is converting sinners, seem to me like the breezes from the heavenly city which refreshed the pilgrims in the land of 'Beulah.'"

The time had arrived for the opening of the annual sessions of the Eastern conferences, and Bishop Hamline communicates to Bishop Janes his desire to relieve him of one of them. In reply Bishop Janes says:

"If Bishop Hamline's health permits him to attend either conference, it will relieve me most if he can attend the Maine, which meets on the 9th proximo.

"The conferences will then all be three weeks apart, and I can meet them without embarrassment or over-fatigue.

"I am desirous Bishop Hamline should not feel anxious or expose his health by too early or too great exertion."

Bishop Hamline's regular assignment of visitations for this year was to the Baltimore, Philadelphia, New Jersey, New York, New York East, East Maine, Maine, and Michigan conferences. The reader will see how small a fragment of health was left him which allowed from all these only the attendance upon one conference, and that imperfectly.

His health had begun to improve from about the first of April, in respect of every thing but his voice. Early in May he commenced his long eastward tour to reach his appointment on July 9th. At Morris, Illinois, he halted awhile, and had, as he says, "a turn of illness." June 14th he writes from Schenectady, New York: "We have reached Mr. Ford's (Mrs. Hamline's nephew), near Schenectady, and after four or five days' rest he takes us in his carriage to Hillsdale for some two or three days, and then to Saratoga to spend eight or ten days, and then to the Maine Conference. I am doing well, getting quite black in the sun, and gaining a robust look. I can not use my voice, and can not endure company."

Bishop Hamline reached Maine in due time and attended his conference, "presiding about half of the session." But having finished his necessary business and closed the conference, he retired to his room exhausted, "unable to see those who called to bid him farewell." The effort had been hazardous, desperate, and it was his last. Henceforth he ceased to contend against the laws of life and the now clearly discovered will of Providence. His courage remained, but his body was shattered beyond hope. On his return from conference he writes to his old friend, the Rev. L. Swormstedt, dated Albany, July 18, 1851:

"I have succeeded in relieving Bishop Janes of one conference, but it has been at great hazard. I was able to be in the conference-room about half the time, but when there I suffered much. I was confined to my bed nearly all day on Sunday, being carried to the church in the morning, just at the close of the sermon to ordain the deacons, but could not get out to ordain the elders. I shall not go to the Michigan Conference unless there is great change. My powers of life—the springs—are gone. Paralyzing influences seem to be universal. I have formed no plan for the future, and do not know as I need. The future of this world is with me of little account. Full Gospel hope in regard to the eternal life is all."

From Albany he passed on to the home of his relative, Mr. Ford, near Schenectady, from whence, July 29th, he writes to his venerable friend, Rev. Jacob Young. He says:

"I have presided in one conference, occupying the chair about half of the time, and have traveled seven hundred miles in the cars to reach the conference and return to this place for rest and refreshment. Since my return I have had some serious admonitions that my state will not endure the labors of another conference. If Bishop Morris, therefore, continues in good health, I shall not attempt to reach the Michigan Conference, which is the only one I have on hand.

"I have preached but one sermon since a year ago last Sabbath. I now see no prospect of further pulpit labors. My voice allows me to converse and lead the devotions of the family with difficulty. It required a great effort to put the questions to vote in conference and ordain the candidates."

To his son he writes, July 31st:

"We returned from conference about two weeks ago. We are resting in the greatest seclusion we can obtain in this part of the country, embowered by green trees and surrounded by meadows and corn and outfields, with a tame but beautiful scenery all around us. We are four miles south of Schenectady, thirteen north-west of Albany, and have the Heidelberg Mountains four or five miles to the south, presenting a beautiful variety in that direction. Dr. P. and wife have paid us a visit here, and a rich visit it was in blessings. Two of the family during their stay were brought into larger liberty, and one converted."

An extract from a published letter of Rev. Dr. (now Bishop) Peck, who visited Bishop Hamline early in August, will suffice to show his state of health. He says:

"It has been my privilege to spend some days with this beloved servant of God. He is at the house of E. Ford, Esq., a quiet, lovely retreat for an invalid. I have observed with the utmost solicitude every thing in relation to his health, and the probability of his recovery. He is a part of the time apparently comfortable. He sits up most of the day, rides out occasionally, and when in his best state converses—not without fatigue, however—with familiar friends. His countenance, his voice, and especially his walk, indicate at all times a broken constitution, but the alarming symptoms of a diseased heart, which occur with more or less severity every day, show that he holds life by a very feeble tenure.

"It is evidently out of the question for him to perform the duties of his office, or expose himself in any way to much fatigue or excitement. His experiment in attending the Maine Conference has proved that all hope of resuming his labors must be abandoned.

"The state of his mind is just what would be expected by all who knew him—perfect peace. It is delightful to be in his company. His intellect is clear as light, and there is more of heaven in the room he occupies than in any place I know on earth. What a striking illustration of the power of love in his calmness and rest of spirit, while he is fully aware he is liable at any moment to drop into eternity.

" . . . Let the Church continue to pray that God may spare these valuable lives. He has a controversy with us. Our great men and princes are falling in our sight. Who can tell but if we humble ourselves in the dust he may 'remove his stroke from us.'"

"Our great men" in the last paragraph refers to Bishops Hamline and Hedding. The latter was now also laid aside and gently passing away. He died in great peace and triumph about eight months later, in April 9, 1852.

Bishop Hamline remained in his quiet home, near Schenectady, about a year, using what strength and opportunity he had for the good of souls. Correspondence with friends, sometimes by his own hand, sometimes by an amanuensis, was one of his substitutes for, or rather methods of, preaching. Among his correspondents were persons of all ages. Like those of the apostle John—"fathers, youth, and children." Many sought from him a word of counsel, and, had his strength permitted, this sphere of usefulness might have rivaled his palmier days. A young lady of high culture, daughter of a venerable Presbyterian minister, had been led away by visionary authors, to the great grief and anxiety of her father, who specially desired Bishop Hamline, as an early friend, to correspond with her. He thus writes, August, 1851:

"To Miss E. A. G.—I must confess I shall be disappointed if it do not prove at last that you innocently affect rather than feel admiration of the works of Davis. Your interest in Swedenborg and Bush is quite another thing. They blend the highest accomplishments of mind with an apparent sincerity, which leads me to the conclusion that they are frenzied; that a deep delusion led the former astray, and a serious mental hallucination bewilders the latter. Of this, in the case of Professor Bush, I see not how any one can doubt who has carefully read his ' Reasons.' It was placed in my hands last Summer by a disciple of his in Chicago. Last Winter I read it, and was so utterly astonished that Professor Bush should have been governed by such reasons in his conversion, that I read it a second time, so as to be sure I understood it, thinking that I must have failed to appreciate the force of his reasoning. On reading it a second time I felt assured that a degree of insanity, ' *delirium ad hoc*,' or *mono-dementia*, was the only thing to which the course of the Professor could be ascribed. I must confess, to speak plainly, that I do not believe a jury of any twelve men in this State could be persuaded, by the best attorney, to award twelve and a half cents to a party in court, upon the amount of evidence produced by Professor Bush in favor of Swedenborg's views and mission. If I had been of the party before reading that pamphlet I do think it would have converted me back again.

"You say, 'We must read impartially.' I did more; I leaned to the Professor's side. That is, I was so mortified that he should be converted without even a plausible excuse, that I read it the second time with a sincere desire to find some color of reason for his course; for I had been his special admirer, and had placed his commentary in my library as fast as it issued from the press. And now, my dear friend, you must read impartially also. And I beg you to read the pamphlet again, not as a rhetorician, or he will captivate you, but as a severe logician, blinded to all the charms and attractions of his periods and modes of expression. Do this, and he never will convert you.

"As to Davis, I must say that your venerable father ought to be pardoned for refusing to read him. I have only read his 'Revelations.' His 'Harmonia' I have not seen. But I differ from my dear friend when she says, 'a mine of thought.' I would say (not a 'continent of mud,' that is not bad enough to describe it) a pit of foul abominations. My friend, forgive me when I say you wrong yourself to be the advocate of such a man, of such frauds, (I can not say delusions in his case), designed, I believe, to overthrow the faith of Christians, and actually seducing unstable souls to ruin.

"I should grieve if I thought this honest expression of opinion would lead you to conclude that I am bigoted and incapable of judging, for I desire to gain your ear and patience in a matter of so much moment—of everlasting moment

"You speak of progress. In reading the Apocalypse, do you not perceive that these times (as all respectable commentators agree) are to be characterized by the spread of infidelity, and the prevalence of lying wonders, in an eminent manner? The 'three unclean spirits' (Rev. xvi, 13) are the spirits of 'devils working miracles' or wonders. 'Blessed' now 'is he that watcheth.' How fearful the fact that all Germany, except a small remnant of evangelicals, is turning to atheism! How fearful the fact that already some sixty German papers in this country are now boldly advocating deism and atheism! Some of these, too, are Church papers, professedly so; but, in the hands of rationalists, are disguised advocates of deism. Is it not in harmony ('Harmonia') with such diabolical enterprises against God and his Anointed that some of these enemies to Christianity should appear in the garb of universalism—in the garb of new 'revelations,' 'spirit rappers,' 'clairvoyants,' and such like? O my dear friend in Christ (precious name!), 'let us who are of the day be sober,' putting on 'the whole armor of God.'

"My best love to your parents. They seem almost parents to me. I long to see you all. May grace be with you all."

To the Rev. J. M. Leavitt (now Rev. Dr. Leavitt, President of Lehigh University, Pennsylvania), one of his spiritual children, whose conversion has already been noticed, and who now was suffering from the unkindness of certain members of the Church, he writes:

" AUGUST 25. 1851.

" I am not surprised, nor should you 'think it strange, concerning the fiery trial.' It is no 'strange thing' that has 'happened to you.' And if you can persevere in 'enduring' you doubtless will find that true, 'Blessed is the man that endureth temptation.' Let us endure hardness as good soldiers.

" As to the Church, there is certainly occasion to be tried. 'If it consisted of only myself,' may each member say, 'I should be tried, wonderfully tried, that the Church was so unlike what Christ's redeemed should be. And if in self so much exists to confound, surprise, and distress me, when thousands of others—some of them still less controlled by grace—are added to that self, is it strange that the sum total of unworthiness should be a sight grievous to look upon?' Yet, we should go on to think, God blesses the Church. Sons and daughters are born unto her every day in many places. Her members are passing by hundreds, weekly, in calm hope and holy triumph to heaven. More than the ancient number, seven thousand, have not bowed to idols. I am tried also. The Methodist Episcopal Church has much in herself to mourn over. But whither should we turn? On every hand there are grievous things found in the midst of the tribes of Israel."

In October, 8th, Bishop Hamline again writes:

" I am about the same in health. I am two and a half miles from meeting, four from post-office, and *very* retired—not too much so. If I ever improve in health it must be in a very retired position, away from all company. We are delightfully situated as far as family, room, table, and beauty of scenery are concerned, with all the comforts of a rich farm—and all that the ocean can supply. We have *family prayer*-meetings, and are blessed with a *family revival*. God is good. Jesus is *precious*. We may not leave here, until (if able) the General Conference comes; or we pass over Jordan. But we leave that to Providence."

On the subject of his health, he writes, October 19th.

" I am declining in health, and can not flatter myself with a long stay in this 'vale of tears.' My disease is what would

29

generally be considered *alarming* and extremely *unpleasant*. It robs me of much sleep, and loss of sleep affects my nervous system very unfavorably. My breathing is also much interrupted at night, and often when I compose myself to rest, I am aware that I am *peculiarly* liable to awake in another world. How thankful I ought to be that in this condition, I often feel, not barely acquiescence but joy in the near prospect of eternity."

An extract from the same letter will show the feelings of his heart toward the lamented, the great, the good Dr. Stephen Olin:

"I am the more moved to this style of meditation and writing from a recent occurrence, namely, the death of a dear friend, Dr. Olin, a man who, more than any other on earth, shared my admiration and love, a man whose equal in intellectual majesty and sanctified fervors I never saw, nor ever expect to see again in time. Indeed, he was so transcendently above all other men I ever knew, in any Church, or even among our great politicians—the most eminent of whom I have often heard, in the senate chamber and on popular occasions—that a comparison between them can scarcely be instituted. The most hasty and unstudied efforts of Olin excelled the most elaborate efforts of the Websters, the Calhouns, and the Clays."

Between Hamline and Olin there existed the strongest friendship and spiritual communion. In the fall of 1844 they met at the session of the Genesee Conference in Vienna (now Phelps), and the biographer of Olin thus records of them:

"One afternoon they paced to and fro in the small garden of the house where the Bishop lodged, in earnest conversation. Their communings were not at that time of the interests of Zion, so dear to them both, and upon which they so often conversed, but upon the inner life of their own souls. He expressed his surprise that the Bishop could bear to be engaged two or three hours consecutively in fervent devotion. Dr. Olin said that his own brain would not allow him to indulge in such prolonged seasons of importunate prayer. He spoke of the ardor and intense feeling he had at first carried into religious things, and how he dedicated the entire Sabbath to high meditations—how he longed for deep religious enjoyments, and how God had led him by a way that he knew not, so that he was satisfied to have his soul kept waiting on God."

Such was the union of these two great men. Their views on the great and engrossing subject of entire sanctification, then specially exciting the attention of the Churches, were harmonious, and experiences were freely rehearsed and reviewed. Neither could preach without, in some form, bringing in the doctrine, and they always proclaimed the gospel from that interior stand-point. On Sabbath of the same conference about five thousand people were computed to have gathered. Both preached in the grove—Olin for two hours and a half to an entranced congregation. Those sermons are yet remembered— will never be forgotten.

But to return to our narrative. No material change in Bishop Hamline's health was perceptible, except a slow, insidious advance of his disease.

To Rev. Jacob Young, November 3d, he says:

" It was a great relief to us to receive your note, and find you could write a few lines with your own pen. Praised be God for his great goodness! I had no doubt but death would be gain to you, but to remain in the militant Church awhile seemed needful to thousands in Zion. I have long admired the grace of God, as exhibited in the last years of such patriarchs as Pickering and Bangs, whose last years seem so glorious a comment on the doctrine of ' perfect love.' When you informed us of the strong confidence you had attained on this subject, we felt a great desire that your district might experience the full and protracted benefits of your fresh experience on that subject. We now believe it will. I know not but God has raised you up for this special purpose. O may he crown the year to you with his goodness, may his paths drop fatness! May the whole district be as a Pentecost—in a flame of revival, and may your last days be far your best days!"

In a letter to Bishop Waugh he says:

"I have many reliefs in my sickness. I have books, and can read about four hours in twenty-four. I stay with a very pious family, and have family religion around me, which is a great satisfaction. Best of all, I trust I am resigned to the will of God more than I formerly supposed I could easily be if deprived of the privilege of preaching the word. O how thankful should poor, dying sinners be for Christ and the Holy Spirit! I have nothing now to look for in time but what would be called 'inglorious rest,' some suffering, and patient waiting till my change come. Yet much of the time I am peaceful and happy. And when clouds arise they disperse again and leave a brighter sunshine.

"I have not been unmindful of the severe labors inflicted on the effective superintendents this year. We have tried to remember them in prayer, which was all we could do. True, I reached one conference in my anxiety to save Bishop Janes, but I ministered very feebly, though by the kindness of the brethren we got through comfortably. Probably my health suffered some by the effort."

In another letter to a very dear friend he gives this interesting reminiscence of himself:

"I often think of Peter's request (as tradition teaches) to be crucified with his head downward, as unworthy to be crucified in the form that his Master was, and it seemed to me I understood something of his feelings. It was in this state I labored so hard in 1842–43, preaching from four to six times a week, besides all my editorial duties, feeling that he who blessed such a sinner ought to have my very life. These labors were cut short, you may remember, on the 6th of January, 1844, by the beginning of my illness, from which I have never yet recovered. And though I have not said it to go abroad, I have no doubt my present sinking state is traceable to these labors, and the accompanying and succeeding intense exercises of my mind. My unexpected position in 1844 [referring

to his election to the superintendency] was a fiery trial. As I
had made it an invariable rule for years not to have any thing
to do with my own allotments, but leave myself wholly (like
clay with the potter) in God's hands, and at his disposal, I
could not then say yes or no to control my destiny without for-
feiting, as I supposed, that great blessing which implied entire
submission to God's will. On my knees I said from hour to
hour : 'Lord, it is thy business, not mine.' 'Thou knowest all
my weakness ; see thou to it.' I think this was in a spirit of
deep humility and submission. I can not write more of the
history now. This has cost me several efforts, and I am
completely exhausted. O may Infinite Mercy send strength
to us all for Christ's sake ! "

Writing to Bishop Janes, he says :

" It is very grateful to have an interest in the prayers of
the Church, and of God's servants. I am thankful for it. I
trust you have finished your conferences without permanent
injury to your health. You have had a year of wonderful toil.
Thinking of you as I last saw you, very feeble, and unable to
preach, I have feared exceedingly that you would break down,
and perhaps fatally. Surely God has helped you, and I join
with you to bless his holy name."

To Bishop Morris he says :

" As to labor, I do not think of it any more. I resign all.
I know that I was ever unfit to be honored as an instrument
of saving souls ; but God called me, I believe, to preach, and
to occupy for a season the general pastor's office. Why he
should have done it he will permit us to 'know hereafter.'
Now he calls me to surcease, and this I think it easy to understand, and he renders it easy to accomplish. I am not unhappy in rest, though labor never looked so desirable as it
now does. I have great conflicts, but great comfort. I think
I can safely affirm, 'I know that my Redeemer liveth.' O
how wonderful that I am permitted, enabled rather, to feel
and say thus !"

The decision of Judge Nelson, of the Supreme
Court of the United States, awarding to the Meth-

odist Episcopal Church, South, their *pro rata* share of
the Church property, had been delivered November
11, 1851. In a letter to G. Goodrich, Esq., December 14th following, Bishop Hamline thus speaks:

" I expected the decision of Judge Nelson would take you
by surprise. I care little about it (*per se*), but as an indication of the *character of our Federal judiciary*, so lately considered ' above suspicion,' under the control of an almost immaculate (officially) Marshall, it grieves and mortifies—nay, it
alarms—me. ' *Et tu, Brute !*' What, the incumbents of the Supreme Bench . . . ! Please forget these hints. I will predicate
them of *your* opinion, and make you (if you please) responsible for them. What right have Dr. Peck, Dr. Simpson, and
above all, what right have I, to intermeddle with law decisions? I give it up. If *you* feel tolerably sure that your
views are correct, what a sad picture does our government present, with its *judicial* department, where, above all, we look
for incorruptible and unflinching integrity, and an almost infallible discrimination, rendering and *reasoning out* decisions,
which not only the bar, but the people deem, not merely erroneous, but grossly derelict. I will not say that I, one of the
people, maintain this opinion. But I hear this said, and see it
written on every hand. I wish a lawyer would review the decision in the *Western Christian Advocate* that I may be better
prepared to judge. I write *rashly* if my words are to go
abroad ; please, therefore, to consider all ' *sub rosa.*' I have
desired to *speak*, and this was my first safe opportunity. I will
say in conclusion, I wish the South to have the money—but I
did not expect they would obtain it from the United States
Court if appealed.

" My health is very poor. I do not go to meeting at all,
but the preachers come to the house and preach once in two
weeks. I am unable to speak above a whisper much of the
time, but I have great peace. O the blessedness of *pardon*—
of an indwelling Christ—of fellowship with the Father and
with his son Jesus Christ ! Let us be sure, my dear brother,
to keep a witness of these blessings every moment. It is
equally necessary for *all*. May God help us to be faithful unto
death."

November 15, 1851, he writes to his beloved and faithful physician :

" I give up all hope of more labor in this world, and wait my appointed time for my change. The last fifteen months I have preached but once. Now I can not use my voice in public or private, even in gentle conversation, without producing distressing symptoms."

To a ministerial brother who had been much aggrieved at being suddenly removed from a loving people before the expiration of his allowable term of service, he writes, December 31, 1851:

" The things referred to in yours are certainly a great trial, not only on your own and your family's account, but as peril to our Church interests. But we will try to check our fears by reflecting that God rules and overrules. If there be wrong he can turn even *it* to good account. Perhaps in this case he suffered impure motives somewhere to prevail, for your greater good, or for the greater good *on the whole*.

" Never think of locating. Remember it is more honorable—respectable—to *leave* a society where they desire your *return*, than to *stay* where they desire your *absence*. The former is your happy lot. Take courage, then, I beseech you. I trust this may be a year of fatness,—that God will do great things for you and for the people of your charge. My health is exceedingly poor. I do not go out, now, at all. I can read, think, and converse a little. Writing tries me. I am, with all my afflictions, enjoying the winter very much. Seclusion suits me in my feeble state. I could look back with regret (do, indeed), that I have done so little for my Savior. But 'Covered is my unrighteousness.' I have faith in Christ,—

    " 'T is all my hope and all my plea,
      For me the Savior died.' "

CHAPTER XXII.

[1852.]

GENERAL CONFERENCE OF 1852—RESIGNATION OF HIS EPISCOPAL OFFICE.

THE year 1852 marks an epoch, not only in the life of Bishop Hamline, but in the history of the episcopacy of the Methodist Episcopal Church as well. In that year, at the General Conference held in Boston, Massachsetts, Bishop Hamline tendered his resignation as bishop, and retired to the rank of a superannuated elder of the Ohio Conference. The doctrine of the Church, as to the nature of our episcopacy, had always been that it was an *office*, and not a distinct clerical *order*, but no act or precedent had ever occurred to give it practical and administrative sanction. Aside from ecclesiastical considerations, the spiritual loss to the Church by the retirement of such a man from the episcopacy was accepted with universal regret as a common affliction. The simple and only ground of his retirement was want of health. We have seen how he has carried with him a disabled body from the beginning, but his excessive labors had at length so impaired and exhausted his normal powers that, with his organic disease aggravated, the necessity of rest became imperative. The sequel proved that his constitutional force was unable to rally. He might have superannuated as a bishop, but this would not release him from a relation to Church care and authority which would prove to him a constant occasion of unrest and solicitude.

We have seen him retire from his visitation of conferences in 1850 with alarming physical prostration. The rest of intervening months fails to restore him, and in 1851 he is able to adventure upon public duty but once, and this at the hazard of life. Clinging to the forlornest hope, he writes, May 24, 1851, to M. Barney, Esq., a friend of his boyhood, "I have some hope that I may yet get to work." But it was vain. The experiment in the following July decided the case forever. As late as March 25, 1852, in a letter to a ministerial friend, he says: "My health is gone, so that I have attempted to occupy the pulpit but once in almost two years, and not once for the last fourteen months. The disease is of the heart, if physicians report correctly, and is often very tedious, accompanied with faintness and often faintings, which threaten dissolution. I find such a state involves trial, over which I sometimes trust grace enables me to triumph, but at others the conflict is severe."

The eventful year of 1852 opens, with Bishop Hamline, with solemn thanksgiving and covenant:

"O thou Infinite Father of my spirit, in whom I live and move and have my being, and from whom cometh every good and every perfect gift, help me this day to renew my covenant with thee, and thereby consecrate myself afresh to thy most holy service, by thy Holy Spirit, through Jesus Christ thy Son! Help me to apprehend the solemn nature of this act, and to be deeply humbled and affected in view of the parties to this transaction. Thou, O Lord, who condescendest to regard thy servant in this solemn hour, art infinitely pure and perfect, and, therefore, infinitely exalted above the loftiest of thy creatures. 'Behold, I am vile.' All my nature is corrupt, and without the cleansing power of thine Omnipotent Spirit there is no soundness in me. Yet thou hast condescended to reveal thyself to me in the most wonderful relations. Thou art my creator, and I am thy creature. As thy subject thou art my King, and as thy probationer thou art my Teacher and my Judge. As a sinner I may call thee my Redeemer, in which relation thou hast done, and (be astonished, ye heavens), hast suffered for me, as neither my thoughts can conceive nor my trembling pen declare.

"How unspeakable the benefits which I have received as the fruit of Christ's sufferings thou, O Lord, and thou alone, knowest; as well as the terrible and eternal wrath due to my sins, instead thereof! Blinded by sin, thy Spirit has in some measure enlightened me, and shown me thy law, and laid upon my conscience the burden of my transgressions. Dead in trespasses and sins, thy Spirit did quicken that conscience, so that its burden should become intolerable, and cause my soul to cry for relief to thee. Helpless, and unable to escape from my burden, thou didst receive me and call me to life. Full of misery, thou didst send to me the Comforter to abide with me forever. Polluted in all the depths of my moral being, thou didst descend into the loathsome sepulcher of my affections, and not with 'hyssop sprinklings,' but with the blood of Christ, commence the purifying of my unclean heart. And, amid the frequent and guilty wanderings of twenty-four years, thou hast not utterly forsaken me; but with as frequent and with as powerful calls, reproofs, and drawings of thy love, hast restored and comforted my weak and wounded soul. Thou knowest, O Lord, what thou hast done for me in all these marvelous instances of thy mercy; and full well thou knowest how impossible it is for the finite to comprehend the Infinite of thy pardoning, preserving, restoring love toward one most ungrateful and vile.

"And now, O blessed God, thou crownest thy patience and pity toward me by causing me to taste at this present time the sweetness of thy comforts, and to feel that thy hand is not withdrawn from me; but that thou witnessest to me, as well by thy Spirit as by thy Word, that thou forgivest iniquity, transgression, and sin. Therefore, O Lord God of Hosts, Father, Son, and Spirit, I give myself to thee, now and forever, to serve and glorify thee; to be subject unto thee cheerfully and constantly, in all states which may serve thy will and glory, through Jesus Christ my Lord. Amen!"

In such a divinely serene and devoted state of soul he looked out upon the untried scenes of the coming year with the dignity and the resignation of faith. In this trying hour the marked feature of his Christian life—supreme concern first for his own soul, then for the Church and humanity—derived new luster from the deepening shadows of his affliction. He could "decrease" if thereby Christ should "increase." With unabated zeal for the pulpit and the battle-field, he could remain content with his confinement, "the prisoner of the Lord." But if about to be released from service in the field, he was not exempt from the practice of arms in camp. His trials and conflicts were chiefly necessary incidents of his infirmities, while his victories were astonishing even to himself. Writing to Rev. L. Swormstedt on business, he closes with a glance at the coming General Conference and himself: "Many plans are on hand," he says, "as to presiding elders, lay representation, pewed houses, etc. I suppose something is said, too, about offices. For my part, the only agreeable thing I would desire is to get back into an annual conference, travel two or three circuits, have a glorious revival, see a few hundred souls converted and deeply pious, die in peace, and go to heaven. Who knows but a gracious God may grant it? I would be very willing to have you for my presiding elder."

During almost the entire itinerant life of Bishop Hamline, Rev. L. Swormstedt had been his presiding

elder. Thus they were thrown much into each other's
society, and, being nearly of age, a warm, brotherly
attachment sprung up between them, which added
years served but to increase. They were as David
and Jonathan of old, and, perhaps, to no other person did Bishop Hamline talk and write more freely
on confidential matters than to him.

To his children, Dr. and Mrs. Hamline, he thus
writes, February 19th.

" DEAR CHILDREN,—We rejoice exceedingly that you are
thoroughly convinced the world can not make you happy.
This conviction, if it be thorough and continually deepened,
will be an important step toward real happiness. Yet do not forget that we may resign the world in general, but still pursue it
in detail. We may resolve against it as a whole, yet seek
and seize it by parts and parcels. To reject it as a whole is
easy, because as a whole it has many things really repulsive,
even to our unsanctified hearts ; whereas, divided up by Satan
into baits of temptation, portions of it may look very alluring.
The trout dreads the bearded hook, and persuades itself that
the whole affair is to be dreaded ; but the skillful angler lays the
tempting bait around its shady nook until all the fear is forgotten, and death is greedily swallowed.

" If we can fix the purpose to reject the most alluring
things of earth, we may succeed. to eschew all. But this we
can not do without religion. We are so constituted that we
shall choose the best apparent good. To the irreligious that
' apparent good ' is the world. Religion does not appear good
for present entertainment unless we possess it. When we
lose the relish for it, we can not remember how sweet it is.
When we possess it, we wonder how we can forget its sweetness ; but if we lose our relish we do, and always shall, forget
it. Now, dear children, choose, pursue, obtain, enjoy all the
religion God will grant you, and you will be in no danger from
the world."

" *Wednesday, March* 3.—The powers of darkness have been
repulsed. I have been joyful all the day. What a mercy !
What a miracle I am ! It seems impossible that I should be
thus blessed ! My trials have for some weeks been very great.

" *Sunday evening*, 7.—I have had a blessed day. I am almost afraid to say so. I am surprised to find myself repeating, 'My God, the spring of all my joys,' etc. My conflicts and struggles have of late been very great.

"*Sunday*, 21.—My flesh trembleth under a sense of his mercy. How wonderful are his blessings! It seems as though my Savior was trying every possible method to bless me; as though Infinite Wisdom would exhaust itself in expedients to bless and save me. I would love to tell all the world the height and depth and breadth, the bottomless abyss of mercy that saves sinners."

Mrs. Hamline had been speaking to him, at one time, of his making an effort the next week to go and meet the bishops, and thence to attend General Conference. Talking of it, she says, agitated him, and now that he felt he must resign his office, urging him to attend General Conference distressed him, and he seemed to sink. Mrs. Hamline expressed anxiety, upon which he said:

"You ought not to be anxious; may be the Lord will take me away before that time. I felt last night as though I might be baptized for the grave. I had a deep and peculiar blessing last night. What a wonder that such a sinner can look calmly at death and even long for it. And it is not the impudence of self-confidence, but the gush of heart-felt trust in Christ. I am reminded of the rainbow round the throne—it is all rainbow. If we were to depend on justice, what could we do? But it is mercy! Mercy! If it please his Infinite mercy to take me now, I will rejoice, but I leave it to his wisdom. It will be right either way. I had a blessed time in secret prayer to-day."

To a friend he said:

" Do you experience any thing which answers to that saying, 'Except ye eat the flesh and drink the blood of the Son of God ye have no life in you?' I think I have now something in my experience which just answers. O the wonders of redemption! Christ die for sinners? Who can think or speak of it?

O the wonder that he should visit such a heart! For some
hours my heart has been like running waters.

> "Well might I hide my blushing face,
>   While his dear cross appears."

To the Board of Bishops, at their meeting in
Philadelphia, Bishop Hamline writes, April 21,
1852:

"Rev. and Dear Brethren.—With some hope that I
may visit Boston, if I make no previous effort, I am compelled
to decline meeting you in Philadelphia. A friend and physician, who is familiar with my state of health, warns me not
to attempt to go either to Philadelphia or to Boston. I may be
compelled to relinquish both; but as I could render you no
service I ought now, I think, to give up the former. If I fail
to reach Boston I shall in due time forward you another communication, with my parchment and resignation, there being
no hope that I can perform any more service in the ministry.

"I have been afflicted to see my dear colleagues laboring
so hard the last year or two to supply my lack of service; but
I am thankful that God has brought you through. I have had
great comfort in my retirement, and precious seasons in prayer
for you and the Church, and I will be thankful for an interest
in your devotions. In the absence of our venerated senior
[Bishop Hedding], removed to the Church above, may God,
even our God, abundantly bless you in all your deliberations
and conclusions!"

To Rev. Jacob Young, he writes, May 6th.

"Beloved Brother.—You said twenty-one years ago, as
we walked together, 'you must increase, but I must decrease.'
I am *now* just as old as you were then—fifty-five. I am unable to preach, pray in family or get to conference; but you,
twenty-one years older than then, can *do all*. Surely 'God
seeth not as man seeth.' . . . I shall forward my resignation in a day or two. I can write no more. I hope to dwell
with you forever in heaven! O delightful thought! Pray for
me. Your son in the Gospel."

The General Conference met in Boston, May 1,
1852. On May 7th, Bishop Hamline sent to that

body a letter, together with his episcopal parchments, and a letter from his physician. On May 10th, the bishops presented the same to the conference, which was read, and referred to the Committee on Episcopacy. The following is Bishop Hamline's letter:

"*To the General Conference of the Methodist Episcopal Church convened in Boston.*

"DEAR BRETHREN.—Doubting whether the state of my health will allow me to reach the seat of the conference, I forward this communication at an early period that you may be informed on one point of moment to your future conference action.

"Many will remember that when elected to the episcopal office I was in poor health. For several previous months I had preached but once, and was incapable of much labor. Traveling so improved my health, that for six years I attended my conferences, and, after a few of the first months, performed considerable labor in the pulpit. But in 1849 my duties were unusually laborious. In the intervals of some of my conferences I took long journeys, and devoted myself with my colleagues to the revision of the Hymn Book; and in addition to my own district, which was large that year, the partial failure of Bishop Hedding induced me to attempt extra efforts. From that year's labor I have never recovered. Through the following winter I was much of the time confined to my room. Towards spring in 1850 my physicians urged me to get released from all official duties and take a sea voyage, warning me that a tour of conferences during the summer would be extremely hazardous and might end my labors for life. But the severe toil likely to fall on my colleagues induced me to proceed, and I reached four of my six conferences, though in the last I was of little service. Since then (September, 1850) I have preached but once. Last summer, I presided in one conference only, which I found, after the excitement was over, greatly aggravated my difficulties. As to the nature of my disease, in 1844, three physicians in Cincinnati gave me their written opinion (urging me in the same not to attend the General Conference) that it was a disease of the heart. Perhaps all but two or three who have carefully examined me since, concur in that opinion. The inclosed letter from Professors Lawson and Comegys expresses the same view of my case in 1850. But whatever my disease may be, it incapacitates me for labor.

"Under my official responsibilities, to be unable to discharge my duties was an affliction, especially as it bore heavily on the effective superintendents. But I was comforted under this affliction, being persuaded that I had done all I could—more than physicians and counseling friends deemed incumbent or even warrantable. I have been much of the time calmly resigned to this trying inactivity.

"And now I think that the circumstances warrant my declining the Episcopal office. Eight years ago I felt that Divine Providence had strangely called me to the office. I now feel that the same Providence permits me to retire. I, therefore, tender my resignation, and request to be released from my official responsibilities, as soon as the way shall be prepared by the preliminary action of the Episcopal Committee.

"Relieved of my official obligations, I think of nothing but cleaving to Christ with all my heart, and in my feeble retirement aiming to promote his blessed cause. I mourn over my unworthiness, personal and official, but trust in one great Prophet, Priest, and King, for acquittal, cleansing, and eternal life.

"Though my heart is moved at severing an interesting relation to the militant Church, to the General Conference, and to my venerable colleagues, beloved in Christ, yet I rejoice in those other relations which I pray may always endure until they shall heighten into the fellowships of heaven.

"'Of heaven!' There the sainted Hedding has found his rest. In his letters of condolence he used to say, 'I shall soon follow you.' He went before me. But we are all going, and shall soon all be gone. Even you, so active in Zion, strengthening her bulwarks and beautifying her palaces, will soon have finished *your* work and have left behind you the traces of your foot-steps in your walks about the city of the great King. When you surrender your sacred trust to a younger generation may the fruits of your present labors move them to rise up and call you blessed. And to this end may the blessing of the Lord your God be upon you in the labors of the present conference, and in the toils of a life-time devoted to Christ's service."

On the 11th of May, the day after the foregoing document had been read in conference and referred to the Committee on the Episcopacy, two events occurred—a private meditation of Bishop Hamline in his room at home, and a public act of General Conference. We give them both. The Bishop thus muses and writes:

"This is the beginning of my fifty-sixth year. Yesterday was my birthday. I desired to record some things yesterday, but was not so secluded as to-day. My dear wife—thanks to thee, Heavenly Father, for this precious gift of thy providence — is abroad for a few hours, and I am alone with God. Let me make my record now. My habitual feeling is, surely I am the chief of sinners. This I believe is not 'voluntary humility.' But I am a *pardoned* sinner. Christ's mercy has reached *me. I feel* his blood applied. I am not now saying, I shall get to heaven. I may fall away and perish. But I am *now* a *pardoned* sinner.

"The General Conference is in session, and its doings affect me. I have resigned my office. I was called by the Church, and thought I was moved by the Holy Ghost to take the office. If my brethren pass me, and leave me uncensured, I shall now lay down the office, and this God approves. Now, O my God, sanctify to me all trials. Support me under all sicknesses, nervous weaknesses. Give me penitence, faith, meekness, love, and all the graces of Christianity, and save me, the chief of sinners, to the honor of thy grace, for Christ's sake. Amen."

At the hour of this meditation the case of the Bishop came before the General Conference for decision. The following is an abstract of their Journal:

"TUESDAY, MAY 11, 1852.

"The Committee on the Episcopacy reported in part as follows:

"'They have had the communication from Bishop Hamline under consideration, and present the following resolutions, and recommend their adoption by the conference:

"'*Whereas*, It hath pleased Almighty God deeply to afflict

our beloved Bishop Hamline, and, *whereas*, he has been laid aside from active service thereby ; therefore,

" ' 1. *Resolved*, That we sincerely sympathize with our beloved superintendent in his afflictions.

" '2. *Resolved*, That after having fully examined his administration for the last four years—his administration and character be and hereby are approved.

" '3. *Whereas*, Bishop Hamline has tendered his resignation in the following language, to wit, " And now, I think that the circumstances warrant my declining the office. Eight years ago I felt that Divine Providence had strangely called me to the office. I now feel that the same Providence permits me to retire. I, therefore, tender my resignation, and request to be released from my official responsibilities, as soon as the way is prepared by the Episcopal Committee." Therefore,

" '*Resolved*, That the resignation of Bishop Hamline of his office as a Bishop of the Methodist Episcopal Church in the United States of America be, and the same hereby is, accepted. All which is respectfully submitted.

" 'P. P. SANDFORD, *Chairman.*
" 'BOSTON, *May* 11, 1852.' "

The discussion of this report, prior to action, presented a scene of dignified sorrow, delicate appreciations, personal sympathies, and stern adherence to Church principles rarely equaled in any deliberative body. On the one hand, to accept the resignation would settle forever the doctrine that a bishop of the Methodist Episcopal Church was an ecclesiastical *officer*, not representing a distinct priestly *order;* while, on the other hand, such an act would be a great loss to the Church and her episcopacy, and a seeming disrespect to the retiring bishop. The thing the conference would choose was that Bishop Hamline might be permitted to retire from active service in view of his loss of health, and still retain his title and rank.

Dr. Sanford, chairman of the committee, said it might be proper for him to say a word or two in reference to the report. The committee had had in contemplation a different report from the one presented, until some brethren, intimate with Bishop Hamline and his afflictions, assured the committee that nothing else, in the opinion of the Bishop, could possibly relieve him from the burden that must incessantly press upon him. Consequently it was the opinion of the committee that this was the only course they could recommend in order to relieve the mind of the Bishop from the extreme pressure that weighed him down in his afflicted condition.

Dr. Bangs said that no man had a higher respect for Bishop Hamline and the episcopal office than he had, but he had other reasons than those assigned by the chairman of the committee for approving of the report. He believed the Bishop perfectly superannuated, and that when he resigned his office he did so in the utmost sincerity. He thought that the present was a fair opportunity to set the precedent that we did not consider the doctrine "Once a bishop always a bishop" our doctrine. It was not so. The principle was recognized in 1844, in the case of Bishop Andrew. If they adopted these resolutions the principle would be carried into practical effect.

J. A. Collins said he could not look with approbation on the resolutions proposed. It was clear that Bishop Hamline's illness was brought upon him by the increased labors of his position. He felt that when a bishop had lost his health through excessive and extraordinary labors, they ought not to accept his resignation. He might get better, and if that were the case, he presumed every one of them would delight to have him perform his functions as a bishop of the Methodist Episcopal Church. He did not wish to place himself in conflict with so able and venerable a body as the Committee on the Episcopacy, and would not be understood as doing so, but he would suggest the following resolution as a substitute for the last offered by the committee:

"*Resolved*, by the delegates of the several Annual Conferences in General Conference assembled, That the bishops be, and they hereby are, requested to return to Bishop Hamline his parchments, accompanied with a communication informing him that this General Conference declines accepting his resignation as a superintendent of the Methodist Episcopal Church, and grants him unrestricted permission, and advises him to adopt and pursue such course for the restoration of his health as his judgment may dictate."

Mr. Griffith said he yielded to no man in his profound respect to the office of the episcopacy as recognized and defined by the Methodist Episcopal Church. He deemed it the most perfect scriptural model of the episcopacy that ever existed in the world. He was, therefore, exceedingly unwilling to come to the conclusion to which at last he did come; but when he came to look at the subject fully, he felt himself forced to grant the Bishop's request. If they would take the communication of the Bishop, they would find that he set forth his case something like this: He was in ill health when elected, and that ill health had been increased and augmented almost perpetually from the weight of his duties, until finally he was reduced to a state of utter prostration. The testimony of eminent physicians was that his disease was that of the heart—a malady of which ordinarily there was no cure. Such was his condition. He also further states that such is his peculiar temperament and constitution of mind, that while there is any sense of responsibility resting upon him he could not enjoy himself. Under these circumstances he had come to the conclusion, that the only remedy was to be released from this sense of responsibility that rests upon him. He felt himself incompetent longer to discharge the duties of his office, and wished to be freed from them; and he thought also that it was a providential dispensation of God, that he had it in his power to establish a precedent that might be of use in future time. From these reasons, said Mr. Griffith, the committee voted as they did.

Dr. Holdich moved that the report of the committee be taken up, item by item, which was carried. The first two resolutions were then taken up and adopted.

Dr. Sandford said he had confidence in the judgment of the brethren who had had recent and intimate communications with Bishop Hamline. They expressed the opinion that it was impossible to relieve his mind from the burden under which he is laboring, except by the acceptance of his resignation. They would not have had a unanimous opinion in the committee on the subject, had they not been assured that there was no other way to relieve the Bishop from his sense of responsibility.

Dr. Cartwright had been in intimate correspondence with Bishop Hamline during the greater part of his afflictions, and he spoke understandingly when he said that it was the Bishop's earnest desire to have the privilege of resigning his office. He also thought it a good time, the set time, to test the principle involved in the resolution.

Mr. Moody was in favor of the substitute. Bishop Hamline's services, before and since his election, had gained for him enduring fame, and entitled him to their most specific and positive regards, and to the honorary relation to that body contemplated in the resolution offered by Brother Collins. While the Methodist Church was racked with discord from center to circumference, he came to the General Conference, and with the might of his arm struck with the wand of his power that huge stalking shadow erst in our midst, and rolled back that portentous cloud which hung darkly over them. He thought that every principle of delicacy and of Christian courtesy would lead them to adopt the substitute proposed by Brother Collins. They knew the particular situation of the Bishop's mind. It was the peculiarity of gifted minds to feel acutely where those of a grosser cast felt not at all, and he believed that if they overrode the resignation tendered, and requested him to use his own time and judgment in seeking the restoration of his health, it would fall like a balm from heaven upon his troubled heart, and would have a more powerful influence in restoring him to health than any other means.

E. P. Tenny said that from the statement of the brother last up it appeared that Bishop Hamline had struck down the shadow of a ghost that had stalked into the Methodist Episcopal Church in relation to episcopacy. Very good; but now they wanted the General Conference to strike down the thing itself, and he hoped the original resolution would pass.

Mr. Pilcher did not rise to make a speech, but only to give a little information. He had a conver sation less than a year ago with Bishop Hamline on this very subject, and he told him he intended to resign, and hoped the General Conference would set a good example by accepting his resignation. He suggested to him that he had better not resign, but take a superannuated relation, and then be left at liberty to pursue such a course as he should think most likely to benefit his health. He told him that that would not relieve the matter at all. The sense of responsibility was too much for his enfeebled frame. If they passed the substitute it would not meet the case, for the weight of the responsibility would still be felt, and he would feel it his duty to relieve his colleagues to the very utmost of his power.

Mr. Shaffer said this was not a question of delicacy nor of sympathy; it was not a question to be decided by resolutions of professed friendship, but it was a question big with the destiny of the Methodist Episcopal Church. One objection which the friends of our system had often to meet was the difficulty that grew out of the ceremony of ordination. The argument that they had but two orders in the Church—deaconship and eldership—and that the bishopric was not a third order, was met by the question, "But why bring forward a distinct ordination like that of the Episcopal Church?" If we had a precedent that an officer could resign, we could at once point to this precedent, and silence the objectors; but why should they crush that good man with the weight of that office upon him? He was in favor of the original resolution.

Mr. Slicer was in favor of accepting the Bishop's

resignation. It would place the Methodist Episcopal Church in the United States upon a vantage
ground which she had long needed. Adopt the substitute, and, although the Bishop might not preside
in an annual conference, or make the appointment
of a single circuit preacher, he would still have his
proportion of episcopal authority and responsibility,
and it would hang as a millstone about his neck.

B. M. Hall said that in 1844 it was his unspeakable pleasure to read the famous speech of L. L.
Hamline, and he felt that God had raised up a man to
meet the crisis which they had reached. He agreed
in every word respecting that speech which had
been uttered by his brother from Ohio. He felt as
though principles were advocated and positions taken
in these days exceedingly injurious to us as a Church,
aided, as he thought they were somewhat, by the
effect of our service of ordination to the office of
superintendent. He did not blame the outsider for
insisting that they had three orders in the ministry
before he was fully initiated into its policy. He
really believed that the speech was worth more than
could be estimated in dollars and cents. That speech
made him a bishop. He went out to the Straits of
Thermopylæ just at the time to save us, and fought
nobly. Now, he would beg the brother from Ohio
not to dim the glory that encircled the head of that
man, nor the reflected glory that falls upon his conference, but let the low Church principles of that
speech be carried out to their consummation by the
very man who originated them. Then, he thought,
the Ohio Conference and Bishop Hamline would have
a double glory; then the Methodist Episcopal Church

would receive a benefit from that man which they had not received from any other living man.

Dr. Holdich thought this was not a fair case for a precedent. He was in an infirm state of health when elected, and had worked himself down by a devotion to the duties of his offic. He thought the failure of his health was not a sufficient reason for accepting his resignation, and he favored the substitute.

Dr. Durbin asked himself the question, "Will it be well for Bishop Hamline that we accept his resignation?" He believed it would be best for him. Brethren who knew him had told him it would be, and on their judgment he relied; and, therefore, it was due to Bishop Hamline that they grant his request. Bishop Hamline was competent to resign, and the conference was competent to accept his resignation.

At this point in the discussion a letter from Bishop Hamline to Jacob Young, then just received, was presented and read. An extract is as follows:

"SCHENECTADY, *May* 8, 1852.

"To REV. J. YOUNG,—Yours is just received. But for some peculiar difficulties I could get to General Conference, and wish I could, for I greatly desired to see you. But for your difficulty of sight I would have written to you a long letter asking your advice; but as I have forwarded my resignation, and, I trust by divine guidance, come to my conclusions, I will only say, when my resignation comes before the conference I hope you and all my friends will vote for it promptly. I am embarrassed by the office, and I believe in the principle of resigning, and wish to set an example. Free from office, I may yet rally in mind, and then in body, and preach a little more. I should like to fall into the conference with Revs. Jacob Young, Trimble, Heath, Connell, etc., if God so orders.

"I sent on my parchment and letter of resignation yesterday.

"To-day I am wonderfully blessed. It is one of the happiest mornings of my life. I think God approves."

Mr. Clark added that he recently had an interview with Bishop Hamline, when the Bishop told him he should resign at the next General Conference; that the Bishop said he should consider it almost a sin to retain an office the duties of which he could never hope to perform. Mr. Clark said he was convinced that if they would soothe his spirit, and place him in a position to recover, they must grant his request.

The case was now clear, no ground was left to further advocate non-acceptance. By motion of Rev. Wm. Reddy the "substitute" was laid on the table, and the original form of the report was taken up. We quote from the journals of conference:

"It was ordered to consider and act upon the report item by item.

"The first resolution of the report was unanimously adopted by a rising vote.

"The second resolution was unanimously adopted.

"The third resolution was adopted.

"The report was amended by appending the following resolution submitted by J. A. Collins, and adopted by the conference:

"'Resolved, by the delegates of the several annual conferences in General Conference assembled, that the bishops be, and they hereby are, respectfully requested to convey to Bishop Hamline the acceptance of his resignation as a superintendent of the Methodist Episcopal Church by the General Conference; accompanied with a communication expressing the profound regret of this body that the condition of his health has, in his judgment, rendered it proper for him to relinquish his official position, assuring him also of our continued confidence and affection, and that our fervent prayers will be offered to the throne of grace that his health may be restored, and his life prolonged to the Church.'

"The preamble of the report was adopted, and then the report as a whole, and as amended, was adopted.

The following is the letter of the bishops to Bishop Hamline, accompanying the record of the action of General Conference in the case, pursuant to to their order:

"CONFERENCE ROOMS, BOSTON, MAY 13, 1852.

"REV. BISHOP L. L. HAMLINE. *Dear Brother,*—In compliance with a request of the General Conference of the Methodist Episcopal Church, we herewith transmit to you a certified extract from their journal setting forth the action of that body in accepting your resignation of your episcopal office.

"In performing this duty we take occasion to join with the General Conference in expressing our 'profound regret' that Bishop Hamline's health has led him to feel it necessary to tender to the General Conference his resignation of his episcopal office. Most deeply and fraternally do we sympathize with him in his severe and protracted sufferings. Most earnestly and frequently do we invoke the blessing of God upon him. We also avail ourselves of this opportunity to express to Bishop Hamline the high satisfaction which his association with us in the superintendency of the Methodist Episcopal Church has afforded us, and the sincere regret we feel at losing him from our number. Be assured, reverend and dear brother, that in retiring from the episcopacy you bear with you our high esteem, our warm fraternal affections, and our best wishes for your future welfare.

"We remain your affectionate brethren in Christ,

"EDMUND S. JANES,
T. A. MORRIS,
B. WAUGH."

The regrets of the Church at the necessity of this resignation, and for the public loss sustained thereby, were universal. It was a day of mourning. A bright star had set. It was as "the day of his burial." It would be unseemly to publish the regretful letters received by Bishop Hamline on this occasion, but two we may not withhold from the reader, the first for its sweetness, the second for its historic insight, and both as representing the sentiments of the Church. From the seat of General Conference, Dr. E. Thomson, president of Ohio Wesleyan University (afterward Bishop) thus writes. The letter is dated May 9, 1852, two days earlier than the acceptance of the resignation, but when the inevitable result was fully foreseen:

" MY DEAR BROTHER,—I was deeply grieved to learn of your state of health, and especially that it is such as to forbid your continuance in the episcopal office. Permit me to say that I love you, that I feel under great obligation to you, that if at any time I have caused you pain I am very sorry for it, and that if at any time or in any way I can serve you, I shall be pleased if you will point it out. Most sincerely do I pray that your health may be restored, that your peace of mind may be uninterrupted, and that, whether you live long among us or die soon, you may be filled with all the fullness of God.

" Remember me, dear brother, to your excellent wife, and ask for me an interest in her prayers. I intended to call upon you when you were in Peoria, but the boat did not stop. You will do me a great favor if you will write me, and still greater if you will pray for me. I shall always value your friendship. Accept my thanks for your kindness. No bishop has been more courteous to me than yourself.

" Yours, truly,   E. THOMSON."

The following is from the Rev. Dr. J. T. Peck, President of Dickinson College, Pennsylvania (now Bishop). Those who attended the General Conference of 1844 will readily recall the discussion on the nature of the Methodist episcopacy, and corroborate the views taken in the letter of Dr. Peck. The letter is dated eight days after the final action of the conferenceon "resignation :"

"DICKINSON COLLEGE, *May* 19, 1852.

"MY DEAR BISHOP: I must beg you to allow me the use of this word as a title of respect to which I have become accustomed, and which I feel to be eminently due. Indeed, I do not know how I can reconcile my feelings to any other style of address,.for *you are my bishop*, and shall be so long as we both live. I am very well aware that you have no fondness for titles of any kind—that you are above being flattered by a name, and you will understand me fully as giving expression merely to my own feelings of profound respect, a privilege which I hope you will continue to allow me.

"To me this is a day of mourning. I find that in spite of all the evidences to the contrary I had still, almost unconsciously, retained a strong hope of your reviving again and entering to some extent upon the labors of your office. Now it comes home to my heart that your services as superintendent are lost to the Church. It is the day of your burial to me and I doubt not to thousands. But I have my consolation. It seems to be the will of God. You have been almost miraculously sustained to do what you have done. Evidently to my mind you had a distinct mission to perform in this field. God raised you up from a sick-bed; brought you to the General Conference of 1844; nerved you to make the clearest demonstration of the limits of our episcopacy on record, one which will be referred to as authority in all the future history of the Methodist Episcopal Church; secured your election to the episcopacy; gave you strength and grace to illustrate, in a brief period, throughout the length and breadth of the land, the eminently spiritual and religious character of the office; and then withdrew that supernatural strength, leaving you all the clearness of intellect and control over your own volitions as well as the disinterestedness requisite to seal by your own act those great principles of Methodism, to the support of which you had given all the logic of language and of a consistent life. *It is of God.* I have not a doubt of it. Any reflecting man acquainted with the genius of ecclesiastical power, who thoroughly examined the state and tendencies of our episcopacy as they developed themselves in 1844, could not fail to see where we were drifting. To the

surprise of most of us, when the *officer* (Bishop Andrew) was
called in question, he was found to have silently and imper-
ceptibly intrenched himself in an *order*, which was the negative
of the whole system, and which we had been in the habit of
repudiating openly and constantly from the first. Fortified in
this position by the high-Church notions of the senior bishop
(Bishop Soule), and a large number of leading men, it was
already a difficult and perilous matter to define our episcopacy
by the laws of its institution, and throw off the new construction which had been the silent growth of years of uninterrupted
prosperity. The disunion came on, and I honestly believe it
was timely. The right to remove an officer when he had dis-
qualified himself for the office was demonstrated. The assertion of degradation, in such a result, was repudiated, and by a
mysterious train of providences, in which you have been the
prominent instrument, extending to the right of resignation, by
the concurrence of the appointing power, we have obtained at
last a definition of Methodist episcopacy, which is immortal in
history, which no sophistry can evade, no art can render equiv-
ocal. None but God can foresee the immense practical importance of this achievement. I hail it as one of the providential
indications that he has yet a work of immense importance for
the Methodist Episcopal Church to do.

"And may we not hope, my dear brother, that this relief
from the burden of work and responsibility will be favorable to
the recovery of your health? It will certainly give you quiet
of mind, and remove much perplexity from your correspondence. Oh that you might be favored with returning strength !
How I should thank God to see you rising again—to hear your
voice once more on Zion's walls. Take courage, my brother,
it may even yet be so. It will be so if God has yet another
work for you to do. But be this as it may, you will be sweetly
in the hands of your kind Father. I was gratified to observe
the feeling of tender regret, in General Conference, for your
illness, and for the loss the Church had sustained in the failure
of your health. If you had not urged the case in a private letter they would have been importunate for the withdrawal of
your resignation."

The feelings of Bishop Hamline, after the deter-
mination of his case by General Conference, were

those of thankfulness, satisfaction, and rest. The
agony was now over. The critical point of his history was passed. To him and to the Church, it was
grateful to know that, if it must be done, it had now
also been well done. The great change had taken
effect under such prudent counsel, and discreet and
dignified action, that both in the principles and the
personal feelings involved in the method of accom-
plishing the delicate work, it had secured the greatest
satisfaction. He had accepted the office unsought,
and as a cross, under a marvelous sense of duty, and
now, after eight years of overwork in great infirmity
of body, he had laid it down, by providential order,
as a burden he could no longer bear. "I feel," said
he in a letter to Rev. L. Swormstedt, "that a mountain load has fallen from me. I regret some erroneou-
ous statements in discussing my resignation, but it
can not be helped, and I am free from this office. As
to *orders* I am as much a bishop as ever, but I am
not called to superintend '*at large.*' I know I was
never worthy of the office, and *you* know I never
sought it, nor thought of it." Again he says: "The
'acceptance' was received on the 13th (yesterday),
and gave me comfort. Others who crave the honors
of office are welcome to them. I have more comfort
in leaving than in receiving office, when I can leave
conscientiously, as I now do. I am now a 'local
preacher,' and if I could only preach I would be very
busy, I assure you. But my power of speech, and
almost of breathing, is gone. I will wait on the Lord,
and be of good courage." Bishop Morris writes to
Bishop Hamline, July 27th: "The acts of the late
General Conference, with a few exceptions, accord

with my views of propriety. . . . Had I been similarly situated in regard to health, I think I should have pursued the same course you did. I never doubted the doctrine that a Methodist bishop, in good standing, might resign his office, that the General Conference might accept it, and allow him to return to the ranks of the eldership for an appointment, or for such relation as his health required."

The resignation of Bishop Hamline was the subject of criticism, not entirely friendly, by the Church South. The case of Bishop Andrew, at the General Conference of 1844, as we have seen, forced the Southern delegates upon the ground of at least moderate Puseyism. Indeed, they never defined, logically or theologically, their own doctrine further than that it was assumed that in ordination the episcopal candidate received something which he thenceforward held through life, or till "excommunicated by due process of trial:" According to this his rank must be priestly, not simply ecclesiastical ; held *jure divino*, not *jure humano*; belonging to the essence, not the economy of the Church ; made to stand upon an exact parity with the order of elder, only a grade higher.

According to this theory a bishop might, perhaps, resign his jurisdiction, or the active functions of his office, but not his parchments, as, on the same principle, an elder from failure of health may resign the pastoral function without surrendering his ordination papers. But the cases are not parallel. A bishop of the Methodist Episcopal Church, in resigning his episcopal parchments, resigns only the pastoral function, or jurisdiction of office, not his priestly order. All that distinguished him from the presbyter was the extent and authority of his ecclesiastical jurisdiction. This governmental power was all that was conferred in the solemn form of his ordination, and this surrendered, he retires ecclesiastically to the simple rank of a presbyter. His episcopal parchments are only his vouchers for the legitimate investiture and exercise of this new prudential power. The form of episcopal ordination is not, therefore, evidence of priestly rank, but only of the solemnity, greatness, and legitimacy of the new jurisdictional function. The question proposed · to the episcopal candidate, in ordination, touching the distinguishing feature of his office, is not the same as in the ordination of deacons or elders, but simply : " Are you persuaded that you are truly called to this ministration according to the will of our Lord Jesus Christ?" The "call" is to a "ministration," which is elsewhere defined as belonging to the ecclesiastical economy of the Church, and the specific work, and his call thereto the candidate professes to believe to be "according to the will of our Lord Jesus Christ." This office being prudential, the officer is subject to the judgment of General Conference, by whom he was elected, not merely for his moral conduct, but for the legality and discreetness of his administration, and his acceptability before the Churches. This view does not derogate from the dignity and solemnity of the office.

There was a moral grandeur in the act of Bishop Hamline, in resigning, of great significance, and, while the Church regretted the fact, they approved the principle involved in it. The right to resign, and of General Conference to accept, was according to the doctrine of Wesley, of Asbury, and of the Methodist Episcopal Church; and no act, simply ecclesiastical, has ever occurred in the history of our Church of broader import or more decisive influence upon its polity in the generation to come.

CHAPTER XXIII.

[1852 to 1854.]

RETIRES TO PRIVATE LIFE—THOUGHTS OF TRAVEL—WEALTH AND LIBERALITY.

AFTER the General Conference of 1852 Bishop Hamline removed to Hillsdale, N. Y., where among his family friends he enjoyed retirement for about one year. The change of official relation to the Church wrought no change in his solicitude and sympathy for his active brethren, and for the cause of the Redeemer. To Rev. Dr. Roe he writes, September 16, 1852:

"Your remark that 'life seemed a failure' has been thought of almost daily since you wrote to me. But, my dear brother, if we get to heaven, probation will not be a failure; and then, in that blessed world, God will employ us in serving and glorifying him, and life, immortal life, will not then be a failure. Let us, therefore, lift up our heads and rejoice. Our redemption is nigh if we steadfastly believe."

To the Rev. John M. Leavitt, his son in the gospel, whose conversion has been already given, he writes (November 13th), to strengthen his heart in the great decision he had made in resigning the legal profession for that of the gospel ministry:

"May grace, mercy, and peace be with you in all your work and all your labors of love, so that God's vineyard may prosper more and more under your culture. It is a great but blessed enterprise of immortal moment in which you are engaged, and to which you have consecrated life. And do you not, in the light of transpiring events, congratulate yourself and adore Christ more and more, that you are snatched from the world and placed on the walls of Zion? Look at the great Webster, fading away and forgotten as a dream. Not one of his works, lauded as he is, is of so great moment as to have been the means of plucking one sinner as a 'brand from the burning.' Surely, in the light of such a close of such a life, God's humble ministers should renew the praises of him who brought them out of darkness into his marvelous light, and commissioned them to teach others the new song.

"May you long continue a messenger of life to poor dead souls! We have peace through the blood of the Lamb; 'peace which passeth all understanding.'"

Various expedients were proposed for the benefit of his health, among which was a voyage to Europe, in which Dr. Palmer, of New York, kindly volunteered as a medical companion. In a letter to the same, April, 1853, Bishop Hamline says:

"Your most unexpected offer to go to Europe and bestow on me by the way your most grateful Christian society and prayers, and a watchful care of my health and comfort, has greatly affected me. It is just the mode of traveling I should have desired of all conceivable modes, and when your letter came to hand I had scarcely a doubt but that I should go. True, I was in a most difficult position to tear myself from, and saw it at the first glance; but the object seemed so momentous that I supposed there could hardly be a question as to the propriety of my acceding to your generous proposal. The point of difficulty, however, is the oppression of confinement and company. When you were last here this was in a measure palliated, but has returned upon me with great severity. Last Sabbath (a precious Sabbath to my soul) I attempted to lead in the prayer-meeting; broke down; had one of my worst turns; and since then I can scarcely endure to be in the house at all, and feel comfortable only while in the fresh air abroad. I stay, probably, from twelve to fourteen hours in twenty-four, either in the garden and field, or at my open window, with the fresh chill breezes of April fanning me. How, then, can I endure the cabin or the state-room, with a hundred passengers, less or more, around me, and the horrors of seasickness superadded? I believe I should die. I can not go."

A residence in Palestine was suggested. He says:

"I have long inclined to the opinion that the Jews will be literally gathered into Palestine; that either personally. or spiritually Christ will reign over them there; that before their gathering occurs they will be, generally, converts to the Christian faith; that their dispersion, not their gathering, will facilitate their conversion, just as Chinamen in America could be more easily Christianized than in China. Of course, I incline to think that you could do more for them in New York than you could in Palestine. But I only incline to this view.

"As to myself, I am totally superannuated. I might get to Palestine if on shipboard, but I should be a nuisance on its soil, with scarcely power of locomotion, and scarcely power to be at rest. If being there could enable me to show how deeply I am a debtor both to the Jew and to the Gentile, I would freely go for that end. Yet if it were the mere show of conscious indebtedness it would not be wisdom to go. I will wait on the Lord as to my future, and hold myself ready to follow all the openings and leadings of his Providence. Pray that I may be willing to be guided."

At this time considerable attention was drawn toward Palestine, and some, under a belief that Christ was soon to appear there, had actually taken residence in the Holy Land to prepare the way and to welcome his coming. The ardent soul of the Bishop, caged in a broken and falling tenement, struggled to be free. Though no enthusiast, he would have traversed the wide world in quest of the "lost sheep." Writing to Rev. L. Swormstedt, December 5, 1853, he says:

. "You have now a great missionary meeting. What would you think, if I should turn missionary, on my own hook, to Italy, Palestine, or India? There is no great hope, however, for age creeps on apace. 'I am,' as Brother Quinn said in

1843, 'a feeble old man.' O may we all be ready to be crowned! Jesus is precious, and we may get very near to him."

But he was a full believer in the rapid fulfillment of prophecy and the near coming of Christ. In January 3, 1854, he writes to Dr. and Mrs. Palmer:

"The new year opens pleasantly upon us. Jesus is precious. We may expect great things this year. Prophecy unfolds; veils are being lifted; our God will soon come and will not keep silence; a fire shall devour before him, and it shall be very tempestuous round about him. We trust to be gathered with his saints, for we make a covenant with him by sacrifice. How warm my heart grows as I write these broken words; but we go where joys shall flow in equal numbers. Praise be to God and the Lamb!"

Parental care and solicitude were mingled in all his prayers and thoughts, and often found expression in loving family epistles. To his son, who had now graduated and taken the profession of medicine, he thus writes:

"HILLSDALE, *January* 6, 1854.

"To Dr. L. P. HAMLINE: *My dear Son*—We were very lonely after you left us. Our prayers followed you on your way. I trust you roused up and was cheerful on your return home. We are in a world of suffering, and must have our share with others. We can find no true refuge but in Christ. In youth, as well as in old age, we need a Savior. O, my son, my dear son, rest not but on the bosom of Jesus. I can scarcely write this evening, but it seemed a little like talking with you to write a few words, and I thought I would attempt it, for after you went away I found it so lonely without you, that I regretted your departure, even though reason approved it, seeing I expect you down again soon. I will add a little in the morning. I trust you will be blest through Christ our Lord."

Though unable to go out to war as in other days, Bishop Hamline's heart was toward them that offered themselves freely to the Lord's army, and his sympathies were alive to the progress of the Redeemer's kingdom. This appears in all his letters, whether of friendship or on business. "I hear of great revivals among you," he writes to Rev. M. P. Gaddis. "Praise God for this. Revivals are the great hope of the Church. There can be no Church without them. May the people and preachers never forget it. I pray that Brother Caughey may be a son of thunder in Ohio. He is a heavenly-minded man, unlike some who went before him as revivalists, and, I think, worthy of great confidence."

On April 20, 1854, Mr. Hamline left Hillsdale and returned to his relative, Mr. Ford, near Schenectady. Here he records:

"*Sunday*, 23.—At Mr. E. Ford's, Rotterdam. Attended Church in P. M., but felt unusual dryness. The local brother gave us a good sermon, however, and here is a people devoted to God.

"*Monday, May* 8.—The Lord has blessed me this day. I feel that Jesus is unspeakably precious. My soul breathes after him. 'Whom have I in heaven but thee!' is the exclamation of my soul, visited by the Spirit of the Son sent forth into my heart, crying, Abba, Father.

"*Tuesday*, 9.—'I will extol thee, my God, O King, and will praise thy name for ever and ever! With my whole heart will I praise thee.' This has been a day of precious blessings to my soul. Lord, thou knowest if I am thine. Let me know myself, and not mistake where eternity depends."

As an experiment upon his health, after a few weeks, he removes for a time to Sharon Springs, a pleasant village and watering-place in Schoharie County, New York. His stay was about two weeks too short for any permanent effect, though he says: "I trust the waters have done me some good." While at the Springs he writes:

"SHARON SPRINGS, *Sunday* 14.—This lovely Sabbath is spent without any but closet privileges; but these are precious.

There is a chapel half a mile off, occupied by the Lutherans
and Methodists alternately. This is the Lutherans' day. It
seemed to me it would be a feast to my soul to hear the Lutheran,
but was too ill to go. I am here at a hotel, but the family is
very kind. . . . Lord, give me this day the waters of life.

> 'Insatiate to this spring I fly,
> I drink and yet am ever dry.'"

He left the Springs May 27th and returned to his
residence near Schenectady. On Sunday, June 11th,
he records:

"The holy Sabbath. Have felt humbled under the mighty
hand of God. Life with me is almost past; but a fragment
remains. I have attempted to serve my God for many years,
yet when I bear these services into the presence of God's law,
and compare them with its stern and righteous requirements, I
am confounded, and cry out, 'God be merciful to me a sinner!'
O Lord, I am ashamed to lift up my face in thy presence! I
lie in the dust, I put my hand upon my mouth. I beseech thee,
O God, to show me, this day, the malignity of sin and the fullness of the Savior—his power and willingness to deliver me
from sin! Thou hast brought me to taste the sweetness of pardon and freedom in Christ. Convey, I beseech thee, to-day,
while I wait before thee in prayer and in communing with thy
word, a fresh witness of thy favor, which is life, and of thy
loving-kindness, which is better than life. O bless with thy
salvation, thy full salvation."

In a letter to dear friends, June 12th, and allud-
ing to their notice of fulfillment of prophetic signs
preceding the coming of Christ. He says:

"Your last deeply interests me—us; but amid the coming
events we forget not 'Glorious things are spoken of thee, O city
of God!' Jews and Papists will all disappear by ingrafting into
Christ, or wrath from his judgment sentence. May the little
Jew be a shining light! My mind is comfortable. I rest in
Him who says, 'Ye shall find rest.' I find it."

In his diary he thus writes:

"*September* 1.—Reading Baxter's 'Saints' Rest' a few days
has greatly refreshed me. It and Wesley's incomparable ser-

mons (the Bible first), and hymn book, are a precious Christian library. I believe I have seen more clearly into my own heart of late, more clearly, too, the preciousness of Christ. O what a vile heart! O what a precious Savior! 'His name shall be called Jesus, for he shall save his people from their sins.' I need yet further and fuller discoveries. I desire such a view of my sins always as, but for divine support and comfort, would destroy me; and then such views of Christ, that if my sins were ten thousand times more, yea, more than those of the whole world in all its generations, I could instantly by faith cast them all on Him who bore them all in his own body on the tree. Such views are needful for me. By these, endeared each day more clear and more affecting, must I grow in grace. Each step in the knowledge of Christ must be a step also in the knowledge of myself; just as increasing light, thrown on a painting, renders more distinct the background as well as the features and finish of the portrait.

"*Sunday*, 3.—I am very feeble to-day, too ill to visit God's house; breathe with difficulty, feel as though I might easily expire in a few minutes; yet, by my earnest request, Mrs. Hamline is at meeting, and I am glad she is there. If I should expire and reach heaven before she returns, how wonderful it would be. I do not dread the journey more than she does her return, nor am I alone. Christ is with me and in me."

As it was during the years 1853–4 that Bishop Hamline's property interests and bequests came more prominently before the public, it seems proper to here pause and survey rapidly both his financial ability and his habit of benevolent giving. This is the more proper, partly because he has been misunderstood by some at this point, but chiefly because "pure religion and undefiled before God, even the Father," is declared in Scripture to be unworldly and unselfish, and is universally thus accepted among men, whether Christians or unbelievers.

No part of the life of Bishop Hamline more beautifully illustrates the depth of his experience, and the sincerity and strength of his Christian character than his practice of disposing his temporal affairs. In his earlier life he was ambitious of wealth, and by his marriage came into possession of a comfortable estate, which, with his profession gave him ease and a qualified affluence. But his conversion changed the whole plan of his life. Within a year after this event he began to preach, and when settled in his convictions that this was his calling, he immediately "left all to follow Christ."

As to his temporal affairs, they gave him no concern. The time he gave to them scarcely equaled two days in a year. As early as convenient, after entering the itinerancy, he committed all his property interests to the trusty hands of Daniel Brush, Esq., President of the Zanesville Bank, himself a Methodist and a gentleman of high standing for probity and prudence. Later this care fell to Mr. Brush's son-in-law, Mr. J. Taylor, and still later to Grant Goodrich, Esq. (now Judge Goodrich), of Chicago. His agents were always faithful and competent. This enabled him to turn to his one work, "knowing nothing among men save Jesus Christ and him crucified." It is interesting to know how lightly the cares of this world sat upon him, and how true was his Christian conscience to acquit himself faithfully as the Lord's steward. When it became necessary, on account of his itinerant life, to dispose of his property in Zanesville, and to invest elsewhere, he had no plan or thought to do more than preserve what he already had by simple loans on interest. But after earnest advice and solicitation he consented to invest, especially in consideration of his son's growing family, and the probable wants of his faithful wife if she should survive him. After full consultation with Mr. A. Garrett (whose widow afterward founded the Garrett Biblical Institute at Evanston), and with Hon. Grant Goodrich, to whom he had now committed the agency of all his fiscal affairs, an investment was made in real estate in Chicago.

In a letter to Mr. Goodrich, December 14, 1851, he thus expresses his concern at the amount of care which necessarily devolved on him in managing his affairs :

"I fear these various matters, small and great, invade your time too much, considering how arduous such professional researches—'*viginti annorum*,' etc.—are, which the lawyer is compelled to by severe necessity. But I do not see, in my present sick state and remote position, how I can otherwise attend to the business which (I trust not without providential favor) now lies at Chicago and in your hands. But if it is a serious annoyance do not hide it from me. Be sure to let me know. Unless there is a radical improvement in my health, I shall (*inter nos*) positively decline my present office in May; and if I have strength enough to do any thing, I can contribute a little counsel in my business. Be assured, however, I shall never attempt to be a business man, or approach that character. My face is strongly set in another direction. And I can not sufficiently praise God that he gives me neither the disposition nor the necessity to mingle in the affairs of this vain world. Blessed be his goodness !"

It was late in Bishop Hamline's life before his property investments had largely appreciated so as to entitle him popularly to the rank of a moderately wealthy man. It was not till 1853 that he was estimated to be worth one hundred thousand dollars. But even this was not all productive. A liberal subtraction from available income must be made for unproductive property, for taxes, repairs, insurances,

payment of agent, etc. As to his salary as bishop
he says: "After paying traveling expenses, all goes
back to the Church." As to his donations he says,
May, 1854, "I have been giving about one thousand
dollars annually, one-half my income, in small donations here and there, and tried to think I was doing
my part; but of late I have felt dissatisfied, and
began to feel I was 'laying up,' or Providence was
laying up for me, and that it might be my duty to
invade the principal." In another place he says: "I
did not sleep last night till twelve o'clock. The Lord
greatly blessed me. I think I shall do more for the
Church, pecuniarily, at least." Thus his thoughts
ran. When it was first announced to him that his
real estate was valued as above, he retired and upon
his knees in prayer and thanksgiving consecrated it
to God. But it was a large trust and could not, by
human wisdom, be suddenly disposed of. The cause
of education in the West had been much on his mind,
and he desired to aid the more distant West as being
less able to sustain colleges and institutions of the
higher grade. With this view he. opened a correspondence with Rev. D. Brooks, of Minnesota, and
Rev. G. B. Bowman, of Iowa Conference, to ascertain what were their plans for education and what
their needs. At this time he had no knowledge of
any existing colleges in these conferences, but simply
sought information with a view to the most judicious
disposition of his means.

To the Rev. C. Kingsley (afterward Bishop Kingsley) he writes, April 17, 1854:

"I have sought for some months to concentrate my pecun-
iary means of usefulness at some very needy point, with the

purpose of a very special effort, on an extensive scale, to furnish the means and facilities of education to a large number of young persons. For this end I have been in correspondence with frontier ministers, where the field is comparatively unoccupied, and yet is so filling up with emigrants that no time should be lost. To accomplish this enterprise I have pledged to a friend, who joins me in it, all that I can possibly spare for years to come in this good cause—more than one-half of my yearly income—and ultimately about half of all my possessions."

To Rev. C. W. Sears he writes, May 17th:

"I have felt a great desire to do something in the cause of education, especially in a way to promote missions."

These extracts are from letters to the above brethren who were agents for colleges, and had communicated with Bishop Hamline.

The brethren, Brooks and Bowman, above named, waited on Bishop Hamline at an early date, and the result of their visit is thus given by Bishop Hamline in his diary:

"*May 25,* 1854.—Have been visited by Rev. David Brooks, presiding elder of St. Paul District of the Methodist Episcopal Church in Minnesota. Have donated twenty-five thousand dollars for the university in Minnesota. This is about one-fourth of my estate. I have done it in a wholesome dread of such scriptures as 'How hardly shall they that have riches enter into the kingdom of heaven.' God has prospered me without my own agency, and added to the value of my possessions.

"*Tuesday,* 30.—Brother Bowman, agent of the Mount Vernon Institution, Iowa, has been with me since yesterday morning. I have pledged him another twenty-five thousand dollars for a college at Mount Vernon, if he succeeds in getting a charter, and the Iowa Conference and North-western University separate. Thus, within one week, I have endeavored to consecrate half I have on earth to my blessed Redeemer. I should have no comfort in this but for the strong hope that, when I am gone, some of God's gifts to me shall be my voluntary gift to his blessed cause. O how condescending in him to seem to make something mine, that my heart, moved by his own goodness and Holy Spirit, may seem to return something to him. How fondly do I hope that in after time a Judson, or a Wesley, or a Nast, or a Jacoby may be nourished up for the Church in the very institutions which I feebly assisted to rear. I rejoice that my dear Mrs. Hamline is so cheerfully, cordially, and forwardly united with me in these considerable donations of fifty thousand dollars. We have still fifty thousand dollars left. In view of my son and his family, and of two families (a brother's and sister's) which I have principally to support, I think it will be right for me to keep my estate at about its present value. If it increases, or lands advance in value, Lord, help me to watch against riches! And now, O Lord, show me thy glory in the face of Jesus Christ! Amen."

As the Institution in Minnesota was named the "Hamline University," and as public notice of the gift was forbidden by Bishop Hamline (according to his habit in bestowing benefactions), it went abroad that the gift was bestowed in consideration of giving the Bishop's name to the college. But this was untrue, and it is just to his memory to correct the error by giving the following extract from a published letter of Dr. David Brooks, dated Red Wing, May 10th, 1855. In the letter he says:

"Having seen an article in the *Western Christian Advocate* asking for information as to a donation of twenty-five thousand dollars given by our beloved Bishop Hamline, I wish to say Brother Hamline wrote to several brethren in Iowa and Minnesota—to me among them—stating that he proposed to appropriate fifty thousand dollars of his estate to colleges in the far west.

"I happened to be the first to respond, and to visit him. I found him at Sharon Springs, New York, where—though scarcely able to see company—he received me very kindly, examined the posture and prospects of our university, just then chartered, and, without a word of persuasion, gave us twenty-five thousand dollars, about one half of which is in hand, to be used in putting up college buildings.

"In this transaction there seemed a singular coincidence. We had just got our university charter, and, without a syllable of correspondence with Brother Hamline, had given it his name. We had never notified him that we had even thought of a university in Minnesota till I received his letter. If he desired the honor of giving a *name* to the college, that was secured to him without a donation, as the institution was already chartered. But to the fact that I visited him before the Iowa brethren, who were a week later, I owe it under Providence that I obtained the first subscription, and not to the *name of the college.*

"Some conditions were annexed to his subscription, as, for instance, a portion of it should form a permanent endowment fund. Bishop Hamline insisted, also, that no public notice should be given of his bequest, which is the reason that hints only have crept into the press. But now, as many are inquiring on the subject, and some erroneous notices have been before the public, I presume it is right and proper to give this explanation. Red Wing is in Minnesota, and not Wisconsin."

In writing to Rev. E. S. Grumley, August 25th, 1854, Bishop Hamline says:

"Yours received. I have given twenty-five thousand dollars to the Minnesota University, but the name was all unknown to me, and was given it before they expected any thing from me. I wish the name was changed. I will write again soon. I will give no institution any thing for a name."

Bishop Hamline's income was never large. From two thousand dollars it increased to "less than five thousand dollars per annum;" but when from this he had met his necessary foreign claims, the amount left was "between five hundred dollars and six hundred dollars," and this at a time when within the five months previous his benevolent donations had amounted to five hundred and eighty-five dollars. He generally anticipated his income. Writing to Bishop Janes, September, 1851, he says:

"I find they are about attempting a German Church in Albany. I hope to be able to give something toward it during the winter, but must wait a little, as I find I have given almost three hundred dollars (mostly in the West) within eight weeks, and as I can only spare at about half that rate consistently during the year, I shall be compelled to check my hand."

This shows that his habit of giving at that time was at the rate of nearly one thousand dollars per annum, which was more than half his net income at that time. His agent, Mr. Brush, asked him for a donation of two hundred and fifty dollars for a chapel for the Ohio Wesleyan University. Bishop Hamline sent him a list of his donations for the few preceding months "and asked him to say if he thought he ought to give it?" to which he promptly answered "*no.*" He gave it, however, with addition, a little later. Another brother, a college agent, wrote him, and " thought he ought to give a thousand," intimating that it was considered he lacked in liberality. Two hundred and seventy dollars he had recently given to the same institution. In reply, and after a courteous explanation of his affairs, Bishop Hamline says :

"I trust always to receive in a proper manner the admonitions of my brethren on every point of duty. In regard to donations I am told by some valued friends, acquainted with my circumstances, that I am too lavish. I infer from your letter that yourself and some around you think me far otherwise. I can have no hope of meeting the views of both parties, and perhaps ought to think myself happy in the middle course. . . .

"I must add one more remark. I can not purchase reputation from brethren who accuse me of covetousness, while I am probably laying out less expense on myself and family than they are, and am giving not one-tenth, but six-tenths or seven-tenths of all my income to the Church. I would not for any thing pay a price to such to hush their 'gainsayings.' Above all, I would not buy from these brethren the verdict that I am pure and good. I am not willing, therefore, that my name should appear on your list of subscribers. I will request you, therefore, to have the one hundred dollars alluded to by you, credited as a subscription by my friend Dr. C. Elliott, and the one hundred and seventy dollars, forwarded to Mr. Brush some weeks ago, when paid, credited as a subscription of one hundred dollars to L. Swormstedt, and seventy dollars of it pay the subscription of Rev. Jacob Young. May our Heavenly Father bless you for Christ's sake.

"Affectionately L. L. HAMLINE."

The rebuke of this letter needs no comment, and the sharp edge of it, in the spirit of dignified meekness and charity, is thoroughly characteristic of the writer.

In 1856 Bishop Hamline was appealed to for personal aid by a stranger, recommended by several friends. In reply, he confesses that "the statement of his condition was a clear case to call forth Christian sympathy." But after courteously detailing the reasons for declining aid—which, indeed, was impossible without a forced sale of real estate—and stating "I never yet received [from my estate] two thousand dollars per annum, clear of taxes, repairs of buildings," etc., he says:

"My dear sir, I answer thus at length, because I fear to decline a call of this kind without such reasons as will do to present in the judgment to Him who says, 'Inasmuch as ye have done it unto my brethren, ye have done it unto me,' shall be made a test of fitness for the benedictions of that swiftly coming day."

Writing to a beloved brother, an agent, on business, in 1855, he drops these words:

"I am now without a hundred dollars in the world above the necessary provision for family current expenses, living very economically at that, and I do not expect any surplus income for two or three years to come. I can not purchase me a home, having no means for that object. It is not very probable I shall feel it my duty (or privilege rather) to give much more to colleges. Yet if the same advance should be realized on Chicago property for six years to come, as for five years past, I might give more to that good object. Then I will, if Bloomington should be under your care, and you still advise it, remember that young college."

It is an interesting evidence of his Christian sincerity in giving that in 1864, when he had relieved himself of the heavy obligations assumed for other institutions, he remembered that in 1855 he had been applied to for aid for a seminary in Maine, which he was then forced to decline. Being now in condition to respond to the call, he is still embarrassed at having mislaid the letter. Not being able to recall which institution had made the application he writes to each of the Methodist seminaries of that State to find the one desired. In his letter he says,—"I have hope that I shall be able to resume my benefactions abroad very soon, if I live, and if I do not live—which seems now likely—I wish to have my last will and testament in such a form as seems to harmonize with providential indications, and my own former purposes when I could judge better than in my present weakness." This was a little over a year before his death.

To various literary institutions, too many to mention, from Maine to Minnesota, he contributed in smallers sums of from one hundred to three thousand dollars. To Dr. Scott, for the Irish educational fund, he gave one thousand dollars. To Churches he has lent aid in a similar ratio as to literary institutions. His aid to the German missions in this country has already been noticed. His stated annual subscription to the Methodist Missionary Society was one hundred dollars, which sometimes went up to two hundred and fifty dollars. To the Bible Society he was a liberal patron, and left an annuity of one hundred dollars, with a further bequest of one thousand dollars; and the same to the Methodist Missionary Society, and the Ohio Wesleyan University, at Delaware, Ohio. These often required the sale of real estate, as his correspondence shows. He also left directions for various other bequests, to be executed by his surviving partner, some of which have been paid, and all provided for. To individuals his benefactions were constant and unnumbered. Toward his aged brethren, less favored with worldly stores, he was drawn in true practical sympathy, not only in personal benefactions, but by making benevolent donations in their name and to their credit, or by assuming their subscriptions, thus keeping up their social status. Yet, as we have seen, there were not wanting those who thought him parsimonious. Rumor had given an indefinite, and imagination almost a boundless, extent to his means, and applications flowed in upon him for aid from all quarters, and almost for all objects. To courteously answer these involved an amount of correspondence which his later years could not well sustain; while declinatures were construed as evidence of penurious tendency, a common liability of infirmity and age. His friends understood the case, but strangers and illiberal minds were left to their sinister suspicions. It would be to expect too much of human nature to require that a disappointed applicant should return well impressed and lovingly disposed. Bishop Hamline's habit of life was always simple and frugal, comparing well with the average fare of his itinerant brethren; but even this, though adopted for conscience' sake, and as a necessary condition of benevolent liberality, was sometimes imputed to an unworthy motive by those who could not penetrate the mystery that "it is more blessed to give than to receive."

In his first years in the itinerancy he was in the habit of giving to his brother ministers whatever he received from the Church, they being in greater necessity. In a letter to his sister, accompanying a valuable remittance, he says:

"I have been careful all my days, or I should have been a pauper now. I fear I am almost the only one of the family that always had a place for every thing and every thing in its place. I never throw any thing down, but put it in its place. When I have ten dollars I study what I can do without and buy little, and then what I want most. . . . I want my nephew to receive and practice this lesson."

This was Mr. Wesley's habit. His well-known maxim was, "Make all you can honestly, save all you can, give all you can." Wesley wore no fine clothes, allowed no useless expenditure, was the chief support of his father's family, gave away fortunes. Bishop Hamline's heart and his house were open and hospitable, and he was in sympathy with every good work. There were other claims than his own, as we have seen, upon the family estate, and the fluctuations of

value of property might at any time reduce his possessions to a moiety of their then estimated value.
Indeed, his revenue fell off more than two thousand
dollars in one year (1860). Much of his property
was inherited from his first wife, and due to their son
and his family.

Upon a candid review of his course it must be
conceded that he acted wisely. As a steward of the
Lord he used the proceeds of his capital, and not unfrequently portions of the capital itself, for beneficent
and Christian ends, adopting the maxims to help the
most needy when equally worthy. To have wholly
dispossessed himself to enrich others would have been
only to cause the same capital to change hands. This
might have (as in the fable) only destroyed the source
of the "golden egg," and in any wise it would not
have been in harmony with the Lord's method to
take the talent from him who improves it to give to
another, but only from him who buries it and abuses
his trust. There is no reason to suppose that the
same capital could have been made more productive
of aid to the kingdom of Christ in any other hands.
By the Church he must be accounted a true son of
John Wesley, as we doubt not he is by Christ pronounced "a good and faithful servant."

CHAPTER XXIV.

*RETIRED OCCUPATIONS—"ALWAYS ABOUNDING IN THE
WORK OF THE LORD."*

THE opening of the year 1855 finds Bishop Hamline still at his residence near Schenectady, to
which he had returned from Hillsdale, April 20th,
1854, and where he continued till the spring of 1857—
about three consecutive years. Here, as his strength
permitted, he employed his time in reading, meditation, and prayer, in social meetings at his house, in
visiting and talking with the neighbors, in correspondence with friends abroad, in attending the usual
Sabbath services and class meetings, and in such
extra meetings as he was able to sustain by help from
visiting ministers, and in receiving his numerous calls
from friends abroad. As his life was quite retired
and himself greatly burdened with infirmity the
events of his history were few.

The rural home of Bishop Hamline is thus de-
scribed by his venerable and faithful friend, Rev. J.
B. Finley, in a letter to the *Western Christian
Advocate:*

"I write you from the beautiful cottage of our mutual
friend, Rev. L. L. Hamline, situated on a public road leading
from Schenectady to Albany, and where the turnpike and
plank-roads to that city intersect. It stands on a beautiful
eminence, and is indeed a most lovely spot. The cottage is
forty-eight feet, in front and twenty-six back, containing five

rooms below, two large pantries, and the office of his son—Dr. Hamline. Four chambers above were finished as bedrooms, with a room containing his unbound library, one hundred volumes of the *North American Review*, with all of the Methodist Reviews, and a large number of the Biblical Repositories, with much other useful American literature. Bishop Hamline's entire library contains about eleven hundred volumes of choice books. The cottage is neatly but plainly painted; every room carpeted, nearly all of them papered very neatly, and furniture corresponding to the plain neatness of the house and the piety of its inmates. A fine piano stands in the parlor, and daily discourses cheering music.

"It will be a treat, no doubt, for many of Brother Hamline's ardent Christian and other friends, to know that in the midst of all his bodily affliction he is comfortably situated; his health is various—sometimes it permits his being up and taking some moderate exercise; at other times he is confined entirely to his room; his disease is *angina pectoris*, with others, which often bring on a state of suffocation; his nervous system is much shattered, yet he is as devoted a Christian as he has been ever since he professed to be born of God. His mind is still vigorous, and he is looking forward in joyful expectation of an eternal rest. My good and kind sister Hamline, with whom I have been acquainted for thirty-five years, still retains her uniform piety, and is now the center around which her family circle revolves. Nothing reigns here but peace and religious influence."

His state of mind is thus given in a letter to friends in New York, January 1, 1855:

"A 'happy new year' to you both, and to your dear children. We are happy in Christ, the portion and dwelling-place of all the truly blest; out of whom none can be happy, and in whom none can be miserable. We are happy in the Holy Ghost—the Comforter—in the Father of our Spirits, God over all, blessed forever. May the fresh and full anointings of the Spirit all the year long be on you and yours, like the plentiful, priestly unctions on Aaron; nay, like the unctions of Him who is our great High Priest, in the days of his suffering for us, for it is your privilege to be partakers of the same anointing with your elder brother, that like him you may conquer and triumph."

Again later, to the same:

"I trust you are winging your way *upward*, and still striving to bear others along. I doubt not you are. Letters from the West notice glorious revivals. What developments are opening and impending! In the history and progress of events, students of the Bible must feel a lively interest. Crowding events must throw a flood of light on the prophecies, and are calculated to excite high expectations in the public (Christian) mind. May the blessed Master prepare us for the future, both of time and of eternity."

The year of 1855 was one of great and unprecedented trial to Bishop Hamline, offering a severer test of his faith and Christian graces than he had been called to hitherto.   As his affliction came through the false faith of professed friends it was the more difficult to bear, and being unprovoked and without cause as the sequel proved, he could only refer it to God.   It is beautiful to witness how he demeaned himself in this hour of darkness, and how through prayer and faith he sublimely rose above its hurtful power.   As if thrown back upon first principles he reviews his providential and Christian life, and then renews his covenant with God.

"SCHENECTADY, *Sabbath, September* 30, 1855.

"It will be twenty-seven years on the 5th day of October, now at hand, since God, through Christ, pardoned all my sins, and gave me the 'glorious liberty of the sons of God.' In about six months, without asking or seeking it, I received license to exhort; and in about a year, license to preach. In October, 1830, I was called to Short Creek Circuit, as an assistant to the venerable Jacob Young, and in 1831 was again invited to take an active sphere of labor on Mount Vernon Circuit, with Rev. James M'Mahon, a most devout and lovely man, who, like my precious Brother Young, was a father to me. In 1832 I was received on trial in the Ohio Conference, and sent to Granville Circuit with that holy man, Rev. H. S. Farnandis, in charge, and a good young brother, Stephen Holland, as a third man, on a six weeks' circuit. Here God wrought wonders in a revival at Newark. In 1833 I went to Athens Circuit, and was again blessed with the companionship of Rev. Jacob Young as my colleague. And who ever had a better counselor or friend? Here my health failed. In September, 1834, I was sent to Wesley Chapel at Cincinnati, and had for my colleague that able and faithful minister, Rev. Z. Connell. Long may he live and labor. In 1835 I was returned to Wesley Chapel with the lamented W. B. Christie, of precious memory; but before the year closed was placed in Columbus by Bishop Morris, to fill the vacancy caused by the sickness of Rev. E. W. Sehon. In September, 1836, I was ordained elder by Bishop Soule, and elected assistant editor in place of the worthy Rev. William Phillips, deceased, where I remained till 1840. In 1840 I commenced the *Ladies' Repository*, and continued it till 1844, when I was ordained superintendent, which office I resigned in 1852. I have now been almost four years at rest, and three years on the superannuated list of the Ohio Conference. This morning, under trials of no ordinary kind I have a deep sense of unworthiness before God—yea, such as my pen can not describe. But I must add, I have a wonderful sense also of the presence and smile of God. No tongue can describe how Jesus blesses me to-day. What I esteem a very gracious act on God's part, I have the most unexpected comfort and peace of soul, in a sweet submission to all the will of God.

"And now, O my God, I desire this day, by thy Holy Spirit moving me thereto and enabling me, to make a new dedication of myself to thee, and enter anew into covenant with thee. And I do yield myself afresh up to thee, O God, Father, Son, and Holy Ghost, as a 'living sacrifice, holy and acceptable unto God, through Jesus Christ my Lord,' for ever and ever to be *thine*, and thine *alone*. And herein I record this my unworthy but sincere purpose to fear, love, honor, serve, and praise thee, living in strict obedience to thy pure law, and in humble subjection and cheerful submission to thy holy will and providence in all things. Nor do I (so I trust and purpose) propose to serve and submit to thee, blessed God, on condition that I am saved out of the hand of my cruel foes (whom I pray thee to bless and bring into thy kingdom); but, whatever thy wisdom shall permit to come upon me, I pray thee for grace to keep this covenant, even passing through that valley of the shadow of death which such affliction must open before me. O Lord, even then, above all times, help thou me, that I may not only cry on the Mount of Transfiguration, 'It is good for me to be here,' but also in the Gethsemane of sorrow and in the judgment hall of offense, buffeted and spit upon, or bleeding with the agony at every pore, I may be able to cry, 'Though I walk through the valley of the shadow of death, I will fear no evil: for thou art with me; thy rod and thy staff they comfort me.' So, O Lord, even now 'thou art with me.' Amen and Amen. Eleven o'clock A. M."

On the evening of the same day he writes:

"Since I made the foregoing dedication of my all to God, I have been kept in great peace. My mind has been much exercised daily on the subject of faith, in connection with perfect love. This has led me to cry to God for some days for a specific faith in regard to it. I have not cried in vain.

"I now perceive that I have depended too much on emotions; that I have not adverted to faith as distinctly as I ought; that I had more faith than I supposed; that I needed, by some divine discipline of soul, to be taught more clearly the importance of faith in connection with this great blessing, and that some loss of comfort and strength has been a method of instruction in the great mystery of faith. But the best of all is, I do now reckon myself to be dead indeed unto sin, but alive unto God. Yes, it is gloriously true. 'My hallowing Lord hath wrought a perfect cure.' Amen."

To Dr. and Mrs. Palmer, he writes, October 15, 1855, speaking of the great blessing he had received, he says:

"On Thursday, October 4th, this visitation became, it seemed to me, almost miraculous. For about five hours I scarcely changed my position ten minutes (which, at another time, I could not have endured without great difficulty for an hour), and yet I was no more weary than though I had been reclining in perfect health on a bed of down. This memorable day of days must not be forgotten."

Three days later he writes to his venerable friend, Rev. Jacob Young:

"O my dear brother, like Jacob delivered out of the hand of Esau, I have in my wrestlings received what I was not specially looking for—a wonderful and glorious work of God in my own poor heart. I have never enjoyed such peace and fullness as I now do. The heavenly Master is preparing me to ' enter into the joy of my Lord.' His Word has such a sweetness in it as I can not describe. Oh, how I exult in the thought of meeting you in heaven, and there, in the full light of eternity, with expanded powers and spotless affections rehearse the marvelous works of God."

Through conflicts and victories a great lesson of faith was learned. "Satan," he says, "mostly assails my faith. I take it as a proof that he knows wherein my strength lies. Faith gone, Christ is gone, and, of course, all is gone, for Christ is all." But in this "good fight of faith" he was not alone. The sympathy and prayers of thousands had been awakened in his behalf. In him the Church felt an unspeakable interest, and many were the words of cheer and loving sympathy given him by those who could not see his face. Not the least among these goodly words were those of his old and beloved Ohio Conference, who, at their recent session, sent him their greeting, with a resolution unanimously passed, "expressive of their unabated confidence and affection."

In his Patmos of retirement the visitation of old friends was doubly grateful. With this he was often cheered. The Rev. Dr. Elliott, with others of Cincinnati, returning from New York, November, 1855, turned aside to greet their time-honored friend. He says:

"Messrs. Swormstedt and Poe, and ourself deemed it our duty, on returning home, to visit our much esteemed friend, Bishop Hamline. We found him in improved health. He sometimes takes part in religious meetings, by exhorting and concluding. He visits, prays, and talks with his neighbors, much to their spiritual advantage. Through the aid of Brother

Cox, from Jersey, last summer, meetings were conducted in a pine grove near his house, much to the edification of believers and conversion of sinners."

It was the policy of Bishop Hamline to utilize all gifts of visiting friends for the direct promotion of vital religion. It was in pursuance of this policy that the Rev. Henry Cox was engaged during the summer of this year for a series of grove-meetings every afternoon and evening. At the closing "meeting of the series," writes Dr. Carhart, "after sermon the Bishop arose, and, though scarcely able to stand without assistance, made an application of the sermon, and an appeal to the people, such as I have never heard equaled. The Holy Ghost fell on us; weeping was heard in every direction in the vast assembly; sobs and cries for mercy followed; and, as the speaker continued, and even before the invitation was given, penitents crowded around the rude altar, and the whole assembly, rising to their feet, seemed drawn toward the speaker, and to melt like wax before the fire. When the invitation was given to those seeking Christ to come forward, it seemed to me that the whole audience moved simultaneously, while some actually ran and threw themselves prostrate upon the ground, and shouted, 'God be merciful to me a sinner!' The memory of that scene can never be effaced from my mind."

Thus in varied labor, suffering, solicitude, and triumph, the year of 1855 wore away. A suffering sister, dying by the slow process of cancer, drew upon their loving sympathies and care, and shadowed the domestic life. She passed away in triumph. It was a year never to be forgotten, of which a bright

record was made in the religious histories of many
converts, in the grateful hearts of many friends, but,
above all, in "the Lamb's Book of Life." On receiving a great strengthening of joy and faith, Bishop
Hamline thus records, December 6, 1855:

"Jesus is precious, unutterably precious. Oh, what can he
not do for poor dying souls! for souls that believe. Never before did I see such a beauty in faith. It is the mode prescribed
by Infinite Wisdom for the reception by sinners of all the blessings of salvation, and, if Infinite Wisdom prescribed it, there
must be ample reasons for the prescription; and, as religious
influence gains power over the heart and understanding, of
course that method of salvation which God has prescribed will,
in all its parts, be more and more admired by the soul thus
saved. Faith works by love, and purifies the heart. And, although they who exercise it have no merit on its account (because even faith is wrought in them by the Holy Spirit), yet it is
a grace most comely in the eye of God, and one that he com-
mends in the strongest terms. No sin is so severely condemned
as unbelief, no Christian virtue so eulogized as faith. That
makes God a liar, this honors him above measure. Of this
it is said, 'He that believeth shall be saved;' of that, 'He
that believeth not shall be damned;' but how little is it considered that unbelief is so great a sin that it hinders the pardon of all other sins; that all prayers and cries for mercy
are utterly vain unless faith supplants unbelief in the soul.
How many are striving to please God and reach heaven by
various resolutions and efforts of amendment, while unbelief holds possession of the heart, and the struggling soul is
every moment sinking lower under its influence."

"*Tuesday, January* 1, 1856.—Comfortable morning. Christ
is precious. Company interrupts a little. I spent the time
from ten A. M. to three P. M. at E. Ford's, and dined. Had a
comfortable day. I covenant afresh with Jesus. Amen.

"*Wednesday*, 2.—Company—Brother B. Isbell and daughter. Good prayer-meeting at night. O Jesus, thou art precious!
Come near to my poor soul; dwell in me the hope of glory;
reign in me for evermore; set me as a seal upon thy heart.
Glory be unto thee, O Lord most high!

"*Saturday* 5.—Arose this morning dull, but in private

prayer, about nine A. M., the clouds fled.   A glorious day broke in upon my soul. Oh, how sweet and precious this heavenly light! Lord, abide now with me forever. Increase my faith, I pray thee, a hundred fold."

To his friends in New York he writes, January 30th:

"If Jesus walk with us on the stormiest seas we need not sink.   Like Peter, he bids me come to him on angry waves, and, though the first impulse was dismay, I was caught up, as it were, from the 'beginning to sink' by his Almighty arm, and now I am calmly and delightfully walking on the troubled waters close to his bleeding side; and never did conquering prince or monarch in his triumphant chariot, amid applauding millions, enjoy what I do.   I invite you not to mourn and lament over me, but to praise, rejoice, and give thanks. Glory be to God on high!   I am weary or I would dwell on the theme. 'Farewell."

Many sought words of counsel from his pen, which had not been entirely disabled by his infirmity.   The Rev. Dr. Leavitt, who ever reverenced and loved the Bishop as his spiritual father, was now in the flush of manhood.   His religious experience, which had very much taken the type of that of Bishop Hamline, had served to intensify his desire of Biblical knowledge in the direction of philological study.   The new spiritual trial to which this exposed him he thus unfolds in a letter to the Bishop:

"— To what next shall I refer? My inner life? Here is, indeed, a boundless theme.   Yet, how often have I poured its history into your ear. You know its beginning, and its progress. Permit me, however, to say, that my experience has undergone some change. That freshness, that simplicity of Christian joy which for more than two years have marked it, have been in some measure modified. I am far more painfully alive to my own defects. The self-confidence of my nature is diminishing. The point of view in which I see myself has varied. My sermons are more studied, and elaborated. I am more bent on the improvement of my intellect. I lay more stress upon the training of the intellect. I am prosecuting with more zeal my favorite plans of acquisition in the Latin, Greek, and Hebrew languages. O, sir, I burn with consuming desires to read my Bible fluently in these tongues, and to preach the Gospel with more efficiency and power. These feelings have embarked me in courses of study of which I formerly never dreamed, and they have been working a silent change in my religious life. I can not now be contented with that simple elementary training which I once esteemed all-sufficient. I confess to you I wish intellectually to be thoroughly furnished for my work as a minister, and I know that this aim is gradually dissipating that *simplicity* and *contentedness* which once characterized my experience. At the same time I must say that my purposes are stronger, my consecration is more entire, my views of duty are more clear, my love to Christ is deeper, my faith is more unwavering, and my witness, although not so joyful, is steady and abiding. My communion with God continues. In the pulpit, if I do not have as much lively satisfaction, I think I do more real good—What has produced these changes? Is it neglect of duty? I am not conscious of any. Is it the work of the devil? I have often asked myself the question, 'Am I in a snare?' This I have tried to settle. Is it the result of my more accurate, and laborious habits of study as a teacher? These have doubtless exerted an influence. Is God preparing me by this modification of my inner life for more extensive usefulness? The future must answer. I must tell you, also, that I look upon thorough and extensive preparation for the ministry with far more favor than formerly. Truly, sir, when I reflect upon the matter these changes startle me. I feel they are giving my character its impress for life. They are ushering me forward in a new and unexpected direction. Have I made myself intelligible? Perhaps these things have all occurred in your own history, and are familiar to you. Will you please drop me a word of advice, and help me to take my bearings? Life is a dark sea, and we must often take our reckonings. Help, dear sir; I need help. It just occurs to me that I have been more and more careful about confessing in public the blessing of full salvation. I have been solicitous to guard and shield the doctrine from ridicule and reproach. Perhaps this has been a snare."

It would be difficult to describe in language more clear and beautiful the exercises of a devout heart, while pursuing a course of intellectual study, and the difficulty of guarding against formalism, and of preserving a fresh glow of spiritual ardor in connection with the absorbing demands of the reflective and logical understanding—in fine, to harmonize high feeling with cool thinking. Every Christian student, every devout and spiritual young minister, has grappled, more or less, with the same perplexing problem; and the answer of Bishop Hamline which follows, though clothed in general terms, may safely be pronounced to contain the sum of human wisdom on the subject:

"SCHENECTADY, *September* 20, 1856.

" To REV. PROFESSOR LEAVITT,—Yours was duly received; but my laboring pen is slow to answer it. Broken machinery will not work. I am thankful that I can write a little. As to study, you must feed the soul with knowledge ; and if you do not allow either ambition or mere intellectual taste to control your devotion to literature so as to cool your desires after God, your keen relish for prayer and praise, you need not fear. The Spirit will always give some signal of alarm when we are in danger. All we need is to keep a lookout for the token. He does not always give a very bold signal, startling the soul and arresting careless observation, which renders it the more necessary that we 'watch.' As Christians, we should not rest without making an observable progress in faith, love, hope, peace, joy, zeal for good and the salvation of souls, and, in a word, in all those branches of heavenly-mindedness which belong to redeemed sinners, in a world like this. As ministers, we must have our eye on our great commission, and the heavenly tempers which belong to and befit it. We ought to have more faith than Abraham, more love and religious heroism than Daniel, more close walking with God than Enoch, more meekness than Moses, and more patience than Job ; for our dispensation is far richer than theirs in all the means and motives of piety, while our hearts are no more corrupt than theirs, for these means and motives to operate upon and subdue.

"Now, dear brother, press on in literary pursuits as earnestly as you please, only taking care to be ready to offer up your son whom you love, as Abraham did; to keep your head on Christ's bosom, as John did; to be ready both to be bound and die at Jerusalem for Christ's sake, as Paul was, and, if I may depart from Scripture examples, feel, as Olin said, ' I can conceive of no degree of physical suffering which I would not endure for the privilege of preaching Christ crucified.' "

In all his sufferings and personal exilement from the busy hum of public affairs, Bishop Hamline never lost his interest in national politics and doings. The political excitement on the subject of slavery reached its maximum in the fall of 1856. The nation, the very earth, seemed to heave and rock in dreadful portents of an eruption and catastrophe. Our great men knew not what to do, and men looked in every quarter with apprehension, "their hearts failing them for fear, and for looking after those things which were coming on the earth." Four years later the crash came. In his prison of infirmity Bishop Hamline could only think and feel, but his apprehensions were those of a seer. In writing to a friend he says:

"Your last was full of refreshing news of the salvation of souls—the progress of the kingdom. Amidst so many alarms it is good to hear that Christ's work is being accomplished in the hearts of men. We seem to be entering on a time of trouble. Perhaps we have gloried too much in our 'Great Republic,' and God is teaching us, 'He that glorieth let him glory in the Lord.' "

To the Rev. B. Isbell he writes, November 10, 1856:

"We trust that your hopes of a good revival will be realized. This, after all, is the hope of the Church—the only hope of the world. A successful election in favor of sound morals is most desirable, and I have both desired and prayed for it. But God is wise, good, mighty, and what he permits or works must be best on the whole. He may permit slavery to work out its dire effects. We deserve it as a nation, though hundreds of thousands are clear, and he will cover them in the shadow of his wing until the calamity be overpast.

"There are signs, I think, that the slave-holders are to eat the fruit of their own way, and be filled with their own devices. Thirty years ago scarcely a man in the South justified, but simply excused, slavery. Now nobody there excuses, but justifies, it—and '*O tempora! O mores!*'—by the Bible, perverted to that base end. 'It is time for thee, Lord, to work; for men make void thy law!' We rejoice in the brilliant success of E. and A. May the Father's choicest blessing rest upon them, and you all, forever! Amen!"

To Dr. and Mrs. Palmer, December 2d, he writes:

"We greet you in Christ's name, who bore our griefs and carried our sorrows; who was wounded for our transgressions and was bruised for our iniquities; who bore the sin of many, and made intercession for the transgressors; who was oppressed and was afflicted, yet opened not his mouth; who now sees in us, and multitudes around us, the travail of his soul, and is satisfied. Unto him who hath loved us and washed us from our sins in his blood be glory for ever and ever! Worthy is the Lamb that was slain!"

A fitting benediction for the dying year.

Chapter XXV.

[1857-65.]

REMOVAL TO MOUNT PLEASANT, IOWA—LAST YEARS OF LIFE.

IT had not been the intention of Bishop Hamline to remain so long in his Eastern home. He had purposed to return to Ohio, the State of his adoption, at an early day; but his great exhaustion, after his resignation in 1852, made it necessary to remain in quiet retirement till nature should recuperate. This delay was still further prolonged by the illness of his son, then a student of medicine in Vermont. He had been fishing upon a beautiful lake when the boat was upset, and he and his associate remained three hours in the water, holding to the bottom of the boat. He escaped drowning, but a severe and prolonged sickness followed. Three years were thus added to their stay near Schenectady. It had been a grateful home among friends and kindred, and, like the house of Obed-edom, where the ark abode, was signalized abroad for the blessing of God. But it had always been considered as temporary, and the time had now fully come to depart.

Cincinnati was the objective point most naturally selected. There he had spent nearly two years as pastor and eight years as editor. It had been regarded as their home for several years after his election to the episcopacy. There he had numerous friends, and to the place he felt a home-like attach-ment. But, after so long a residence East, in a more Northern atmosphere, his physicians warned him it would be unsafe to adventure into Southern Ohio. Various places opened to his view where a cordial reception would have been given, but his thoughts now turned to the more distant West. Mount Pleas-ant, Iowa, was about the same latitude as Schenectady, with a healthy climate most suited, it was judged, to his state of health. It was the seat of the college he had helped to establish, the president, Dr. L. W. Berry, a warm friend, and the surroundings every way inviting. Thither, at length, his mind tended. The citizens had tendered a most cordial memorial for the honor, signed by Christians and the leading public men in the various professions, ''believing,'' as they said, ''he could not be more pleasantly sit-uated as to health and society than in Mount Pleas-ant, and his residence among them would be, to them, a high privilege.'' All things thus concur-ring, their guiding star seemed to rest over Mount Pleasant.

But they would not be going among strangers. Friends awaited there. There, too, the Rev. Dr. Elliott, his editorial *confrere* for eight years, and his devoted friend, had anticipated settling. Drs. Elliott and Berry were projecting a new Biblical school for the more practical culture of clerical candidates in connection with the college. Elliott abounded in all good works. Open, frank, and generous, he was singly devoted to the public good. To him and to Dr. Berry the thought of Bishop Hamline's removal to Mount Pleasant was joy and gladness. Full of plans of Christian, scholarly work, he writes to Bishop Hamline: "On praying and reflecting on the subject of your removal to Iowa, my best judgment is that it would be better for your family and the Church." Of his writing, he says:

"I am glancing over Corpus Juris Canonicæ, culling out all the principal items on political Romanism, and, at the same time, am perusing three leading Canonists, namely, Danti, in three volumes, octavo; Reiffenstuel, in six volumes, folio; and then Espen or Espenius, in six volumes, folio. These, with Bellarmine, are, after all, the principal standards."

On his favorite project for opening a Biblical school, he adds:

"I am still purposely intent upon attempting a little school on plain Methodist principles, without attempting to make great scholars. I should rejoice, indeed, to have you there to consult as an adviser and coadjutor, that we might do something towards preserving the simplicity and purity of our holy Methodism. Perhaps it might be to you a work that would be a substitue for a long life of service. . . . It will lengthen my day to have you within reach of me, and I must think that the associations of Mount Pleasant will, with God's help, do much to render life agreeable, and prepare for a blessed future. Brother and Sister Coston will be pleasant associates. Grace, mercy, and peace be with you both. I wrote to Dr. Hamline. I want him for a neighbor."

Coston, here referred to, had resolved to accompany the Bishop. He was the same that eighteen years before had ridden seventy miles to see Mr. Hamline, and assure himself of the reality of his conversion. He had earned a high repute in the itinerant field, a man of great heart and noble aims, and a close friend. His wife, too, was a lady of distinction and culture, of a brave and generous nature, and an experienced Christian. Her father, General

Gibson, was one of the commissioners who sat on a log where the city of Zanesville now stands, and received from the mouth of Logan his celebrated speech ("Who is there to mourn for Logan?"). Her early associations were with President Jefferson and his class. Her first husband owned the estate known as "Braddock's Field," and there they entertained General Lafayette, with his *suite* of eighty men, when, on his visit to America, he had gone there to see General Gibson. Mrs. Coston was a sincere Christian, and, on her second marriage, as she told Mrs. Hamline, "she married a Methodist preacher to get further out of the world." But many of her old friends, of the style of her early life, clung to her till the last. She died in triumph, April, 1864, and her husband took part in the funeral services of Bishop Hamline a year later.

It was in April, 1857, that the family settled in their beautiful Western home. Bishop Hamline had intended to extend his journey either to the Upper Mississippi or the lakes, but the heat of approaching summer caused him to relinquish the plan, "and, from the salubrity of the climate," he says, "I judge it was best." The little colony of kindred hearts settled upon the same village block, or square. Bishop Hamline and his son, Dr. L. P. Hamline, with their families, in separate mansions, occupied the south side of the block, and Elliott and Coston the north side. Facing oppositely, their yards connected; and, as no other buildings were on the square, their room was ample and airy, and their intercourse through garden gates, easy. To human eyes their Paradise might seem restored. But it was not worldly ease they sought. A little chapel was subsequently erected adjoining the Bishop's house, and they were ready for the work of the Master. "I have enjoyed the summer remarkably well," he writes to a friend, August 18th, "considering all things; and Mrs. Hamline has been in her element (religiously) with a class in our house, in which several have professed the 'special salvation,' and give unequivocal proof of possessing it. A female prayer-meeting, one square off, is equally blessed, and even the Protestant Episcopal and Congregational ministers' wives are attending, and weep as though their hearts would break. 'Why, what beautiful hymns you have,' said the latter. Being the daughter of a New England Congregational minister, she has never known any thing of Methodism until now. Pray for us that no light may be quenched or obscured."

To another he writes:

"Our religious privileges are great, there being six hundred Methodists in this little city, besides Presbyterian, Congregational, Baptist, and Episcopalian churches. Our two churches are excellent, and we must have another soon. Our college is doing well. There are some twenty-five preachers here; pretty well for a city of five thousand souls. The place is growing slowly, and may reach a population of ten thousand."

For several years after settling at Mount Pleasant, Bishop Hamline was able generally to attend one public service on the Sabbath, which he did by sitting in an easy chair near the door, not being able to endure the more confined air near the pulpit, and leaving immediately after sermon. A Church class met every Sabbath in his little chapel, also a female prayer-meeting on Thursday evening. These he

attended regularly, when able, and, when not able,
he came to the door and gave his testimony, or exhortation, and retired. Occasionally, when able to
listen, a sermon was delivered there, and not unfrequently the sacrament of the Lord's-supper. His
regular example of Church attendance, when able,
and often when not able without great pain and hazard, was one of the marked features of his Christian life.

So, also, his fidelity to class-meeting. It was not
to him an empty form, but a lively means of grace.
Its obligation was woven in his religious conscience,
and, as a spiritual help, it was cherished in his warm,
Christian affection. With him, experimental religion
was the foundation of all worship, and all practical,
spiritual life; and class-meetings, or something an-
swering to them, were an essential part of the cultus
of that life. He taught that class attendance was a
prominent part of the specific Church covenant,
which, as Methodists, they had no moral right to
omit more than any other contracted obligation, and
that to train the conscience to the habit of neglect
in such positive engagements, was self-abuse, a moral
delinquency which could not consist with a healthful
Christian character. He admitted the case would be
different where there had never been such a formal
obligation assumed, as in other Churches. But in
such cases there would be a loss to spiritual life and
encouragement.

Wherever Bishop Hamline lived he put himself
at once upon a "war basis" for aggressive movement for saving souls, and helping others to "fight
the good fight of faith." Like David, he gave him-

self no rest "till he found out a place for the Lord, a habitation for the mighty God of Jacob." It was hence he and his ever faithful wife, being of one heart and mind and purpose, were always found in sympathy and efficient subsidy with every Church movement of a truly revival character. Thus he became a strong help to the regular and active ministry. No part of his life shines out more beautifully than these last years of suffering. In August, 1859, the Rev. P. P. Ingalls, pastor of Asbury Chapel, Mount Pleasant, in writing his annual letter concerning Bishop Hamline "to the Bishop and members of the Ohio Annual Conference," says:

"DEAR FATHERS AND BRETHREN—It is with great pleasure that I speak to you of our beloved Bishop Hamline. I can not tell you how highly we appreciate his presence and influence among us. It is beyond my expression. He is not able to labor in any of the ordinary ways of an itinerant minister, and yet labors very efficiently in promoting revival influence and building up the Church. I am fully satisfied that with regard to health, he is constantly on the very verge of eternity, and remains with us only by the most exact prudence and greatest care.

"While you have his name and conference relation, we hope to have *him* while Providence permits his stay upon earth."

He could still, occasionally, write a little. Here, too, was an opening to do good. With the bereaved and suffering he always, since his own experience of sickness and death in his family, felt the liveliest sympathy. To the Rev. C. W. Sears, on occasion of the death of his wife, he writes, December, 1857:

"True religion may sometimes intensify *grief* as well as *joy*. But the joy yields such *strength* to the heart of the sufferer—the strength not only of *hope*, but of unspeakable *fruition,* that sufferings otherwise insupportable, become not only *tolerable,* but *grateful.* When the devout father in Zion was asked how he endured the loss of his loved wife, he said, 'I can not deny that I feel it most keenly, and that it cuts me to the quick, yet I have a joyful acquiescence in God's will.'

"So, then, if religion, by quickening our sensibilities, occasions us sharper sorrows as well as joys, those are so assuaged by these that the soul fortified to endure exclaims, '*I glory in tribulation also!*'

"But such poor words as mortals can supply are inadequate on this theme. Inspired phraseology suits it. The joy is '*unspeakable* and full of glory,' and under its cordials the soul exclaims: 'These *light* afflictions, which are but for a moment, work out for us a far more exceeding and eternal weight of glory.'

"My dear suffering brother, may this bright sunshine —long bright to thee and the departed one—become now so intense to thy soul that, though the clouds will not *disperse,* they may be *all gilded* by the beams, and make a mild and mellow light amidst the night of grief surrounding you."

A pleasant episode to the monotony of sickness Bishop Hamline found in the friendship and correspondence of the Rev. T. Stearns, a Calvinistic clergyman of the old school. He, like Bishop Hamline, was laid aside by sickness. They enjoyed frequent interviews, rode out together almost daily, and often communicated in writing. Mr. Stearns was an educated, clear-headed thinker, open, frank, candid, courteous, independent. The subjects of investigation were doctrines, prominently entire sanctification, and on both sides for practical, spiritual ends. Bishop Hamline, having been brought up a Calvinistic Congregationalist of the olden type, could well understand his friend, and the method of his reasoning. The intercourse ran along through several years (till Mr. Stearns removed), and their warm friendship till the close of life. We can not give the correspondence, but a hint or two, illustrating its tone and tenor, we may not withhold. As illustrating the views of an honest Calvinist, we give one letter from Mr. Stearns:

"Mt. Pleasant, *February* 15, 1859.

"Dear Brother,—I am greatly obliged to you for the loan of Dr. Geo. Peck's work. I have read it with deep interest. The question on which I had been so long in doubt is now settled clearly, as to what you believe as a denomination. I am pleased to see the difference between your views and those of Mahan and Finney. To their views of legal perfection I have felt and do feel insuperable objections, and also to a view prevalent in portions of New England twenty or twenty-five years ago, that the sanctified ones become so united to Christ that their acts become his acts, and so they could not sin even if they broke every commandment in the decalogue, as it was Christ, and not they, who did it. But to evangelical, or Wesleyan, perfection, as explained by Dr. Peck, I feel no objection. Dr. Peck, on page 47 of your book, and on pages 50 and 53–4 from Wesley, and page 57 from Fletcher, shows most plainly that you do not claim to keep the Adamic or Mosaic law perfectly. You mean, therefore, scarcely any thing more than we do by 'full assurance of hope,' or 'full assurance of faith.'

"The perfection which Dr. Snodgrass is opposing *is legal*, or absolute union to Christ, *not Wesleyan*. And from remark and observation I know the impression very generally prevails among Presbyterians that you believe in legal perfection. And it seems to me your writers are not generally quite guarded enough to distinguish this point. Even Dr. Peck often uses language so that, if I had not just before read his strong expressions, I would be compelled to think he defended legal perfection.

"I think his language is unguarded when he speaks so often of the person living without sin, by which he means *voluntary sin*. But, from Lev. iv, 27–29, and v, 17, 18, and from I John v, 17, *involuntary sin* is, in the Bible, called sin, as well as by Calvinistic writers.

"I also feel that his language is too sweeping on pages 135–6, when he speaks of Rom. x, 4, as though Christ had abolished the law, and we are not required to keep it. We suppose it is set aside as a law of salvation, but, from Matt. v,

17, 18, and 1 Tim. i, 8, that it still remains to convict of sin and tell us of duty, and thus send us to Christ.

"It seems to me that the least satisfactory part of the whole book is that part of chapter 7 where the doctor meets such texts as Eccl. vii, 20, and 1 John i, 8, etc., and also, on his own principles, the most useless part. I can not see why he may not just let those texts stand in their full force, as he intimates on page 47. For I think he there gives just what they mean, and that they are not in the way of Wesleyan sanctification.

"One word on your tract. While it is truly valuable, it seems to me, though I may be wrong, that the criticism I suggested is important. Because, from what it was predicted of Christ (Isa. xlii, 21), and what he says (Matt. v, 17, 18), it seems to me it was just as requisite he should *obey* the law as *suffer* its *penalty;* and, from Heb. ii, 10, and v, 8, 9, that he suffered for us all along, before the final conflict, and thereby became perfectly qualified to be a sympathizing high-priest for us. In relation to our terms, 'full assurance of hope' and 'full assurance of faith,' both are Scriptural. See Heb. vi, 11, and x, 22.

"I was deeply interested in the 'Experience of German Methodist Ministers,' and am greatly obliged to you for it. It will do good, as from the simple experience of so many of them it will effectually show that they are not still German Rationalists, or cold-hearted formalists. I am glad to have so satisfactory a refutation of that imputation.

"I shall read with pleasure the 'History of Methodism,' and will return as soon as I have read it.

"One more remark. I wish the difference between Wesleyan and legal perfection were more generally understood, because I am persuaded it would greatly increase love and confidence between you and Calvinists. For, as you mean so nearly the thing which we believe attainable, we certainly will not object to your choice of a word to express it. I trust the perusal of these works has given me more charity, and led me to desire more conformity to the will and spirit of Jesus, our Lord. Pardon my freedom in writing, and remember me when you come near our precious Savior.

"Fraternally,   T. STEARNS."

The propriety of using the terms "entire sanctification," "perfect love," etc., to denote a state of grace in this life, had been before them. Mr. Stearns objected to the use of them because, according to their technology, and certain errors that had risen up, they would be likely to be misunderstood, and hence mislead. Bishop Hamline replies:

"I still find the question presses on me, why not apply the words '*sanctified wholly*,' or '*perfect love*,' to some gracious state of the soul? I have no objection to predestination and election; none even to imputation. Mr. Wesley does not hold your explanation of them to be correct, much less the terrible Antinomian view which you so strongly object to in the New England Perfectionists. And you will think more charitably of his views expressed in the history and elsewhere, perhaps, if you considered what Antinomianism had done to ruin the Churches of England, and almost blot out religion in his day. You think your views of sin and holiness forbid the use of these phrases. But the question arises in my mind, have we a right to embrace any views of sin and holiness, or any other theological point, which will render it inconsistent or erroneous in us to apply Scripture phrases according to apostolic usage? We claim that we do use 'predestination' and 'election' after the *usus loquendi* of Scripture. You would not drop the use of the word repentance because Arminians apply it to convicted sinners, rather than to the generous grief of the regenerate. You do not ignore the phrase 'born again' because Pelagians deny total (congenital) depravity, and other errorists hold it to be a mere *outward* reformation or an outward form (baptism). Why, I pray you, give up the apostolic terms applied to *mature believers*, merely because a horrible and blasphemous clique in New England proclaim themselves too holy to need prayer or the Sabbath, and say when they sin Christ does it? Nay, even if Wesley and Fletcher and Peck and Finney and Upham, and ten thousand others, make a wrong application of these phrases? The learned divines of the Calvinistic Church ought to rescue these Scripture phrases from such abuse, if abuse it is, and help to turn a pure language upon Zion. I fell in company with old Dr. M'Calla in 1849, and had *heart* communion with him in the stage half a day. He wept like a child, and talked of Jesus till it seemed like rising to the third heaven. I know not how uniformly he evinced this heavenly spirit, but if always I should say he is made 'perfect in love.' Now, which has the best authority from Scripture—to call it 'perfect love' or 'assurance of faith?'"

The friendship of these two ministers of Christ was intimate and hallowed. Their manner of life was similar. Both rose early, and spent a long time in reading the Bible and prayer; and both lived in full sympathy with the age and the progress of events till the close of life. They died within about three years of each other.

During all the prison-life of his confinement the mind of Bishop Hamline was ever active, and his heart enlisted in the progress of Christ's kingdom. In a letter to Rev. J. Young, January, 1859, he says:

" I am now old and gray-headed—locks almost white. I am feeble and sore broken; all my bones (as it were) out of joint. My mind, like my body, is enfeebled. The grasshopper a burden, the wheel just ready to break at the cistern of life.

"As to public and Church interests, I find my affections all awake concerning them. New phases of society in India and China, as well as in Japan, suggest serious and solemn meditations as to the state, resources, and obligations of the Church amid such clear indications of Christ's approaching reign. Italy, France, and Austria, to say nothing of Turkey and other nations and principalities, are evidently nearing another earthquake period, and both hopes and fears are quickened at the approach of some terrible convulsion, out of which may spring good or evil in regard to the progress and prevalence of Christ's kingdom in the earth, though, whatever may be the immediate results, the remoter effects must be good. For

'Jesus shall reign where'er the sun
Does his successive journeys run.'"

In another letter he says:

"O that the Church were prepared to meet all these favoring tokens, and send forth thousands of missionaries to the harvest-fields so earnestly inviting the reapers! But we may hope that the Master will prepare the way, and soon produce in the Church a temper and a conduct in harmony with his other movements abroad.

"It is a comfort to see the things which we behold, even if we must be mere spectators, and not actors, in such scenes. Like Simeon in the temple, you must feel like exclaiming, 'Mine eyes have seen thy salvation.'"

But in his "decrease" he enjoyed not less than John Baptist had in his castle-prison among the mountains. An oasis of privilege was still left. "We have a large class-meeting," he says, "in our own house Sabbath afternoon, and often fifty persons present. It is the best class I ever saw assembled, and I can give you no idea how sweet it is to my poor soul. Sabbath week we had Dr. Elliott, Professor Whitlock of Victoria College, Canada, Professor Kelly, brother Coston, two other traveling, and four or five local, preachers. Yesterday we had the class-room filled, so that I believe not another chair could have been put in the room. But 'the best of all is, God is with us.' O what a mercy to us in our old age to have such a privilege! On Thursday we have a female prayer-meeting in the same room; generally about twenty-five to thirty present; and, though I do not see, I hear the sisters' fervent prayers and praises. Except in an annual or General Conference, I have never seen the same number of persons as well trained in experimental and practical piety as in these two meetings."

Among the peculiar trials of this period of his life was that of witnessing the departure of friends and compeers. In a letter to Jacob Young, March, 1859, he writes:

"David Young has followed Finley, and I gloomily say to myself, Jacob Young goes soon in the course of nature, and what early friend have I left? Say what we will of death, and of heaven in view also, there is a deep gloom in this breaking up of earthly ties. I mean not to complain of the economy; it is all right. When transferred to the other side of these Christian death scenes, a new light will doubtless so illustrate and beautify them that all the gloom of them will vanish; but surveyed on this side the dark valley, we must now and then behold them under those guises of sadness which render them solemnly mournful."

The sympathetic strain of this extract is as true to nature as to triumphant faith, and honors both. Perhaps no one feature of Bishop Hamline's character is more worthy his profession than his deep and generous sympathy with the afflicted, as his numerous letters in this department show. Jacob Young, above referred to, died a few months later. He was, as we have seen, Bishop Hamline's first colleague on the circuit. His wife was of the Kent family, with whom Bishop Hamline resided when he was converted. In his letter of condolence to her he could only say:

"Mrs. Hamline requests me to write. Alas! who shall comfort *me* while I strive to comfort others. My father and your husband is in the grave. No, is in heaven. But we can not see his face nor hear his voice. Lord Jesus, help and bless and comfort us!"

In the opening year of 1860 he records:

"I have spent thirty-two years in the ministry of God's holy word. For eight years I have been superannuated, and God has 'tried me as silver is tried;' but he has often sweetened those trials by his presence in a marvelous manner, and now, day by day, 'my fellowship is with the Father and with his Son Jesus Christ.' Though almost helpless, and dependent on my devoted, affectionate wife for personal attentions, which her exemplary patience never wearies in bestowing on me, (thanks to thy name, O my God, for such a gift!) yet I am far more contented and cheerful than in the best days of my youth. O thou adorable Redeemer, who hast bought me with thy blood, and new-created me by thy Spirit, grant that this record of thy love and mercy to one so unworthy, may be a blessing to my children and children's children when I am gone the way of all flesh, for Christ's sake. Amen."

To the Rev. L. Swormstedt, February, 1860, he writes:

"I have been confined all winter almost entirely to my house. Have been off of the square but once in three months, but my confinement has been as a paradise. My soul never dwelt so fully under the shadow of his wing as it does now. It seems as though only a thin veil separates my soul from glory; not from God, for I dwell as near to him as my humanity can bear, and sometimes I am ready to cry out with Fletcher, 'Lord, withhold thy hand!' And like him, I cry, 'O for a gust of praise to go through the universe!' 'God is love.'

"O, my dear brother, this faith is a wonderful power in the soul. 'Believe, only believe,' the Spirit whispers in my heart. I believe, and, glory to God! I am saved. May the Lord bless you more and more for Christ's sake!"

To Rev. J. T. Mitchell he writes:

"It seems to me I am nearing my heavenly home and can not stay long below. If otherwise, my words will do no harm; and if so, let me say to you, Farewell!

"I have peace with God and with all mankind. I am, if not greatly mistaken, ready to depart and be with Christ, and should I depart suddenly, you may indulge the hope that I am gone to the land of the pure and the blessed. The Spirit bears witness with my spirit now, and nearly every hour and moment, that I am a child of God; and the Spirit of his Son is sent forth into my heart, crying, 'Abba, Father.'"

Such is the strain of his letters and diary entries at this period. The following letter may suffice to indicate his opinion of so-called "spiritualism," rather and more properly *demonology*. The letter dates December, 1860:

"To MRS. H. H. BIGELOW,—Tell H. to be sober, devout, and diligent, and his youth of poverty will be a blessing to him.

But if he, like too many of our 'stark-mad' Yankees, leave the pure, 'blessed Gospel of the Son of God' for chaff, and for the 'cunning craftiness of men;' for witches, necromancers; for 'wizards that mutter and peep,' as the Bible calls them, he will live (and probably die) a fool.

"I found here a venerable and well-educated Methodist brother out of the Church, who had been a fine physician near forty-five years, given up to 'spiritualism,' and mad with credulity on the subject. I labored with him two years, when he recovered his peace with God, renounced all its 'filthy communications' in 'circles,' etc., denounced its deceits and abominations, and now is clothed and in his right mind, wondering at the audacity of his apostasy, and the mercy of his restoration to Christ, and has present 'joy unspeakable and full of glory.' I suppose worlds would not tempt him into a 'circle' for five minutes. His wife led him astray as Eve did Adam of yore. She died in mercy, and he returned to that Jesus whom he had crucified (as he says) in his heart.

"We are right in the midst of that period referred to in Rev. xvi, 13, and the 'spirits of devils working miracles' will 'multiply wonders and deceive the nations.' The Lord in mercy save us in the trying hour."

It was in the year 1860 that Bishop Hamline drew up and presented to the Trustees of the Iowa Wesleyan University a plan for liquidating its debts. The university was badly involved. Several attempts had been made to extricate it, especially in the year 1856, but despite all efforts the buildings were likely to be sold at public sale to cancel its debts. The plan of Bishop Hamline was so practicable and so well guarded the subscribers and donors against the possibility of losing their money in case the effort failed, and so equitably provided for the different claims so that no creditor should be wronged, and as a legal instrument so adroitly prepared, that courage revived and a vigorous effort was again made by which the total amount was secured on paper. But the war and other causes embarrassed collections, so that actual payment was not effected till 1864, through the energetic agency of Rev. Mr. Bradrick. But the plan of Bishop Hamline was the ground and opportune means of finally rescuing the college from its embarrassments.

In the midst of labor and sufferings, with numerous calls and visitations of friends, Bishop Hamline is cheered with the fraternal letter of his former colleagues, the bishops, from their meeting at Springfield, Ohio, December, 1861:

"Convened for our annual consultation, we avail ourselves of the opportunity to write you a fraternal letter. Though you have long been deprived, by want of health, of the privilege of participating in the active duties of the ministry, we doubt not but you still feel greatly interested in Zion's prosperity. We remember with pleasure the days of other years, when you shared with us the responsibility of the general oversight, when we consulted and prayed, preached and exhorted, wept and rejoiced together. Since you retired from the field to seek rest and health, we have toiled on, as God enabled us, with humble reliance on our Heavenly Father. The result is before the public. In the mean time we have deeply sympathized with you in your sore and protracted afflictions, such as we suppose would long since have brought your final release. That you yet live, is proof of supporting grace and cause of devout thanksgiving to God. We pray that the Lord may be with you to the end of life's painful conflict, then bring you to the heavenly inheritance. We hope to join you there.

"Wishing many blessings to Sister Hamline, yourself, and children, we are, dear brother, as ever and for ever, yours in he love of Jesus,

"T. A. MORRIS,	M. SIMPSON,
E. S. JANES,	O. C. BAKER,
L. SCOTT,	E. R. AMES."

CHAPTER XXVI.

[1862 to 1865.]

LAST YEARS—CLOSE OF LIFE.

WE have already said that Bishop Hamline took a lively interest in Church enterprise and public affairs. The political and military movements in Europe and Asia from time to time drew from his pen and lips opinions and expressions which evidenced his insight into prophetic Scripture and current history, and his heart of true humanity. Our country was now in the depth and darkness of civil war, and an ardent patriot could not be still. Christianity illuminates and intensifies the moral principle of truly defensive war, and makes it the sword of God "to execute wrath upon him that doeth evil." The following letter will suffice to show how thoroughly he penetrated the perils, necessity, and true policy of the hour :

"*January* 21, 1862.

"To Hon. James Harlan,—I seize the first scrap of paper I find to say that it seems to me the best way, if not the only way, to meet the rising tide of treason in the West, is to arm and train one hundred and fifty thousand blacks as soon as possible. They will be in the field as one hundred and fifty thousand loyal Republicans. If the war takes a turn that so many can be spared from the field, the white Republicans can return and vote. If they can not be spared, then it will save a draft, and perhaps great difficulty. I know it is a bold measure, but such measures are often the salvation of a people, a dynasty, a government. You remember the language of Junius : ' If the prophet had not armed himself with boldness, he would have been hung for the malice of his parable.' Boldness is in the advancing success of traitors ; boldness has carried this rebellion forward to the formidable stage it has now reached ; resistance, on the other hand, has been temperate, prudent, and if not now made to shape itself into an aspect bold and fiery like their own, I fear we are lost. The boldest measures are now safe, I think. We have prudence and humanity enough for history, we need boldness for triumph. Arming three hundred thousand blacks would make traitors, North and South, hate us no more, but would cause loyalists to distrust us far less. To seek, by mild measures, to conciliate the former is hopeless policy. The government must address itself to the fears, not to the hopes or favor of the Benedict Arnolds of the age.

"Pardon me for dogmatizing. I forgot, in the passion of writing, that I addressed a Senator who knows so much better than I do. I write with pain and confusion in my head, too, so that I can scarcely see my pen-marks.

"Mrs. Hamline says : ' Please remember me affectionately to Mrs. Harlan, and be assured yourself of our respect and prayers.'

"P. S.—Suppose it comes to the worst, and some hundreds of thousands in Illinois and elsewhere attempt a bold revolt, would not the armed blacks be a formidable force to put down revolt and save the country ?"

An extract from Senator Harlan's answer to this may not be improper, dated Washington, 27th :

"DEAR BISHOP HAMLINE,—Please accept my sincere thanks for your excellent and patriotic letter of the 21st inst. I agree with you fully in relation to the policy that should control the Administration. The President, I think, is initiating measures to carry it out. But every thing moves so slowly ! The Lord only can know how much the nation must suffer on account of the delays in carrying out a policy admitted by all earnest lovers of the country to be not only right, but absolutely necessary. Colored men are being enlisted for service on land and sea—but the work drags—drags."

As a further specimen of Bishop Hamline's deep and patriotic interest in the war, we add the following letter:

"*September* 28, 1862.

"To Mrs. H. H. BIGELOW,—A paper from your place gives me reason to conclude that your son has enlisted. I did not feel like urging his enlistment, but will now say I most heartily approve of it. I think every young man in America of right age and good health should give himself to his country. My son is not very young nor very vigorous, but if he chooses to go I will not say a word. He has offered as a surgeon, and has been examined and approved; but there are so many pressing their claims on the governor that he who does not urge himself forward has no chance; besides, many doctors are poor and without practice, and are appointed in compassion to their families, while they know that my son is well off from his mother's estate."

The events of Bishop Hamline's life during confinement were few, and our principal remaining task is to follow along the even current of the days and observe the symmetry and uniformity of a character which had hitherto been contemplated in connection with the honors and publicity of office, and the brilliancy of talent. The habit of early rising remained with him till the last. His first employment every day, even when most feeble, was to pray, remaining on his knees as long as his strength permitted. He then read his Bible lessons, consisting of several chapters from the Old and New Testaments. Then, especially during our country's war, he read up the news. With him public events were the footsteps of Providence. He always read secular subjects from the religious stand-point. During one year of his illness he was unable to read at all, and a member of the family read to him as long as he was able to hear. Subsequently his sight improved, but the intense suffering of his brain forbade his hearing any reading, and then he read his large type Testament and Hymn Book, as strength allowed, placing them open in a chair by his side that he might read a few verses at a time. It was in this position they were found when he died. When his health had allowed he commonly spent hours on his knees. In 1848 he attended a dedication at Lexington, Ind. The preacher there, who lodged with him, observed his habit of private devotion, and said to him: "Bishop, do you have to pray so much always?" In relating it to Mrs. Hamline afterward he said: "The dear brother did not know that I was enjoying a heaven upon earth on my knees." Mrs. Hamline says: "For years it was his habit to kneel at his arm-chair, bending low over its seat and remaining so long perfectly still that, having been often assured by physicians that from the condition of his heart he was imminently exposed to sudden death, I used to go up softly to see whether he was not dead on his knees—*whether he breathed.*"

The hour of female prayer-meeting in his little chapel he always kept sacred in his apartment, and it was during such a meeting, while the ladies were praying, that his spirit took its flight from earth. His favorite lines of one of our incomparable hymns, which he often repeated when retiring, were:

> "Safe in thy arms I lay me down,
> Thine everlasting arms of love."

It was while they were singing these lines that his wife Eliza's spirit departed.

To Rev. L. M. Vernon he writes, March, 1863:

"I have longed to write to you for a year or more, but my eyes, head, and nerves almost wholly prevent my writing. A letter from Bishop Morris has remained unanswered for months.

"'Preach the word, be instant in season and out of season.' Work night and day for our adorable Lord. 'I am now ready to be offered,' quite on the verge of heaven.

"Dr. Elliott just bade me farewell, and I expect to see his face no more until 'death is swallowed up in victory.' O, I feel the victory, even now, through all my inmost soul!"

Rev. Dr. Eddy, editor of *North-western Christian Advocate*, returning from a visit to Bishop Hamline, July 1, 1863, writes:

"We enjoyed a pleasant interview with this venerable and eminent minister. He looks older than when we saw him years ago. His hair is white, his beard is of silvery hue, but the tones of his voice are as in days long since. His health is frail. Providentially on Saturday he was unusually well, and we had several hours' interesting conversation. Old days, past scenes, mutual friends, the country and the Church were spoken of. His spiritual sky is clear. For the Church he has strong faith, for the country unswerving loyalty, with deep loathing of home traitors and spurious patriots. Mrs. Hamline is also in frail health, and, with her husband, is looking for the better home. We will bear with us the memory of our interviews and the meeting at the mercy-seat.

"They have made a liberal arrangement for the benefit of the Park Avenue Mission Church, for which they merit the gratitude of the Church."

To Rev. Z. H. and Mrs. Coston, Bishop Hamline writes, April 10, 1864:

"I have been very happy to-day, yet weep much. O how precious is Jesus! 'the sinner's Friend,' when, broken-hearted and believing, we cast ourselves on him for ever and ever. We are not afraid to trust in him.

"Old age, sickness, sorrow, death near at hand, all can

not drive me from thee, blessed Jesus! The more they gather and center on us, the more closely and confidingly we trust in thee, O thou Lamb of God, who takest away the sin of the world! Praised be the name of our God for ever and ever! And let all the people say, Amen!

"Sister Swormstedt, of Cincinnati, is with us for a few weeks. Her dear, precious husband, whom we loved so much, is in heaven, and she in weeds of sorrow, yet full of faith and 'of the Holy Ghost, waiting to pass over."

Mrs. Coston was at this time sick and near her end. Nine days after she died in holy triumph, and as the previous letter was one of saintly victory, the following is one of brotherly condolence:

"MOUNT PLEASANT, IOWA, *April* 19, 1864.

"TO REV. Z. H. COSTON,—Yours of the fifteenth instant arrived this morning, and its affecting news was read with such emotion as you would expect from the pleasant chastening society we enjoyed with you and your sainted wife. I drop a note to say you have our deep and prayerful sympathy. We both, you know, have passed through those cypress shades, and know, better than you ever did until now, how dark the vale, cheered indeed by no light but from that Sun of Right-cousness, which shed his beams so brightly on the death scene at which you just now gazed with tearful admiration. We catch the blessed song from her dying lips, 'Glory to Jesus!' Be comforted, my mourning brother, with 'very full comfort' while you bear those words in your very heart's memory along to the same joyful translation scene which awaits you, and I trust us also, and for which and its issues we wait in hope.

"Mrs. Hamline joins in all these expressions of sympathy, and in prayers for your hourly peace and comfort in Jesus, our foundation and strength."

It was a trying hour to Bishop Hamline. His close friends of other years were fast departing. Finley and Farnandis and David and Jacob Young and Dr. Berry and Swormstedt, with others, had gone. Elliott was absent, and now Mrs. Coston, a

noble spirit of their household circle, had been called
away. But while it saddened his earthly life it had
no such effect upon his heavenly outlook. A year
before, when quite sick, he says to Mrs. Elliott:
"Tell Dr. Elliott that I am perfectly happy; I feel
as though I was in Paradise—never was more cheerful." "If Mr. Elliott hears how ill you are he will
come home," says Mrs. Elliott. "He must not,"
replied the Bishop; "I can die without him if I have
my Savior with me; could even die without my wife
and children, though it would be pleasant to have
them by my side, if Christ is with me. But would
be glad when I die to have Dr. Elliott before I am
buried, if possible."

The General Conference of 1864 met in Philadelphia. On May 26th the bishops sent to Bishop Hamline their fraternal greeting and sympathy:

"REV. L. L. HAMLINE, *Dear Brother*,—Accept our fraternal salutations in the Lord. Those of us who had the privilege
of being associated with you in the cares and duties of the
episcopal office and work remember with great satisfaction the
fellowship of labor and love of those eight years. All of us
remember, with interest and high appreciation, your association
with us in the holy and active ministering of our Lord Jesus
Christ.

"We are very thankful that, since your retirement from
the effective ranks of the ministry, you have been enabled in
so many ways to serve your fellow-men and to honor God.

"We are grateful to our Heavenly Father that in your years
of superannuation you have been so divinely sustained and so
greatly cheered and comforted by the Holy Spirit.

"It is with us, also, a matter of praise to God that you have
been so exempted from acute sufferings, and that so many
years have been added to your life upon earth.

"God has also been very merciful to us. He has given us
sufficient health to enable us to meet our official obligations so
as to be approved by the General Conference, and we trust

also to divine acceptance. He has also given us the great happiness of seeing the work of the Lord prospering in our hands. We have also enjoyed much of the divine presence in our journeyings and labors, and great spiritual peace and comfort in believing.

"You will be pleased to learn that Rev. Brothers D. W. Clark, Edward Thomson, and Calvin Kingsley have been elected and ordained bishops during this session of the General Conference. You will unite with us in hailing these brethren welcome to the office of bishops in the Church.

"You have learned from the official papers how greatly God has prospered his Church. It is certain God is still with his ministers and people. We are, with you, looking and praying for the glory of God to fill the whole earth.

"With Christian salutations to Sister Hamline, and commending you both to the grace of God, we remain yours fraternally in Christ Jesus our Lord,

"T. A. MORRIS,	E. S. JANES,
L. SCOTT,	M. SIMPSON,
O. C. BAKER,	E. R. AMES."

"The undersigned heartily concur in the foregoing expressions of esteem, good will, and high appreciation of your services to the Church. We entertain severally a grateful remembrance of the pleasure and profit we have derived from your ministrations, and our earnest prayer shall be that God's richest blessing may abide with you.

"D. W. CLARK,
E. THOMSON,
C. KINGSLEY."

Bishop Janes, in acknowledging the gift of Bishop Hamline's seal of office and letter press, for which the latter had now no further use, says:

"I am greatly obliged to you for the very useful gift. It was not, however, its intrinsic value that made it so desirable to me, but the fact of its having been possessed and used by yourself as one of my colleagues in the general superintendency of the Church. As mementos, your seal and letter press have great interest to me. I desired very much to possess some memento of yourself. The circumstance of our being elected and ordained together always gave me a peculiar regard for

Bishop Hamline—a sort of class-mate feeling. So far as I am conscious, there never was the least rivalry or jealousy to mar our fellowship of labor or love. . . .

"God has given me health to work, and a heart to work. I delight in his service. I thank God he has kept me, in my administration, from ruinous errors, and given me much favor with the people. He has been my wisdom and prudence and success. I bless his name continually. I pray God to spare you from suffering, and continually to cheer you with his presence.

"Mrs. Janes joins me in affectionate regards to Sister Hamline. I desire to be remembered to Dr. Hamline's family.

"Yours fraternally in Jesus,   E. S. JANES."

To his dear friend, Moses Brooks, Esq., on receiving the news of the death of his wife, Bishop Hamline writes, October 10, 1864:

"AFFLICTED BROTHER,—I have not for years been so anxious to write a letter as to you, my dear afflicted friend. I greatly desire to dwell a moment on the sanctified, glorified, redeemed one who just ascended from your presence to her God; and then on that infinitely glorious Redeemer who bought her and us with his blood, and has made her, and will soon make us 'kings and priests unto God.' But my head is so distressed and confused that I must give up the pen to my dear wife. In such affliction I rejoice that you have such a home to fly to as you will find with our dear Brother and Sister Leavitt. Give to them the assurance of our undying Christian love. Please write often. Farewell! . . .

"Tell Brother Brooks that I do not expect to live to write another letter. This is my farewell."

A few days before, Dr. Elliott having come in, Bishop Hamline said: "I am not able to converse," but he desired Dr. Elliott to write on a slate which he handed him. The doctor wrote, "The will of the Lord be done." The Bishop wrote underneath, "Amen." Dr. Elliott wrote again, "Amen! Amen!" and added, "In heaven we shall not need slate and pencil to converse." The Bishop took the slate, and added, " No; nor tables, nor light, nor a temple, for the Lord God is the temple, and the Lamb the light thereof;" and, taking up the Testament, turned to Rev. xxi, 22, and handed the passage to the doctor, saying: " 'T is beautiful! glorious! glorious!"

Sunday, October 2.—Feeble as he was he read the sermon of Monod on the faith of the Canaanitish woman, and was greatly blessed. He said: " Were I forty-seven instead of sixty-seven years old, it seems to me I would bend all my energies to the subject of faith, praying, preaching, talking, and writing about it."

October 4.—At evening he said: " To-morrow will be the 5th of October. Thirty-six years to-morrow since the Lord revealed himself to me the hope of glory." On the fifth, to his little grandson, he said: " To-day I am thirty-six years old." The child was puzzled, and said: " Sixty-three you mean, grandpa." The Bishop explained in a most interesting manner. Afterward he said: " The Lord has sometimes wonderfully blessed me during the last Summer" (mentioning particularly a sermon preached in his class-room by Rev. G. B. Jocelyn), saying: " I received a great blessing under that sermon. I went up stairs weeping aloud, and going through the chambers. I knelt before the Lord first in one place, and then in another, confessing and praising." He then spoke of a season of suffering which followed. He said: " I ought to suffer and die meekly, patiently. How is it that he so blesses me?"

October 16.—To Mrs. Hamline he said: " The weary wheels of life stand still. I know what that means, the weary wheels of life;" adding, "I feel a wonderful peace pervading my whole being.   Christ is so near me as I can not describe.   He answers me by Urim and Thummim.   Light pours from his breast into mine.   I dwell not in a world of glory, but a world of love.

> " 'O love, how cheering is thy ray!
>   All pain before thy presence flies.' "

After kneeling some time in silent prayer, he said. "Such blessings are poured upon me when I kneel to pray that it seems as though I can not live.   'Tis wonderful thus to live in a furnace."

October 27.—After suffering great pain, he said: "What I have suffered to-day I think has taught me a useful lesson—has been very profitable.   I have thought of my Savior's sufferings as I never did before."   After dwelling some time on this theme, he asked his wife to show him the hymn (in the old edition of our hymn-book) which contains the stanza beginning with the line,

> "See how his back the scourges tear."

The year 1865 dawned upon the setting of one of the brightest luminaries in the militant Church. Memorable is that year, and sacred in the calendar of the Church, above, below.   But we should not call it a setting sun.   It is so, as in nature, only in appearance to us who dwell upon the earth's surface. In reality the departing of earth's great lights is only constellating a new hemisphere with stars of rare and enduring glory.   Until the soul of our lamented Bishop "passed into the heavens" he continued to shine with increasing luster, as a star in the right-hand of "Him who liveth, and was dead, and behold he is alive for evermore, amen; and hath the keys of death and of hades."

On Sabbath evening, January 4th, Bishop Hamline thus writes:

"DEAR WIFE,—Deprived of the privilege of the class, I hereby give you, in brief, my testimony. My sins are all pardoned through the blood and righteousness of my Lord Jesus Christ. The great work of inward purification and Christian edification is gloriously progressing. I feel that, living or dying, I am my Lord's. Press onward, my beloved, after Christ and heaven. Should I die soon, follow me to the grave with holy transports as an attendant on joyful scenes, for I go to the 'marriage supper of the Lamb,' to your God and my God. I wait your coming there. O may the dear children and grandchildren (how my eyes gush forth in tears as I write of them!) meet us there! Ever, ever yours, and Christ's above yours.

"'And if our fellowship below
In Jesus be so sweet,
What heights of rapture shall we know
When round his throne we meet!'"

At another date he writes:

"I have not recently recorded my joys and sorrows; but now, knowing my end is near, and that I shall soon go to my blessed home, and having strength to write a few words for your comfort when I see you no more on earth, this morning I am so filled with 'joy unspeakable and full of glory' that I can scarcely contain the bliss. Heaven is so near. I am near to God, and near to my eternal home. O, I wish I could explain how Christ now appears! but I can only say, 'Expressive silence muse his praise.' Again, 'He that believeth on the Son of God hath the witness in himself,' 'the Spirit itself beareth witness with our spirits,' etc.

"'My guilt is washed away
By my Redeemer's blood,
And by the Spirit I can say
That I am born of God.'

"O blessed assurance! My dear wife and son, 'Behold, I ascend unto your Father and my Father, to your God and my God!' Glory be to the Father, and to the Son, and to the Holy Ghost! Amen!"

Sunday, January 22.—Unable to attend the class-meeting in his little chapel, he went to the class-room door, and gave the following, which proved his last class-meeting testimony. He said:

"I am not as happy to-day as I was last Sabbath, and not as happy as the sister I heard shouting just now. I am not able to speak to-day, and at first thought I would not try. But I have had a solemn day; was greatly affected while reading my morning lesson. I read where Jesus prayed, 'Father, forgive them, for they know not what they do.' I thought he could not pray that prayer for me if I lived short of the fullness of the blessing of the Gospel, and it is a solemn thought. Dear brethren, our blessed Lord can not pray that prayer for *you* if you live without his full salvation, for you know what you do. O brethren, get this fullness, this perfect love! Dear brethren, get perfect love!" etc.

Dwelling most earnestly and affectingly on the believer's duty and privilege, and retiring, as he often did, under the apprehension that it might be his last opportunity to speak to the class, he said: "I would like to go home to-night; O, I would like to go home to-night! I am ready."

After a suffering night of family alarm, his children, Dr. Hamline and wife, coming in in the morning, Mrs. Hamline said: "Father, I am sorry to see you so ill this morning." He replied: "It is all right; just as the Lord pleases. His will be done, and the will of no other. His infinitely holy Providence does every thing right. He gave his Son to die for me; that is enough to all eternity. Glory be to the Father, and to the Son, and to the Holy Ghost!"

In the midst of these celestial joys and mortal conflicts, and the assiduities and affections of visiting friends, he is cheered by the remembrance of his former episcopal colleagues, now sitting in council at Cleveland, Ohio, who lovingly send him their last joint fraternal greetings, February 22, 1865:

"Rev. Bishop Hamline. *Dear Brother,*—The undersigned, having learned through Rev. Dr. Elliott of your severe illness, desire to express to you our deep sympathy with you in your sufferings, and also our grateful joy to learn that in your affliction you are abundantly sustained by the grace of God, and cheered by a consciousness of the Divine presence. We desire to renew our assurances of high esteem and fraternal love in Christ. While thus cherishing you in our affections, we also remember you in our prayers, earnestly beseeching our heavenly Father to bestow upon you all the blessings your soul and circumstances may require.

"With affectionate salutations to Sister Hamline, we remain your affectionate and sympathizing brethren in Christ.

"T. A. Morris,	E. S. Janes,
L. Scott,	M. Simpson,
O. C. Baker,	E. R. Ames,
D. W. Clark,	C. Kingsley."

Bishop Morris, also, in a personal note, writes:

"Dear Brother and Sister Hamline,— . . . We sincerely sympathize with you both in your painful and protracted family affliction, but 'reckon that the sufferings of this present time are not worthy to be compared with the glory that shall be revealed in us.' We are hopeful as to the final success of Methodism in the world, also as to its results in our own case as individuals.

"We shall write to Sister Palmer for the 'Guide' to help us.

"I send you a copy of my talk on the 'Spirit of Methodism.'

"Please give our love to Dr. Elliott and family, Dr. Hamline and family, and accept for yourselves the prayers and Christian affections of yours, ever, T. A. Morris."

Friends were speaking their last words now, and the certain nearness and probable suddenness of death prompted from his pen what might be his final testimony and advice as to his burial:

"March 6th.

"MY DEAR WIFE.—In 1844 I did not desire the 'office of a bishop,' never thought of it, never connected my person and that office even in my wildest imagining; but I desired then, as you must remember, a 'good work;' that is, the work of saving souls; and how wonderfully God endowed me with strength for that work in 1842 and 1843, until stricken down by disease. Now, this very day, I feel the burning desire, kindled by the Holy Spirit, to engage in that 'good work;' but there is a difference. Then, I desired to die and go to Christ, whom I loved with such a glowing love, but also desired the good work, not the office; but now, with the same desire to save souls, I have no expectation of it. Of course I am not 'in a strait,' as Paul was, but my desire to depart and be with Christ is unrestrained by conflicting desires. I infer that my time is close at hand, and that I shall soon be 'absent from the body and present with the Lord,' so I give you in writing a few words of affectionate advice: Procure a plain, modest monument for my grave, with no letters on it but the name, date of death, or the like. If convenient, let this be inclosed with an iron railing large enough for a few family graves. I would advise you to stay with the children. Be with them daily, and you can counsel and comfort and help guide their dear little ones to Christ. And now, finally, thanking you with a warm and grateful heart for your labors, patience, and prayers for me these twenty-eight years, gone forever, I commend you to God in Christ Jesus, who is able to build us up, and I am persuaded will bring us to meet before his throne. His holy religion has been our solace and strength on earth amid many toils and trials, and I trust we are to be numbered with those who came up out of great tribulation, and have washed their robes and made them white in the blood of the Lamb."

The few remaining days of his conflict were spent in the usual order, rising early and with help, attiring himself for the day, then spending a season in his sitting room in prayer, after which his hymn-book and Bible were placed for his use during the day in a chair by his lounge. Wonderful were his sufferings, and transcendently wonderful were his victories of faith and joy and hope. His living was "quite on the verge of heaven." He said: "I do not want one thought that is not fit for heaven. I have of late thought much of that." Some of his spiritual exercises seem almost more than belong to the honor of human nature in this life. The Monday before his death his son, Dr. Hamline, went to Chicago on business, to return the following Saturday. But on Wednesday, being strongly impressed that he was needed at home, he hastily returned before his time, and just in time to be present at the scene of parting. Wednesday, the 22d of March, Bishop Hamline was able to attend to some business matters. At family worship he offered a short prayer, but after breakfast was taken with severe spasms, from which, however, he revived and seemed as comfortable as at any time for the past two months. In the afternoon his violent symptoms returned. "That pain is coming back," he said, "and I do not see how I can live through another such spell as I had this morning." The business to which he was giving attention was suspended. Handing the papers to Mrs. Hamline, he said: "I can not attend to that now. If I live till to-morrow I will attend to it."

His agony increased rapidly, the perspiration streaming from his face. A messenger was dispatched with all possible haste for the family physician, and very soon another, who ran to bring the first physician he could find. He often exclaimed: "O agony unspeakable! I never knew what pain was before!" He could not keep one position a moment; but, extending his hands for aid several times, rose and stepped a few steps, and then sank back again to the lounge. He said, "Pray that I may be relieved." Two short, earnest prayers were offered for his relief. When a third commenced, he said pleasantly, "There, now," it being all the voice he could endure. During all this time he was perfectly calm in mind and collected. Remembering the feebleness of Mrs. Hamline, he said to her, "Sit down, they will do all I need;" and when she extended her hand to help him rise, "No," he said; "let them help me." At length he exclaimed, a glow spreading over his agonized features, "O, children, this is wonderful suffering; but it is nothing to what my Savior endured on the cross for me." This was his last effort to speak. He had said a little before, "I feel the pain approaching my heart;" and now the agony, which exceeded in intensity any thing the beholders ever witnessed, had reached its climax in the spasm of the heart. When the doctor arrived, consciousness was apparently gone, and a few brief moments closed the scene.

Thus passed to its heavenly rest the redeemed spirit Thursday, March 23, 1865. As he lay dressed for the grave, friends who visited the remains, exclaimed, "What a picture of rest!" The agony being over, and the noble features having settled back into natural form and expression, the countenance looked more like devotion than death.

Three days had passed, when, on the 26th of March, the solemn *cortege* moved along the way to Asbury Chapel, the doors and pulpit of which were

draped heavily in mourning. The crowd around the
door gave way for the procession, and the officiating
minister, as they passed down the aisle, pronounced
the service, "I am the resurrection and the life."
In the pulpit were Dr. Elliott, Revs. Z. H. Coston,
T. Corkill, A. C. Williams, and H. M. Thomas, the
latter four taking part in the service. Dr. Elliott
gave an excellent discourse from Pslam xxxvii, 37:
"Mark the perfect man." After divine service the
remains were interred temporarily, according to the
forms of the Church, upon his own grounds, whence,
subsequently, they were removed to "Rose Hill
Cemetery," between Evanston and Chicago, where
they await the voice that shall call them forth to
"the resurrection of life." "They that be wise
shall shine as the brightness of the firmament, and
they that have turned many to righteousness as the
stars for ever and ever."

Chapter XXVII.

GENERAL RETROSPECT.

OUR labor of love, though properly ending here, might seem to be incomplete without some general retrospect. The facts of the life we have delineated we have endeavored to spread out truthfully and impartially and in their just proportions upon the pages of this volume. Yet the different features and phases of the character portrayed, we have been able hitherto to consider only separately, which the reader may not be able to arrange in their true relations and harmony. Few men, in any age of the Church, have attracted more attention, or won more admiration, or commanded a more positive influence over men and councils, over individuals and the popular mind, than Bishop Hamline. It were but natural that he should be judged of variously, and that his principles of action should sometimes have been misunderstood and misapplied. The history of the world familiarly shows that the man who, by native genius and talent, rises above the average of his fellow-men becomes a mystery to his age in proportion as he transcends other minds. It is so, and has been so in all ages, and in all professions and departments of society. As a sequence of superiority, office and honor often fall in train, and these expose to envy and the selfish passions of men. What is the secret of success? is a question which curiosity prompts, whether from good or evil motives. The power of Bishop Hamline, as an individual mind, apart from office, can not be doubted. The secret of that power is readily seen by those who thoroughly know his history and mental structure, and understand the words, "ye shall receive power after that the Holy Ghost is come upon you."

One undisputed fact stands out in full relief upon the canvas of his life—from his early boyhood he was a leading spirit in whatever circle he moved; and as clearly does it appear that moral principle, reverence for God and his Word, and cultivated manners marked every period of his life. Not less notable is the fact that in every responsible position of maturer years he was successful. As a lawyer, as a candidate for the ministry during the years of his first essays, as a preacher and pastor, as an editor, as a bishop, he was not only successful, but eminently so. In writing, in preaching, in debating, in Church administration, in council, he held a leading influence, and this without seeking or intending to make himself public, or aspiring to distinction. There must be something remarkable in the intellectual, moral, and æsthetic character to sustain and account for all this. But greater than all, when, by premature affliction, he was laid aside, retiring from public life to pine and suffer and waste away in the seclusion of the sick-room for a period of fourteen years, he developed a greatness, a resignation, a living sympathy for the salvation of souls, a degree of positive usefulness, which showed him superior to adversity and thoroughly penetrated with the doctrines which he professed and taught.

His religious experience was strongly marked, both in the change it wrought and the evidences by which it was attested. Great were the transitions in his conversion and in his experience of perfect love. They were the epochs of his history; they were the gates of ingress to the spiritual mysteries of God; they were as keys of the kingdom of heaven. His whole after life pointed back to these marvelous events. From thence arose his power with God and with man. The convictions which preceded in both cases made the changes more real, left no shadow of doubt of that reality. He could always say, "That which we have heard, which we have seen with our eyes, which we have looked upon, and our hands have handled, of the word of life, declare we unto you." He had now passed beyond the region of the speculative, by which in earlier life he had been entangled, and had attained the positive. This, also, gave power and effect to his teaching and preaching.

The doctrine of entire sanctification which he preached was not a speculation, nor a mere dogma, but an experience in consciousness, attended with the "witness of the Spirit," with "signs following" in corresponding fruits and effects. With Bishop Hamline this conscious experience was the great conservative, aggressive, balancing power of his life. His whole character was recast in this mold. To those who had seen and heard him but once or twice, or occasionally on public occasions or social meetings, he might seem to carry this subject to an extreme; but those who knew him long and intimately saw and knew that what he appeared to be occasionally, he was really and daily. "He believed,

therefore he spoke;" and that faith was, indeed,
"the substance of things hoped for, the evidence of
things not seen"—"the faith which is of the operation of God." On this subject he spoke not as one
that "beateth the air;" but words had a meaning,
because the things which they represented had entered into his inmost soul and liveliest apprehension.
His teachings on this subject, and on every subject
of experimental religion, will be a legacy to the
Church, and a way-mark to Wesleyan theology, in
all ages. What he might have been had he never
been converted, or what he might have been had he
never entered fully and deeply into the experience
of perfect love, is not our prerogative to guess; but
this we may clearly and safely say, had it not been
for the great baptism of the Holy Spirit abiding with
him, he never could have left the record he has.
True, he had uncommon natural talents, without
which the Holy Spirit would not have chosen him
for the particular sphere which he filled; but it was
the Spirit using these talents which made him mighty.
And this is the New Testament idea of "gifts of the
Holy Ghost," which served the ends of miracles,
namely, natural talents wholly sanctified, wholly
brought under the will of the Holy Spirit. The souls
which he was instrumental in reaching with the light
of conviction, and effectual teaching on the higher
truths of the spiritual life, may be reckoned by
thousands.

Bishop Hamline did not always preach alike elo-
quently, though always to edification and profit to
those who sought after truth and grace. His early
life was shadowed by sickness and suffering, which

followed him into manhood. The effects upon his nervous system from excess of study and mental action while yet a youth were felt more or less till the time of his conversion. After conversion his preaching and spiritual labor several times prostrated him, up to the spring of 1844, and twice to the extent that his life was almost despaired of. He was never well but in the comparative sense. His excessive labors in 1842–43 came near carrying him off, and laid the foundation of his premature infirmity and retirement from public work. Few, very few, even of his friends, knew the cost to him of his great sermons, and his unremitting toil. While the multitude would be discussing the merits, and speaking in praise of the sermon, he would hasten to his chamber, exhausted, to receive the special ministrations which a loving wife or Christian friends might bestow, for the soothing or the reanimation of an exhausted system. At such times, too, bodily infirmity would induce a mental suffering over his inability to preach Christ worthily. He never preached for fame. Reputation as a pulpit orator, the applause of men, were lost sight of in the absorbing thought of saving souls. Most emphatically could he say to the Churches, in the language of Paul, " For neither at any time used we flattering words, as ye know, nor of men sought we glory, neither of you, nor yet of others, God is witness." His sermon on " The Witnesses " was prepared in his earliest ministry for the purpose of reclaiming a senior fellow-lawyer from his skepticism. As his friend did not habitually attend Church, he carried the skeleton of his sermon in his pocket week after week, hoping to find him in the house. At last he gave up hope of his being present, and decided to preach on the subject. As he rose to announce his text he saw his friend in the congregation. His soul went out into the subject, and God gave point to the truth. His friend was much affected, inquired after that when Mr. Hamline would preach, was checked in his course, but not long after suddenly died of accident.

The meekness and humility of Bishop Hamline's character were a marvel. He often startles one with his bold expressions. He says: "I find myself often adopting Edwards's expression, '*infinitely vile!*' responding even to the clear and most manifest visits of the Comforter. How canst thou dwell in a heart infinitely vile, and fill it with such jubilating joy? Often my bursting raptures mingle with a most grateful grief, that Jesus should condescend to dwell in so loathsome a heart as mine is, and employ his omnipotent Spirit to purify what is so corrupt. Who can speak in proper terms of such condescension of such a Savior?" His humility and self-abhorrence were grounded in a deep sense of native depravity and the exceeding sinfulness of sin. It was no affectation. He saw with eyes illuminated by the law, the throne, the nature, and attributes of God. What was he? "Now that mine eyes see thee," says Job, "I abhor myself, and repent in dust and ashes." Bishop Hamline's joys, which often seemed more than the human frame could sustain, were commonly accompanied with a view of the depravity of our nature, and the ill-desert of sin inversely profound. Perhaps in this he has few equals.

Perhaps no feature of his Christian life was more

open to unfriendly criticism than his uniform seri-
ousness, his general restriction, in conversation, to
subjects of experimental religion, and his habit of in-
troducing seasons of prayer in social parlor gatherings.   It is, however, enough to know that he never
ignored the claims of social intercourse where the
themes of conversation were instructive, edifying, or
needful.   But where the occasion dwindled into what
the apostle calls "insipid talking " or "jesting," or
any form of unprofitable communications, he considered a few minutes spent in prayer was the surest
and best method of recovering the hour, and putting
things upon a right course.   If lightness or frivolity
discovered itself in an annual conference, his prompt
and ready voice recalled them to watchfulness and
prayer in a manner that could not offend a Christian spirit, and could only be unsavory to a worldly
mind.   He never joked nor talked idly.   In the pulpit and in the social circle he was alike intent upon
the cultivation of his own soul in Christian grace, and
saving others.   His faith seemed to apprehend Christ
as really always present, as though he were so in
visible form.   He lived "as seeing him who is invisi-
ble," and adjusted all his habits of life to the proprie-
ties of such a fact.   That he was sometimes sad and
despondent is true, but it was not the fruit of any
peculiar cast of his piety, but the force of his complicated infirmities, and these seasons were brief and
always succeeded with glorious visions of faith, and
joyful experiences.   He was never ascetic, much less
misanthropic, and never violated the law of love and
sympathy.   He was simply earnest, upright, sincere.
In the midst of sufferings which, in common eyes,

might excuse him from all active interest in the welfare of others, he sustained a continuous system of efforts for the salvation and temporal good of his neighbors and fellow-men, and this for a period of fourteen years. There is no mistaking the sincerity and integrity of his religious profession.

If the reader has carefully noted the steps or processes of his mind in his awakening and conversion, and afterward in his new and more profound consecration of himself to God, his experience of perfect love, and his habit of renewing this consecration and carefully retrospecting his life from time to time, at New-year, birthdays, or on occasions of special affliction, he will discover the ground and secret of his strength. Although he never had occasion to "lay again the foundations" of his Christian character, he often recalled, reviewed, rehearsed, and confirmed them in solemn form of covenant; and the lively remembrance of what he was, and what grace had done for him, threw him newly and fully upon that ever-needed grace. As the ship is carefully examined often before putting out upon a new voyage, to know that her timbers are sound, that her fastenings remain sure, and that all is safe and "seaworthy," so did he in regard to his habits of faith and love and obedience. This habit of self examination was a marked feature of his life, and only when he knew himself by the light of the Holy Spirit, who "searches the deep things of God," and by that Spirit was assured that he rested only and wholly in the atoning blood, did he feel safe. The condescending love of God to him, and a sense of his own natural vileness and demerit, were the balancing forces of his character.

Bishop Hamline was no quietist, mystic or mo-
nastic. If his rules of life exceeded those of a
worldly Christianity, they were not out of harmony
with the oracles of God and the example of Christ.
He was thoroughly churchly in his principles and
habits. His reverence for, and faith in, the written
word of revelation was an integral element of his
religion. He sought no artificial methods of humiliation, or forms of life. He was no recluse; he lived
in the world, grappled with its realities, conformed
to its innocent customs, and entered into hearty sympathy with its real duties, relations, and trials. The
depravity of man, the blood of atonement, the regen-
erating, sanctifying, witnessing Spirit, the authority
and fullness of the written Word, were the formative
dogmas of his creed.

As to his talent as a preacher and a writer, the
reader is referred to the "Introduction" to Volume I
of Bishop Hamline's Works, where the subject is
fully stated.

And now, in taking leave of this work, which was
undertaken with a humbling sense of inadequacy, yet
for the love of God, it only remains to say that an
intimacy of three years with Bishop Hamline's writings, in preparing the two volumes of his Works,
and this of his biography, added to a personal acquaintance with him during the term of his episcopal
office, the love and esteem which the writer of this
had for him from the beginning have become more
intensified and settled upon a surer ground of knowledge, and the symmetry and beauty of his character
have been more clearly appreciated as this knowledge
has increased. The unused manuscripts are laid aside

with feelings something like those of burying a
friend, but thankful that the heart has been brought
into closer communion with one whom the Lord
loved. Many have been the seasons of joyful fellowship, not unfrequently accompanied with tearful
thanksgiving, during the preparation of this volume.
And if the effort to help in placing the voice and
character of this "angel of the Church" back in
their true place in the Church shall be in any good
degree successful; if the reader shall derive as much
profit in reading as the editor in preparing this volume; if, in a word, God shall approve and "further
it with his continual help," then shall we all unite to
"glorify God, who has given such power unto men."

THE END.

www.ingramcontent.com/pod-product-compliance
Lightning Source LLC
Chambersburg PA
CBHW031057110726
47900CB00003B/965